ANEW

The Scattered Seeds Series

Based Upon:
THE QUILT
SHATTERED SEEDS: "SOFIA'S STORY"

Maura (Clu) Gallagher

ANEW

THE SCATTERED SEEDS SERIES, Vol. I
THIRD EDITION
2 August 2013

ISBN-13: 978-1480178083
ISBN-10: 148017808X

EDITOR: KATHLEEN SUKALAC
ACKNOWLEDGEMENT: LINDA LAFFERTY
Mainstream Accessible Fiction

Based on the Original Manuscript: THE QUILT
Written by Maura P. Gallagher
31 August 2007

Self-Published as:
SHATTERED SEEDS: 'SOFIA'S STORY'
CLU GALLAGHER (PEN NAME)
12 March 2011
The following are previously self- published Editions:
SHATTERED SEEDS: "SOFIA'S STORY" SPECIAL EDITION
6 December 2011
SHATTERED SEEDS: "SOFIA'S STORY" SPECIAL EDITION II
12 March 2012
SHATTERED SEEDS: "SOFIA'S STORY COLLECTOR EDITION
5 November 2012
ANEW, THE SCATTERED SEEDS SERIES FIRST EDITION
12 November 2012
ANEW, THE SCATTERED SEEDS SERIES SECOND EDITION
6 March 2013

DEDICATION

BARBARA (FERRANTI) MAUS
(1948- 2010)

"Your time in this world did not go unnoticed, my friend"

CONTENTS

CHAPTERS

CHARACTERS

(In order of appearance)

Bill McDeenon
Janene McDeenon
Sophie Simon/Sofia Gunther
Clarissa
Corporal James Robinson
Randy
Private Dwayne Johnson
Private Reynolds
Jeffrey Anderson
Frau Frieda Kraus Schmidt
Herr Heinrich Schmidt
Herr Adam Schmidt
Herr Gerhard Gunther
Frau Alexandra (Schmidt) Gunther
Sofia Gunther
Franz Gunther
Fraulein Esther Rosenfeld
Frau Claudia Schultz
Officer Felix Fuerst
Maximilian Felix Fuerst IV
Ana Alexandra Fuerst
Frau Helena Stein
Margo
Wilhelm Miller
Harold (Hal) Schneider
Annie Schneider
Mary Long
Attorney Marcus Stern
Jacqueline (Stern) Mansfield
Stephen Mansfield
Michael Stern
Frederick Felix Fuerst
Raymond
Allison (Allie) Tyler
Mr. Corcoran
Simone Lawrence
Mai-Linh Tai
Nhu-Suong Tai
Binh-Ly Tai
An-ly Tai
Tamika Johnson
Sister Mary Agnes

PREFACE

31 AUGUST 2008

Janene McDeenon, a young writer/editor for a magazine in Atlanta is writing an article on "Adoption in America'. The research on the internet leads her to 'SOPHIE SIMON', a famous writer and the founder of a well-known worldwide chain of adoption centers for needy children known as 'W.O.O.Q' or the 'WORLD ORGANIZATION OF QUILTS'. Janene, adopted in infancy by an American couple, Bill and Madeline McDeenon, is the orphaned bi-racial daughter of a Vietnamese woman and an African American soldier serving during the American War in South Vietnam.

Growing up in America in the loving home of the McDeenon's, she had never wanted to know about her roots until after Madeline had died in 2006. Now, at age thirty-something and still grieving Madeline's death, she wants desperately to find her biological mother and hopes that the research for the article will serve two purposes.

Promising to share some information about a Vietnamese orphan whom she thinks may be of interest to her, Ms. Simon invites Janene to her home for an interview. With great apprehension and the continuing support and help from Bill in her quest to find her Vietnamese mother, Janene plans a trip to Pittsburgh to meet with the famous author/ philanthropist.

CHAPTER 1
THE WOMAN ON THE CLOUD

As they exit the dimly lit 'Fort Pitt Tunnel' on the last leg of their journey, Janene McDeenon is dozing, slumped in the front passenger seat of her adoptive father's mini-van. A bright ray of the autumn morning sunshine blasts through the windshield, warming her eyelids, giving her a gentle wake-up call. Not wanting to leave her dream, she opens her eyes, but only to a crack, hoping not to disturb the familiar image of the stunning Asian woman dressed in colorful silks blowing in the wind.

The woman rides a white puffy cumulus cloud and her oval shaped eyes summon Janene, who is more than willing to go to her, but the cloud darts away, hiding behind one of the many glistening structures of the city of Pittsburgh. Clusters of concrete, steel, and glass structures, nestled against the banks of three adjoining rivers, form a unique triangular design, a magnificent creation accomplished by the union of Mother Nature's Bounty and man's ingenuity.

Pulling herself up and pressing her cheek against the car window, mesmerized, she studies the site. "Are we there yet, Dad?" she asks in a childlike whisper.

Bill McDeenon's blue eyes twinkle in the blinding glare of the sunlight coming through the windshield, reminding him to replace his sunglasses to their rightful place on his face. He had removed them before entering the tunnel, placing them on top of his head of sandy colored hair. "Yep, we're here, Neeny," he says using the nickname that his biological son, Brian, had given Janene when he had been barely able to talk.

"It's about time. I thought we would never get here," Janene sighs opening her eyes wider, watching as the cloud passes overhead, and

13

allowing the familiar vision of the woman to fade into the recesses of her mind again.

"That reminds me of our trips when you were little. You must have asked that question a hundred times before we had finally reached our destinations. You never did have much patience for the waiting," he says as his freckles dance across his nose with the movement of the dimples in his cheeks. The twinges of gray hair along the sides of his face and his receding hairline betray his youthful appearance and bear testimony to his age of sixty-two.

"I remember," she smiles.

"We're now passing the junction of the Allegheny, Ohio, and Monongahela Rivers," he announces acting as if he is their tour guide.

"So, this is Pittsburgh," she says looking to the right and left. "That first view of the city as we had exited the tunnel onto this bridge certainly was an amazing one."

"It sure was," Bill agrees.

Following the directions of his GPS, a gift from Janene when she had decided to begin the search for her biological family, Bill guides the car to the far right lane, exiting the 'Fort Pitt Bridge' onto '376 E' taking them to their destination, the home of the famous writer, 'Sophie Simon'. "Hmm, I had always heard that Pittsburgh was a dirty town. The loss of the steel mills must have changed that," he notes adjusting his sunglasses again. "They certainly have named the downtown area of Pittsburgh correctly. . . 'The Golden Triangle' describes it perfectly."

"For sure," Janene agrees as the view changes and the van finds its way along the boulevard bordering the banks of the Monongahela River. "I hope this trip doesn't prove to be another let down. I'm afraid I've run out of patience searching for my roots," she frowns. Tossing a lock of her long dark wavy hair over her shoulder and lost in thought, she studies the calm river beneath the bridge. Its quiet waters remind her of her life as the adopted mixed-race daughter of a loving American couple. An orphan, the daughter of an African American soldier and a Vietnamese woman, she had spent the first thirty-some years of her life not wanting to discover the mysteries of her birth, afraid of what she might find. Now, she can think of nothing else. As she glances at her adoptive father, she smiles thinking that no matter what she discovers about the circumstances of her birth, he will always be her one and only 'real' father.

"I have a good feeling about this trip, Honey."

"That's what you said about the last one."

"Yeah, but this one is in Pittsburgh."

"How do you know so much about Pittsburgh?"

"It's a big sports town and I'm one of their biggest fans."

"What kind of sports?" she asks turning to look at him.

"Not any that you would recognize. They didn't have 'team-basket-weaving' the last time I had checked."

"Could I help it that I was too short for basketball? Besides, you had the boys for that," she quips picturing her petite body dressed in her gym clothes, running out onto the court in middle school.

"You know I'm kidding. I've always been proud of your interest in the Arts. I can still see you tapping away at your first dance recital and hear your squeaky performance on the violin," he smiles. "How could I ever forget the celebrating we had done when you had won that 'Certificate of Achievement' for the story you had entered in the 'Junior Literary Awards."

"I knew you weren't serious, Dad," she says turning her attention back to the river, watching as they pass a large barge loaded with coal. Its disappearance from view reminds her of her childhood, now a collection of memories. A picture of her two adoptive brothers, Brian and Kevin, Bill and Madeline's biological sons, as they had successfully shot baskets in the final championship game, replaces the one that had reminded her of the failed try-out for the girls' team.

A favorite photograph of her family appears in her mind, bringing a smile. She sees Bill and Madeline, smiling and standing tall behind her, Brian, and Kevin. "Blonde and blue-eyed brothers and parents, I certainly do stand out," she thinks comparing her mixed heritage with that of her adoptive family. Noting her own dark wavy hair, brown skin, and oval eyes, she is positive that no one would doubt her heritage, and she is even more certain that some might think she doesn't even belong in the picture. However, she is certain of one thing – *Dad wouldn't be one of them*

"If it had been up to Dad, I would still be eight years old," she thinks as she feels her stomach begin to churn. She pictures Bill and Madeline in her mind, recalling that time when she had won the award for her essay. Bill is smiling his special smile and she feels the warmth of Madeline's embrace. Even though it has been two years since her adoptive mother's death, she still misses her. Time has not diminished the pain of losing the only mother she has ever known.

"I wish Mum were here," she says as a tear forms.

"Me, too, but I'm sure she's here in spirit," Bill smiles searching the road signs, making another lane change.

Her mind travels to her job at the magazine and the special assignment for which she had volunteered. Writing an article on 'The New Face of Adoption in America' had seemed to be the perfect opportunity for her to combine work and the pursuit of her greatest wish, one that has become her main focus now, finding her biological family. 'Thirty-something' on her last birthday, she had never been interested in finding any information about her heritage, not even the exact year that she had been born. However, the contentment of her earlier years of not wanting to know about her birth can't compare to her current high level of anxiety in finding even the slightest detail about her beginnings.

"I hope I did the right thing by volunteering for this assignment, Dad."

"I have a feeling about this interview with Sophie Simon, Neeny."

"Do you think I have waited too long, Dad," she says with a twinge of anxiety returning. Her excitement had escalated when her research for the article had revealed a promising lead that would not only help her with the assignment, but also with the search for her biological family. The information had led her to 'Sophie Simon', known for her books made into animated movies for children. She had uncovered the little known fact that Sophie Simon's real name was 'Sofia Blackburn-Anderson', the founder of the largest chain of adoption centers in the world.

"It's never too late, Neeny. Maybe Sophie Simon can finally give you some answers. Look, there's another tunnel," he notes as he reads the sign announcing the entrance ahead into the 'Squirrel Hill Tunnel'. "I'm pretty sure that we should exit before this tunnel. I hope this GPS knows what it is talking about, after all of these wild-goose chases, I don't want to get lost now."

"Wouldn't it be something if I found my family here?"

"It would. You've had enough disappointments."

"That's for sure," she says studying the scene out of the car window, captivated by the appearance of yet another one of the many bridges connecting the banks of the river. The beautiful Vietnamese woman appears before her again, riding high on the cloud above the bridge. This time, the woman is holding a baby in her arms, securely nestled against her breast. An African American soldier enters the picture, gently wrapping his arms around her, pulling her close, and kissing the baby on the forehead before the vision fades from Janene's mind. She isn't surprised that the vision fades when the soldier appears. She had always feared finding any information about the man who had fathered her. Unraveling the truth about how an American soldier fighting in Vietnam could have impregnated her mother had been one thing that had always terrified her.

As she concentrates on the next instruction from the GPS, she puts her former fears aside, permitting a renewed eagerness to uncover more information about her roots. She watches anxiously as Bill exits off the parkway onto a ramp taking them to the prestigious city neighborhood of 'Squirrel Hill'. She checks the streets and house numbers, comparing them to her notes. "You've arrived at your destination," the high-pitched female voice of the GPS announces.

Her heart beats fast.

Beautiful homes line both sides of the tree-lined street, but Janene looks to the one with the blue cloth awnings and the wide circular driveway in front. "Just as Sophie Simon had described," she thinks remembering their phone conversation. As goose bumps run down her arms, she wonders if they are the result of finally seeing the large home with the well-manicured lawn, or if they are the result of the continuing mental pictures of the Vietnamese woman in her dreams. "This must be it," she says as she compares the address in her notes to the spectacular mansion.

Her heart jumps again.

"It certainly is impressive, Neeny," Bill says pulling the van up to the gate and pushing the button on the intercom.

"May I help you?" a voice asks.

"Ms. McDeenon to see Ms. Sophie Simon," Bill replies as he focuses on the gate. Slowly, the large black wrought iron gate opens wide. He coasts the van down the driveway across the tree-lined grounds of the mansion. At the end of the long winding drive, the huge home stands majestically cuddled between two tall oak trees.

"Wow!" she says softly as her jaw drops and her eyes get big. "I knew she was wealthy, but this is really something. The royalties from her books explain this mansion, not to mention the blockbuster films, but I still can't believe I'm actually interviewing the famous 'Sophie Simon' or that she may have some information about my roots."

"I've never been interested in children's literature – that had been your mother's department, but even I had known that all of those hit movies about that quilt had been based on her book, THE MAGICAL QUILT," he says parking the car under the portico in front of the stone walk leading to the front door.

"The biography on the internet had said that she had established the international children centers through her philanthropy. If her centers hadn't become so successful, I might not have ever made the connection of the famous writer to the largest chain of centers for needy children in the world." Her stomach flips; she feels nauseous.

"How do I look, Dad?" she asks reaching for the visor mirror, but changing her mind and not wanting to look. Those same self-esteem issues, ones that had begun in childhood, still nag her, making her feel anxious.

"Maybe today will be the day that I'll be able to look in a mirror and know who I really am," she thinks as she does a mental check of the preparations she had made earlier, hoping to insure that she will make a good first impression.

"You look wonderful."

"Are you sure? I don't want to scare her away," she says reaching down to the floor for her briefcase.

"Don't be silly," he says with a click of his tongue against his teeth, making a snapping sound.

As he gets out of the car and comes around to open the door for her, he says, "You're beautiful. You wouldn't scare anyone if you tried." Thoughts of the unsuccessful searches fade now, quickly replaced by a feeling of exhilaration as she anticipates the meeting that has occupied her mind for weeks. Moving toward Bill, she feels a sudden urge to wrap her arms around him and kiss his cheek.

"Thanks so much, I love you, Dad," she whispers in his ear.

"For what?" he asks with his usual grin.

"Thanks for just being you – the best father in the world."

"Do you want me to come in with you?" he asks releasing her.

"No," she sighs hoping that this meeting is different from all of the previous disappointing ones. She recalls that, even after all of the leads of her two-year search had turned to dead ends, Bill had insisted that they never give up.

"This is one that I'll do on my own," she says with determination.

"I promise; I won't say a word; I'll just listen."

"I'll be fine; don't worry," she reassures him while still trying to convince herself.

"I'll check into the hotel. Call me on my cell when you're ready and I'll come back for you."

"Okay."

As she walks the path leading to the long porch lined with a row of white wooden rocking chairs, memories of her adoptive family's smiling faces accompany her, warming her again, taking away a little of her nervousness. She looks out to the grounds, noting the rows of yellow and orange chrysanthemums bordering the walks, reminding her that the flowers had been Madeline's favorites; their familiar sight warms her, giving her a new energy. As she approaches the large oak door, her attention goes to the wrought iron plaque of a patchwork quilt, marked with the letters 'W.O.O.Q.' staring back at her. Recalling her research for the article about adoption, she sounds out the meaning of the abbreviation in her mind, *World Organization of Quilts*.

Her curiosity about the adoption agency's name edges out her anxiety, but only slightly. She takes a deep breath, feels her stomach flutter, and presses the doorbell. Just as quickly, as if a bolt of electricity had struck her hand, she takes it back. Waiting, standing as still as a statue in front of the door, her mind whirls reviewing all of the steps she had taken to research the article as well as find her family. She recalls that the information about the W.O.O.Q. agencies was easy to uncover; it had been the most prominent one on the internet.

As she studies the large piece of metal etched with the faces of children from all parts of the world, memories of the many books she had read by her favorite childhood author, Sophie Simon, come to mind. Scenes from the movies about the magical quilt flash, bringing fond recollections of those times when she and Madeline had attended each of them. The conversation she had had with Sophie Simon prior to her inviting her to Pittsburgh had led her to believe that Sophie's center in Vietnam would provide information that would be beneficial to her in her research. In addition, Sophie Simon had mentioned that she knew of a Vietnamese orphan whose story might be of interest to her. It pleases her to know that she is about to meet the woman who had provided her with such childhood happiness, but her anxiety about what she will tell her about the orphaned Vietnamese child escalates. "What's taking them so long?" she questions – just as the door opens.

"May I help you?" asks a middle-aged woman wearing a black dress and apron piped in white.

She swallows hard, takes a deep breath, and stammers, "My name is Janene McDeenon. I am here to see Ms. Blackburn-Anderson."

"She is expecting you, Miss. McDeenon. Please come in," the woman says with a sweep of her arm.

She takes a step, but not before catching a final glimpse of Bill sending her a kiss on a wave. She smiles, sending him one back, before entering the foyer.

A shiny round table in the center of the huge entrance hall explains the odor of furniture polish but, for Janene, it doesn't override the familiar smell of the chrysanthemums arranged in a large hand-painted porcelain vase resting on an intricately crocheted tablecloth. Memories of Madeline spin in her mind. She sees her working in her beloved garden, gathering the flowers for a bouquet to place in the center of their supper table. The chrysanthemums are in full bloom and Madeline is smiling her extraordinary smile.

The familiar aroma of the mums brings to mind a fleeting memory of the last time she had seen Madeline, picturing her in her coffin, adorned with the bouquet of mums with the white satin ribbon displaying the word 'Mum' that she had placed there. Her heart aches. 'Mum' had been the name she had called Madeline. Janene also grew to love the flower and her love for Madeline had increased even more after Madeline had lost her struggle with breast cancer, taking her life two years earlier. She dismisses any more negative thoughts, replacing them with positive ones as she moves farther into the room.

"May I take your coat, Ms. McDeenon?"

"Perhaps, the mums which fill Sophie Simon's home are a good omen," she thinks as she begins to struggle with her overcoat. "Thank you," she answers switching her briefcase back and forth between her hands, removing one arm of her trench coat at a time, and freeing her navy-blue blazer. After handing her coat to the servant, she fixes the collar on her white blouse and straightens the wrinkles in her red pencil skirt.

"Please follow me," the soft mannered servant says draping the coat over one arm, leading her through the entrance hall and down the long corridor decorated with photographs framed in gold and showing a multitude of children from different countries of the world. The center of attention is a large quilt hanging on a wooden pole, centered on the wall above the landing of the majestic wooden staircase. Janene looks up at the quilt, staring at it in awe. It consists of hundreds of squares, each printed with the face of a child and arranged around a center pattern of pink squares, displaying the letters, 'W.O.O.Q.'. Fascinated, she studies it, wanting to get closer. Instead, she walks as if in a trance, wondering about the many children Sophie Simon had helped and the story she had promised to tell her. At the end of the hallway, the woman servant opens the double doors. The first look astounds her.

She stares through the doorway into the dimly lighted room with the high ceiling; its walls lined with shelves filled with hundreds of books. A tiny stream of colored light breaks through a crack in the drawn drapes, revealing just a hint of the stained-glass window behind them. The narrow beam of light crosses the room as if it has been programmed, shining directly on a framed portrait hanging above the baby grand piano, showing a handsome African American soldier standing beside a hut near a rice paddy. Her heart beats faster as she studies the picture. The picture reminds her of the ones she had conjured in her mind during the many times when she had imagined her own biological father. Her eyes move from the picture to the only occupant in the room, a woman sitting in a chair in front of the large stone fireplace. The woman appears to be thinking. "Sophie Simon?" she questions as she studies the old woman.

Confused, she glances around the room, searching for an explanation, but the small reading lamp on the end table, casting a light on the woman's face, draws her back to her. The folds of a multicolored shawl cover her shoulders, hugging her arms. Her curled fingers lay on the pink-colored patches of a thread-worn quilt covering the bottom half of her body. Janene thinks the tattered quilt doesn't seem to fit in the ornate room, or on the elegant woman. Only the ring finger of her left hand wears jewelry, a large round diamond set upon a gold wedding band glistening in the light of the lamp. The light accentuates the woman's white hair, pulled into rolls, and pinned around her pale face. The finger-shaped wrinkles around her eyes, the burrows along the sides of her mouth, and the layers of ivory skin under her chin, seemingly held up by a large rhinestone pin attached to the collar of her heavily starched white blouse, reveal an old woman, one from another time and place.

A book rests in her lap; its title, ANOTHER NEW BEGINNING, stands out on the cover in bold, blue lettering. She strains to read the name of the author, written in much smaller print underneath the title. "Jeffrey Anderson," she reads silently wondering about the book and the author.

Suddenly, she hears a woman's voice calling out her name, distracting her. She looks at the old woman in the chair, but she has not moved, still sitting with her eyes closed. "Ja-nene," the voice calls out again, disturbing the eerie silence of the room. She looks around the room and checks to see someone has entered, finds no one, and turns to study the woman again. The woman sits with her eyes closed, not moving, not responding to her servant.

"Soo-fee-aah," the voice calls louder, startling her. She looks to the servant, who makes no response to the voice, acting as if she has not heard it. Janene feels her heart beat even faster as the servant moves toward her employer and she hears the voice again, this time saying, "An-Ly." She jumps. She can't understand and feels frightened. Taking a deep breath, trying to calm herself, she studies the woman in the chair, wondering if she is actually Sophie Simon. The pictures she had found on the internet had shown her as a much younger and healthier woman. Although the old woman seems to be in a deep sleep, Janene's heart sinks when she entertains the horrifying thought that she might be dead.

"Miss Sofia, Miss McDeenon is here to see you," the servant says.

As Janene waits, she tries to reassure herself that her active imagination has just gone wild again but, as her stomach juices begin to come into her throat, she isn't successful. She swallows and steadies her body, remaining frozen in place, except for her eyes, which move back and forth between the servant and the old woman. Staring at Sophie Simon's chalky-white face, her mind screams, "No! Please, no!"

"Miss Sofia?" the servant says again, in vain. She turns to Janene, displaying a look of helplessness. Janene moves to help her, but suddenly stops when she hears the voice again. "Bin-Ly," the voice speaks in barely a whisper. Janene freezes, unable to move. Her heart beats faster; she feels faint; her body goes limp.

A look of terror appears on the servant's face. She turns away from Janene and moves toward her employer, calling out "Miss Sofia" repeatedly in a louder voice several times before touching her forearm. Getting no response again, she reaches for the 'Call Button', but before she can press it, the old woman opens her eyes. Her vivid light blue eyes shine for only a moment behind a set of gold reading glasses, which once had set perched on her nose, but now fall down landing on the book in her lap. Looking up, she finds Janene staring at her as if she is in a trance and their eyes lock. Neither woman seems able to look away. Upon realizing that the woman is 'Sophie Simon', Janene feels unnerved and tries to gather thoughts, eliminate the confusion, and break the strange fascination and the mysterious spell that has overcome her. "I . . . huh . . . I talked to you . . . the phone. I called to tell you I would be late," she says in almost a whisper, her voice quivering, her body shaking.

The two women study each other as if they are puppies trying to understand a new command from their master, turning their heads from side to side before settling into a mutual stare. "Will there be anything else, Miss Sofia?" the woman servant says with a deep breath, dispelling the bond between them.

"Yes, Clarissa, bring us the refreshments and open the drapes," Sofia answers in a soft voice, but never taking her eyes from Janene.

"Yes, Miss Sofia," says Clarissa moving toward the window.

Clarissa pulls hard on the cord of the wall-to-wall brocade drapes covering the large picture window, causing them to open wide, revealing a picture from the first movie about the magical quilt, set in carefully placed pieces of stained glass. Streams of colored lights flood the room, defined by the penetrating sunlight through each piece of the glass set in lead. A beautiful blonde princess sits sidesaddle on a large white horse; a handsome young prince holds it reins.

She wears a fluffy, white silk gown and rests on a multi-colored patchwork quilt, cloaked across the back of the horse. The prince is leading the horse that carries his princess toward a drawbridge that crosses the quiet waters of a moat, complete with a flock of swimming swans, and offering protection for his stately castle snuggled in the shade of a grove of tall trees under the bright sun of a cloudless blue sky.

The colored light pouring through the window brings the famous author's form into full view and at the same time casts a spotlight onto her visitor's pretty face. Clarissa moves toward the door, closing it behind her, leaving the two women alone, staring at each other.

Neither of them moves; both appear frozen in time.

After a few moments, Sophie speaks first. "I remember our phone conversation, Miss McDeenon. Was your trip a pleasant one?"

"It was a very long one, but pleasant," Janene replies breaking just a little smile, one that only slightly relieves her nervousness. However, the strength of Sophie Simon's voice offers her some reassurance as she considers the manner in which she should address the famous author. She is puzzled as she considers the propriety of calling her 'Ms. Simon', 'Ms. Blackburn-Anderson' or perhaps be bold enough to call her 'Sophie'.

While she reflects on the possible titles, she watches as Sophie Simon continues her survey of her, scanning her from head-to-toe, making her feel even more uncomfortable. Undaunted, Sophie continues inspecting Janene, apparently not aware of Janene's discomforts. She examines Janene's slight body, touring it from the top of her head and finally finding her slender legs, fitted in navy blue high-heel shoes. Not satisfied, her eyes travel back to Janene's face, stopping on her almond-shaped-ebony-colored eyes that glisten with a brilliant blue glaze. She studies the golden-brown strands on top of Janene's dark hair, almost serving as a crown as well as highlighting the waves that trail down to her waist, outlining the shapely curves of her body. "She seems captivated by me," Janene thinks comparing Sofia's study of her to one done using a microscope.

Feeling very unnerved, not understanding Sofia's reaction to meeting her, she feels her cheeks redden and her body begin to shake. Again, she looks away, bowing her head, and resting her chin on her upper chest, hoping to get some control over her own body.

"I'm sorry if I have come at a bad time," she says as her fingers fiddle on the handle of her briefcase. "We had planned to be here yesterday but, as I had explained in my call to you, construction delays, detours, and a major traffic accident had forced us to stay over at a hotel."

"The important thing is that you are here," Sophie smiles.

Janene feels queasy again as she ponders the remark. A feeling of great anxiety descends upon her, reminding her of the one time that she had earned a trip to the Principal's Office in middle school. Trying to offer some excuse for her misbehavior, she says, "I am sorry for not getting here at the appointed time."

"Please, Ms. McDeenon, it is I who should apologize for not being prepared to receive you. It is just that I was dreaming. You remind me of someone in my dream – someone whom I had loved very much."

The remark strikes Janene. Her heart flutters as the image of her own dream of the Vietnamese woman races through her mind again. She looks back at Ms. Simon, but she can't focus her attention for long before she has to look away, trying to dismiss the uncanny feelings of unknown familiarity.

"Please, won't you sit down, Miss McDeenon? I am truly sorry."

"Thank you," Janene says moving toward the chair opposite her.

She flattens out the wrinkles in her skirt with one hand, slowly lowering her body into the chair, and placing her briefcase down on the floor beside her before crossing her legs tightly in front of her. She looks up to see Sophie Simon still watching her every move.

"May I call you 'Janene'?" she asks with a smile.

For the first time, as she folds her hands in her lap, Janene stops trembling. "Yes, please do," she answers relieved that her anxiety seems to be fading.

As she studies Sofia, her attention immediately goes to her eyes, noting that Sofia and the soldier in the portrait share the same very unusual eye color. His differs from Sofia's in that his are several shades darker. Sophie's are a very light color blue, reminding her of frosted glass. "Is it a coincidence?" she wonders contemplating the identity of the soldier in the picture that holds such a prominent place in the famous author's home. Even though she realizes that Sophie Simon and the soldier are of different races, she considers the possibility of a relationship between them.

The comparison also causes her to consider her own eyes, surprised by her conclusion that the soldier's eyes are the same color as her own. She remembers the many times in the past when others had commented about the qualities of her eyes, noting their uniqueness, sometimes a dark blue ebony, almost a deep violet, glistening with shades of a shimmering topaz to a cool midnight blue. However, she decides that the shape of her eyes greatly contrasts those of the bi-racial soldier in the picture in that the shape of her eyes broadcasts her Asian ancestry. Sofia interrupts her thoughts about the soldier, his identity, and his relationship to Sofia.

"Please, call me 'Sofia'," she says as her fingers grasp the quilt in her lap, seeming to automatically gravitate to one thread-worn-pink patch, repeatedly stroking it with her index finger in a circular motion.

"I would be honored, 'Sofia'."

Janene watches as Sofia continues to caress the same pink patch located in the center of the quilt. She shifts her body in the chair and glances at the pictures in the room again, but her attention keeps returning to the portrait above the piano of the smiling face of the soldier. Each glance seems to lessen the nauseous feeling, diminishing her fears, but she can't stop the sensation that she has met him before, not knowing where or when.

Her experiences in the past with the phenomenon known as 'Déjà Vu' had always made her feel uncomfortable, but never to this degree. She compares these feelings to those types of perceptions she had had in childhood making her feel insecure then and now adding to her growing feeling of apprehension. She is relieved when Clarissa enters the room again, hoping that her reappearance will direct Sofia's attention away from her. Clarissa carries a silver tray, holding a teapot, two china cups on saucers, a creamer and sugar bowl, and a platter of sugared crullers. She places the tray on a small serving table between Sofia and Janene.

"Will there be anything else, Miss Sofia?"

"Hold all of my calls, Clarissa; Tell 'Mr. Jeffrey' that our guest has arrived; our visit may be a long one," she smiles in Janene's direction, followed by another stare.

"I'll tell him, Miss Sofia," Clarissa replies moving toward the door, closing it quietly behind her.

"May I pour you some tea?" Sofia asks lifting the teapot.

"No, thank you. I'm anxious to hear the story about the orphaned Vietnamese child, the one you had mentioned during our phone conversation when I had contacted you about the article I am writing."

"I'm just as anxious to tell you the story," Sofia says lifting the cup from its saucer, taking a sip.

"Do you mind if I use a recorder?"

"No, of course not, the story is quite long and it is one I think you will want to remember," Sofia says placing her cup on its saucer. "If you are ready, I'll begin."

Janene removes the device from her briefcase and sets the recorder on the end table beside her. After sitting back in the chair, she smiles at Sofia, nodding her head, suggesting that she is ready. Sofia moves the book on her lap to the end table and straightens the folds of the quilt, positioning it so that it is exactly in the middle of her lap. She places her hands on the center squares and begins her repetitious stroking. After clearing her throat, she begins.

*

"It was 1972 in the jungle of South Vietnam, along the Mekong River, not far from Saigon. A young American soldier, Corporal James Robinson is serving his country . . ."

*

"She seems to be telling the story as if she is reading it," Janene thinks as she listens. Confused, she looks up from her notebook and faces her, trying not to make eye contact, but their eyes lock again.

Forcing her gaze away, she looks around the room searching for some hidden script or clue to the way that Sofia is telling the story.

Unable to find anything that would confirm her curiosity, she recalls the steps that she had taken as she had researched the article, ultimately bringing her to Sophie Simon. Although, she had spent considerable time investigating Sofia's centers, she had not spent much time probing her personal life, nor had she looked into her professional life as a writer. Wondering if she may have overlooked some important information, she contemplates interrupting to ask some questions, but resists the urge for fear of offending her. The faraway look on Sofia's face arouses her interest and she smiles back when Sofia sends one her way. Realizing that her mind isn't on what Sofia is saying, she turns her attention back to her, thankful that she had decided to use the recorder.

The tensions in her neck and shoulders subside and she feels less nervous. Deciding that she will not need the pen and notebook, she leans back in the chair, folds her hands in her lap, and gives the storyteller her complete attention.

As she listens, Sofia's words transport her to the same time and place, the jungles of South Vietnam in 1972:

"He hates guard duty," Sofia says. "The monotony of the constant watching and listening for long periods of time works on his mind, making it drift to the same place, bringing vivid memories of home. Just as he had done on previous occasions when he had served guard duty, he can't stop thinking about his first hunting trip when he was eight-years old.

His father had liked to hunt deer in the nearby forests of northwestern Pennsylvania and he had looked forward to the time when he would think that his only son was "old enough to handle a gun." However, the trip had been disappointing one for him, not only because he had failed to kill a deer but also because he had contracted a rash from an exposure to 'Poison Ivy'.

The name of the plant that had caused him so much discomfort back in 1959 had also been the title of a [1]popular song. Despite his experience with the itchy rash on that first hunting trip, the song had become one of his favorites while growing up and he can't seem to dismiss it now. The words and the melody repeatedly play in his mind.

> *Poison iv-y-y-y-y . . . Poison iv-y-y-y-y*
> *Late at night while you're sleepin', poison ivy comes a'creepin'.*
> *Poison iv-y-y-y-y . . . Poison iv-y-y-y-y*

The words always seem to accompany his every rub of an unrelenting itch, a condition that had started soon after his arrival in South Vietnam. "Too many bugs in this damn country," he thinks as he swats his arm, hoping that the itchy sensations are from bug bites and not from an Asian variety of the plant. The fact that only he can hear the song is a good thing – the slightest sound could mean disaster for an American soldier standing

---

[1] "POISON IVY", THE COASTERS, 1959, U.S.A. Words and Music by Jerry Lieber and Mike Stoller lyricstime.com

guard outside of a United States Army Base on the outskirts of Saigon in 1972. The air hangs like a dripping-wet shower curtain, blanketing the area, stealing his oxygen, smothering him.

As they make their journey past his eyebrows and onto his eyelids, beads of perspiration glistening in the mid-August moonlight dribble down his forehead. While still trying to maintain a firm grip on the butt of the military-issued M16 rifle, he grasps the green towel he had tied around his neck earlier and uses it to wipe the sweat from his face. He steals another scratch, aiming at the itchy spot on his left forearm before lifting the binoculars by their cord hanging around his neck. He positions them toward the boring view of the clusters of green vegetation, standing so still in the moonlight, harboring a potential threat from the enemy. Another itch and another scratch bring to mind the ruined hunting trip back in the forest of Pennsylvania. The memory is one that has repeated itself many times since he had left home, becoming a soldier.

He pictures himself back home again, covered with the itchy rash, frustrated by the overwhelming need to scratch and hoping his father would have a solution. Back then, before reaching for a bottle of pink lotion and applying it lovingly to his only son, his father had said, "I think you've managed to contract the worst case of poison ivy in the history of Mercer County, Jimmy."

Now, he wishes for a bottle of his father's misery-stopping lotion but, realizing the unlikeliness of that happening, he wills himself to think of something else besides his urge to scratch. His mind travels to the first day when he had arrived in the Asian country torn by a civil war. He feels a twinge of homesickness, and he scratches his forearm again. As if programmed, his diversionary thinking takes over, making him reach for his other compulsion – chewing tobacco.

He had arrived in Vietnam preferring cigarettes, but had quickly followed the lead of the veterans in not wanting to draw attention to their positions, abandoning the smoking habit, one that he had started in high school. "That is all I would have to do, light up our position like a Christmas tree, or give it away with the smell of a smoke-signal," he thinks as he anticipates the reactions of the other soldiers if he would light up. The image reaffirms his commitment and prompts him to pull out a plug of tobacco from his shirt pocket.

As he chews, he surveys the area again, gripping the glasses tighter with one hand and tightening his hold on the butt of the rifle with the other. Aiming the binoculars at the mass of green foliage just beyond the clearing, he performs a visual sweep of the area, only stealing an occasional look at the littered ground covered by the discarded lumps of mush that had helped take the time away.

"It is a slow night. Just the way I like it," he thinks as he allows his mind to stray, taking him down that melancholy lane again, but this time his thoughts turn to his grief, missing Randy, his friend and fellow soldier.

Memories of the past ten months as they had fought battles together culminate with a final image of Randy's helicopter crashing in the jungle, killing him and his crew of five. His eyes mist as his heart thumps and he reviews the scene of the body bags, as they had been loaded onto the transport plane for their final trip back to the United States. A dangling log on the end of the crane had found his head instead of its place on the clearing, knocking him unconscious; earning him a trip back behind enemy lines for medical care, making him unavailable for the assignment, avoiding the same fate. The images force him to consider the fact that he had escaped their fate only because of a "streak of luck."

"Maybe it was 'Divine Intervention' as Mom had said," he thinks as he contemplates his mother's letter; written to him after he had sent her a letter telling her what had happened to Randy. As he recalls the freak accident that had determined his life, he thanks God for allowing him to avoid the same destiny.

Bursts of conversations he had had with Randy echo in his mind. They had become friends quickly, a fact that he had found odd because he had never been able to make friendships with other men. Randy had been the first Black man he had ever met. He remembers how easy it had been to bond with him, becoming best friends in a very short time. Thinking of the plans that they had made for the time after their discharge when they would be back in their homes in their mutual state of Pennsylvania, he wonders if a graveyard will be the ultimate location of their reunion. A strange noise distracts him, taking him out of the moment.

Positioning his binoculars for a perfect view of the clearing bordering the far edge of the jungle, he watches as a form emerges from out of the darkness into the moonlight. For only a moment, he likens the scene to an actor who is making an entrance onto a stage, complete with an orchestra playing the jungle noises as background music. As he focuses on the figure approaching him, it takes only seconds for him to abandon his diversionary thinking.

It's a woman – just a girl.

He sees her pretty face come into view. Her long-jet-black-hair hangs down to her waist from under a 'Cooley', a conical straw hat. The hat and the loose-fitting-pajama-style pants under a long shirt known as an 'Áo bà ba' are the typical attire for women in tropical countries. She carries a small child who appears to be sleeping. "Maybe it is dead," he thinks as he watches her approach. Her steps are strong, determined, and moving with purpose – as if she is on a mission.

The memory of a previous operation pops into his mind. It had occurred when his squad had been out on patrol – his first assignment as a combat infantryman. The squad had just passed a group of rice paddies when they had come upon a clearing in a little cove, surrounded by tall trees, littered by hanging brush and vines. From behind a slight mound in the hillside, three Vietnamese women had appeared; one held a child in her arms. As the platoon had moved toward the women, Sergeant Egan, the soldier in charge, motioned to his men to halt and hold their fire. The Sergeant and several soldiers approached the women with guns drawn. A grenade attached to the apparently dead child exploded just as a squad of enemy soldiers opened fire.

After a fierce gun battle, he and the surviving soldiers found Sergeant Egan, the women, and the child in pieces scattered on the ground. All of the enemy soldiers were dead, but shrapnel and gunfire had left several Americans injured. Through some kind of a miracle, he had not been one of them. The memory brings reality to the situation at hand, one of potential danger, as well as acting as a catalyst for his next move.

Studying her as she moves closer, he allows his binoculars to drop on its cord around his neck and places both hands on his weapon. He stares at her down the barrel of his rifle as he positions his weapon and points it directly at her head, zeroing on a spot in the middle of her forehead. Confident of his mark, he executes a visual check of the baby, looking for signs of explosives.

Finding none, but not convinced about the potential outcome, he focuses on the oval eyes staring back at him, standing motionless, glaring, and ostensibly undisturbed by the rifle pointing at her. He senses softness in her eyes, but he concentrates on the previous mental re-enactment of the gory scene of Sergeant Egan's body parts scattered in pieces. His stomach turns. As he positions his finger on the trigger, he hears only the Sergeant's voice whispering in his ear.

Fire your weapon, Robinson.

He ignores the order deciding to watch her, staying poised to react, and pressing tighter on the trigger.

"Take," she orders lifting the quiet child, offering it to him.

"No . . . No take," he answers with a slow shake of his head.

" . . . America . . . you take . . . 'merica," she pleads.

He stands frozen like an ice sculpture, melting in the heat of a sauna, sweat dripping down his forehead, over his eyelids, and down onto his cheeks.

She doesn't move. Again, he studies her outstretched arms holding the still child; he never flinches as he turns his head from side to side, again, confirming his negativity.

What am I going to do with a baby?

He considers his own question, his mind drawing several possible scenarios – none very appealing. He concludes that he is stalling, listening to the voices in his head, not concentrating on the reality of the situation. He wills himself to stay focused and his eyes never leave hers as he squeezes the trigger tighter.

The baby lets out a deafening scream – the jungle goes silent.

It is alive.

For a split second, he and the woman seem as one, both of them staring at the noisy child, now squirming, screaming hysterically, crying in the woman's arms with huge tears flowing down her cheeks, matching those on the face of the woman.

He steadies his trigger finger, halting any further motion.

The woman lets out a sigh, her bottom lip quivering as she takes a deep breath . . . and waits.

Hoping that her next move will force his decision, he also waits, watching as the screaming baby continues to serenade them.

In what seems like an hour, but is only a fraction of a second, he replaces the image of the Vietnamese woman with the one of *the beautiful doe protecting her little fawn* – the same one that had eluded him on that first hunting trip in Pennsylvania so long ago. Back then, he couldn't pull the trigger, making his first kill – nor can he now – despite hearing Sergeant Egan's voice shouting an order in his ear.

Shoot her Robinson!

She moves her lips as if she will speak, but the sultry air carries no words. Instead, it brings a light rain, washing over them as if the heavens had started to weep. The baby stops crying . . . leaving only the sound of the silent jungle. As if frozen, he can only watch as the woman suddenly bolts toward him. In one motion, she throws the baby at him, turns, and runs toward the jungle.

The baby lands with a thud onto a pile of dried brush in front of him and begins screaming again the top of its lungs, flinging its arms, and kicking its feet. Thinking that the baby is booby-trapped, he falls to the ground and braces himself for the explosion, but his body barely touches the ground before he changes his mind.

Remembering the *'little fawn'* from the forest of Pennsylvania and likening it to the baby, who is now thrashing like a whirling dervish with screaming accompaniment, he drops his weapon, scrambles to get upright again, and dashes toward the baby all the while praying that he will not find a grenade or that a sniper's bullet will not find him.

He lifts the baby up, frantically searching it and the area around it. "Damn it! I should have shot her when I had the chance," he curses under his breath as his eyes team with his hands, finding every part of the child's small gyrating body.

His hands trembling, but finding nothing, he picks the noisy baby up and runs back, diving behind the sand bags, falling on top of the baby, shielding it.

His heart pounds as he feels the child beneath him on the wet ground, now just whimpering. Seizing his weapon again, he assumes his position behind the stack of bags, scanning the area with his rifle pointed toward the jungle. He looks down the barrel of his rifle as his nostrils fill with the odor of green vegetation soaked in rain. Moving in a half circle with his rifle pointed, he searches the unknown, looking for the enemy.

Finding nothing, he relaxes and he positions his binoculars again, seeing only the quiet darkness beyond, providing him with the last glance of the woman before the jungle consumes her – just as the dark forest in Pennsylvania had consumed that doe so long ago, hiding her in the same ambiguity from which she had come.

He hears his heart beating outside of his body as he searches the horizon. After a thorough check, finding nothing, reassured that the woman had acted alone, he allows his glasses to fall onto his chest, lowers his rifle, and turns his attention to the baby, now hanging onto his boot, still turning, twisting, and very much engrossed in its own discomforts.

Another search of it provides nothing.

He breathes a sigh of relief.

"Thank-you-God," he exhales. Another deep breath brings an inexplicable desire to help the child. He runs his fingers over the baby's body, checking for broken bones, looking for any lacerations, and concluding that *it is crying more from fright than injury.*

Wondering why someone down the line has not responded to its cries, he signals with their designated whistle. The shrill but soft sound startles the baby, stopping its crying. It looks up at him, sending him a smile through its tears.

He stares at it, trying to explain the weird sensation of having met the baby before, not able to understand the feeling, thinking of it as belonging to the enemy but something about the color of the baby's eyes hypnotizes him.

After only a few moments of trying to connect his thoughts to the baby, he shrugs off the feelings of familiarity and centers his attention on the little face, now studying him with the curiosity of a kitten. Its almond shaped eyes, bright as star sapphires and shining with tears, reflect the diminishing moonlight. As the last of the tears roll down its brown cheeks, he notes the child's darker skin, wavy-hair, and unusually colored eyes, seeming to glow with the same color blue as the Vietnamese sky.

It isn't pure Vietnamese.

He decides that an African American, *probably a soldier,* may have fathered it. As he speculates about the possible scenarios of the child's conception, flashes of accounts of warring American soldiers interacting with the Vietnamese women appear in his mind. The mental pictures disturb him as he studies it further and considers the fact that Randy had done two tours and had had plenty of time to interact with the native women. The thought opens up the remote idea that *Randy may have had a relationship with a Vietnamese woman, leading to fatherhood.* He looks back at the child and sees Randy in its little face.

Could this be Randy's kid?

He considers the fact that *Randy had never mentioned any Vietnamese women,* quickly shaking his head in disbelief. *Not happening – Randy would have told me.* As he turns his attention away from the child to inspect the area again, he dismisses the possibility of the child belonging in any way to Randy.

After another survey, seeing nothing, and hearing only the sound of the child's sobbing, he checks it again. It is sitting up now, trying to climb his leg, wrapping its small arms around his calf.

What's taking them so long?

He speculates the possible reasons why no one has recognized his signal and decides to whistle again.

The bird-like sound of his whistle distracts the baby. It stops whimpering, looks up at him on his six-foot-two perch, and pulls itself up, grabbing onto his thigh.

"You are probably not even able to walk," he thinks as he considers his inexperience with babies and the likeliness of the baby having any previous experience with an American.

He watches as the baby turns its bottom lip down and starts to cry harder, bringing him to the conclusion that he is scaring it to death. He pictures himself as the baby is seeing him, noting his large frame, freckled face, and crop of strawberry-blond hair. "Hello, my little lost friend. My name is James . . . I wonder what yours is," he whispers.

Responding to the soft tone of his baritone voice, the baby coos as its stare finds his face. The serious expression on the baby's face turns to a smile, making him think that it is trying to say something to him. "I don't understand much Vietnamese and yours sounds like Vietnamese babble," he thinks as he studies the child further, unable to stop looking at it, deciding that their introduction now changes his former concept of the *baby-enemy-with-the-grenade.*

After studying the dark sable-colored waves of dark hair becoming curls surrounding its small face, he notices that its feet are bare, poking out

32

of the legs of some wet pants. A dirty shirt and the pants are its only clothes. He decides to check under the pants and finds a cloth diaper prompting him to notice the large puddle surrounding his boots.

"Great, Diaper Duty," he mutters with a smile and making a funny face, trying to make the child stop crying.

"I can't change you right now, Buddy, even if I knew how," he whispers. For the first time, he feels compelled to investigate the gender of the child. He looks inside the wet diaper.

His face blushes.

"Wow! You are a SHE," he sighs as he quickly stops looking and closes the diaper.

She looks up at him with a serious expression, matching the one on the woman who had abandoned her.

"I'm not going to hurt you, Baby," he whispers.

She smiles back, melting his heart like a torch in a snow bank.

He lowers his weapon, picks her up with one hand, and bounces her lightweight body, trying to comfort her. "Hush. You're okay. You'll wake up Saigon if you keep it up," he pleads as he places his hand on her back, pats it, and whispering soft words of comfort.

Holding her small body in one arm close to his chest, he places his weapon in front of her, trying to protect her. His hips sway, moving in rhythm to a humming sound inside his head. Only a few of the words of his mother's lullaby come back to him, but the melody rings clear.

[2]"Lull-a-bye and good-night," he sings no louder than a whisper.

For the moment, he is no longer a soldier and *she isn't the enemy.*

His mind travels back to former times, ones when he had been in the company of those he had loved, and who had loved him. A picture of Madeline, the woman he had left behind to another man, explodes before him, bringing a sweet memory of her kisses. His heart aches as he recalls their last good-bye and he longs to be home, feeling her arms around him. The sound of a male voice startles him, taking him away from his yearnings, bringing him back to reality.

"Hey, Robinson, what's this . . . Looks like [3]'Romper Room'."

He looks up to see the smiling faces of Private Johnson and Private Reynolds, soldiers in his platoon positioned farther down the line. He feels his cheeks get warm.

---

[2] Johannes Brahms's Wiegenlied: Guten Abend, gute Nacht ("Good evening, good night"), Op. 49, No. 4, published in 1868 and widely known as Brahms's Lullaby, wikipedia.org/Brahm's Lullaby

[3] Romper Room, a long running children's television series . . .in the United States . . . Canada . . . from 1953 to 1994 wikipedia.org/wiki/Romper_Room

"Yeah, some woman dropped her off."

"We heard the cries and your signals," says Private Reynolds.

"What took you so long?"

"We wanted to make sure that 'The 'Stork' wasn't making any more deliveries," Johnson finishes with a straight face.

"Give it to me . . . I'll take it back to the base," offers Reynolds.

"No. I'll take her," he says pulling her closer as he straightens his shoulders and tightens the muscles in his jaw, hoping to show the demeanor of a combat infantryman – *not the one of the troubadour babysitter.*

"It's a 'HER'?" Johnson asks.

"Yeah . . . Finish the guard duty," he orders giving them a stern look and squeezing her tighter.

"Corporal Robinson, you aren't getting soft on us, are ya, Bro'?" Johnson teases.

"Don't worry about it," he says walking away.

As he walks toward the compound, carrying her, he reprimands himself, feeling guilty because the others had found him slacking in his soldierly duties. However, despite hearing their chuckles as he makes his way back, he doesn't find fault with his actions but, as a sudden downpour drenches him, he can't dismiss Johnson's innuendo.

"Getting soft" . . . yeah . . . that's right."

"Damn rain, that's all it does in this god-forsaken-country," he mumbles under his breath as he moves toward the base. Hiding her face under his arm, pressing her small body closer to him, he tries to protect her from the onslaught of the heavy rain. As he takes some carefully planned steps, trying not to slip on the muddy ground, he considers his actions and tries to justify them in his own mind, deciding that he had acted appropriately and that the incident had a good outcome in that no life was lost. However, now, despite his efforts to act soldierly, he can't resist the urge to rock her. His mind inundates with feelings of gentleness and kindness – ones he had thought he had lost since coming to the battlefield. It takes only a few rocking motions before the 'star-sapphires' make their final retreat behind her eyelids, but he thinks it will take more than a few graceful moves before he will forget them, or her.

As he nears the gate, he can't stop thinking about Randy. He looks down at the sleeping child, pictures Randy sleeping with the angels just as peacefully, and catches her smiling in her sleep. "The dimples in her cheeks dance when she smiles – just like Randy's," he remembers as he recalls some earlier conversations he and Randy had shared. One in particular comes to mind – the first time they had shared their backgrounds after becoming friends as well as fellow soldiers.

"I had volunteered to come to Vietnam, James," Randy had confided.

"Not me, Randy. The Draft is the only reason I am here. When I had lost the student deferment at the Community College, 'Good, old, Uncle Sam' was right there with the draft notice."

"I had scholarships to at least a half dozen Ivy League schools."

"You enlisted, instead?"

"Yeah . . . After pilot training school, they sent me to Guam and then here. When my first tour had ended, I asked to be deployed here again."

"You must love punishment?"

"Not really, I wanted to make my country proud," Randy said with a glint in his eye.

"My parents had struggled to pay the tuition . . . They had wanted me to go to college . . . not my choice. It would have been really something for them if I had graduated college – the one thing that I could have done to really make them proud of me, but I flunked out."

"Well, I had disappointed my mother when I had become a pilot instead of going to Harvard. I guess we have something in common."

"My parents are second generation German/Irish, farmers in Mercer County, just north of Pittsburgh. What about yours, Randy?"

"My mother was German, raised in Berlin. Her father had arranged her marriage to a Nazi."

"Was your father a Nazi?"

"No," he grinned. "Haven't you noticed? I'm not blue-eyed and blond. My father was Black, a pilot, the second marriage for my mother. I've wanted to be a pilot for as long as I can remember."

"I had always dreamed of becoming a farmer, just like my dad. I wanted to stay in Pennsylvania, grow fruits and vegetables, get married, and have a bunch of kids."

"We have 'Pittsburgh' in common, too, James. I was raised there."

"Really, maybe when we both get out of here, we can go see a baseball game together?"

"Maybe, but, when my tour is up this time, I want to come back to Vietnam again – as a civilian," Randy shared.

"Not me, I never want to see this place again. Why would you ever want to come back?"

"I guess we all have our own dreams."

Remembering his private moments with Randy is painful for him, especially the one when he and Randy had made a mutual decision to exchange letters to their next of kin in the events of their deaths. When they had gotten word of Randy and the others, the chaplain retrieved the letter that he had written to his parents from Randy's personal effects and had given it back to him. He fulfilled his promise to Randy by sending the letter he had written to his mother to her. He had also written a letter of his own to her, expressing how much he had admired her son. Writing that letter to Randy's mother had been one of the most difficult tasks that he had ever done.

His thoughts return to other conversations he had had with him, ones that had bonded them, bringing him to the conclusion that Randy had indeed been the older brother that he had always wished for, but had never had. Since the day that he had learned of Randy's death, he had felt a part of him had died, not able to imagine a time when everything and everyone wouldn't remind him of Randy.

His mother's words as she had kissed his cheek and said good-bye at the airport pass in his mind. "Things happen for a reason, Jimmy. Fate never determines your life. Divine Intervention does."

His mother's words bring a feeling of finality for him.

"You're not the enemy," he whispers looking down at the baby, now sound asleep in his arms. Her lips move, but her eyes never open as the corners of her mouth turn up. Touched, he answers his own question with another.

"Who cares who your father is?"

"You should be raised in the greatest country on earth," he whispers as Randy's smiling face appears in his mind again.

"I'm going to make sure you are," he breathes into her ear.

"Randy would want it that way."

*

Her eyes wet and her voice cracking, Sofia stops reciting her story.

As evidenced by the tears streaming down her cheeks, the story has affected Janene as well. She sits glued to the chair, only her eyes move, finding Sofia, and waiting for an explanation.

Sofia swallows hard and explains.

"I had written that story in 2006, Janene, after I had attended a Memorial Service for Vietnam Veterans. Corporal Robinson had been the keynote speaker. At the reception, we had a long conversation about his time in Vietnam. I had wanted to continue talking with him after the event and we had agreed to get in touch to set up a time. Unfortunately, he died before we could meet again . . . only a few weeks afterward from a sudden heart attack," she shares relaxing her shoulders, but tightening her grasp on the cluster of pink squares in the center of the quilt.

Janene is compelled to look away, again staring at the portrait of the soldier. Suddenly, as if a light goes on in her mind, she remembers the searches she had done through the Department of the Army and the name of the one soldier whom she had been trying to find after quizzing Bill about the circumstances of her adoption.

Corporal James Robinson.

"What are you saying, Sofia?"

"I'm Randy's mother. The portrait on the wall and those on the piano are of him. He had wanted to be just like his father, my second husband, Randolph Robert Blackburn II," she says pausing to wipe her tears.

"It seems that he has managed to achieve just that, following him to an early grave."

"I'm so sorry, Sofia."

"Thank you, Janene, but I think I should be offering you condolences as well. You see, I believe that we are related," Sofia says barely louder than a whisper.

Janene swallows hard, preparing for what she is now certain that Sofia will tell her, but is afraid to hear.

"I am your grandmother. As one might call me in Germany, I am your 'Oma', and you are my son's daughter," she shares as she slowly rises from the chair and extends her arms out, moving toward Janene, already on her feet and trembling.

"Your name is 'An-Ly Tai Blackburn'," Sofia whispers putting her arms around her, pulling her close.

" . . . I was told that you were dead . . ."

* * * * *

CHAPTER 2
FAMILY

After Janene and Sofia had taken a few minutes to regain composure, Sofia says, "I would like to tell you more about your family."

"That would make me very happy. This seems unbelievable. I don't know how to thank you. Until Madeline had passed away, I grew up having no interest in finding any information about my roots. I regret that now. I had prayed I had not waited too long and I was optimistic about this meeting with you. Now, I am very grateful that I have found you."

"I'm just thankful that your job at the magazine had demanded some research and that it had revealed information about my centers. I am very proud of them."

"You should be, Sofia. They are a great accomplishment and a testimony to your strong character."

"Thank you, but I wasn't always strong, Janene. After I had lost Randy, my life needed a purpose. I found one when I had opened the first center for the children."

"I noticed that you had used a quilt as your logo?"

"Yes. If not for my quilt, I would never have had the inspiration to begin the centers. Maybe you would like me to tell you why I have such a strong affection for this old and tattered blanket?" she asks tugging it closer and smiling.

"I would like that very much."

"I couldn't tell my story without a mention of the quilt. That is how important it is to me. It continues to be the one item in my vast estate whose future, after I am gone, perplexes me."

"Oh my, Sofia, you aren't ill, are you?"

"At eighty-nine, one doesn't take anything for granted, least of all the calculation of your days here on earth. The disposal of some things is easier than for others. I have specified that this old blanket, which means so very much to me, is to be buried with me," she says looking down lovingly at the quilt.

"I don't have anything in my life that I would consider that important. That is, important enough to bury it with me."

"Some might think I am a crazy old lady," she smiles.

"I don't think that."

"You see, Janene, the quilt has been in and out of my life since I had been five years old. To me, it is a reminder of my past, a relic of the earliest times in my life when those whom I had loved had molded me according to my country's traditions and culture. It is the one unifying link in my life of so many 'new beginnings'. Perhaps, once I tell you my story, you will understand."

"The pictures of the children printed on the quilt in your hallway tell a remarkable story about the woman who had established the worldwide centers for needy children. My curiosity about that had peaked the moment I had seen the plaque on your front door."

"Oh, yes, you noticed the metal sculpture. One of the parents at the first center had given it to me. He had made it himself. At the time, he was a struggling artist who had lost his wife in an accident, no longer able to care for his two-year old son. After the center had cared for his son and he had been able to resume his parental role, he had presented me with the sculpture as a token of his gratitude.

"I'm feeling overwhelmed, Sofia. I can't believe all of this. It just doesn't seem real."

"I couldn't believe it at first either; I mean about you and my son and his time in Vietnam. I had first learned of you and your Vietnamese mother after the Department of the Army had notified me of Randy's death in July of 1972. Shortly after I had received that notification from the Army, I received a letter from an orphanage in Saigon, telling of a Vietnamese woman who had identified Randy as the father of her daughter. Sadly, the letter further explained that the woman and her child had been killed when the North Vietnamese had destroyed her village."

"I know little to nothing about my birth, not even the exact date. Apparently, I was born sometime in late 1971, possibly even early 1972. They had guessed at my age. Bill and Madeline had adopted me on the third of February in 1973 and they had celebrated my birthday every year on that date."

"I only know the date of Randy's death – July 31, 1972," Sofia replies. "Until a month ago, when you had inquired about your biological family, I had believed that you and your mother were dead and that I would never be able to unravel all of the mysteries of Randy's time in South Vietnam. I had spent many years trying to deal with the senselessness of his death. However, deep in my heart, I had always had this uncanny feeling that things were not what they had seemed."

"I thought it had come from my unwillingness to believe that he had died, but something about that report from the orphanage never felt right to me. Of course, the letter from Corporal Robinson, as well as the one from the orphanage, had given a certain degree of authenticity to all of the accounts from the Army but, after years of dealing with the horrible grief, I had never really accepted his death, or the story of his time there. Your recent inquiry to my center in Vietnam had generated a new interest, precipitating a new investigation on my part. I hired a special investigator to work with my center there in the hopes of discovering any new information."

"I'm so glad that you did."

"No more than I am. The investigator had found an ex-nun who had worked in an orphanage near the base in the early 1970's. She verified that Randy did have a relationship with a Vietnamese woman, one whose family had lived in a little village outside of Saigon, not far from the base. She said that the Viet Cong had destroyed the village and many of those who had lived there. This was the first that I had heard of any information, as Randy had never shared any details about his time there, which never surprised me. I had been deeply against his enlisting in the service. Perhaps, that is why he never told me."

"Your son never told you that he had fathered a child in Vietnam?"

"No . . . I had no idea until I got word after his death."

"Do you have any reason to question the validity of the story?"

"Not at this point. I believe the story to be true. However, the investigator is still looking for more clues but he has assured me that what I have just told you is accurate. The baby who had been given to Corporal Robinson by the woman in the jungle was indeed Randy's child," she says with a pause to take a deep breath.

"There is something else, Janene – something that I am sure that Corporal Robinson and Bill and Madeline McDeenon didn't know," Sofia says tears forming again.

Janene's eyes open wide.

"You are an identical twin, Janene."

"What?"

"Yes, it's true. Randy had fathered more than one baby."

"You mean that I might have a twin sister out there somewhere?"

"Yes, if she is still alive."

"This is unbelievable."

"Actually, it didn't surprise me as much as you might think. They say 'twins run in families' – my mother had a twin brother. I can imagine your surprise. If only Randy had told me, I would have moved the earth to get my granddaughters home."

Janene feels a lump in her throat.

"What else do you know?"

"When I had met James Robinson, he had told me about his experience while standing guard shortly after Randy had died. He said that he had never forgotten the little girl because her eyes had reminded him so much of Randy. Now that I've met you, I can see why," she says smiling and looking into Janene's eyes.

"He also said that the experience had prompted him to recall a conversation that he had had with Randy several weeks before the fateful night when his helicopter had been shot down. Randy had told him that he had wanted to 'go back to Vietnam after his second tour had ended and he was worried about the war and its impact on his ability to do that. He never shared with Robinson any of the reasons why he had wanted to return. However, James had said that the experience with the woman and the baby had haunted him until he had been so moved by it, that he had approached his friends, Bill and Madeline McDeenon, with the idea of adopting the little girl."

"Was my mother the woman who had given the baby away?"

"I don't know the answer to that question. The investigator is still trying to piece it all together. "If she was, Robinson couldn't verify it. He admitted that he had always felt some connection to the woman and the baby, but he had no proof except for his own vivid imagination. In the end, he had concluded that it had been his grief over losing Randy that had generated a need for him to make the comparison of the baby to Randy."

"Did Corporal Robinson tell you any more about my adoptive parents?"

"Robinson also told me that his friends, the McDeenons, had said that they wanted to work with a Catholic organization to adopt the child. After finding out that they had been successful in adopting the child given to him in the jungle, he put the entire incident behind him. My investigator has revealed that the orphanage in Saigon had papers identifying the baby as an 'Identical Twin', but the records are very inconclusive. He is still trying to unravel it all."

"I'm shocked, Sofia. Is your investigator certain?"

"Yes, he said he was very certain. In addition, I have hired him to continue the investigation, telling him not to stop until he can provide me with every detail available about my son's time in South Vietnam."

"Has he made any progress?"

"Not yet, but he is encouraged by the information he has been able to gather, mostly as a result of contacts through my children center there. I can't help but believe that some type of 'Divine Intervention' must have been in play, just as Robinson had concluded. The center in Vietnam wouldn't exist – none of them would have, if it had not been for this old tattered quilt," she said looking down at it lovingly.

"What makes you say that, Sofia?"

"It is a long story and one I hope to tell you. I would like to invite you and Bill to stay here with us for a few days so that we can get to know each other better and I can tell you more about your father and your family."

"That is so very nice of you."

"It is the least I can do for my granddaughter."

"You must miss Randy very much," Janene stutters feeling a new sense of belonging.

"One can never explain the feelings of a parent who has lost a child. Right now, I am thinking about Randy and all that he had lost. He had lost his life while trying to achieve his goal of serving his country. The fact that he had also lost the opportunity to see his children grow up had never occurred to me until now. That makes me very sad, but what makes me even sadder now is the revelation that you and your sister never knew him. Now that I have found you, I am not concentrating on losses. I am rejoicing. An old woman's dream of living long enough to finally know the truth is now a reality."

"I wish I had known him."

"You may not have had the opportunity to know him personally, but I assure you, I plan on doing everything in my power to make certain you will know everything about him. That means beginning right now," she says as she hands her the framed picture of Randy that she had hidden under the folds of the quilt.

"Oh, my," Janene says taking the picture in her hand, studying it.

"I'm also investigating further into your Vietnamese family besides finding out what had happened to your sister. I'll not rest until I have found her and any other members of your family. You are part of our family, Janene. I want you to know everything about us. Not only do I want you to hear about our German family, but I also want you to know about your African American side."

"I appreciate that, Sofia."

"I regret that I had never had the opportunity to know the Blackburn Family as well as I would have liked. Before their deaths, they had played a huge part in Randy's earlier life. They are all gone now, but I'll share their family history so you will have a total picture of your very rich heritage," Sofia says reaching for the leather-bound album on the side table with the cover marked 'Randolph R. Blackburn II and Randolph R. Blackburn III' in gold letters.

"Thank you," Janene says taking the book in her hands, holding it as if it is a carton of eggs, leafing through the pages, looking at the pictures of her father when he had been a boy and his father as a young Army pilot in World War II. She feels a pang in her heart when she sees the face of the American soldier in the jungle of South Vietnam.

"I'm overwhelmed, Sofia. I don't know how to thank you."

"Randy would be very proud of you. I want to tell you about him."

"I would like that."

"Then, I'll begin at the beginning – always a good place to start," Sofia smiles sitting back in her chair, relaxing her shoulders, and taking a deep breath before beginning her ritual again, stroking the pink square in the center of the quilt.

*

"A very long time ago, a little girl lived in Germany at a time when there was great unrest in her country. Her father was a poor baker and her mother was the daughter of a peasant farmer. Her name was 'Sofia' . . .

*

Noticing the surprised look on Janene's face, Sofia stops speaking and looks to Janene, waiting, as if expecting a reaction from her. Almost on cure, Janene asks, "The story is about you, Sofia?"

"Yes. It is. I know you want to know more about your father, but I can't explain him without telling you my story. I believe that his understanding of my life had influenced his decisions about his own life and, sadly, they were ones that had led to his untimely death."

"I see. Forgive me for interrupting."

"Please don't apologize. I can see where you might be confused. I thought it best to begin my story by telling you about my grandparents – yours as well. In Germany, we refer to a grandmother as 'Oma' and a grandfather as 'Opa'. I hope you will feel comfortable enough to call me 'Oma' sometime. It would be a great honor for me."

"It would be an honor for me if you would call me by my nickname, sometime. Only my family and my closest friends call me 'Neeny'," Janene whispers casting her eyes down, feeling shy, and uncertain. "I've never had a grandmother. Bill's and Madeline's mothers had died long before my adoption," she smiles.

44

"Well then, I'll begin again, Neeny."

"Your great-great-grandparents were 'Heinrich and Frieda Schmidt'. They loved God, Germany and each other very much. They had been hard working farmers in a community of designated fields in the rural area just north of Berlin – that is until 1924 when Oma had come to live with us."

As Janene listens to Sofia's story, the accuracy of it, especially the part about having a twin sister begins to bother her. *Is it the truth or just another wild goose chase?* Confused by the sudden burst of information, she considers her past efforts to find her biological family.

Maybe it is curiosity just getting the best of me.

She has that feeling again, the one in the pit of her stomach. She studies Sofia's face noticing that her eyes, still glazed with moisture, seem to focus on something or someone not present in the room.

It is as if she has removed herself to another time and place.

She sends Sofia a smile. To her surprise, Sofia smiles back, obviously paying particular attention to Janene's reactions to the story when only a moment ago, her mind seemed to be back in Germany in 1924. Sofia's smile gives her a sense of belonging for the first time.

Maybe she really is my grandmother.

However, the manner in which Sofia has elected to tell the story still arouses her curiosity. *How could she possibly memorize the story word for word?* The fact that Sofia seems to have memorized her story and can recite it perfectly seems remarkable to her. The feat would be a difficult one for a much younger person, but seems highly questionable for a woman Sofia's age.

Her attention turns again to Sofia as she contemplates reasons for why Sofia would choose to tell her about her biological family by relating the story from memory. She sits back in her chair, waits, and listens, finding it hard to concentrate on the story when she can't stop asking questions about the storyteller. Looking to the recorder, checking it to make sure it is working, the glow of the green light reassures her that she will have an accurate account of 'Sofia's Story'. However, she still has many unanswered questions and she watches Sofia closely for clues that will answer them.

Why is Sofia constantly glancing at that quilt?

She is unable to understand what Sofia could possibly get from an attachment to an old tattered blanket. Deciding to pay closer attention to her story, she wonders about the role that the quilt must have played in Sofia's life.

Why would she hold it in such high esteem?

As Sofia pauses, taking a deep breath, Janene's concern for her rises. "She seems so weak," she thinks as she considers asking her if she would like to take a rest and resume at another time. However, a new strength seems to energize Sofia and her voice gets stronger. Deciding that Sofia must have deliberately willed herself to go on, Janene changes her mind, inspired by Sofia's strength.

Listening carefully to Sofia, she turns her attention to another time and place, one that seems very important to Sofia's story, a farmhouse just north of Berlin in 1924.

"The light of a new October day slips through the window of the old farmhouse, catching the eyelids of sixty-five year old, Frau Frieda Schmidt, reminding her of the day that she had been dreading," Sofia says.

"Where are the roosters?" Frieda mumbles opening her eyes.

The birds had always been her alarm clock and their absence disturbs her, but only until she remembers that her only son, twenty-four year old 'Adam', had sold them to Herr Schuler yesterday. The recollection makes her stomach turn. Three generations of the Schmidt and Krause families had endured immense hardships over the years, but they had always managed to hold onto their fields – until now.

She pictures her only daughter, 'Alexandra', Adam's twin sister, holding her newborn son, 'Franz'. Alexandra's five-year old daughter, 'Sofia', stands nearby. As she considers them, the next generation of Germans, she wonders about their futures. Her own questioning reminds her of Sofia, who *is always asking questions, one after another.* The little girl with the vibrant-blue, inquiring eyes, and thick-blonde-wavy hair had become a great source of joy to Frieda. As she reflects on the German birthright of her children and grandchildren, she considers all that she had learned of the German traditions as she had grown up in the same house that she has to abandon now.

That legacy from her beloved family had provided her with a wealth of strong morals and beliefs, giving her a sense of pride in her family, church, and country. Recalling scenes from the earliest times of her upbringing when she had asked questions about her ancestors, she wonders if Sofia and Franz will grow up asking some of the same questions, wanting to know about their heritage. She considers the fact that she had been that way as a child, always asking questions. Her memory takes her to the many times she had sat on her father's lap, asking him *one question after another.*

Thinking about the past saddens her, while contemplating the future brings her great anxiety. She had not always felt this way; she is sure that her present sense of insecurity had started after Germany had lost the war. She knows little about the politics of the past or the present, but she is certain about one thing, their lives had changed dramatically after the soldiers had walked away from the Front and had come home, defeated, demoralized, and depressed about their futures.

She likens the changes in Germany to those of the life cycle of the caterpillar – *in reverse*. She thinks about the metamorphosis that must occur before the dull and gloomy bug can transform itself into the beautiful butterfly, whose symmetrical wings designed with glorious precision cut shapes take it skyward, leaving its earthbound existence. Comparing the butterfly to the country's magnificent monarchy, now in its demise, she considers the fact that the country has returned to a former dark time. The contrast makes her heart ache for the country of her parents and grandparents. "Life had seemed better back then," she thinks as she reaches for the quilt she had made, rubs the patch of fabric that had belonged to her mother, and reflects on the times when she had felt safe and secure in her arms, looking forward to her future, not longing for the past.

She had made the quilt from remnants of her family's clothes and textiles when she had been just a girl, keeping it close to her over the years, feeling as if it had possessed some magical powers. The mere act of caressing it to her cheek and calling to mind one of the many stories about her deceased relatives had always given her comfort. Over the years, it had become her source of refuge, a hiding place from the realities of the day, bringing fond memories of the past, and giving her a renewed sense of strength. However, now, as she lay wide-eyed in the dimly lit bedroom of the only home she had ever known and contemplating never seeing it again, her quilt does nothing to relieve her overwhelming sadness and anxiety. The lyrics of a monotonous song, one describing their pending doom begins again. The song, one of a round of questions with no answers, just repetitious scores of dread and doom had begun, a day in early March when Adam had shared the bad news with her.

*

Six Months Earlier

It had been a cold and windy day, another in a string of them that had brought a yearning for nature's renewal, a new beginning, and an end to the long winter. The embers of the pieces of scrap wood that Adam had managed to hoard had burned to a soft orange glow, giving them the last hope for some warmth. Dressed in her coat and wool scarf, Frieda sits at the table across from Adam finishing the last of the meager meal she had managed to provide; some beans canned last summer and made into a soup. The light of a burned down candle flickers, revealing Adam's face.

Their eyes meet. Her heart flutters, remembering the last time that she had seen that look on his face had been nine years earlier, the day that her beloved Heinrich had died.

"I have some bad news, Mutti."

"What? You look as if you have seen a ghost."

"Maybe I have."

"Just tell me."

"The price of seed is too high and we have no money," Adam shares with a blank face.

"I don't understand."

"Money is worthless. Even if I had been able to save from last season, it still wouldn't be enough. I would have to spend it as soon as I had made it. Even a one-day delay makes a difference. The prices keep getting higher every day, sometimes in the same day," he says slowly moving his head from side to side in disbelief.

"Perhaps we should burn our money. Use it as fuel. It might be more economical," he says sarcastically. "That is the way it had been pictured in a political cartoon in the newspaper in town. Hmm, since we have no money or fuel, it really makes no difference."

"What does it mean, Adam?"

"If I can't produce a crop this season, Mutti, they will take back the fields – give them to another, one who they believe will," he says casting his head down, not able to look at her.

"Lose the farm? How could this happen?"

"I am truly sorry, Mutter, but there isn't anything I can do," Adam says petting the back of her hand softly. "We will just have to walk away. I can't stop them – they have their own agendas," he mumbles letting his body sink into the chair and raising his hands in desperation. "I am powerless to change this."

Frieda sits staring at him, not able to find words. She watches as he gets up from the table, puts on his hat and coat, and walks out without saying another word.

That was when the song had first begun to play in her mind, continuing its annoying repetition every day as she had tried to brace herself for the possibility of losing her home.

How-can-it-be . . . Lose-the-farm . . . How can it be?

Frieda had begun to think of it as her 'lullaby' . . . it had sung her to sleep each night. Its monotonous verse repeated itself continually until she would awake terrified, turning her dreams into nightmares. The sleep deprivation during the night brought extreme fatigue during the day. The song became background music for her every thought, creating great anxiety for her as she awaited their destiny, feeling powerless to prevent it.

The impending doom of having to leave the only home that she had ever known haunted her every waking and sleeping moment.

March turned to April and the rains had softened the fields. Adam planted the heirloom seeds that he had saved from the previous year, hoping that they would produce a bountiful crop, enough for him to gain permission to keep the farm. However, all of his hard work and tender loving care only produced a barren field. No amount of rain, sunshine, or Adam's diligence – or Frieda's prayers – would make those shattered seeds grow. By the end of August, they knew their fate

*

Moving Day
4 October 1924

Frieda wants to make her body move from her bed, but she can't dismiss the melancholy thoughts of her past life, nor the terrifying ones of a homeless future, which are keeping her from rising and facing the new day. The song of heartbreak plays in her mind again. The music weighs her down, making her efforts to rise seem impossible.

Time has not been kind to Frieda. The effects of years of hard work and the onslaught of arthritis show in her twisted joints and distorted bones, replacing her youthful look. It had developed over time, but its arrival had been marked with a vigorous display of afflictions, hallmarked by severe stiffness and pain, becoming a challenge so great she questions the strengths of her coping skills. Yearning for the young, vibrant, beautiful body of the girl she had once been, she misses the comforts of her youth, something she had always taken for granted. Depression grips her as she forces her mind to jump past the sad memories, wrapping itself around strong feelings of determination, borne from her strong maternal instincts.

Her body moves, lifting upright, revealing an old woman's torso which has been ravaged by a harsh life, first as the daughter of a farmer and then as the wife of one. With a newfound strength, she sits on the side of the bed, dangling her feet onto the cold bare wooden floor. Pain radiates up her legs. When the cramp in her left leg turns her toes backward, she cries, "Damn it." Somehow, cursing the crippling arthritis gives her strength.

"Grandma Krause would turn over in her grave," she moans covering her mouth. "Quiet. You must not wake up Adam," she whispers to no one.

She can't stop thinking about Adam, picturing her strong handsome boy who had worked to run the farm in the absence of his father. Her stomach aches remembering the ashen look on his face when he had told her he had lost the farm. The loss had ransacked the vibrancy of his youth, leaving his face stoic with bewilderment and distrust.

"Adam needs me now, Heinrich," she whispers in the darkness of their bedroom. She looks for him, as she always does.

"I know, Frieda. I'll be waiting for you," she hears him say.

She sees the empty side of the bed and her sinks again.

Images from their childhoods provide her with a welcomed feeling of strength, helping her to rise from the bed, which she had once shared with the love of her life, Herr Heinrich Schmidt. Even though he had died nine years earlier, thinking of that day still makes her sad. Tears flow down her cheeks into the burrows of her flesh that had become hardened wrinkles. Years of working on the farm had taken their toll, but the last years, since losing Heinrich, had been the worst.

Thinking of her dead husband and her past life had become her morning ritual, but the finality of this morning, the last one in their home, takes on a special significance. Every morning when she had searched for the warmth of his body, the sweetness of his kiss or the sound of his breathing, her tears had made their trips down her cheeks, leaving permanent marks on the once flawless complexion of the beautiful girl, 'Fraulein Frieda Ana Krause'.

Reaching for the clothes that she had placed on the chair beside the bed the night before and wiping her tears, she begins her morning ceremonies, lost in thought about the past. She sees Heinrich again, remembering every detail about him as she had done every day since his death. As she pulls on the string of her white cotton nightgown letting it fall to the floor, she looks away, lowering her chin, still reacting to his gaze as if she is still the shy bride on her wedding night.

She imagines him reaching for her, taking her hand in his and pulling her back gently, his lips finding hers. His hands search her as their bodies meet in rhythmic motions. They lay locked together for only minutes before his fields beckon him, but the knowledge of their oneness and the belief that he has planted his 'seeds' sustains her and contributes to her overwhelming feeling of satisfaction.

As she reaches for her clothes, she still feels his warmth inside her. Thinking about those lost, intimate, marital moments is the most painful part of being a woman, *a woman left behind.* The long, black dress with the buttons down the front looks back at her with defiance. The garment reminds her of the burden that dressing has become. Like everything else in her life, the task of dressing is one of humiliation, despair, and regret. "Nothing is easy for me anymore," she thinks as she spreads the dress out in front of her, steps into it, and pulls it up so that she can slide her arms into its sleeves.

She moans as she hopes for success in completing the simplest of tasks as she draws the sides of the dress together with stiffened arms, contemplating the next burden, possibly the hardest, the arduous buttoning, and always a special challenge for her twisted fingers. One by one, she wraps her fingers around each wooden button, trying not to cry aloud. "Only seven?" she whispers asking no one, expecting no answer.

There might as well be seventy.

She lowers her body onto the side of the bed, trying to reach her naked foot with her hands, fumbling with the cold stockings. "Oh, I saved the best for last – the stockings and shoes," she mumbles sarcastically.

Her foot wrestles each stocking, anticipating its lack of readiness for its slide into the waiting sturdy shoe. The dark-weathered shoes reveal their age. Time and wear has molded the shape of her foot into each, a visual story of her harsh life as well, paralleling the one described by the wrinkles on her face. She had made it a habit of taking her time in dressing, knowing that if she does, the simplest of tasks would be easier. However, today she spends more time than usual, hoping to delay what she has dreaded, her final visit to Heinrich's grave.

The ritual of taking her dead husband a bouquet of his favorite flowers had started the first autumn season after his death in 1915. The chrysanthemums were always in full bloom by late summer. She remembers how Heinrich had always loved the flowers from the first time they had planted them, years earlier. The fact that the plants had reproduced themselves, returning year after year, had always surprised her. The space in front of the small farmhouse burst with its annual display of glorious colors of dark red and gold every autumn without fail and without any special skills from her. Thinking of the past makes her heart sink; she contemplates never spending another season on the farm that she loves so dearly.

"I wish Heinrich had been a mum," she thinks as she lifts her body from the bed.

He would come back to me every autumn, just like the mums.

After tying the other shoelace, she plants her feet firmly on the floor and steadies herself. "It's hard enough dealing with the stiffness, but this pain will be the death of me," she thinks with a wish that today would be that day. Focusing on her task, she moves toward the door and tiptoes down the hall past Adam's door, listening for the familiar squeak of the floorboards, hoping it doesn't arouse him.

She stops in front of his door and listens. Convinced that she hasn't awakened him, she continues past his door into the front room. Its emptiness brings more sadness; she tries to overcome it by visualizing the room as it had once been. She sees the upright piano standing against the wall next to the stone fireplace. Heinrich's chair waits for him in front of the window. The cuckoo clock pops its head in and out with its familiar cry. The windows, draped with her grandmother's crocheted curtains, allow the light of the lingering moonlight to shine through the glass of the drawing room window, giving an eerie view of shadows and forms, hidden in the grassy meadow where Heinrich once had worked.

She squeezes her eyes shut, trying to see clearly, finding the image of Heinrich pulling the plow toward the north field. As she passes his chair, she feels a chill. The scent of his pipe fills her nostrils. Her heels click on the hardwood floor, sounding echoes, and her knees creak in rhythm as she walks along the empty hallway. The sounds, sights, and smells bring back a flash of memories. She knows every nook and cranny of the house as if it had been her own body. Childhood explorations had revealed all of their secrets, providing an adventure for her inquiring young mind, but a visit to the attic had always proved to be a special treat.

She remembers how three generations of the Schmidt and Krause families had stored bits and pieces of their lives in that space. The fact that Adam had cleared all of the families' relics yesterday hadn't caused her sadness, and her inability to climb the steps hadn't added to her distress. However, memories continued to haunt her and the prospect of her task, facing her relatives one last time, weighs heavily on her mind. Today, she plans to face them, dreading the moments that would fulfill the promise she had made to herself upon hearing the news that they had lost the farm. Before she leaves the farm, she plans to go to the graveyard to tell those who had loved it as much as she has that it will no longer be.

The Schmidt and Kraus family 'seeds' will never be planted here again. As she pictures the scene that will occur later when she moves to her new home on the second floor above the bakery owned by her son-in-law, Herr Gerhard Gunther, she feels a pending doom. She pictures Adam having to carry her up the steps and her stomach turns. "I suppose once I make my way to the second floor, I'll just have to stay there," she says as she rubs hard on her hip, trying to thwart the pain. She is conscious that she is doing what Adam had accused her of doing – *talking aloud when no one is there.*

"Now, I am answering myself," she laments walking through her kitchen.

She removes her sweater from the hook near the door and eases each arm into its sleeve. The wool scarf, ready for its triangular fold, waits to cover her long silver braids, tied in a knot on the back of her neck. Fumbling with the fold, tying the ends of the cloth under her chin, and grasping the doorknob are the last of the preparations, ones that would seem simple to others but are monumental to her.

When she steps outside onto the wooden porch, the scent of the cool morning air mixes with the bitter aroma of the chrysanthemums, reminding her again of her intentions. Bright yellow, orange, and white blooms look up at her, bringing Heinrich to mind again. She feels his presence, whispers to him, and visualizes him hovering in the misty morning air.

"I almost forgot. You will be waiting for your autumn bouquet," she whispers to him as she picks the tallest flowers, not bending, but reaching into the flowerbed.

"I was able to get down on my knees the first autumn we had planted these, Heinrich. It doesn't seem that long ago to me, but I guess it was. The tallest ones are easy to pick; they are the gold ones, your favorites," she says gathering the flowers into her arms.

From out of the mist, the tall handsome man with the blond hair and flaming blue eyes, the one who had taken her heart so long ago, appears in front of her. Frieda looks into her husband's eyes and suddenly she sees all of the family members gather around him. They are all smiling, except for Heinrich. "He has the same look on his face as the one he had when he had buried each of our sons," she thinks as her heart skips a beat.

Even though she knows the visions are not real, she is unwilling to relinquish them, believing that if she does she will lose all memory of the past and that the visions are her only means of enduring the present as well as facing an unimaginable future. She sees Heinrich walking toward the path to the cemetery and watches as he holds out his hand, motioning her to follow.

She walks with her head down behind his ghost. Fog obscures the path to the cemetery, which usually is very visible. She is the only one responsible for the path; her daily trips had created it. She could have walked it blindfolded, but the mere slice of a bright, yellow ball rising on the horizon brings flashes of light and the slowly retreating moonlight guides her. The dim light casts strange shadows on the ground from the tall linden trees that mark the final resting places. Heinrich's ghost fades from view but her memories take her down one lane, the day her beloved husband had died.

*

It was the tenth day of May in 1915. The roosters had started the day as usual, a typical morning on the farm for the Schmidt family. After a breakfast of eggs, Heinrich shared his plans for the day. "I want to get that beam in the barn fixed before I go out to plow the north field. There is a storm brewing. If I go now, I may get both done," he says before putting on his hat. "I have sent Adam to the east field, Frieda. He should be able to finish the plowing that we had started yesterday by early this afternoon."

Frieda and, Alexandra go to the well to get water to wash clothes. After filling the buckets, they carry them back to the back porch to the large tubs and begin their usual routine. Frieda scrubs the garments against the washboard; Alexandra rinses them and wrings them with her hands, putting them in the bucket. When washed, they hang them on the lines in the backyard. "I hope we can get these dried before nightfall," says Frieda.

"Vater says there's a storm brewing, Mutti."

"Yes, but there is a warm breeze," she says as she presses her nose to Heinrich's shirt blowing on the line. She loves the smell of the clothes after the warm air of the countryside has dried them. Her mind is a million miles away as she hangs Heinrich's socks on the line.

"Mutter, Mutter, come, quick. It is Vater. He is hurt badly. The beam in the barn is on top of him," Adam shouts as he runs towards Frieda.

She is in motion before Adam finishes telling them about finding his father. When they arrive at the barn, Heinrich is lying on the ground with a deep gash in his forehead. The cut sprouts a pool of blood onto the bed of hay supporting his lifeless body.

"Hurry, Adam, get Herr Weiss," Frieda shouts as she rushes to his side. "Alexandra, get some rags," she cries.

She feels his face and wipes the blood from his forehead, but the moment she had seen him on the ground with the large gape in his head, she knew her efforts were in vain. She cradles his head in her hands, trying to stop the bleeding, screaming his name, praying for a miracle, but none comes. By the time Adam and Alexandra return with Herr Weiss, she has already said her tearful good-bye.

Now, thinking of that day brings Frieda to tears.

She has harbored the thoughts for years, ones brought on by her overwhelming sense of guilt, a feeling that had overcome her long before Heinrich's accident. She had believed that Heinrich's death had been the result of her inability to give him more sons. She deemed that *another son could have helped Heinrich in the barn that day and he may not have died.*

Now, she places the blame for losing the farm on herself, believing that a brother could have helped Adam and they wouldn't have lost the farm. The day of Heinrich's burial comes to mind, bringing more sad thoughts. The family plots of the Schmidt and Kraus families set side-by-side in a small cemetery in the grassy meadow, one that all of the farmers hold in common. She sees Adam and Alexandra listening to Pastor Hauptman as he had said his final blessings before they had lowered the coffin into the cold dark hole.

"The next generation of Schmidt children will own this farm, my dear husband, I promise you," she had vowed to Heinrich. At the time, she had no idea how she would accomplish that promise, but she never doubted the certainty of her conviction.

"Adam had seemed wiser than his fifteen years, then. He never should have blamed himself. He should have had a brother," she thinks now as she makes her journey up the path and recalls his vow, promising that he would run the farm, keeping the fields in the family. His insistence on taking the blame lingers on her mind as she nears the top of the ridge.

She knows that he is blaming himself and she feels the frustration of not being able to convince him otherwise. As the tall linden trees, age-old icons of German mythology, come into view, she thinks that the trees are like giant soldiers standing guard over the tombstones of her ancestors and her family. She recalls the day that she and Heinrich had visited the cemetery together for the first time as husband and wife.

"It is good that the linden trees had been planted around this cemetery, Frieda. They are appropriate for a graveyard for those patriots who have loved Germany so much," he had told her so long ago. Now, she wonders if Adam feels the same love for his country that his father and grandfathers had felt.

She thinks not.

"Since losing the farm, Adam has changed," she considers, remembering that he wouldn't talk about the circumstances that had led to losing it. She sensed it had something to do with the loss of the war and the changes that have occurred since, but she knew her place and she wouldn't question him.

However, she would never blame Adam for losing the farm. She just wished that she could convince him that its loss was indeed her fault. As she looks up and sees the picket fence surrounding the cemetery, her mind drifts to the past again. She remembers that Heinrich had been the one who had wanted to build the fence, telling her that he "wanted to honor the previous generations by securing their burial ground." She remembers that day in the month of April following their wedding the previous summer.

It had been an unusually hot month. Frieda was heavy with their first child and uncomfortable by the premature heat. Heinrich and their neighbor, Herr Weiss, one of the others in the communal farm and their neighbor, had volunteered to help Heinrich with the project. The two men had been working for several hours without relief. When she had seen Herr Weiss walk back to his house, she became concerned about Heinrich who was still in the field. She filled a glass pitcher, a wedding gift, with water from the well, and decided to take it to him.

It was a long walk from the house to the cemetery on the far meadow. She waddled up to him and was surprised when he reached out to her, laying his hand on her shoulder. "Frieda, you shouldn't have come out in this heat," he smiled, releasing his hold and then, surprising her even more, he moved his hand, placing it on her swollen belly.

"I'm fine, Heinrich," she answered while trying to recover from his public display. Even though they were alone in a field far away from any eyes, she felt nervous about his obvious departure from propriety.

"I saw Herman returning; I was worried about you without any water out here," she explains relishing the lingering look on his face, one that she had come to expect from him whenever she would show concern for him.

"Thank you, dear Frieda," he smiles – the same one that she had worn on their wedding day.

"Oh!" he shouts as his hands moves. "I felt him kick."

"I do believe the heat has made him take loss of his senses," she thinks as he smiles again and keeps his hand on her belly.

"So, it is a boy I am carrying, is it?" she asked coyly while pouring the water from the pitcher into the tin cup.

He takes the cup from her hand and drinks the water down in one gulp. "I'll give both of you a good life. I promise, Frieda," he vowed putting the cup in front of the pitcher and waiting for her to refill it.

She watched him down it as quickly as the first. As he pressed his hand down on her waist slightly, holding it there, he gazed into her eyes and then kissed her on the mouth, catching Frieda completely off guard. It was a moment that she secured in her memory, cherishing it forever. The two of them walked hand in hand back to the house, content with the prospect of having a family . . . and a new fence.

One month later, Frieda had given birth to a son, just as Heinrich had predicted. However, Heinrich had not foreseen burying his first born on the same day on which he had been born. He had not counted on his son dying in his mother's belly but, unlike Frieda, he wouldn't allow his sorrow to overcome him and would never question "God's plan." On the other hand, Frieda questioned 'God's plan', wondering what she could have possibly done to prompt a merciful God to take her son away.

A few months later, Heinrich rejoiced when Frieda had shared with him that she was pregnant again. However, secretly she worried that her joy would affect the outcome of the pregnancy in a negative way and she would not rejoice in the news.

As she nears the gate, thoughts of losing her first son make her legs grow weak. She hears a voice call out of the fog saying, "Frieda, if he had lived, he would have fought in the trenches and have died anyway."

The mysterious devil's advocate shouts so loudly that Frieda stops in her tracks to survey the landscape and listen intently, trying to identify it.

She sees no one and hears nothing.

The voice questioning her dead son's future causes her to wonder about the way she and Heinrich had handled their grief. Losing their first-born son had overwhelmed them, but the loss of their second son had been devastating and incomprehensible. She remembers a conversation with Heinrich after they had buried their second son in the old graveyard next to his grandparents.

"Surely, God wouldn't be cruel enough to take all of our sons . . . Would he, Heinrich?"

"We must not question God's plan, Frieda. Our Faith will show us the way."

When they had lost their second son, her questions had turned to complete and utter despair and, again, Heinrich had stood steadfast in his acceptance of 'God's plan'.

Two years later, when their third son had been born dead, an angry Frieda wouldn't allow any questioning. Watching silently as Heinrich had lowered the perfect body of her newborn son into the ground, placing the tiny box next to those of his two brothers, she vowed never to speak to Heinrich or anyone about the actions of 'a merciful, compassionate God'. Depression veiled her and held its gnawing grip on her for months afterward.

Now, she feels that same sense of despair and desperation, just as she had then, remembering that guilt had been all that had to offer Heinrich and that he couldn't offer her any comfort. Despite his tenderness, she was afraid to get pregnant again, preferring to wallow in her losses, retreating from him, not wanting to please him, or herself. She had relinquished herself to the unrelenting sorrow, but Heinrich had never abandoned her, nor did he give into his own grief. Instead, he used it to carry on the life he had always valued, loving his wife, never giving up hope, guided by his Faith in God and his country.

Several months after their third son's death, Frieda realized that she was pregnant again. Heinrich's frowns had turned to smiles when she had told him, but not so for Frieda. Still questioning God, she wouldn't allow any feelings of joy or happiness, fearing they would just perpetuate another loss, but when the twins had been born after a long and difficult labor, she wanted to jump for joy and shout from the rooftop: "We have not one, but two live babies!" Instead, she whispered, "Thank you, dear God, thank you."

"God has been good to us, Frieda. He has given us a son and a daughter together. We will do the best with what God has given us. I'll work hard and God will reward me for my efforts," Heinrich had whispered with his eyes filled with tears and his voice quivering before placing his cheek against the face of each of his children, trying to feel their breaths.

Confident that they were both breathing, he lifted the newborn infants into his arms and brought them over to Frieda, placing them on her breasts, kissing them, and then pressing his lips to Frieda's forehead. "Thank you, Frieda. We will call him 'Adam' because he's our first son to live, but he will be our only son," he had said in a very serious voice.

Frieda's face had turned as white as the sheet.

"Doctor Wolman has said that the twins are healthy, but they will be your only children, my dear Frieda."

Her brief joy again met the depths of sorrow as tears rolled down her cheeks.

"What name will you give our daughter, Frieda?" Heinrich asked with a stronger voice and a new sparkle in his eyes.

"Alexandra Julia," she whispered.

"It is done then . . . 'Adam Heinrich Schmidt' and 'Alexandra Julia Schmidt' . . . welcome to the world . . . You are German! You will make your family and country proud . . . so help you God."

"Amen," Frieda said in a stronger voice.

"God has chosen to give us three dead sons and now a son and a daughter who live," Frieda whispered. "I am grateful for a merciful God."

However, the question of 'Why?' would haunt her and temper her joy in the years that followed.

*

As she pulls her body up the hill toward the fence, Frieda contemplates the future.

"Adam is strong, like his father and he still has his youth to sustain him," she thinks as she wonders how she will ever deal with losing her home. As she places her hand on the latch of the white-picket gate, she entertains the thought of suggesting to Adam that they repaint the cemetery fence before the onslaught of winter.

You won't be here this winter.

Her stomach flutters.

"A confession to those who have gone before me, admitting my guilt, is the only way I can move forward," she decides. "I need to tell them that the one possession that they had all worked so hard to keep is gone and that I had failed in my promises to them . . . I could not give them the sons who could have prevented this."

She doesn't know what words she will find to express her feelings to her dead loved ones who had expected as much from her as she and Heinrich had expected from their own children. However, as she takes a few steps toward Heinrich's grave, she knows that she must. She drops the bouquet of mums next to his tombstone, nestling them closer to the marker with her shoe, fighting back tears as she reads the inscriptions. "Rest in Peace," she repeats reading as she stands before each of the other markers on the graves of her ancestors and those of her three babies.

How could you possibly rest in peace after I tell you?

Suddenly, a picture of each of the wooden boxes, her dead sons' coffins, appears in her mind. As she sees Heinrich lowering each box into the ground again, she feels the same sense of failure and abandonment that she had felt then. "You promised me a good life, Herr Heinrich Schmidt!" she screams at the top of her lungs, causing an echo through the valley.

Why did you leave me?

She moves toward Heinrich's marker, touching it, feeling his face in the cold hard cement, hoping her gesture will erase her previous harsh remarks, but still relieved that she had vented them.

The stone reminds her of Heinrich's dead body, lying deep in the ground. As tears roll down her cheeks, she caresses the stone, rubbing her lips across it, trying to feel him again. "I have some bad news, Heinrich. I don't know how to tell you," she whispers as her eyes survey all of the stones standing patiently beside his.

She sees all of her family's faces and tries to put their collective expressions of disappointment out of her mind. She desperately wants to be relieved of her guilty feelings, but she can't find absolution for herself.

"How can I expect it of them when I can't of myself?" she thinks dropping her head down, her chin on her chest, closing her eyes, and sobbing.

A cold wind whips at her, fluttering the skirt of her dress.

She opens her eyes to find that the soft morning sky is as dark as midnight. A thick, dense fog covers the tall trees, transforming the small cemetery into a large white cocoon.

"It is that 'caterpillar' again, the one who will never complete its life cycle, becoming the beautiful butterfly," she thinks as she sees a form crawl out of the fog toward her. Indistinguishable at first, it changes into the figure of Heinrich.

He stands before her, holding the first of their dead sons in his arms, alive and smiling at her. As she gazes in disbelief at her dead husband's ghost, the images of their dead parents join his. Her mother holds the second of her dead sons. His mother holds the third. All of them are smiling at her.

"The jury of my peers," she mumbles casting her eyes down. Clearing her throat several times in an effort to find words, she can only sob, hoping that the foggy morning mist will dissuade the ghosts from finding disappointment in her, changing their smiles to frowns. A rustling of wind captures her attention, causing her to lift her eyes.

Words fail her.

She waits; hoping one of them will help her, but not one of them offers, only staring back at her from the holes where their eyes should be. The holes penetrate her like a hot poker. However, an inexplicable sense of empowerment overcomes her, forcing her to hold her head high, casting her eyes upon the sunken ones of the forms before her.

"Soon, I'll be with all of you in the same place that you are now. I know it is a far better place than here. I'll never rest here with you under the linden trees and that will be my eternal punishment," she shouts at them in a strong determined voice. For the first time, a deep feeling of acceptance replaces that of her overwhelming guilt. With her head held high, she watches as each of the forms melt into the mist. Heinrich's is the last.

The fog lifts, revealing an autumn spectacular, intersecting the horizon in colors of gold, red, and green, crowned with a bright yellow sun. However, as quickly as the fog recedes, steel-gray clouds and a cold east wind replace it, suggesting the impending doom of another harsh winter ahead.

That caterpillar won't make its transformation.

"It is too late," she whispers to herself. "The butterfly will never be," she thinks as she walks the familiar path back to the farmhouse. It seems shorter than the one taking her there. The hem of her dress hangs heavy with moisture. She reasons that the wet garment explains why each of her steps feel as if she is lifting twice her weight, but she knows better. It had been the ordeal of visiting the graveyard for the last time and the anticipation of this dreaded day weighing on her – not the dew.

Pictures of past years, when the farmers had worked their fields living in harmony in the small community, replay in her mind as she walks the path down from the meadow. Images of her impoverished fellow citizens, still reeling from the war, replace those of the past. As she nears the house, she notices that some of the men are beginning a new day, already in their fields working. Envious of those who had managed to keep their fields, she remembers Adam's words.

"Their time will come."

Bright bursts of yellow against a clear, blue sky suggest the promise of a beautiful new autumn day. She takes a deep breath, wanting to feel the moment, hugging her eyelids closed.

"If only I could save this picture," she wishes opening her eyes, wanting to capture one more memory.

By the time she reaches the farmhouse, she realizes the memories would always be with her, just behind her eyelids," Sofia says stopping her story and reaching for the teapot.

*

"Would you like some tea, Janene? I'll have Clarissa warm it."

"No, thank you. I'm fine."

"I told you the story was long. Would you like to resume another time?"

"No, please don't stop on my account. I'm anxious to hear more. That was such a sad time; such a beautiful story."

"Telling you the story of your ancestors pleases me, Neeny," Sofia smiles. "I remember telling it to your father, but he had been much younger."

"It pleases me, too."

"Oma had been the heart of our family. Her memory lives forever in mine," Sofia shares moving her hand across the quilt to her heart before finding her spot on the quilt again.

"When Oma and Uncle Adam had lost the farm, it had turned out to be the best thing that could have happened to me because it had brought my dear grandmother closer to me. However, it had proved to be a slow death for her and for the country that she had loved so much."

"I had always regretted that I had never had any blood relatives who could share the family history, traditions, and cultures of South Vietnam."

"That is why I am so very anxious to tell you everything. You see, I believe that a deeper knowledge of your past will guide your future. There was a time when I had denied my heritage, too hurt, embarrassed, disillusioned, and feeling guilty because of the monumental historical events of the times in which I had lived, ones that had destroyed my life and the lives of so many others. My parents had taught me to place my faith in God, my family, my country, but, despite my devotion to those three, there was little joy in my life, rather it had been about loss, pain, and doubt.

Because of the way my life had turned out, I found fault with my legacy as a German and had come to detest it. I denounced all connections to the country of my birth. However, the opportunity to look back and assess your past, hopefully building bridges into the future, is one of the more positive things that comes with living this long," she smiles.

"Oh, my, I am getting ahead of myself. Where did I leave off?"

"Oma Frieda was moving in with you."

"Yes, you HAVE been listening," she smiles.

Janene nods her head in agreement; she smiles back and feels her cheeks get warm.

"It is God who we should blame!" Sofia shouts in a louder voice as she continues her story. "That was what my Oma had decided when they had lost the farm," she says as tears form again.

"Now, I know she must be telling a story she has memorized," Janene thinks with a smile. "Why else would she keep referring to herself as 'Sofia' and not use 'I' as she has just done?"

Thinking that someone else may have written the story and Sofia is reciting it, her curiosity urges her to interrupt and question her, but she decides against it, still not feeling very comfortable with the revelation that the renowned writer, Sophie Simon, is actually her grandmother. "All in good time," she thinks as she settles back into the chair, concentrates on listening, and giving her new grandmother her full-undivided attention as she continues to share her story.

"Frieda sits in the kitchen, thinking about its emptiness, wondering if it really had belonged to someone else. Its nudity makes her feel as cold as she had felt in the cemetery. Except for the few remaining items on the table, two chairs, and some boxes that are ready for the cart, the room is bare. Adam had broken up some of the chairs last winter, using them as firewood and he had already taken a few of them to the bakery. Yesterday, she had packed her grandmother's curtains into a box, which now waits at the door, ready for Adam to carry to the wagon.

The sideboard now graces the kitchen of Frau Weiss, her dearest friend and neighbor. She had always hoped that the furniture that had once belonged to her mother and her grandmother would one day belong to Alexandra. However, Alexandra has her mother-in-law's furniture in their apartment. She had looked forward to the day when Adam would take a wife and a new daughter-in-law would occupy the house. She feels the sting of losing his legacy again. It gives her comfort to know that Alma's kitchen will be the new home for the piece of furniture that had served them so well and that the apartment above the bakery will host the curtains and the two remaining chairs.

She removes her sweater and, hangs it back on its hook. The aroma of eggs frying in the skillet fills the room. From his place in front of the pot-bellied stove, Adam is making their final breakfast. "Oh, Mutter, I thought you were with someone," he says turning toward her but not waiting for her reply. "I guess you have been talking to yourself again," he continues returning his attention back to the cast iron skillet.

Frieda ignores his remark about talking to herself. She removes her scarf, places it on the hook, and slides her body down wearily into one of the two remaining chairs.

"I was worried, Mutti. I got up and didn't see you but I looked out of the window and I saw you on the ridge coming back from the cemetery. The tea is brewing and the eggs are almost finished."

"I had decided to get up early today to pay my final visit to Vater's grave," she answers secretly noting Adam's use of the word, 'Mutti' instead of his usual 'Mutter'. She remembers with pleasure that he had called her that in his boyhood, only occasionally using the term since he had grown up, and only then when he had seemed to slip away from his manhood, becoming the little boy he had once been.

"You must be chilled. You were out there a long time. Maybe you should have waited until after the sun had warmed up the meadow."

"I didn't want to rush you. I still have some things to pack."

"You would have had plenty of time. We will not be leaving for a while yet. I still have some things to finish before we leave," Adam explains turning the eggs.

"We will have to remember to pack the skillet and tea kettle. We should give them to Alexandra to use in her kitchen," she reminds him. Thoughts of the pots remind her of her childhood. The old teakettle had sat on the iron stove for as long as she could remember, becoming a permanent fixture. She sees her mother standing in front of the stove and wishes that she could feel her arms around her again. The look of disappointment in the cemetery on the face of her mother's ghost quickly puts those thoughts out of her mind. She doesn't want to endure the pain again. She starts to clear the one end of the table holding the remaining remnants of household items that are awaiting their fate.

Adam continues making breakfast at the stove, offering no comment about his grandmother's pots. Frieda sits down, exhausted from the earlier tasks, her mind swirling with thoughts of Adam and ways to convince him that losing the farm isn't his fault. She thinks it would help him to discuss his feelings, but she knows that she has always found it difficult to get him to talk. Remembering that his father had been the same way, a man of few words, helps to relieve her frustration, but not her determination to help him with his misplaced guilt.

"When I had made the decision to go to the cemetery early today, Adam, I wanted to tell Vater that I had lost the farm, but I couldn't tell him. I knew that he would be so disappointed in me," she blurts waiting for his response as he brings the hot teapot to the table.

He moves Frieda's cup closer to her, pours the tea, and then places the kettle back on the stove. "Mutter," he says laying his hand gently on her shoulder, "Vater wouldn't have been disappointed in you. I am the one who has disappointed him. I am the one who is responsible for losing the farm – not you," he says as he pours the tea into his cup, carefully avoiding her eyes.

Frieda focuses on her son while he finishes the tasks of presenting breakfast. Their eyes meet for only a moment before he casts his away. She says nothing. *Nothing I've done or said so far has helped him to deal with his guilt.*

Even though Adam is still her little boy in her mind, he is a grown man. Raised in the German tradition, she knows that a woman shouldn't question a man, *even if he is her son*. Realizing that she must respect his manhood, she casts her eyes away and concentrates on the food in front of her. Her heart is aching for him. She wants to run to him and wrap her arms around him as she had done when he was little. Instead, she considers her words and begins again.

"Adam, dear Adam, you have done everything you could. You tried your best. That is all your Vater would have expected."

He offers no response.

"I went to the cemetery feeling guilty and to ask your father to forgive me for losing the farm. The farm would still be ours if I had been able to give him more sons. If your brothers had lived, Vater may not have died," she says not giving up, but casting her chin down onto her chest. From under her eyelids, she watches him as he sits down across from her at the table.

"I did live. I could have helped him with that loose beam in the barn that day. Instead, Vater had sent me to the pasture."

"Adam, Vater always needed more help, but he was too proud to ask. He wouldn't even ask the other farmers for help and they had a shared interest in that barn. He insisted on carrying the burden himself. He sent you to the pasture because he thought that he needed you there more than he needed you in the barn."

"I became the 'first born son' because my brothers had died. If one of them had lived, the farm would have been his legacy, not mine, but I am the only son who had lived. The responsibilities are all mine, Mutti," he says placing the dishes down as he sits in the chair at the table across from her.

"If your brothers had lived, they would have helped Vater. They would have had fields of their own and they would have helped you – we wouldn't be losing the farm," she continues trying to plead her case.

"Brothers wouldn't have made any difference last year, Mutter. For that matter, except for the first born, your additional sons would probably have met their fates at the Front."

"It is my fault entirely, Adam," her eyes filling with tears.

"Mutti, we have been over this and over this a hundred times. You aren't responsible for Vater dying. It isn't your fault that the farm is gone now."

"Yes, Adam. That is my point. I know that, now. Neither you, nor I, are responsible. Your father would tell us that. He always had told us to do our best and God would do the rest. So, if we are to blame anyone, 'IT IS GOD WHO WE SHOULD BLAME'," she shouts waiting for the bolt of lightning to strike her for her blasphemy.

"Mutter! You surprise me! I've never heard you speak in such a way," he says suddenly taking his attention from his first forkful of eggs.

"I have never felt this way before," she says lowering her voice to almost a whisper, her words surprising her as well.

"Well, then, I guess we are finally in agreement, aren't we Mutter? All three of us: God, you, and I – WE ARE ALL TO BLAME!" Adam says lifting his fork toward his mouth again.

"Adam, what can I say to make you understand? You are not to blame!"

"Nothing, Mutter, there isn't anything more to say. I can't turn back the clock and make the farm ours again."

"It will always be my biggest heartache that the farm isn't yours. It was supposed to be your legacy," Frieda says watching him as he swallows another mouthful.

"There are many other Germans who won't have their legacies, either. I'll be fine . . . I am a 'Schmidt' . . . remember? Don't worry, we will all be fine," he says as he lifts his teacup and lowers his voice.

"Come now, Mutti. The tea is getting cold."

They eat their eggs and drink their tea in silence, neither one of them finding any more words to share. When they finish, Adam clears the dishes and washes them in the dry sink. Frieda sits quietly at the table, gazing at the few items on the table that need to be packed.

"Can you fit Oma's tea kettle and the skillet in that box, Mutti? If not, I'll put them in the back of the cart," Adam asks as he wipes the skillet dry.

"Yes, they will fit nicely into this large box. Put them here."

"Good. I have a few more things to put in the cart, then I'll be coming back to take these boxes. With any luck, we will be at the bakery by late-afternoon."

"I'll be ready," she tells him, knowing that she has lied.

I'll never be ready.

"I'll be outside getting the oxen and cart ready," Adam tells her as he puts on his flannel jacket over his farmer trousers and places his corduroy cap on his head.

Frieda nods in return and turns her attention to the linens.

She picks up the embroidered tablecloth, which had belonged to her mother, and presses it to her nose, still hoping to smell her. She folds it neatly and places it in the box. It joins the other linens she had packed last night, all of which will have to endure the same ritual before achieving their special places in the old wooden box.

The wooden table, where she had served hundreds of meals to her family over the years, holds a collection of remnants of her life on the farm. It sits in front of her, firmly fixed, as if in protest of the impending event. The large planks of oak secured on the sturdy base had been a patient staple over the years, never moving, never complaining, always present, and listening.

Its virtue will be its own reward.

It will remain with the chrysanthemums.

"I wish I was the table," Frieda whispers to herself as she quickly wipes her tears on the sleeve of her dress and returns to the task of packing, deciding that it is best for her to move some of the boxes so she can get the remaining items packed. Adam had specifically told her that he would lift the heavy boxes but she decides that she will do it anyway. She struggles to lift the largest box with his warnings ringing in her ears. Thoughts of Adam's reminder bring to mind a conversation that they had after he had attended some political meetings in town.

"The meeting was frightening, Mutter. Herr Weiss told of some of the men from the city digging in his fields, stealing his produce. We are not the only desperate Germans. The reality of the situation is simple. The farm is gone and nothing we can say or do will ever bring it back. I have failed you and Vater, and I have failed myself, but, most of all, the government has failed us and all of those who have ever professed our loyalty." As she reflects on Adam's account of the meeting, she concludes that Adam is indeed correct, a reflection that even surprises her.

Our country has let us down . . . It is Germany . . . Yes; Germany is who we should blame.

Her statement, although only to herself, shatters her strong feelings of patriotism, ones that she has savored her entire life. "I can't think about Heinrich any more. He is dead. I can't think about the dead. They are all gone. Nothing will ever bring them back. I'll not think about the past. I'll not worry about the future. I'll only think about today," she shouts in a strong voice. This time she doesn't wait for the bolt of lightning.

"I shall not waste my energy on the dead – only the living."

Her immediate family is foremost in her thoughts. Herr Gerhard Gunther, her son-in-law, who has offered her a place to live, comes to mind first, but she worries about his ability to do that, knowing that he is also having financial difficulties. His father, who has owned a bakery on the outskirts of Berlin, had groomed Gerhard's older brother, Hugo, to take over the business, a customary practice for the first-born son. Law had mandated that he wouldn't have to serve his country and go to war. The government had reasoned that the family needed the first-born son to help at home when they had set the law. Accordingly, Gerhard and Alexandra had been married for only a few months before he had to leave for duty in the trenches. Shortly afterward, Gerhard had gone off to war.

However, Hugo didn't like the idea of becoming a baker like his father. He decided to run off, leaving his father with only his new daughter-in-law, Alexandra, to help with the business. About a month later, Alexandra discovered she was pregnant. She took on the role of helping her father-in-law in the bakery in the absence of her husband and his brother.

It wasn't long before her father-in-law's condition had deteriorated and Alexandra had difficulty operating the business on her own. In her sixth month of pregnancy, she suffered a miscarriage, a son. Meanwhile, an inhalation of toxic gas had injured Gerhard in the trenches. He had spent time recuperating in a medical hospital and then returned to the Front. However, he had only been back to duty for a few days when the war had suddenly ended. There had been so much confusion when the soldiers had learned that the war had ended and that Germany had lost it, they had just walked out of the trenches, weapons in hand, and had gone home. Gerhard arrived home to a dying father, a wife suffering from postpartum depression and a collapsing bakery business.

Soon after he had returned, Alexandra was pregnant again, giving birth to their first child, 'Sofia Alexandra Gunther', on September 6, 1919. Gerhard's father never lived to see the birth and Gerhard had no time to recuperate from his wartime experience before he had found himself running the bakery in a struggling economy.

Moreover, the country's population had experienced a huge loss in adult males killed in combat. There was great unemployment; very inflated prices for goods and services gripped the country. All of this contributed to a general tone of depression as the country tried to recover from the losses of the war.

In addition, the Peace Treaty had assigned huge financial reparations to Germany for their participation in the war, throwing the country into a financial crisis as a result. Like most of the Germans after the war, the Gunther family had struggled and had little about which to rejoice.

However, the birth of Sofia proved to be the first ray of light and hope for a better future.

"You have a baby girl, Herr Gunther," the Doctor had said. "She is small but appears to be perfectly healthy. Your fears of something happening to the baby because of your gassing at the Front apparently seem to be unfounded. Frau Alexandra Gunther is doing fine as well," he said as he shook his hand.

"Thank you for giving me a grandchild, Gerhard. I hope that Sofia's future is free of the heartaches that have plagued you and Alexandra," Frieda had told Gerhard five years ago when he had placed the newborn baby in her arms. Secretly, Frieda had wished that the baby had been a boy.

"I'll work hard to make sure of that, Frieda, and with God's help, it will happen," Gerhard had told his mother-in-law.

Frieda thought for a moment that she was hearing Heinrich again. She couldn't help but notice the similarities between the three men, Heinrich, Adam, and Gerhard. The three of them were examples of God-fearing, law-abiding, patriotic German men who had one thing in common. Circumstances beyond their control, the historical events of the times in which they had lived, had changed the course of their lives.

However, despite everything her family had endured, Frieda knew God had blessed them, just as Heinrich had always predicted. Another generation of strong Germans had begun with the birth of Sofia and now, in late August of 1924, with the birth of their second child, a son, Franz Heinrich, the boy for whom Frieda had prayed.

She smiles as she remembers the look of pride on Gerhard's face when he had held his baby son for the first time. "I would never have dreamed that becoming a grandmother would be so wonderful. Sofia has been the light of my life and now, I have been blessed with a grandson, too," Frieda exclaimed as she had held baby Franz for the first time.

"My living with you and them will be the one positive thing coming from all of this," she had said to Alexandra and Gerhard when Gerhard had invited them to come and live with them. "It will be good for Alexandra to have her mother living with her as well, Gerhard. I might be old, but I'm not ready for the pasture yet!"

Adam returns to the kitchen interrupting her thoughts about the past and the prospects of a new future living in Berlin above the bakery.

"I told you not to lift any of those boxes, Mutti," Adam reprimands when he notices that the biggest box is now sitting on the floor and not on the table. She had hoped that he wouldn't notice that she had lifted the heavy box down from the table.

"This one was entirely too heavy for you to lift," he says moving toward the door with the box in hand. "Now, Mutter, you know Gerhard has said there isn't a lot of room in the apartment. You should be selective about the things that you pack."

"Adam, I know what to pack for the garage and for the apartment; I am not senile."

"I am not saying that you are incapable, Mutter. I am just reminding you," he says staring back at her in surprise.

Frieda considers the fact that she had never voiced any personal opinions during her lifetime. "Except for what I had planned to cook for dinner," she mumbles – hoping that he doesn't hear.

"Adam, I have been very organized in my packing. I marked the boxes with a 'G' to show you that those were the ones to go to the garage and the others should go to the apartment to share with Alexandra."

Adam looks at her, shakes his head, and smiles. "Well, I am glad that you finally decided to tell me about your system. I thought the 'G' stood for 'Gerhard'. Since I am the one who is delivering the boxes, it would seem that all of the items you have so designated to go to storage in the garage would be in the apartment. All of those things that you had wanted to go to Alexandra will now be in the garage," he replies trying to hide his chuckle and showing some respect.

Frieda sits with her mouth open, looking at him in total surprise, offering no rebuttal. Adam walks over to his mother and kisses her cheek, something he had not done since achieving his manhood. "Now, please, don't lift the boxes, Mutti. I'll carry each one and I promise I'll make sure each one arrives at its proper destination."

He is such a good boy. She continues packing and thinking of how much she loves him and the kiss on her cheek, still warm, serves as a reminder.

*

Several Hours Later

Adam follows his mother as she leaves the farmhouse, closing the door behind her. Frieda pretends not to hear the small thud as the door shuts. She wants to open it again, rush back inside, and wake up from the nightmare. Instead, she reminds herself again of her promise.

I'll be strong and I'll not look back.

Adam places his hand on her elbow and leads her down the walk to the cart.

Frieda, taking steady steps, afraid that she will collapse, reviews the packing in her mind one last time. "Oh! What about my quilt, Adam?" she asks turning to face him recalling that she may have left it in her room.

"Not to worry, Mutti. I put it in a gunny sack and packed it into the back of the cart."

"I guess we have everything, then?" Adam asks as his eyes find hers.

She turns her head away, casts her head down, and answers, "Yes, Adam, we have everything – we have each other."

He lifts her up onto the bench in the front of the cart that holds the final pieces of their lives and positions his body beside her. After several hard pulls on the reins, the oxen pull the cart away. As the animals pull them down the lane and onto the road, they sit in silence.

The sun is shining brightly and there is no breeze, but Frieda tightens the strings on her bonnet and pulls the ends of her shawl together before locking her hands. As they near the meadow and the site of the family cemetery on the ridge, she closes her eyes, thinking of Heinrich, choosing not to look.

The hoofs of the oxen thump the ground in rhythm with the turn of the lopsided wheels of the cart, playing a repetitive melody. She doesn't hear that tune which had bothered her earlier. As she opens her eyes, takes a deep breath, and looks into the sunshine, she hopes a newer, happier one will replace it . . . and she never looks back."

*

Sofia sighs and rubs on the same pink square. Her eyes fade off into space. Janene is alarmed, worried that the task of telling her story is too much for Sofia but, after only a few moments, Sofia says, "Janene, are you getting tired of listening to an old lady tell stories?"

"No, I'm good. Thank you, Sofia, but I am worried about you. Are you sure you are up to continuing?" she asks with a click turning the recorder off.

"Yes, I'm fine. I'll let you know when I can't go on. God willing, I'll be able to tell you the whole story," she smiles. Janene smiles back at her and watches as Sofia takes a drink of water and then, waiting for Sofia's cue, she starts the recorder again.

* * * * *

CHAPTER 3
THE BAKERY

Pappelstrasse Street

"After an uneventful trip from the farm to the bakery located just outside the city limits of Berlin, they arrive at their new home, a little neighborhood bakery on the corner of the main boulevard into the city and a quiet side street called, 'Pappelstrasse'. Adam directs the oxen around to the alley behind the store and then orders a halt stopping at the back door.

"Do you want me to carry you up the steps, Mutti?"

"No, Adam. No one will carry me into my new home. I'll walk," she answers looking up at the long flight of steps, feeling pain and stiffness from the long trip, and wondering how she would manage. As she takes her first step, holding onto the banister, using all of her strength to lift one leg onto each step, she counts each one of them. "Thirteen of them – I suppose they will just have to be my penance," she mumbles trying to catch her breath when she reaches the second floor.

Breathing in the aroma of the freshly baked bread, she gives Gerhard a smile when he opens the door and embraces her. Alexandra stands behind her husband holding her arms out, smiling. "I hope you will be happy with us, Frieda. We're glad to help you and Adam," Gerhard says leading her into the kitchen with one hand under her elbow. He helps her to one of the chairs from the farmhouse, which Adam had brought on a previous trip. Frieda is relieved as she relinquishes her weight into the familiar chair.

"Thank you, Gerhard," she gasps, breathing deeply. "If you had not offered to help us, I don't know what we would have done," she says trying to get another breath.

"I can't believe that I'm homeless. I would never have imagined this happening to me."

"Now, Mutti, it's not good for you to keep going over this again. The farm is gone and we are here. Let's try to think of pleasant things, now. You shouldn't dwell on those things that have made you so sad," Adam interrupts coming into the kitchen, his arms loaded with boxes.

"Adam is right, Mutter. We're happy to have you living with us," Alexandra says placing a reassuring hand on her shoulder. "The apartment is very roomy, large enough for everyone. May I make you a cup of tea, Mutter? I've already put the kettle on."

"Oma!" five-year-old Sofia shouts running into the room, her long blonde braids flying behind her. She throws her arms around Frieda's neck, burying her head into her chest.

"Sofia! I was wondering where you were. I thought maybe you had forgotten that I was coming today," Frieda said putting her arms around the little girl, pulling her close.

"I didn't forget, Oma."

"You didn't?"

"No. I was in my old room; the one Mutter had said would be yours now. There is a surprise for you there."

"Well, aren't you the nicest girl to surprise your Oma?"

"That's because I love you, Oma."

"And I love you more, my darling," she says with another hug.

"May we play now?"

"Sofia, let Oma be. She has to catch her breath. Come and sit here," Gerhard directs taking Sofia by the hand and leading her to the chair beside Frieda. "We're going to have a special treat to welcome Oma." Safely seated next to her grandmother, Sofia's eyes get big as she looks at the sweets lined on the tray in the middle of the table. Alexandra places a glass of milk and a dish with one of the sweets on the table in front of Sofia. Sofia waits for permission.

"Go on, Sofia . . . You may have your special treat now," Alexandra says. She returns to the stove to bring the kettle for their tea.

"I'll help Adam with the remaining boxes," Gerhard says as he and Adam walk out of the kitchen.

"The tea would be lovely, Alexandra," Frieda says. "We shall have our tea and then you can show me the rest of the apartment and I'll play with you afterward, Sofia. For now, I think I need to just sit for a while and catch up."

Alexandra, Frieda, and Sofia enjoy the tea and some fresh baked pastries filled with jam that Frieda had canned months earlier. While they make small talk about the move from the farm, Sofia sits munching.

Soon, jam covers her face. While the adults talk, Sofia sips on a glass of warm milk. After she finishes, she can't hold her excitement back any longer. "Come, see my new room. Come quick, Oma," she shouts jumping down from the chair and pulling on her Oma's arm.

"You have your own room, Sofia? Well, you certainly are a big girl!"

Frieda allows Sofia to pull her up out of the chair. They walk together into the parlor and begin inspecting the new living arrangements, led by Sofia acting as their guide. The first stop is showing Frieda her room.

The lack of a smile on Frieda's face shows her disappointment. She had anticipated sharing a room with Sofia and tries to hide her reaction, but isn't very successful. Alexandra notices.

"I thought you would be more comfortable if you were in your own room, Mutter. Sofia is a light sleeper. I was afraid she would interrupt your sleep," Alexandra apologizes.

"I wouldn't mind," Frieda says in a soft voice with her eyes downcast.

"Oh well, we can always make changes later," Alexandra says as her face flushes.

Frieda spots a single sheet of paper on the bed and assumes that the drawing must be one Sofia had done. A large circle with curly lines on top and two smaller dots inside with a line under them, resembling the letter 'U', brings a smile. The letter 'S' signs the bottom right hand corner of the page.

"Do you like my surprise, Oma?"

"Oh, thank you, Sofia, the picture is lovely," she says picking up the drawing and examining it.

"You are welcome, Oma. It is a picture of me," Sofia says throwing her shoulders back and trying to be taller.

"Yes, I figured as much. I see you are smiling."

"That's because I am so happy that you and Uncle Adam have come to live with us," Sofia hugs her.

"I am too," says Frieda giving her a big hug.

"I'll keep Baby Franz in our bedroom. That way, Adam can have the small room beside ours that we were using as a nursery. Since I am nursing him, it is better that way," Alexandra interrupts.

"Thank you, the nursery will work just fine, Alexandra. On the other hand, I could just as easily take the divan here in the parlor. I am not sure how long I'll be staying anyway," Adam says as he comes into the room carrying a box of Frieda's things. Gerhard is behind him carrying another box.

"Adam, you never said anything about leaving. Where are you going?" Frieda gasps.

"I didn't want to worry you, Mutter. I am not sure what my plans are but I know I can't impose on Alexandra and Gerhard and stay here forever. I have some ideas that will take me out of Germany, but not just yet."

Frieda's face freezes.

Adam is leaving Germany.

"You're welcome to stay as long as necessary," Gerhard reassures him, not showing any surprise to Adam's remarks.

"Thanks, Gerhard. I appreciate it. I'll not forget your generosity. I know this isn't an easy time for you, either."

"Come see my new room," Sofia shouts again.

"Show me your room now, Sofia," Frieda says taking Sofia by the hand. As she walks, her mind is on Adam and his decision to leave Germany, something that had shocked her, never imagining that he would ever leave his native country.

*

One Week Later

It doesn't take Frieda long to adjust to her new home – *except for the steps.* The bathroom and the kitchen are in the center of the apartment and are equipped with indoor plumbing, an improvement from the detached outhouse, which had once serviced the old building. The kitchen, large enough for a table and six chairs, presents an easy access to the dining room, which displays the old furniture once belonging to Gerhard's mother. An ample drawing room in the front of the house looks out onto the street.

The scents and smells of the freshly baked breads, rolls, and sweets permeate the apartment, but despite all the comforts of her new home, Frieda misses the farm. She feels as if she is a visitor in another woman's home and constantly thinks about the past, putting the memories away, but they remain, haunting her.

*

In the weeks that follow, Frieda settles into the new routine at the bakery. Every time she gets upset over losing the farm, she reminds herself of all of their blessings, rather than their losses. Rationalizing that the move was for the best, she decides that she really had no choice. She didn't want to spend another winter on the farm like the last one when they had run out of food and fuel. She feels the chill of those cold winter days last year, remembering when Adam had resorted to taking down some inside doors to use as fuel for heat. It had been a long winter and a short spring. Their money had run out before they could plant any seed.

Stop it, Frieda; that is all history.

She prays that it will be different now and orders herself not to think about the past. "Adam is right," she thinks. "It's not good to dwell on things that make you sad."

Their situation had looked very optimistic when they had first arrived but that was short-lived. By late December of 1924, the bakery business had dwindled to nothing. The state of the economy post war with the escalating prices had prohibited Gerhard from buying the bakery supplies. The supply and demand forced him to raise prices, which in turn had kept his customers from affording what little he had been able to produce. One day, as she watched Alexandra hold baby Franz close to her breast trying to get him to suckle, Frieda listened as Alexandra shared what she had been thinking.

"I am very worried about having enough milk for the baby, Mutter. I feel my supply is drying up."

Frieda feels pain for Alexandra's plight, believing that she is responsible for the premature aging lines on her daughter's face. She is certain that their coming to live with them had been a burden to them, compounding Gerhard's situation even further.

"You have never had time to recover from his birth, Alexandra."

"I know, Mutter. Gerhard doesn't know what to do next. We have nowhere to turn. We have no money. No amount is ever enough. The prices are so high. People can't afford to buy a loaf of bread and we can't afford to bake them. The coal is almost gone. We will have no way to heat the house or fuel the ovens. We are almost out of food," she confided.

Frieda sat listening, not saying a word, just trying to comprehend it all and hoping that she might be able to give her a solution. Each day as she had watched Gerhard trying to provide for his family, she had worried more. Yesterday, she had watched as he had rationed out a small portion of food for Sofia, a smaller portion than she had received the day before. Sofia's cries had torn Frieda's heart.

"There is no more color in her cheeks," she decided becoming more and more concerned. She knew Sofia was very sick. Her abdomen was protruding and the bones of her ribs looked as if they would burst through her chest. Deep shadows lay under her eyes and her hair was lusterless.

Sofia is starving to death.

She refuses to sit idly by and watch as her family starves. She had looked desperation in the face in the past and she would do it again. The look of helplessness on the face of her children told her one thing for sure.

My children need me.

She knew she would have to take it upon herself to find a solution. Her head starts to spin. The image of death stays with her throughout the night, greeting her again with the first morning light.

*

The Next Day

Frieda and Alexandra are in the kitchen, rationing the last potato. Frieda is still thinking of ways to solve her family's crisis. Gerhard interrupts her thinking when he enters the room and stands silently before Alexandra, studying her as she cuts the potato into smaller pieces. "Alexandra, the coal is gone. We will need to burn something from the household. I didn't want to choose until I had talked to you," he says in a firm voice.

"Burn my rocker, Gerhard," she returns without a wince. She puts down the knife and looks her husband in the eyes. "We have to do what we have to do."

Frieda looks at her daughter's sad face, lined with premature wrinkles and dark shadows. She knows that Alexandra had a special attachment to the rocker, once belonging to her grandmother Kraus. "I'm sure if my Oma were here, she would do the same. We have to burn something. The rocker isn't a necessity. Burn it, Gerhard," Alexandra says again turning away, returning to her rationing. Sofia buries her face into Frieda's apron, but her eyes find her mother's face. Tears stream down their cheeks.

For Frieda, the discussion about the rocker generates thoughts of the harsh winters living on the farm when she had been a child and when she and Heinrich had taken it over after their parents' deaths. She pictures herself sitting in the same rocker with her quilt wrapped around her babies, rocking, and singing to them in the cold sitting room of the farmhouse, praising God that he had blessed them with a son and daughter after years of grief over her childlessness. Heinrich sits smiling at her, smoking his pipe, promising her that everything will be all right. The picture renews thoughts of Frau Schultz, the rich woman for whom Frieda had worked as a domestic when she had been a girl, waiting to become of age and betrothed to Heinrich.

Frieda had learned how to make the quilt by watching the rich women make one at Frau Schultz's home. She remembers that she had decided to leave the quilt in the garage when Adam had mistakenly neglected to bring it into the house on moving day. "Alexandra had placed a very nice covering on the bed," she thought remembering that she had not wanted to offend her by replacing it with her old quilt. Besides, she had too many

76

painful memories of it on the bed that she and Heinrich had shared. Although she longed for it, she dreaded the walk up and down the steps, still trying to conceal her inabilities and too embarrassed to share the fact that her packing plan had gone awry.

While Alexandra and Gerhard busied themselves with the rocker, making it ready for the furnace, Frieda puts on her outdoor clothing and walks down the steps to the garage in search of her quilt. After a brief look into several boxes, she finds it.

"It's like a reunion with an old friend," she notes as she starts to formulate a plan. The empty wicker basket with the strong wooden handle sparks an idea. Her mind whirls as she carries both the quilt and the basket back to the house. She has finalized her plan by the time she reaches the door. She places the quilt down inside the vestibule and walks back out into the cold night air, carrying the empty basket with her hands linked securely inside its handle. She is weary from lack of food, stiff from the walk down the steps, and her whole body aches.

As she walks down the street, her plan energizes her. Her destination is the home of her former employer, 'Frau Berta Schulz', a rich Jewish woman whose family owns several textile factories. Her intention is to pay her a visit, but *it will not be a social call.* "I never thought that I would ever have to beg, but tonight that is exactly what I intend to do," she thinks as she walks toward the opposite side of town in the direction of the farm, but with the destination of the Schultz's mansion.

"This would never have been an option for you, Heinrich," she mumbles, "But, if begging is what I have to do, then so be it." She puts her pride aside as she walks the long blocks toward the old neighborhood where she had once worked as a young girl in the homes of some of the city's richest citizens.

The mansion is located in the most prominent section of the city almost a mile from the bakery. The Berlin winter had driven its residents inside and the deserted streets echo the sound of the strong, howling wind. The Pappelstrasse neighborhood shows little signs of life. The late afternoon light is fading and the chimneys stand cold and stark against the dark sky, blending with the icy bite of the winter air. The wind whips at her cheeks, taking away what little breath she has. She tugs at her scarf, trying to make it snug, and pulls on the cloth belt of her long wool coat, cinching it tighter.

Each step is more painful than the last. The sleeves on her coat hang down over her bare hands, offering them little protection from the frigid air. Within minutes, she feels as if her hands have frozen to the handle of the basket. She braces her body for each new gust as the pain in her spine and knees intensifies and she worries that she will collapse before she gets there. Grasping the handles on the basket tighter, holding it squarely in front of her, using it as an anchor to keep her body steady, she keeps her face down, staring at each cobblestone.

It had been years since she had been to her employer's residence. She pictures her, remembering the kindnesses she had shown her then, hoping that she will offer the same now. The memories of those past times guide her steps. Her sturdy shoes with her now frozen feet inside provide little warmth. The appearance of a newly shoveled sidewalk encourages her and she looks up to see that the chimneys now have smoke billowing from them. Just when she thinks she can't go any further, she arrives at the beautiful home with the wide front porch.

"Nothing about it has changed," she recalls thinking of that earlier time when she had been one of the young girls on the Schultz family domestic staff. She sees the faces of the rich women who had gathered at the house for their monthly sewing group and again feels envious of their luxury of free time. She had never had the privilege of getting together with other women socially, *unless you include the meetings at the church social events.*

She had learned how to make the quilt by watching the women make their own. Curiosity had made her steal away from her domestic tasks, sneaking a look from behind the heavy curtains on the drawing room door. As she pictures the quilts that the women had made, she wonders if they had ever used their quilts, or if they had just hung them in their homes, totally without function, only admired for their artistic qualities.

She had made hers with the intention of using it to wrap her future children. Her parents had arranged her marriage to Heinrich when she had been born. Heinrich was eight years older, but they had grown up knowing that they would someday share a bed. Frieda had loved him from the moment that she had been old enough to feel an emotion, not even knowing what it was. Heinrich had always studied her with a special look. Their childhood innocence had become the foundation of their life together as husband and wife, a union that was rich with all of their mutual collections of all of their families' traditions steeped in the German culture.

The puffs of smoke billowing from the chimney, confirmed her belief that Frau Schultz had no need for the quilt to keep them warm. She pictures it high on a wall in the Schultz mansion as she reaches for the latch on the black wrought iron gate. After struggling to free her frozen fingers, which had stuck to the frigid metal, she follows the brick path around the house to the back door, designated as the servants' entrance.

"What do you want? Why are you here?" asks a woman dressed in a long dark dress.

Frieda tries to answer, but she has no breath.

"It's cold. What do you want?" the woman shouts.

Frieda takes a deep breath and tries to clear her throat by forcing a cough, but she is only able to squeak a nearly inaudible voice. "I am here to see Frau Schulz." The woman moves to close the door, but Frieda pushes her foot into the doorway. "You need to tell Frau Schulz, Frau Schmidt is here," she says in a raspy low voice, leaning closer to the door. "I am not leaving until you do."

The woman looks her in the eyes with a stern look on her face. Frieda gazes back at her and with just as stern a look, she removes her foot from the threshold, allowing the woman to close the door.

The woman slams it shut, leaving Frieda standing frozen on the stoop.

She waits.

The wind blows. It tears open the folds of her coat, but she never moves as it whistles through the bare branches of the trees in the garden.

She decides to knock again, but her arm doesn't move. As hard as she tries, she can't lift it. With no other choice, but to wait, she worries that she will collapse before the woman returns, or that *the woman will not return at all.*

The door opens.

"Come in," the woman orders.

Frieda tries to move her legs, but, like her arms, they don't respond. She stares at the woman's face, her eyes pleading for mercy.

"Did you hear me? Are you deaf?"

Frieda's body sways from side to side and her knees buckle.

Suddenly, the woman's face softens; she takes her by the arm, preventing her from falling, reaches under her armpit, and braces her body as she leads her inside.

"Sit down," she orders taking her to one of the chairs surrounding the kitchen table before leaving the room without saying a word. Frieda sits at the table, trying to get her breath back, warming in front of the roaring fireplace.

As she rubs her hands together, trying to warm them, she looks around the room. Nostalgic thoughts flood her mind as she remembers once working in the kitchen, helping to prepare meals for the rich family.

*

She is lost in thought when the woman returns.

"Frau Schultz will see you now," the woman says in a softer tone than her earlier one. "Follow me," she motions with her arm, leading her toward the hallway. Frieda tries to get up but her body feels heavy and she can't budge.

The woman lifts her by the elbow and helps her from the chair. Frieda offers a smile, but her lips don't get the message. The woman guides her by one arm toward the drawing room.

As she follows the woman, Frieda notices that everything is the same as the last time she had been there, except for one difference. The quilt, the one Frau Berta had made, hangs on a wooden dowel on the wall in the hallway. The sight confirms her notion about her employer's ultimate use for the quilt.

Frieda notices that the same elegant furnishings grace the drawing room and it still has the same smell of newly varnished wood. The large fire blazing in the fireplace gives a wave of warmth and the light offers a welcoming aura. The same pair of high back chairs, the ones she had faithfully dusted, still stand in their places in front of the fireplace, one on the right and one on the left. A flash in her mind brings a memory of Frau Berta Schmidt sitting in the one on the right with a book in her lap, and makes her smile.

"Frau Schmidt is here to see you, Frau Schulz," the woman announces with a curtsy before letting herself out of the room walking backwards toward the door.

As she moves into the center of the room, she sees just the back of a woman's head sitting in the same chair that Berta had occupied. She takes a few more steps, slowly moving into the room, getting a better view of the woman. She notices that the woman holds a throw in her lap and that a knitted cape covers her shoulders. She holds a closed book in her hands, resting in her lap. Assuming the identity of the woman as Frau Schulz, but not recognizing her, she moves closer. She offers her hand but stops abruptly, withdrawing it, confused by a sudden look at the woman, not recognizing her.

She isn't Frau Berta Schultz.

"Her hair is a much lighter brown; there are only a few twinges of gray," she thinks as she quickly withdraws her hand.

As Frieda studies her, the woman gazes back and then smiles.

"Hello, Frieda. It is so nice to see you again. It has been a long time," she says extending her hand in a friendly gesture, but not getting up. Frieda takes her warm hand in hers, holds it for a moment, and enjoys its warmth on her cold one.

"I'm sorry for my visit without an announcement. I was expecting to see Frau Berta Schulz. Do I know you?" she asks as she takes her hand away.

"Yes, Frieda, I suppose you would be expecting to see Mutter, but I'm sorry to tell you that she has passed away. I am Claudia. Do you remember me?"

Frieda leans back, surprised. "Of course, Claudia, I remember you. How could I forget you, Frau Berta's beautiful little daughter? She was so proud of you." A picture flashes in Frieda's mind of Berta's only daughter. Claudia had one crippled leg and she had fought very hard to walk after the doctors had told Berta that she never would walk again. . She looks to Claudia's feet, searching for the special shoes with the brace but the throw on her lap hides them. A wooden walking stick leans against the table confirming that she is Berta's daughter.

"And, I am just as proud of her, Frieda. How can I help you?"

"I have a little granddaughter, named 'Sofia', who is about the same age that you had been when I had worked for your mother and I have a baby grandson, too. His name is Franz," Frieda says choking out the words. "They are starving, Claudia," she coughs and tries to stop her body from falling as she sways toward the chair.

Claudia gets up quickly, perhaps too suddenly, she leans as she tries to regain her balance, unsteady because she had not reached for her cane to help her balance her body on her one crippled leg. As she steadies her own body, she moves to help Frieda. She takes the basket out of Frieda's hand and drops it on the floor.

"Come, sit down, Frieda," she says as she helps her remove her coat and scarf, letting them fall onto the floor, all the while balancing herself on her one good leg. She holds onto Frieda's armpit as she drops into the chair. "Frieda, take a moment to get warm and to catch your breath. We will have some tea and then you can tell me more about your family," she says limping back to her chair. She rings the bell for the servant. "Relax, Frieda, we will get you warm, and things will look better, I promise."

The servant re-appears and Claudia instructs her to bring a blanket for Frieda and some hot tea and sweets. After the servant leaves, Frieda takes a deep breath and contemplates what she will say. She watches as Claudia sits back in her chair and gets comfortable. After a few moments, Frieda initiates the conversation.

"Claudia, I have worked hard all of my life and it was never easy. Mind you, I am not complaining but, until now, I have never had to beg for anything, certainly not for food," she continues without making eye contact, holding her head down. "I have had a hard life as Herr Heinrich Schmidt's wife, but I don't regret it – none of it. He did what he could. He passed away nine years ago in a farm accident." Her eyes tear at the mention of Heinrich.

Claudia watches her intently, saying nothing.

"We are desperate. If I can't get food for my family, they will surely die. I came to beg your mother for just a small amount of food, enough to keep us alive until times improve," she explains as her voice quivers.

"I am begging you, Claudia. Please, will you find it in your heart to help us? I'll get down on my knees if I have to, Claudia," she begs and moves to get up.

"No, Frieda, please. You are too weak. Just relax," she says taking a handkerchief from her pocket. "Don't cry," she says as she reaches over and puts the handkerchief in Frieda's lap.

Frieda dabs her cheeks with the heavily starched, perfectly ironed handkerchief that has a scent of lavender. It refreshes her memory of her former employer's personal hygiene and brings flashes of her time working for her, and taking care of her little girl. She gazes back at Claudia, thinking that the little girl she had come to love has indeed grown into a beautiful woman.

"I am sure if Mutter were here, she would certainly help you. I'll do the same," she says cupping Frieda's cold fingers around the handkerchief.

The servant enters, carrying a pot of hot tea and some sugared pastries on a gold tray and a blanket for Frieda draped over her arm.

After she serves them, Claudia instructs her to prepare a donation of food, to arrange for the delivery of a load of coal, and to order her chauffeur to take Frieda back home when they have finished. The servant acknowledges the orders with a nod and a bow, and leaves the room again.

The two women drink their tea and share the sweets while sharing old times, ones that had proven to be good memories for both of them and making them smile and laugh together. Finally, after several minutes of reminiscing, Claudia changes the subject to Frieda's predicament.

I hope you tell me more about your life and your family, Frieda."

"Oh, Claudia, if there's one thing I love to talk about, it is my family. First, allow me tell you about my granddaughter, Sofia. However, I should warn you that you might be sorry you have asked," Frieda says. She feels a sudden burst of energy at the mere thought of sharing her love for Sofia. The two women chat and laugh together, revealing the details of their lives and reminiscing about the past.

After hearing the particulars of Frieda's story, Claudia rings for the servant again and confirms the arrangements for a daily delivery of supplies to Frieda's home until the crisis has ended. She also instructs her servants to deliver the necessary supplies to the bakery so that Gerhard can again bake his goods. Touched and overwhelmed by emotion, Frieda moves toward Claudia and reaches for her hand, trying to kiss it, but Claudia pulls her hand away as she struggles to get upright. The two women embrace and hold each other tightly.

Claudia walks Frieda to the door using her walking stick and waits at the door with her for the driver to bring the car around. She has instructed the driver to drive Frieda home but before she sends Frieda back with the fruits of her visit, she tells her, "If you need further help, Frieda, please don't hesitate to ask."

She watches as the servants escort Frieda to the car and place the basket of food next to her on the back seat. "God be with you, Frieda. Please know you will never have to beg again." As the chauffeur closes the door, she waves goodbye.

It is Frieda's first ride in an automobile.

"The trip back seems much faster than the one getting here," she thinks as the car moves down the long driveway and exits through the gates of the mansion. She watches and looks out the window with interest as the city passes before her, recalling Heinrich's words whenever they would return to the farm after a trip into the city.

"The return trip is always easier than the one going," Heinrich had said.

"He was right about that, too, but this was one trip that he would never have taken – his pride would never have allowed that," she thinks as they arrive at the bakery. "I thank God for blessing me with the humility to swallow mine."

The chauffeur comes around to the passenger side of the car and opens the door. He carries the basket in one hand and helps Frieda with the other. Frieda finds the sack holding her quilt still waiting on the second step in the vestibule, exactly where she had left it.

"Would you like me to carry the basket and sack upstairs for you, Frau Schmidt?" the driver asks.

"Yes. That would be lovely. There are thirteen steps," she says as she starts to climb the steps ahead of him.

"It may take me awhile, but I'll make it to the top. My family needs me."

"Yes, Frau Schmidt. Take your time."

"Thank you."

*

Fifteen Minutes Later

Frieda is still wearing the scarf tied tightly around her head and her long dark overcoat as she walks down the hallway leading to Sofia's room. The small oil lamp on the tray she carries lights the way as the tray teeters in her cold hands. She manages to balance it, saving the lamp and the bottle of milk from falling while still holding onto the sack with her quilt stuffed safely inside. She feels good about the way her mission had turned out and is anxious to complete the final phase of her plan, feeding and warming Sofia.

The house is silent except for Sofia's soft whimpers. She knows that the others had gone to bed, probably thinking that she had done the same. She hastens her steps, picturing Sofia, dreadfully hungry and cold. When she arrives at Sofia's bedroom door, she lets the sack drop onto the floor and uses one of her hands to hold the tray while turning the knob. The lamp tips, but she manages to react quickly. The door handle feels cold in her hands, cramping her fingers, but several attempts allow the door to swing open into the cold, dark room. Only a stream of moonlight coming through the window lights the room, revealing Sofia hidden under a mound of blankets.

Frieda takes several deep breaths as she moves across the room toward the bed. Fearing her energy will expire, she inhales and slowly exhales again, breathing the frigid air deep into her lungs. Dizziness makes her head swoon; her body sways, making the tray teeter, threatening its precious cargo. Again, she reacts, extending her fingers outward. It is enough to balance the tray, but pain shoots up her arm. She winces as she walks toward the chest on the other side of the room, places the tray down, and goes back into the hall to retrieve the sack holding her quilt. She finds her way back into the room by following the light, now casting an eerie shine onto the bottle of milk, pieces of cheese, and the small loaf of bread. She slowly lowers her body down onto the mattress and catches the first glance of Sofia's face.

She is dressed in a blue cloth coat, obviously several sizes too large, and a pink knitted cap pulled tightly down onto her forehead. She sits up rubbing her eyes and crying. Her cheeks are swollen and red. The strings of the cap rest on braids, hanging loosely along the sides of her petite face. She is confused, disoriented, and obviously very distressed. She sobs trying to catch her breath between each gasp. Her breath forms soft, foggy rings of condensation, which float from her blue lips, swirl above her head, and dissipate into the frigid air.

Frieda's heart pangs at the sight of her.

As she catches her breath, larger rings of mist form over her head. They join the smaller ones caused by Sofia's breathing, creating a ballet of sorts, composed of misty surrealistic forms, rising and dissolving in a continually changing rhythm as they dance in the air. The two figures appear to be props in the performance, frozen as if each is a statue emitting the vaporous serenade from a soundless opera. The same unknown conductor is orchestrating the movements of their eyes, turning the props into the two stars of the production, Frieda and Sofia.

Their eyes are almost identical, a crystal light blue, only differing in their size but gravitating to one another as if they were one, locking at exactly the same time. Sofia searches her grandmother's face for a moment but then closes her eyes, enjoying her warmth as Frieda wraps her arms around her, kisses her cold cheeks, and wipes away her frosty tears.

"Don't cry, my darling. Everything will be all right. Oma is here now," Frieda soothes her, murmuring softly, as she warms her with her breath.

"Oma," Sofia whispers.

Frieda pulls her closer, holding her tightly, hoping that the warmth of her body will transfer to hers.

Sofia shivers beneath the layers of coats and jackets. Frieda hugs her tighter, picturing what Alexander and Gerhard must have done earlier, wrapping their children in layers of cotton and wool, desperate to warm them. A picture of the last burning embers of her mother's rocker in the fireplace flashes in her mind.

She reaches for her quilt, wraps it around Sofia, and then places the bottle of milk to her quivering lips. The first mouthful spills out of the corner of Sofia's mouth. Frieda moves quickly, bringing the bottle down under her chin, catching the precious liquid, making sure that not one drop is wasted. She gives her another drink and allows Sofia to continue gulping it.

"Sofia, take it slowly, just one small drink at a time. Take it slowly, my dear," she cautions her.

Just as there seems to be some kind of rhythm developing between the girl, the old woman, and the bottle, Sofia chokes. Reacting, Frieda removes the bottle and pats her back gently. After several more rounds of coughing, Sofia cries, still choking at the same time. When she had finally cleared her throat, Sofia studies her and reaches for the bottle, moving it away from Sofia's reach.

"More?" Sofia asks through her tears.

Frieda offers her a piece of the bread instead, followed by a piece of cheese. "Slowly, or you will make yourself sick."

The only sounds in the room are the chomping sounds of Sofia's jaws as she chews. In between each mouthful, her lips quiver and her teeth chatter. As if she is a baby bird, she opens her mouth another time, allowing the older bird to place one morsel after another into her mouth, chewing it slowly as directed, and swallowing it carefully. The older bird watches as her young chick eats the first meal she has had in days.

When the bread and cheese are gone, Sofia looks to the milk again. Frieda places the bottle into Sofia's tiny hand, making an upward motion with hers, giving Sofia a visual clue to finish drinking the milk.

Sofia needs no encouragement. She lifts the bottle to her mouth and swallows, emptying it, and then she turns the bottle upside down, checking with her hand extended to make sure there is no more. She looks up at her grandmother with a forlorn expression on her face.

"Tomorrow is another day, Sofia," Frieda says taking the empty bottle.

Claudia's promise to deliver more food flashes in her mind. She has no reason to think otherwise, but she prays that *tomorrow Claudia's chauffeur will bring more food.*

"Thank you, dear God. Thank you, Claudia," she whispers.

As Sofia watches, Frieda places the empty bottle on the tray, looking at her precious granddaughter with complete satisfaction. Sofia's gloomy, wet eyes are riveted on hers. At that moment, the two form a special bond, reserved only for them.

Frieda removes the quilt from around Sofia's shoulders, shakes out the folds, and spreads it on top of the bed covers. Placing her hands onto her shoulders and pushing her gently down, she slides Sofia back under the covers, pulls up the quilt, fitting it snugly under her chin, finally tucking it under the mattress. After she has pulled the cap down farther over her ears and has tied it securely under Sofia's chin, she is convinced that Sofia is safe.

"I'll stay with you until you fall asleep, Sofia" Frieda says anticipating her wants.

"Will you tell me a story, Oma?" Sofia asks in a low voice.

"Yes. Tonight, I'll tell you a very special story, Sofia, my darling. I call it, THE MAGICAL QUILT," she says as she makes herself comfortable on the side of the bed. After pulling the quilt up and tucking it under Sofia's chin one more time, she smiles and begins:

> "Once upon a time, a beautiful little girl named 'Sofia' lived in a faraway land with her parents and younger brother. They were all very happy, until one cold winter day when she was very cold and hungry. With sadness on his face, her father shared their misfortunes. He told her that the reason that she was so hungry and cold was that there was no money to buy food or fuel for heat. Sofia became sad and very worried.
>
> One night, a beautiful fairy godmother came to visit her. She brought a basket filled with food and a very special blanket. Her godmother told her that the blanket was no ordinary one, but an heirloom, made from the remnants of her German family's clothing. She said that it had a special name, calling it a 'QUILT'. After eating some

of the food and warming herself with the quilt, the little girl felt better. She shared the remaining food with her family and they all felt better. The next day, just when her belly was telling her she was hungry again, another basket of food appeared. After that, every night she found a newly filled basket of food carefully placed next to the quilt. Before long, she was convinced that the quilt was magical. From then on, she slept with the quilt every night. If she was cold, it warmed her. If she was hungry, there was food. If she was afraid, it gave her courage.

Sofia's story about her magical quilt spread all around the village. Soon, everyone wanted a magical quilt, just like hers. She felt proud that she was the only one in the village who had a special quilt with magical powers. As she grew older, she kept that precious blanket close to her heart. One day, after she had grown into the loveliest young girl in the Kingdom, a handsome Prince came to her house. He fell in love with the beautiful girl and asked her to marry him. On their wedding night, she took out the quilt and told him the story of how her fairy godmother had given it to her when she had been a little girl. She also shared with him that she believed that the quilt had magical powers, ones that had served her over the years.

The Prince and the Princess took the magical quilt with them as they traveled their Kingdom. No matter where they were, in the cities or in the villages, the quilt always generated a supply of food for the people, making them joyous and growing to love their new Prince and Princess for their generosity and kindness. Happiness and prosperity filled the Kingdom. According to an edict by the prince, they made the quilt into a flag, representing the Kingdom. It flew high above the castle and, from that day, there was great peace and prosperity in the Kingdom. Everyone lived happily ever after. The End"

Frieda notices that Sofia's eyelids have closed and she sighs with relief. She pictures her going to a special place where children sing, play, and are not cold, hungry, or frightened. After kissing Sofia's cheek and rising on her stiff legs, she picks up the tray and creeps out of the room.

Walking back to her own room, she thinks about her mission that evening, feeling a great sense of satisfaction.

As she gets into bed, her thoughts focus on her quilt. It occurs to her that the quilt is *truly as magical* as she had portrayed it in the story that she had told Sofia. *If it had not been for my quilt, I may never have thought of begging from Frau Schultz.* She allows sweet thoughts of Sofia to replace the worries of the day, confident that her quilt will now keep her beloved granddaughter safe through the night."

*

"Is the quilt on your lap the same one that your grandmother had given you, Sofia?" Janene asks when Sofia stops telling the story.

"Yes."

"You've kept it all of these years?"

"Yes, all in good time, my dear. As I share more of my life with you, I think you will conclude that the quilt has a story of its own."

Janene is still curious about the way Sofia tells her stories, never using the word, 'I' to refer to herself. It is just one more mystery for her to uncover about the perfect stranger who claims to be her grandmother.

"I was ten years old, but I remember it as if it had been yesterday. It was the day that Oma's quilt had become mine," Sofia says beginning again with that same faraway look, only this time a little sadder.

17 March 1929

Sofia's skin had begun to itch soon after she had put on the jumper over her white stiff blouse. "Too much starch again, Oma," she thinks turning the last button on her school uniform. A quick look at the clock tells her she will not have enough time to change it. She still needs Oma to braid her hair if she is to arrive at school on time.

She reaches for her Reading Primer of German to French and quickly starts toward Oma's room. "I guess I should be able to braid my own hair, but I really like Oma doing it," she considers remembering her father's words. She can't recall the last time that her mother had braided her hair for her. Oma had taken over the task shortly after she had moved in with them five years earlier.

Alexandra helped in the kitchen downstairs every morning, getting the ovens ready, and preparing the baked goods for sale that day. Sofia was glad when Uncle Adam had returned because he helped with Franz. "Franz is lucky! He doesn't have long hair," she thinks as she approaches Oma's door. *I'm luckier . . . I have Oma.*

The sound of her father's voice in the kitchen confuses her. She wonders why he isn't down in the bakery, but she doesn't dwell on the changes in the morning routine, instead she considers what her father had told her yesterday and the family was getting ready to go to church services.

"Sofia, you are old enough to do your own hair. Oma's fingers are much too painful for her to braid," he said when he had seen Frieda's hands on Sofia's long locks.

"Gerhard let her be. My fingers will never tire of braiding Sofia's hair," Oma had replied continuing the twists and turns of the special braids.

"If you say so, Frau Schmidt" Gerhard smiles as he turns to Sofia. "Come on then, we'll be late for the service, Sofia . . . Find Franz and hurry him up . . . . That boy takes forever," he said shaking his head from side to side.

Sofia runs off, hollering, "Franz! Franz!"

"I don't have to worry about Alexandra spoiling that child – her Oma is doing it quite nicely," Gerhard quips with another smile aimed at Frieda.

"You can't spoil a child with love, Herr Gunther. She will be able to braid her hair and give up the other luxuries of childhood soon enough. Let me spoil her for just a little longer."

Sofia wasn't far enough away. She heard the conversation. It makes her happy to know Oma wants to continue braiding her hair. She knows that she can do it herself, but she isn't ready to give up that special time with Oma. "Oma is much happier now that Uncle Adam has returned from France," she thinks as she reaches for the doorknob to Oma's bedroom. She is still thinking about yesterday when she tries to open the door but the knob doesn't turn.

Oma never locks her door.

She knocks again.

"Oma, are you awake? I need my hair braided," she asks trying the knob again. Confused, she turns and heads to the kitchen.

"Where is Oma?" she blurts as her eyes open wide.

Her family is sitting around the table – *everyone but Oma.*

Her jaw drops and she feels her heart beat faster as she stiffens and stares. Tears run down Uncle Adam's cheeks; Franz's face is red, swollen, and wet with tears. Alexandra has her head in her hands, and she is sobbing quietly. Gerhard, with a very serious expression on his face, one that Sofia has never seen before, moves toward her, placing his hand on her shoulder, not speaking, seeming to struggle to find his words.

"Where is Oma?" she whispers looking up at him.

"Your Oma is gone, Sofia. God has called her home," he says in a soft gentle voice while leading her to a chair beside her mother, who continues crying and offers no further explanations. Sofia searches her parents' faces for answers, but neither they, nor anyone in the room, say another word.

Oma went home . . . I thought this was her home.

She dares not speak and sits very still, listening to her father's words repeat again in her mind, still not able to make any sense of them. She wants to go to Oma, but she doesn't know where to go. She doesn't understand, nor can she imagine a life without her Oma. Furthermore, she can't imagine Oma without her. She feels sick.

Oma needs me. I'm her little bird. I'm the one who makes her smile.

She feels a chill that shakes her whole body.

Something is happening.

She feels lightheaded.

A floating sensation lifts her body from the chair. She looks down and sees the others still sitting around the table. A vivid ball of light appears above her and she hears Oma calling her.

"Sofia, come here, my dear," Oma says standing in front of the light, the most beautiful light Sofia has ever seen. It shines on Oma, lighting her hair, no longer tied up, but flowing down her back in beautiful white waves. Dressed in a long, sparkling-silver gown, and her shoulders no longer looking hunched, Sofia thinks she seems taller and much younger.

She looks like Mutter and the way Oma had described the Fairy Godmother in her story of the magical quilt. She reaches her arms out to embrace her, but her hands feel nothing. Again, she extends her arms, but her hands come back empty. Even though she can see and hear her, she can't touch her. Her heart beats faster.

"Sofia, don't be afraid. I didn't want to go before I had said good-bye to you. I know you are sad, but you shouldn't be. I'll always be with you, Sofia. I'll be right here," she says pointing her finger at Sofia's heart.

Sofia stares at Oma's perfectly straight and graceful hand, no longer twisted and deformed.

"Oma, I want to come with you. I don't want you to leave."

"You must stay, Sofia," Oma says turning and walking toward the light.

"I want to come with you, Oma," she pleads following her, but every step keeps her farther away from her.

"I need you. Who will braid my hair? Who will tell me bedtime stories? What will I ever do without you, Oma?"

"You won't need me here, Sofia. You will have my quilt. It will guide you. All you have to do is remember . . . Remember everything I have taught you."

She moves toward the handsome man who is holding out his hand. "Opa and I have to go. It isn't your time. You must stay."

Sofia moves toward her but, as fast as she walks, she can't catch up to her.

"Come, Frieda, we have to go," Opa says with his arms open wide.

Sofia watches as the couple walks toward the bright light. Tears flow down her face, but she stops crying when she sees the smile on Oma's face. Through her sobs, she hears her mother's voice.

"No, Sofia. You shouldn't go. You must stay here," Alexandra says placing her hand on her shoulder.

"Vater and Uncle Adam must go with Pastor Hahn."

Sofia is bewildered. She is back in the kitchen, moving toward Oma's room, following her father and uncle as they walk down the hallway toward Oma's bedroom. She feels her mother's cold hand touch her shoulder and then her arm wrap around it before settling on her hand and grasping Franz's hand. Alexandra leads them out of the kitchen toward the stairway.

As Sofia follows her mother, her father leads Pastor Hahn to Oma's room. Uncle Adam follows behind them. Alexandra leads the children to the bakery. Sofia notices the sign on the bakery door indicating that it is CLOSED. She follows her mother into the kitchen and sits down on one of the chairs around the kitchen worktable. The three sit without saying a word until Sofia breaks the silence by asking one of her questions.

"Mutter, why does Oma want a new home?"

"Why does Oma want to leave us?" asks Franz following his sister's lead.

"My darlings, Oma didn't want to leave us. Oma died last evening while she was sleeping. Oma is with Opa now; they are in Heaven."

"What does 'die' really mean, Mutti?" Franz asks in a soft voice, his eyes wide open. "Where do you go when you die?"

"Remember when Oscar had died last year? Well, Oma has died, too, just like your bird," Alexandra says gathering them both in her arms.

Sofia remembers the time when Oma had helped them bury their pet bird. "Will we bury Oma in the yard, Mutter?"

"No. No. We will bury her in the cemetery. We must arrange to bury her just like when she had helped you to bury Oscar. That is what Vater and Uncle Adam are doing now. They are helping Pastor Hahn to get Oma ready for the cemetery."

"Mutti, if Oma went to Heaven last night, why are Vater, Uncle Adam, and Pastor Hahn getting her ready now?"

"Her soul went to Heaven last night, Sofia. Her body is still here. God created all of us with a body and a soul. When someone dies, it is because God has called him, or her, back to Him. The soul separates from the body, moving on to be with God in Heaven, but only if the person has led a good life. The body dies because it doesn't have a soul anymore. We bury it in the cemetery according to the scriptures."

"What scripture, Mutter?"

[4]"Genesis 3:19. In the sweat of thy face shalt thou eat bread, till thou return unto the ground; for out of it wast thou taken: for dust thou art, and unto dust shalt thou return."

"But, where do we go if we don't lead a good life?" asks Franz.

"They are sent to a terrible place, Franz, and we aren't allowed to say the word," Sofia answers remembering how she had cried when Oma had placed the limp body of her bird in the cardboard box, dug the hole, and covered it over with dirt. She pictures Oma in a box, others lowering it into the hole, and covering it with shovels of dirt. Her stomach cramps and she feels sick.

Oma, I want to go there, too. I never told you good-bye.

Sofia had never seen her mother look so sad. She knew by the expression on her face that she was missing Oma as much as she was. Oma had tried to explain to her about death when Oscar had died and she thought that she had understood then because the explanation had given her comfort, easing the pain of losing Oscar. She remembers Oma's words when they had found Oscar lying at the bottom of his cage.

"When someone dies Sofia, it means that he or she is gone forever. Those who had loved them have only their memories."

Oma's words are still reverberating in her mind when she hears her mother's voice continuing with the explanation. "When someone dies, we can never bring them back; they are gone forever. We need to live a good life so that we can join them in Heaven when it is our time."

"I'm still here, Mutter," Sofia says looking into her mother's wet eyes.

"Me, too, Mutter," says Franz.

Alexandra wraps her arms around them, hugs, and kisses them.

"I know you are, my darlings. We will miss Oma, but we still have each other. Someday, we will all be together again."

Sofia never asked her parents any more questions about death and dying. They never offered any further explanations.

*

Several days later, Frieda's family arrives at St. Luke's Cemetery.

The cold, but sunny morning changes when an unexpected blustery burst of wind and light rain arrives. The crying group of mourners walks

---

[4] http://bible.cc/genesis/3-19.htm

solemnly under the sobbing sky toward the plain, wooden coffin resting before the freshly dug, cold, wet hole. Gerhard holds Sofia's hand and gently pulls her timid body toward the site. His other hand holds a large, dripping-wet, black umbrella. Alexandra, holding an umbrella in one hand and Franz's hand in the other, leads Franz down the path behind them toward the gravesite. Adam walks with his head down, hiding his tears under the third umbrella.

At the graveside, Pastor Hahn motions to them, directing them to form a circle around the coffin. As they stand under the large linden tree near the tall iron fence, Sofia thinks about what Oma had said when they had buried Oscar in the yard. "We will bury your bird in this yard. He won't be lying under the linden trees, but I guess it will have to do." She is happy that there is a linden tree in the St. Paul's graveyard.

The Reverend prays. Sofia doesn't hear his words. Lost in her own thoughts, she is sure that she hears Oma's voice talking to herself again and positive that she hears her say, "I am here, Heinrich." However, this time, Oma isn't talking to herself and she doesn't answer herself, either. "Oma is with Opa," she thinks as she looks down at the white rose she holds in her hand, wishing it were a chrysanthemum, instead. She remembers that Oma had told her how much Opa had loved chrysanthemums. Even though Sofia had never known her Opa, because of the many stories Oma had shared, she feels as if she had.

"Sofia and Franz, these are for you to place on Oma's coffin, today," Alexandra had told her children earlier when she had given them each a single white rose. Sofia didn't say anything to her mother, but she wished that the rose had been a chrysanthemum.

Just as the Reverend was finishing the final prayers, a large dark-colored automobile pulls up on the road at the end of the walk leading to the gravesite. A driver comes around with a large umbrella and opens the door for a middle-aged woman. The woman, braced with a cane, dressed in a simple black suit and overcoat, wearing a black hat with a veil over her face, and carrying a small bouquet of yellow chrysanthemums walks to the graveside. The Reverend signals that he wishes to begin and offers his final homily and blessings.

When finished he motions to the mourners to give their final good-byes. Alexandra and Adam walk to the coffin together, place a bouquet of red roses on it, kiss it, and whisper their tearful parting words, only each could hear.

Gerhard leads Sofia and Franz over to the coffin. They place their single rose on the box. Almost in unison, they whisper, "Good-bye Oma."

The woman places her bouquet on the coffin, standing silently for a moment, before she speaks.

"Good-bye, my dear friend, Frieda . . . Rest in peace."

The Reverend directs the group away from the site. Only Adam remains.

While the group files away, Adam reaches for the shovel and takes a few steps toward the hole. "I pray that the Schmidt seeds are the last of the shattered seeds of Germany, my beloved Mutti," he says as he places a shovel of dirt on her coffin. "But, I fear that will not be the case."

He places two fingers on his lips before touching them to the coffin for the final time. As he moves away from the graveside, he contemplates the decision he had made earlier when he had prepared for the burial with the minister. He didn't want the children to see the coffin lowered into the hole, or to see him place a shovel of dirt on it. "I pray that it will not be so, but I fear that the pain they are feeling now dealing with their first experience with death is only the beginning."

The others have made their way to the end of the walk when the stranger speaks. "I am sorry to be late. My name is 'Frau Claudia Schulz'. I hope I am not intruding. I had only recently heard of Frieda's passing. I wanted to pay my respects."

"I am Adam, Frau Schulz. You are not intruding. Thank you for coming. Mutter would have been pleased." He extends his hand to her, which she accepts and shakes lightly.

"I am Alexandra, Frau Schulz. It is so nice to meet you, finally. We have never really had the opportunity to thank you for all that you have done for us."

"Please, please, Alexandra, no thanks are needed, nor had they ever been required. Frieda's loyalty before and after was more than enough. I have been glad and honored to help you."

"Mutter had never forgotten your kindness, Frau Schulz," Alexandra says.

"Frieda was an exceptional person but you know that, don't you?" Claudia pauses and looks back at the gravesite.

"I am not sure if you had known about it, but she had come back to my home every week after that first night when she had begged me for help. She had insisted on working in the mansion . . . working hard. I had feared for her health, knowing how difficult it had become because of her condition, but I could not stop her from coming. She was a stubborn woman, never taking any money for her hard work because she believed that she should repay me for helping all of you. She said that she had felt indebted to me . . . that no price could ever be put on the lives of her family."

"Thank you for saying that, Frau Schultz," Alexandra says.

"Here is the money I would have paid her. I knew she would never take it, but I have saved it in this envelope, thinking that someday I would give it to her family," she says handing the envelope to Adam. "I am sorry that it has to be today."

"Thank you, again. Your generosity continues to amaze us. We have always wondered where she had gone off to one day each week, Frau Schulz," Adam adds.

"Please call me 'Claudia'. I feel as if I know all of you – as if you are my own family. Frieda had talked about each one of you, describing you perfectly and telling me how much she loved you. She will be greatly missed, Adam and Alexandra. I have always considered her more than a friend – certainly not just the hired help. When I was growing up, she was like a big sister to me."

"She felt the same way about you, Claudia. She always spoke of you as if you were family," Alexandra says choking back tears.

"Perhaps, you would like to come back to our home for some refreshments?"

"Thank you. You are all very kind, but I have a previous commitment at the Synagogue," Claudia apologizes.

"Please remember, you are always welcome at the Schulz home," she says offering her hand to Gerhard, who extends his right hand while still holding Sofia's with his left.

"It has been nice meeting you, Frau Schultz," Gerhard says shaking her hand.

"Know that the doors of our home and the bakery are always open to you, Frau Shultz."

"Thank you," Claudia says with a smile.

"You must be 'Sofia'," she says glancing toward Sofia. "Your Oma had talked about you often. You are just as beautiful as she had described. I hope you know how much she loved you, Sofia."

"I know . . . She loved you too, Frau Schulz. She told me you were the type of person who made Germany proud," Sofia shares.

"Thank you for saying that, Sofia. You're very much like your Oma," Claudia says with a smile, turning, and walking away.

She has tears on her cheeks when her driver opens the car door.

Sofia had listened as Frau Schulz had related the story of how Oma had come to her home to work over the years, but she had already known about the visits. Oma had told her that she was going to help a friend named 'Claudia' but she had never mentioned that it had been Frau Schulz. Oma had also shared that she had loved this friend very much. Sofia figured it out that the friend was indeed Frau Claudia Schultz. .

Sofia had known the story telling of the night that Oma had begged from the Schultz family and how Frau Schulz had followed through on her promise to give them fuel and food until the crisis had ended. "Sofia, there are good people in the world. Frau Schulz is one of them. She has shown great generosity during our time of need. I'll never forget what she has done to save our family," Frieda had told her when she explained what had happened.

"Oma, is Frau Schulz like the Prince and Princess in the bedtime story?" Sofia had asked becoming curious of the friend Oma had faithfully gone to visit each week.

"Yes, Sofia, she is exactly like them. I hope you will grow up to be like them too."

"I will, Oma. I'll use your magical quilt to help everyone," Sofia had promised.

"I know you will, Sofia. You are a very good, little girl. I know that you will make Germany proud of you, too."

As she walks away from the grave with her parents, she decides that Oma would be happy to know that her friend had come to pay her respects. "I'm glad I could lay a rose on Oma's coffin. I didn't want to put a shovel of dirt on her box as I had for Oscar," she thinks as she looks back and sees the cemetery director smoothing the final layer of dirt filling the hole. The group files out of the cemetery with heads down. Sofia doesn't look back.

*

In the months and years after Oma's death, there was no one in Sofia's life who had ever felt it necessary to speak of death or dying again. The lack of further explanation had left Sofia with many unanswered questions, not only about death but also about most things. She tried to comprehend the loss, but every day the simplest things reminded her of Oma's absence. Each day became more difficult for her. Time would help, but she would never fully get over losing her beloved, Oma. However, in order to cope, she decided to push her feelings deep inside her to a place that doesn't hurt or make her feel sad. Just as she had learned how to bury her bird, she let go of her feelings, burying them deep inside.

"I'll bury Oma in my heart forever," she vowed. "But I'll tell no one."

She never forgot what Oma had said when she had seen her in the silver gown walking away with the grandfather she had never known. She did as Oma had told her, always embracing her words, considering them as Oma's legacy, and finding them each time she held her quilt. How could she not? To her, the quilt became Oma.

*

Sofia changed forever after the day her grandmother had died, letting go of her childish ways. She learned how to braid her hair herself, how to translate German to French, and how to starch her own blouse. Every night, she thought of Oma before closing her eyes and caressing her quilt. It gave her pleasure to see her grandmother's face and hear her voice before she would finally fall asleep.

One night, when she had closed her eyes, yearning to see her Oma's face and hear her voice, her body froze. As hard as she tried, she couldn't see or hear her. The only sound was the pounding of her heart. Petrified with fear, she squeezed her eyes tighter but as hard as she tried, Oma's face did not appear.

She sat up abruptly; terrified that she had lost the memory of her. As she squeezed the fibers of the quilt tightly, holding it close to her heart and to her great relief, Oma's face appeared. "I'll never forget you, Oma. You will always be right here in my heart," she whispered to the image of Oma appearing in her mind.

For the first time, she realized she had *not lost Oma.*

She put her head back down on the pillow and gathered the quilt up to her chin, breathing a deep sigh, and smelling her beloved grandmother again. This time when she closed her eyes, she saw Oma standing before her, smiling her special smile, the one she had always reserved for her.

From that night on, she slept with Oma's quilt, finding comfort in it when she had been confused, lonely, or afraid. Every time she held the quilt, she heard Oma's soft voice and saw her sweet face. She talked to the quilt and listened for it to speak back to her, as if it was Oma herself.

"The quilt is Oma and she is everything good about being a German. I'll never forget her. I'll always strive to be the woman that she was. I'll make her proud," she vowed. From that day forward, Sofia never forgot that promise."

*

"I'm so sorry, Janene," Sofia consoles as she notices the tears running down Janene's cheeks and stops reciting her story.

Janene's emotional response means a great deal to Sofia because she is the first person, besides Jeffrey, with whom she had shared how she had felt about the quilt and her German heritage. She hands her a handkerchief from the pocket of her shawl so that Janene can dry her tears. Janene notices the embroidery on it, showing the word 'Oma'.

"I'm sorry, too, Sofia," Janene sobs as she dabs the corner of the handkerchief against her cheek.

"I didn't mean to interrupt your story. It is just that the story of your Oma's death brought back memories of Madeline. I miss her so much. I wish I had had a quilt like yours or something that could give me comfort now that she is gone. Even though she wasn't my biological mother, I loved her so much and I miss her. I actually feel a little guilty in wanting to find my 'real' parents. To me, Madeline will always be my mother and Bill will always be my father. I hope that doesn't offend you."

"That is understandable, Neeny. I regret that I had never had the opportunity to meet her. I would thank her for taking such wonderful care in raising my granddaughter and I know that my son would do the same."

"I wish you had met her too, Sofia. You would have liked her," Janene says as she hands Sofia the handkerchief.

"Please. I want you to keep the handkerchief. It's a token of your German heritage."

"Thank you, Oma," Janene whispers.

Sofia smiles and suggests that they break for a while.

"I think that might be a good idea," says Janene.

*

An hour later, Janene sits across from Sofia waiting for her to continue the story; she recalls the conversation she had with Bill during the break. Bill had expressed some concerns that the sessions might "be too much for Sofia." He said he had noticed at lunch that she had seemed to be showing signs of fatigue. He also told her that Jeffrey had commented that he was worried about Sofia's health. He is concerned that the storytelling sessions are causing her a great deal of stress.

"Are you sure that you want to continue, Sofia? I could easily come back another time."

"I won't hear of that, Janene," she smiles.

Janene smiles back but still worries that Sofia is taxing herself too much.

"I was about to tell you the story about my life after Oma had died," Sofia says beginning again.

*

"After her Oma had died, Sofia had assumed more responsibilities, both personal and family. She had never realized, until then, how important her grandmother had been to her and the role that she had played in her family. Now, she is required to take care of herself completely, doing many of the things her Oma had done for her. However, she surprises herself with how

98

easily she is able to braid her hair, learn her schoolwork without help, and willingly take on all of the housework. In addition, her relationship with her mother deepens. Oma had shown the family an inner strength that had led them through difficult times.

Sofia looks to her mother as the newest matriarch to replace the loss of her grandmother. The closeness between them would never replace that special part of her that she had reserved for Oma. It seems to Sofia, that when Oma had died, a part of her had died as well.

She celebrates her twelfth birthday in 1931 with not much of a celebration. The day before her birthday, her first menstrual period started and she wasn't ready for the change, neither was her mother. When she had found the spot on her underwear, she had approached her mother wide-eyed and worried. She had been horrified when her mother had handed her a set of rags with an explanation of their use. Her mother reassured her that there wasn't anything to worry about and described it as a "new beginning" for her.

"Sofia, you are a woman now," her mother had told her. "Your body is now able to make a baby. With this, comes great responsibility. Remember that it takes a man and a woman to have a baby and this is something that should only be done after you are married." She wasn't sure what that meant, but she knew that parts of Franz were different from hers.

She looked to her mother for further explanation but her mother dropped the subject, saying, "That is all you need to know right now, Sofia. You will find out the rest, all in good time."

She was used to never questioning her parents. She idolized them, thinking that her father was the wisest man in the world and that her mother the perfect example of a German woman. One day, as she brushed her hair and gazed at herself in the mirror, she noticed the strong resemblance she had to her mother. "I look just like my mutter," she mouthed to herself in the mirror.

Maybe I am beautiful, too.

Until then, she had not given much thought to what she had looked like or whom she had resembled and she never thought of herself as beautiful or pretty. She had always admired Oma and her mother and wanted to emulate them. It pleases her to know that the name is also her middle name. She thought that it suggested an elegance and grace reserved only for royalty. *Someday, I hope to have a daughter who has the same blond hair and blue eyes. I'll call her 'Ana Alexandra' after Oma, Mutter, and me.*

As she brushes the waves from her braids, her thoughts dwell on her family, picturing them in her mind. She sees her mother as she had been in her wedding picture, comparing it to now. Her once-blond hair is now a brilliant white, just as Oma's hair had been, tied in a bun on the back of her neck, the same as Oma. Her brilliant blue eyes are not as bright as they once had been; dark rings of folded flesh shadow them and her jaw line, once so perfect, now droops. Her once slender figure had widened over the years. Her shoulders, now showing a stoop, suggest that she has had a hard life of work and worry.

"I wonder what I'll look like when I am old," she asks studying the picture again. Alexandra wears a lengthy veil of hand-sewn lace, trailing behind her long ivory dress. She stands behind her father who is dressed in his military uniform, sitting proudly in a chair. As Sofia studies the picture, which she had seen hundreds of times before, she can't help but think that her parents must have been the most envious of couples in their day. She wishes she could remember when she was very little, but everything back then is hazy. She does remember the day that her parents had presented Franz to the pastor for Baptism even though she had been only five years old. The picture flashes in her mind.

Her father had carried her into the church and her mother carried baby Franz. Her father's shoulder had felt so warm and safe as she had nudged her face into it, hiding her eyes from those who had seemed to be looking at her. She had felt as if she was sitting at the top of a mountain, looking down on the world, always safe and secure in her father's arms, a sensation that had happened every time she had looked into his penetrating blue eyes.

She sees something in her parents that others would never discern. They had a deep abiding love for each other, their families, their church, and their country. She has come to understand their inner most spirits, platitudes, and strengths, characteristics that have enabled them to bear the hardships of their lives. For a brief moment, she feels that she has the same strengths and that her future will test them. The moment is fleeting, giving her a chill. She quickly diverts her thoughts back to her parents and Oma. The stories they have shared with her about their early years, the war, and the changes brought on by the Great Depression stay with her. She remembers the time that Oma had shared the family history with her. At the time, she didn't recognize how important her story would become to her."

*

"It is 1927; Sofia is eight years old. She and Oma are busy working in the kitchen, doing dishes and talking at the same time. The same kind of things they had done every day since Oma had come to live with them. The very warm summer day had greeted them earlier when they had started at sun up. They are uncomfortable in their clothing, especially Oma who is wearing her usual long black skirt and high neck blouse. Her cheeks flush from the muggy air, or the lack of it, in the second floor kitchen above the hot bakery. They both wear one of the white bakery aprons wrapped several times around their waists.

The smell from the pot of cabbage she had boiled earlier still hangs in the air. Oma picks up a large serving platter, places it in the old wooden sink, splashes it with soapy water, swirls it around and rinses it. As she dries the dish with the towel, she stares at it with a strange look on her face. "I had forgotten that Alexandra had this platter. It had belonged to Oma Krause and she had only used it on special occasions. I can still see it sitting on the table – filled with her special Kraut."

"Who is Oma Kraus?" Sofia asks.

"She was my mother and your great grandmother. Her name was 'Julia', the same name I had given your mother. I thought that it was a perfect one with the name 'Alexandra'. Maybe I should tell you the story of our family. I suppose you are old enough to remember now."

Sofia listens as Oma tells the story of the Krause family, going back several generations, but she isn't really too interested until Oma tells the part about her. Some of the information Sofia already knows, but she couldn't bear to interrupt Oma telling the story. She files the information in her memory. When Oma gets to the part of the story about her father returning from the war and then having a baby girl, Sofia pipes in, shouting, "I know, I know, Oma, I am that little girl. That was when Mutter and Vater had me."

"Yes, you are that little girl and a very special little girl you are, Sofia Gunther," Frieda says hugging her tightly. "You are that baby girl born on September 06, 1919. Everyone thought Sofia Alexandra Gunther was the prettiest baby in the world," Oma teases.

They laugh and hug as Oma continues. "Gerhard's father had died just before you were born. He never saw his baby granddaughter. Gerhard took over his father's business. However, times were hard because Germany had lost the war. Keeping the business going was difficult for him. He and Alexandra worked hard. In 1924, another baby came to live at the bakery," she continues

"That was when Franz was born; a baby brother for me."

"Yes, a baby brother for you. Franz was born on August 14, 1924 and I think you know the rest of the story, Sofia. The Gunther family lived happily ever after."

She looked at her Oma, with eyebrows wrinkled and her eyes big with questions. "You forgot the part about how Oma came to live with Gerhard and Alexandra because there wasn't any food and heat at the farm. You forgot there wasn't any food at our house, either and that it was very cold," Sofia says with exaggerated tones on the "very cold" part.

"No, Sofia, I didn't forget that part. I am surprised you have remembered it. You were very little, then. Things are much better now. Your father's business is improving and people are getting over the war. I just wish Uncle Adam was still here and he still had the farm. He had loved it so much."

"Why has Uncle Adam left, Oma?"

"I don't know, Sofia. German women are not privy to politics and of course, we are not supposed to ask, but I know that he had been very disappointed in Germany. He had said that he was going to France to be with some friends. I had wondered why he would want to do that, but I had dared not question him. Women know their place. I hope he will come back soon. I miss him," Frieda says as her eyes moisten with tears.

"I miss him too, Oma. He had always played with Franz and me. It was fun to have him here with us. I'm sad that he has left us."

"He didn't want to leave us. He had wished things could have stayed as they had been before the war but he knew that the times were changing. I think he also feared that the changes were the wrong ones for the country as well as for him. He had always blamed himself for the way things had turned out."

Sofia's thoughts jump to the time when Uncle Adam had returned to Berlin. She remembers that joy replaced sadness that day. *Oma had never asked him where he had been or what he had done.* He never said. He had only been back for several months before Oma had died, and shortly afterward, he had left again. She remembers that her father and uncle had engaged in deep conversations, their faces very serious, but she didn't understand the things they had discussed. She could tell by the expressions of their faces that it was serious. Her father looked very worried.

As Sofia matured, she thought fondly of the time when Oma had lived with them, recalling how much she had always loved growing up on Pappelstrasse. She felt as if she had lived in the one neighborhood that had been the heart of Berlin and its people. The wide lengthy street with the large trees, lining the grassy area in the middle of the street, rambled with the sights and sounds of a busy city. Pappelstrasse, nestled off the main street leading to the downtown section of the large urban city, was a quiet secluded neighborhood just north of town. The bakery sat in the middle of the block surrounded by other shops, markets, and apartments. The neighborhood had the charm of a small community and yet it served the population of a very large metropolitan city. The street was a busy hub for people going about their daily lives, making purchases, visiting churches and museums, or just enjoying leisurely strolls along the avenue.

She enjoyed her place inside the window of her bedroom, overlooking the street. Although she had spent most of her time in the bakery working, much of the remaining time she had spent alone in her room watching the activities on the street below. It was a small room, but the size didn't matter to her. She had memorized every rose bud on the wallpaper and could almost smell them if she tried. She especially liked the large border of pink roses, which 'walked' around the ceiling. One of her favorite parts of the entire room was the chest sitting in front of the window where she had sat and looked out at the world – her world.

Of course, more than anything else, her most precious possession was Oma's quilt. She had never had a doll but she thought that the quilt was the next best thing. At times, she felt as if it was alive -- a real person, talking to it, and sometimes hearing it reply. Of course, when others were around, she talked to it as if it were a dolly. After Oma had died, she started to call it 'Oma' sometimes by mistake . . . or maybe on purpose.

She loved to sit by the window, spending many hours just listening, breathing in the smells, watching the people, and talking to the quilt. She loved the cling-clang sound of the bell as customers went in and out of the bakery, and the chirping of the birds singing in the Pappel trees. The babies, cooing and sighing as their mothers walked them in their carriages, had always made her smile as had the 'clunk-clunk-clunk' of the wheels on the bakery cart loaded with the fresh baked bread and sweets, their aromas bursting through the window each morning. Just as the roosters had become Oma's alarm clock, the smell of her father's bakery goods had become hers.

She remembers when her mother had cleared out all of the boxes in the garage and had brought Oma's things into her room. It had been shortly after Oma had passed. Alexandra had placed them in the chest in front of the window and Sofia had paid daily visits to the chest, lifting its lid, pleased by the greeting of the aroma of cedar. A closer examination of the contents had always made her sad. She missed Oma. She looked forward to the day when the contents of the trunk would all be hers to take with her when she married, as her mother had promised but the thought of leaving her parents terrified her.

I don't even know a boy. How could I ever marry one?

"This chest had belonged to your Grandmother Gunther," Alexandra said one day. "Opa Gunther had given this chest to me on the day that I had married your father. I have filled it with some of the linens from both sides of your family, each of which has a special message of love to you. Someday you will take this chest with you. These things will remind you of your German heritage, a very special one. The contents of the chest will remind you of what it is to be 'German' – that should always make you feel proud."

Sofia reached her hand into the chest, touching each item, one by one. Her hand smoothed the lace on the embroidered tablecloth stitched by her Grandmother Schmidt. She laid it gently aside and reached for the doily, embroidered with the family name. Oma said that her mother had done the needlework and that it had always been a special family heirloom, always having a special place on top of the upright piano that her grandfather had bought for the front room.

"I can still hear Mutter humming each note of [5]"Brahms Lullaby." Oma had always played the lullaby on the piano and had sung the words to me," her mother had told her.

With each touch of one precious item after another, she remembered the story of each, a lesson in her family's genealogy. Sofia believed that someday she would also take her grandmother's quilt and put it into the chest so that she could hand it down to her daughter but she couldn't part with it until that day. She still needed the magic, not able to let go of the feelings she had derived from touching it and thinking of Oma. When she was particularly sad or lonely, she heard Oma's voice as clear as when she had lived with them.

Sofia grew but she never forgot her Oma or the stories she had told her.

*

One day, when Sofia was almost fifteen, she and Esther Rosenfeld enjoyed a special time together. It didn't happen as often now as it had when they had been younger, but when it did, the girls loved it.

Esther's father owned a shop on Pappelstrasse, a jewelry shop called 'Rosenfeld Jewels', four doors away from the Gunther Bakery. Although the girls had attended different schools, Esther and Sofia had walked home together from school each day. Esther lived in a big house at the end of a well-established neighborhood, several blocks away, but many times, she walked to her father's store after school instead of going directly home. Sometimes, her father would allow her to leave the shop and visit at Sofia's house above the bakery.

The two girls sat on the old cedar chest in Sofia's room, watching the sights below and hearing the sounds from outside floating through the open window. "I just love your quilt, Sofia," Esther said. "It reminds me of the one my mother has. She had told me that the Knights of the Round Table had traveled with quilts on their armor. Their 'Ladies-in-Waiting' had made

---

[5] Johannes Brahms (pronounced [joˈhanəs ˈbʁaːms]; 7 May 1833 – 3 April 1897) German composer and pianist. Wikipedia.org/

the quilts for them and had given them to their special warrior when he had gone off to battle."

Sofia smiled and looked down at the quilt on her bed.

"This quilt had never belonged to a Knight. It had belonged to my Oma. She had made it from scraps of clothes and linens she had found in her farmhouse, not for some warrior but to keep her babies warm." As she studies the old, faded quilt, she doesn't see its age or its wear. She pictures the fabrics, as they must have been when used by her relatives as articles of clothing and textiles for their home, remembering all the stories that Oma had told her about her family's greatness. She was positive that Esther must see it that way, too. "The colors may have faded and the threads may have become worn, but it is always perfect to me," she told Esther, as her eyes gazed across the room to the quilt. "Would you like to hear the story of my Oma's quilt, Esther?"

As Esther shakes her head in agreement, her dark brown hair falls gently down over her forehead and she brushes them away from her gray-green eyes to look at the quilt. Sofia envies Esther's dark hair, dark eyes, and perfect face. "We are truly opposites," she thinks suggesting that they move over to the bed and sit on the quilt while she shares Oma's story. She recalls the times when Oma had told her stories from the Bible and she remembers that Jesus had been a Jew – *just like Esther*.

The girls make themselves comfortable sitting on the quilt, laughing, and giggling. Sofia remembers fondly the last time that she and Oma had curled up on her quilt. "Well," she begins sounding just like Oma. "My mutter told me that Oma had made this blanket when she had been just a girl, anticipating her marriage to my Opa. It had always been on my mutter's bed when she had been a child living at the farmhouse. When I was five years old, Oma and my Uncle Adam moved in with us because they had lost their fields. Oma had once worked in the homes of "some very wealthy Victorian women" when she was a girl and that she had watched them as they had made their quilts during their social gatherings. She had learned how to make a quilt by watching them."

"Who were the Victorian women, Sofia? Were they German, too?" Esther interrupts.

"Yes, some were. They were the women who had lived during the 'Victorian Times'. It had been a time in history dating from the middle of the Nineteenth Century until just around the turn of the Twentieth Century. Oma's father had arranged her marriage to my Opa. We studied about the Victorian Era in school. Did you?"

"Yes, I remember now. It was the time when the women had worn those fancy long dresses, big hats, and lots of jewelry."

"Yes, that is the time. Oma had been just a young girl then. She told me that one year she had to go work in some wealthy family's home in town. The women held sewing parties for their society friends, making linens, and other textiles using quilting, needlepoint, and embroidery. "But, I didn't need things to keep my fingers busy," my Oma had told me. "I never had time for any social gatherings, indeed," she says imitating Oma by moving her hands as she talked, just as Oma had always done.

The girls giggle.

"Oma had told me that she had made this quilt using scraps of materials she had cut from shirts, dresses, and linens belonging to my relatives, sewing each square to another and another until she had all of them sewn together, making one large piece of fabric," she says pointing to each square of the quilt. She watches as Esther studies it.

"Oma had known from the moment she had started the quilt that the pink patches had to go in the center of the quilt. They were pieces from the bodice of her mother's wedding blouse and she had wanted them to be the focal point, arranging them in this circular pattern forming a diamond, and adding the other pieces to them until she had one large patchwork design. She had told me that those patches were her favorites because they were her mother's and that she had wanted them in the center touching the others, the same as her mother had touched all of her family and her mother before her had done the same."

"See?" Sofia says pointing to the cluster of pink squares. "These are the squares here; but this one, the thread worn one in the middle, had been Oma's favorite," she smiles as she lifts her finger and allows Esther to touch the patch worn by Oma's caress. "After she had all of these patches sewn, she started another piece of cloth that would become the back of the quilt. Finishing it, she layered some cotton between the two layers," Sofia says turning the quilt to the other side. "You should never use wool, Sofia, never wool – unless the moths will feast," Oma had said. "She said it had been a long process to make the quilt, but that it had been her 'labor of love'," Sofia smiles seeming to enjoy teaching her lesson on quilt making to Esther.

"I remember how my Oma would finger the squares and tell me the story of each one," she continues pointing to one square in particular. "This square came from Opa's shirt," Oma had said in a sad voice with an odd look on her face. 'Heinrich had worn that shirt on our wedding day."

"A single tear would always form as Oma pressed the square to her nose, smelling it, and then reminding me that the square had belonged to my Opa's shirt. His name was 'Heinrich' and I had never known him because he died when my mother had been only fifteen."

106

"This one . . . here . . . is from my Oma's father. It is a square cut from his work pants," she shares fingering the sturdy blue corduroy, obviously worn softer by use.

"I had never known him either, but I feel like I have after hearing so many stories about him from Oma." Sofia takes a deep breath and Esther watches her with great interest.

"Oma would tell me the same stories over and over but I never tired of hearing them. She told me the story of the time when her father had worried about losing the fields because of the drought. The fields had been in our family for generations. Oma said that he had managed to save them and that he had arranged her marriage that same year to the boy next door, 'Heinrich Schmidt'.

Oma had said that she had never known a time when she had not loved my Opa. She had loved him from the first moment she had any memory of him," Sofia sighs. "My Oma had always fingered the patches of her quilt very slowly. She had something called "Arth-er-rite-is" and her fingers hurt all of the time. When she moved them to another square, she would say, "Yes, this is the one," and then she would tell me another story about someone else in my family.

"This one is from the hem of the first dress I had made for Alexandra. Mutter had sewed that dress for me. We had handed it down to Alexandra. Oh, yes, this one with the yellow dots is the one I had cut from the pretty curtains that had hung on the kitchen window in the farmhouse," Oma had said with that strange look on her face, the one that she would always get when she had touched that particular square and before she started to cry.

"Oma would go on and on, recalling each square as if she was sewing it all over again for the first time. Sometimes, she would repeat the same thing twice and on other occasions, she would have a difficult time remembering anything about the square. This seemed to irritate her but she never seemed too tired to share a story with me about her quilt," Sofia says getting very serious.

"After Oma had died, my mutter told me the story of my Oma's quilt. She shared that she had it on her bed when she was little and that Oma had wanted it to be on my bed so it would protect me, just as it had protected my mother. It had provided warmth but not just from the cold. My Oma had believed that it had offered comfort in the knowledge of our family, their traditions, and beliefs," Sofia said smiling down at the quilt and then at Esther.

"She told me that she had promised her mother that she would keep their memories alive in the minds of the next generation and that her quilt would help her do that."

"You are so lucky to have your Oma's quilt," Esther smiled back.

"I want it to be on my daughter's bed if I ever have one . . . I want to tell her all of the stories that my Oma has shared with me."

"Do you think we will ever be mothers?" Esther asks.

"I think so . . . Isn't that what we are supposed to do?"

Esther's face looks sad for a moment before she finds a smile for her special friend and replies, "I guess."

Sofia smiles back.

"I have always known that Oma's quilt is special. Once she told me a story about a Prince and a Princess. Would you like to hear that story, Esther? I'll tell it to you, if you like?"

"Oh, Sofia, I would love to hear it."

The two settle down on the quilt and Sofia begins telling the story, trying her best to imitate her Oma. "Once upon a time there was a little girl who had lived in a faraway land," she begins. Just before the end, she smiles at Esther and announces with enthusiasm, "They lived happily ever after. The End," Sofia says giving Esther a hug.

"I'm so glad we are friends, Sofia. I hope we find our princes when we grow up," Esther smiles and hugs her back.

"I hope we don't have to grow up for a really long time," Sofia says. A knock at the door interrupts their plans for the future.

"You two had better stop all that talking. Mutter wants you to come help her with supper, Sofia. Esther's father wants her back at the store," Franz informs them from the other side of the door.

Sofia opens the door.

A boy soldier who looks just like her younger brother, Franz, glares at her. He is dressed in a uniform, looking much like the soldiers of THE THIRD REICH, only with short pants.

"Is that what you have to wear to school, Franz?" Sofia asks.

"Yes. They issued them today . . . What do you think, Sofia? Do I look like a soldier of THE THIRD REICH?"

"You look like Franz in his school uniform," she giggles – until she looks at Esther's face.

Esther is as white as the white blouse she is wearing.

"I guess you do, Franz. Yes, you do look like a soldier," Sofia says changing her mind.

"Well, that's good, because this school is going to make me into one," he says while walking off toward his room.

Sofia turns to Esther, still curious about the look on her face.

"What's wrong Esther? Are you sick?" Esther swallows hard.

"Nothing is wrong, Sofia. I should go home. My father will be worried," she says jumping up and running out of the door. Sofia follows her but can't catch her before she rushes out of the door.

"We never said good-by," Sofia thinks as she hurries to the kitchen to help her mother with supper, but she can't dismiss the expression on Esther's face. She had never seen her look that way and she wasn't sure what had prompted her reaction.

"Was it the story about Oma's quilt?" she asks herself as she recalls their conversation. As she remembers the look on Esther's face, she is sure that it had been something about seeing Franz, but she couldn't figure out what it had been about her little brother that had frightened Esther so much that she had run off. She wants to ask her mother about it but she was preoccupied with making a hurried dinner because she had been in the bakery longer than she had expected.

"She was probably just worried that her father would be angry with her because she had stayed so long," she thought deciding to put the memory behind her.

After that playtime, there were no more times together for the two friends. In fact, she didn't see Esther at all after that. She never really understood why, except for what her father had told her: "Herr Rosenfeld needs Esther in his shop, just as I need you now in the bakery." She didn't see many people her age after that. Esther remained her only girlfriend, only because she had never made friends with any others. Not because she had not wanted to make friends, but because she had never had the opportunity. Most of the teen-age girls had to work in the homes of the rich or remain at home working for their family. Her father's wish to keep her at home had kept her isolated. Chores in the bakery had taken up most of her time. She never objected because she had preferred that to having to go to work in some other family's home.

Sofia obeyed her parents always, just as they had taught her. She had taken her household tasks seriously, believing that her parents had worked hard to keep the bakery going and she wanted to emulate the other women in her family so that someday she too would be a hardworking, dutiful wife, and mother. She had little contact with others her age, except from a distance when she had seen them walking on Pappelstrasse, or at church services, or in the markets. She was totally accepting of her situation and completely respectful to her parents' wishes.

Even when Sofia had attended school, she had thought the other children had treated her differently. *I think they don't like me because we are so poor.* The parents of the other children *had been as wealthy as the Rosenfeld family but I don't think they ever had to search for food or beg as my Oma had.* She thought that they had always treated her as if she had been beneath them, ignoring her, and never speaking to her. Esther had been the only one of the girls her age who had been nice to her. She always kept her special affection for the little girl whose father had owned the jewelry store.

*

Sofia's teen years could be best described as the same as her preteen ones. She had not seen Esther for a long time, not even walking down the street toward her father's shop as she had done when they had been younger. However, when she had walked home from the market one summer day, the 'CLOSED' sign on the jewelry store caught her eye. She also noticed that there were soldiers in the shop. She wondered about Esther, speculating about what had happened to her. In addition, she had noticed a locket in the window once and was considering asking her father if she could have it for her upcoming birthday. Now that the store was gone, she put that thought out of her mind, especially the idea of putting Oma's picture inside the locket. Several weeks later, she turned seventeen and Gerhard said, "It is time for us to see about getting a husband for you, Sofia."

She wonders where her childhood had gone, thinking about the future, feeling pain in her stomach as she questions whether she will be able to handle what lies ahead. The world of adults scared her and the fear of the unknown terrifies her, but she is certain of one thing: Getting a husband is last on her list.

*

"It wasn't long before I would change my mind about getting a husband, Janene. Actually, it was the twelfth day in June in 1938, just before my eighteenth birthday . . . I remember it well," Sofia said with a smile.

"Was that the day you were married?"

"Yes, it was. By the way, I never asked you. Is there someone special in your life?"

"No, there isn't. I guess I just haven't met the right person yet."

"All in good time, Neeny, all in good time."

"I hope you are right."

"I am sure of it. Now, what part of my story was I going to tell you?"

"I believe it was the part about getting a husband," Janene smiles.

"Oh, yes, I had better get on with it since I have had three of them," Sofia smiles back.

* * * * *

CHAPTER 4
OFFICER FELIX FUERST

"The first light of Berlin's morning sunrise bursts through the lacy pattern of the curtains on the opened window in the little room above the bakery. The light dances on her face as she sleeps, fixating on her high cheekbones, and lighting them with a rosy burst of color. Although the bright light dances on her eyelids, each remains steadfast, resisting all inclinations to respond. Ordinarily, the light would cause her to wake immediately, but not this morning. It would take more stimulus than just the bright light to awaken the sleeping bride, Sofia Gunther, who had gone to bed exhausted the night before.

When the eve of her wedding day had ended, she had wanted to get some well-deserved rest for her weary body, but her mind continued to review every detail of the upcoming event. . Too excited to rest, she hadn't been asleep for long before the morning light had created this tug of war on her eyelids.

"Everything must happen just as father has planned," she thought as she opens one eye and focuses on a picture on her dresser of her future husband, 'Officer Felix Fuerst', once the neighborhood police Officer, but now inducted into the ranks of THE THIRD REICH.

"Felix, Felix," she whispers in her sleepy state of confusion, not wanting to open the other eye and let go of her dream. Suddenly, her mind focuses on the new day, causing her to jump out of the bed, relinquishing the one thing that she has come to love: *Dreaming about Officer Felix Fuerst*. She sees the tall, broad-shouldered, sandy-haired man in his police officer's uniform, the man who had bewitched her by the glimmer in his eyes, the sound of his voice, and his gentle sweet nature.

Fifteen years younger than her father and uncle, and the only man besides them that she has ever known, she has fallen hopelessly in love with him. She has known the mild mannered man for most of her life as have most of the citizens of the tiny neighborhood. Making his rounds in the community every day without fail, she had grown-up noticing the handsome man as a little girl. The fact that his German surname, 'Fuerst' translated to 'prince' had fed her infatuation with him even more. She had drawn an association to the story of the prince and princess that Oma had told her, imagining that maybe he would become her "prince."

She was sure that Oma would approve of her marriage to Felix because she believed that he was exactly like the prince in her story. She often reversed his name in her mind, changing it from 'Felix Fuerst' to 'Fuerst Felix', enjoying the image of Prince Felix and his Princess Sofia. It had been easy to fall in love with him and now, on the eve of their wedding day, she can't stop thinking about him and the reasons why she loves him.

"He always thinks of others first," she remembers recalling the times he had anticipated her wants and needs before she had had the opportunity to express them. One hot summer day, he met her with a glass of lemonade when she had returned from her errands. *No one has ever considered my needs as Felix does – except for maybe Oma*. She also had decided that he would make a wonderful father after seeing him interact with the neighborhood children, taking time to talk to each child in the neighborhood, interacting with them in spontaneous ways – like throwing the ball back to them or pushing them on the swings.

She felt secure in her decision to marry him because her father had approved of him and so had her mother. *He is very determined.* "When Felix makes up his mind to do something, there is no changing his mind," she thinks as she recalls his commitment to his police officer job. She had surmised that he had set his own set of very high standards, stopping only at perfection. She also had faith in her mother's opinion of Felix when Alexandra had told her, "He will take care of you, just as your vater has taken care of you."

Sofia is convinced that her decision to marry him is the best one she could have made. She knew that, when he had decided to become a police officer, that he had used the level of excellence for himself that he had always demanded from others. "His determination and strong will should provide me with the kind of life mother and father want for me," she thought as she remembered that he had told her that he had dreamed of becoming a police officer from his boyhood. She loved Felix with all her heart and she loved him just the way he was.

"I would never want to change Felix and he loves me just the way I am – even though he has never told me so," Sofia thought as she looked at his picture again. She loved his eyes and the way he formed his words when he talked. She listened to him as if she was in a trance, completely captivated by him.

As she gazed at his picture, she noticed that he is wearing the uniform of the police officer she had remembered and not that of an Officer in the Army, a recent appointment. She had little to no knowledge of the workings of the government or politics but she believed that now that Felix was working for the Fuhrer their future would be bright. However, one thing worried her.

She had compared Felix to the soldiers who had taken over the city and all of Germany for that matter and she concluded that the Felix that she knew didn't seem like a good match. As she considers her perceptions of the man she will marry, she wonders why THE THIRD REICH would ever want a man like him to join them. "The soldiers of THE THIRD REICH scare me to death," she decided. However, despite all of her reservations about the new government or the role Felix would play as its newest member, she had no doubts about marrying him.

"I know Felix is older than you, Sofia, but his experience will help you through the difficult times ahead," her father had told her. She knew that Felix epitomized everything that her parents had ever wanted or dreamed for her in a future husband. He was from the 'old school', demonstrating a love for the culture and traditions of previous generations by his words and actions and she believed her parents when they had told her that Felix would provide an easier life than the one they had given her. Sofia respected her father's opinions and beliefs and adhered to his decisions and judgments. Now that Felix worked for the Fuhrer, and was one of 'THE SOLDIERS' as the people had come to call them, Gerhard had approved of the marriage, saying that he had placed his only daughter in "good hands."

Sofia had vivid memories of the previous times when hardships had made their lives difficult and she had believed that it had been the plight of all Germans. Although she had learned some things in school, she really didn't understand any of it. To her, it seemed that her parents enjoyed a much better life now than when she had been little. However, she had been completely sheltered, only knowing what her parents had allowed. They were very private people who had set values revolving solely around a loyalty to their family, church, and country.

"This new leader has some grandiose ideas for Germany, Sofia. He wants to bring the country out of its depressed state and give the country back its pride. He will be the leader who will make his mark in history, a mark which will bring our beloved country to a former glory for the entire world to again see and admire," her father had told her when she had turned thirteen.

Felix had become as much of a constant in her life as her immediate family. He had been coming into the bakery ever since Sofia could remember, making his rounds as the youngest member of the local police department. Sofia knew that he had taken his police officer's duties very seriously, making sure he had visited every shop or business each day. With every visit, he would spend a few extra moments chatting with her father, or if there were others in the bakery, he always greeted them in a friendly manner, asking about their health and inquiring about family members. On several occasions, she had thought she had seen Felix studying her, but her shyness turned her eyes away.

I am just a girl and he is an Officer . . . I know my place . . . just as Oma and mother have taught me.

*

October 1937

Shortly after her seventeenth birthday, Gerhard and Alexandra had decided that OFFICER FELIX FUERST, member of the ARMY OF THE THIRD REICH should properly meet their daughter. They selected the perfect time for the event, one afternoon after most of the patrons had already done their shopping, and the store was quiet. Sofia was busy cleaning the display cases for the cakes and pies. The bell on the bakery door rang, signaling that someone had entered. She looked up and noticed Felix coming inside. Displaying her usual shyness, she peeked at him from behind the case as he walked over to the counter and greeted her father.

"Good Afternoon, Herr Gunther and such a glorious day it is."

"Good Day, Officer Fuerst! I have some wonderful selections for you to consider today," he said directing him to the iced cakes, fruit pies, and tarts sitting on top of the display case while Sofia continued cleaning it. They had always kept the cakes, pies, and tarts in the glass case. However, since Sofia was cleaning the inside of the case, she had placed the three trays of bakery products on top of the case so that she could clean the inside to Gerhard's standards of perfection. Leaning down into the cake case with her head down, deep in concentration, she looked up. Catching a ray of light shining through the glass, her eyes popped at the sight of the face of the handsome police officer smiling down at her.

"The cakes are almost as beautiful as you are, Fraulein."

She felt her face get warm; she looked away. It seemed like an eternity, but her father spoke next. "I have been blessed that God has given me Sofia. She has been of great service to me in the bakery, Officer Fuerst," he said as he raised his right hand, motioning Sofia to rise.

Sofia bows awkwardly and shows a shy smile, before quickly putting her head down, avoiding his eyes. She feels relieved to have the conversation turn away from her and center on the tart, as her father takes the tray of newly baked fruit tarts and offers them to Felix. As she waits while Felix makes his selection, she can't help but notice that his eyes are not on the tarts, but firmly on her.

"The plums are my favorite, Herr Gunther," says Felix.

Soon after that visit, Gerhard approaches Sofia with the notion of inviting Felix to dinner. Sofia is surprised. However, she catches a glance of her mother's face as she stands behind her father. Her mother raises one eyebrow and nods in agreement. At that moment, Sofia realizes that her parents had already discussed the plan. The realization that they had taken the initiative pleased her because, secretly, she had hoped to get to know Felix, whom she thought had shown an interest in her with just a smile, directed to her alone. When Felix makes his visit to the bakery the next day, Gerhard surprises Sofia even further.

"Frau Gunther and I would be pleased if you would join us for Sunday dinner, Officer Fuerst. Frau Gunther is an excellent cook."

As previously instructed by her father, Sofia stands out of sight behind the kitchen door and listening anxiously.

"It would honor me greatly to share dinner with you and your family, Herr Gunter," Felix answers.

"Good . . . then we will expect you at three o'clock?"

"That will be fine . . . and thank you."

"You are indeed welcome," Gerhard replies.

Sofia pops her head out for only a second and sees Officer Fuerst smiling at her. Quickly she disappears behind the door, listening, but not daring to look out again.

When Sofia hears Felix leave with his small bag of sweets, she thinks that she sees him glance her way one more time. Her stomach jumps. She had never felt that way before – except when she *had an upset stomach*. After Felix leaves, Gerhard shares his plan.

"Sofia, your mother and I have asked Officer Fuerst to dinner on Sunday. You need to help your mutter with the preparations."

"I have already started making dinner plans for Officer Fuerst, Gerhard," Alexandra says.

Again, Sofia is surprised. She wanted to ask her mother if she had prior knowledge of the scheme, but the coy smile on her face and her one eyebrow lifted dissuaded her.

"I am certain that Officer Felix Fuerst won't be disappointed with the dinner we have planned for him," Alexandra smiles.

Gerhard smiles back.

Sofia stands speechless, realizing that her parents had arranged the entire event. Further, she suspects that Felix had been in on the planning as well.

Alexandra begins a conversation telling Sofia about each dish that she was planning to prepare. Gerhard interrupts before she can get to the second course. "I am going to prepare one of my special desserts made with plums and cream. The plums are exceptional right now, and I know that this dessert will certainly please Officer Fuerst – some of his favorite selections in the past have been those made with plums."

As Gerhard and Alexandra move back into the kitchen, Sofia concludes that *Officer Felix Fuerst must be an honored guest.* She had only seen her parents make these kinds of preparations on special occasions and *only for their very special guests.*

*

A few days later, Felix arrives promptly for his dinner engagement with the Gunther family, dressed in his uniform as a SOLDIER OF THE THIRD REICH and carrying two bouquets of flowers and two bottles of wine.

"Officer Fuerst, may I introduce my wife, Frau Gunther?" her father says accepting the wine.

"Thank you. Welcome," Gerhard says.

"Thank you so much for the wine. We will serve it for dinner," Alexandra says as Gerhard hands the wine to her.

Gerhard's formality with the police officer who had been coming into the bakery for a long time shocks Sofia. She knows that everyone in the family knows Felix and that Felix knows everyone in the family.

"It is my pleasure to meet you, Frau Gunther," Felix says handing Alexandra one of the bouquets.

Again, Sofia is confused. She knows that Felix has known her mother for some time.

"Thank you, Officer Fuerst" Alexandra replies with her head bowed and accepting the flowers with her other hand.

Felix looks to Sofia, standing beside her mother with her head down as she fiddles with the folds on the bodice of the pink, organdy dress that had belonged to her mother. She had tied her hair into two neat knots on either side of her head, making herself look older. Her cheeks look like she had used rouge on them, but the truth was that the heat in the bakery had flushed them. Felix straightens his shoulders, smiles broadly, and looks to Gerhard, waiting for his lead, which comes in the form of a nod.

"May I present my daughter, Sofia, Officer Fuerst?" Gerhard says as if on cue. Felix bows slightly, places the flowers out in front of him, clicks his heels, and salutes before bowing as he presents the flowers to Sofia.

"I hope you like flowers, Fraulein Gunther," he smiles.

"Thank . . . thank you, Officer Fuerst," Sofia whispers -- only looking him in the eyes for a second before she puts her head down and cast her eyes away from his continued stare.

"Officer Fuerst, please meet our son, Franz," Gerhard continues.

"Heil Hitler," Franz salutes, clicking his heels together and raising his arm.

"Franz, I have been looking forward to meeting you," Felix says after saluting and clicking his heels in return.

116

Franz, who is standing at attention, trying to be taller in his new youth soldier uniform, returns the salute one more time just to be sure.

"Quickly, Sofia, get vases for the flowers" her father orders.

Sofia obeys; relieved that she could leave the room.

"Franz, hang Officer Fuerst's cap on the hook," her father orders motioning with his hand.

"Frau Gunther has everything ready Officer Fuerst. Please join us at the table," Gerhard says with a wave of his hand directing him into the dining room.

They gather around the table. Sofia and Franz remain silent, just as their parents had taught them. Gerhard leads them in a prayer before the meal, thanking God for all the gifts, and for the good life that they now enjoy. He also thanks God for the company of their guest, 'Officer Felix Fuerst'.

At the conclusion of Gerhard's blessing, the Gunther family all chanted an 'Amen' in unison. Felix waited for them to finish, then he followed with a very quiet and sincere 'Amen' of his own.

Gerhard lifted his glass to make a toast. "To a new and prosperous Germany and to the time when the young will inherit a land that will provide them with a life of joy and peace where all of its peoples will live in good-will and harmony."

Gerhard, Felix, and Franz clicked their heels together and raised their arms again, respecting the new leader of the country with a chant of his name. "Heil, Hitler." They tapped their glasses, took a sip of wine, put their glasses down, and helped the women into their seats. Felix pulled out the chair for Sofia; Gerhard did the same for Alexandra. The family began the meal when Alexandra handed the first meat dish to her husband. She beamed with pride as she uncovered each of the dishes.

Sofia was impressed with the food and preparations, knowing that it wasn't their everyday behavior. They dined on a perfectly prepared dish of roast beef, potato dumplings, and red cabbage. The men always served themselves a portion of the meat before any others at the table. Young children were rarely included. Older children waited until after the men had taken their portion, as was customary. Alexandra wouldn't take any portions of food for herself until all of her family and their guest(s) had food on their plates.

Sofia couldn't stop looking at her mother. She watched every motion, noting every action she performed. Thirteen-year-old Franz was bursting with enthusiasm to get the opportunity to ask Felix about his profession of police officer, his new role in THE THIRD REICH as well as sharing his school experiences. However, he waited quietly, taking his cues from Sofia. While their parents and Felix enjoyed the food and talked in between mouthfuls, Sofia and Franz only listened while eating, not daring to contribute to the conversation.

"Tell me, Officer Fuerst, what had first prompted you to become a policeman?" Gerhard asks, beginning the conversation after swallowing his first mouthful. Sofia remembered the rule: "Never talk with your mouth full."

"To answer your question, Herr Gunther, I had always wanted to be a police officer. Since my childhood, I had dreamed of helping others. My vater had been a police officer, but unfortunately he was killed at the Front when I had been just a boy."

"We lost many good Germans at the Front. I'm sorry that your vater was one of them," Gerhard said. "I had been one of the fortunate ones."

"It was difficult for our family, as it was for many German families. Every adult male in our family had been lost. My mutter had to struggle to raise us. Fortunately, our Opa helped us. The inflation and great depression that followed had a great impact. "

"I remember. My father's bakery business had also suffered, but things seemed to have turned around of late – now that THE THIRD REICH has taken power. Don't you agree?"

"Yes. It seems that way . . . Hopefully."

"I am confident that the country will return to its former greatness under Adolph Hitler."

"Would you like more of the roast beef?" Alexandra interrupts, as she passes the platter to Gerhard, who takes another serving before passing the platter to Felix.

"Thank you, Frau Gunther; Roast beef is one of my favorites." Alexandra passed the other dishes. "I must compliment you. This is delicious," Felix said as he took another helping of the potatoes and cabbage. "I haven't tasted anything like this in a long time, not since my mother was alive."

"I'm sorry to hear about your mother. I had not heard of her passing until recently."

"Thank you. She died about three years ago – as she had always wanted to die – in her sleep."

"I think that is the way I would like to go when it is my time."

"Well, let's hope it isn't for a long time, Herr Gunther."

"This conversation seems to have taken a sad turn. Let's talk about something enjoyable. Maybe you would like to try my special dessert. I made it for this special occasion," Gerhard boasts.

"Sofia, get the dessert dishes. We must serve my plums and cream," he ordered reaching for the dish.

Sofia jumps up and helps Alexandra clear the dishes. She brings the cream-colored, edged in cobalt-blue dessert dishes from the sideboard to the table. They all watch as Gerhard serves his prized dessert, allowing Felix to take the first bite.

"This dessert is the best I've ever tasted," Felix said after finishing the last bite.

"I'm glad that you are pleased, Felix. This is my own recipe, one reserved only for a very special occasion, as this one is for us. We hope that it will be the first of many more dinners you will enjoy with us."

Sofia and Franz watched as Felix enjoyed the dessert. They both knew their father was happy, but both remained silent. 'Children should be seen but not heard,' a rule that both she and Franz had learned very early dictated their behavior.

Sofia occasionally caught Felix looking at her, but she quickly hid her face.

When they had eaten all of the main meal, Felix raises his glass to salute. "Please accept my compliments to Frau Gunther for the exceptional meal and to Herr Gunther for the dessert."

After dinner, Gerhard, Felix, and Franz retire to the drawing room while Sofia and her mother clear the table and return to the kitchen to put it back in order. Gerhard tells Felix to bring his glass with him so they can enjoy the remainder of the wine.

Sofia hears Franz whispering to his father. She knows that he is asking permission to talk to Felix about becoming a policeman, but Gerhard shakes his head from side to side and whispers back, "Not now, Franz."

Franz exits to his room leaving the men to talk in private.

Sofia and Alexandra work in silence, clearing and cleaning dishes and taking care of the usual after-dinner duties. After a while, Alexandra removes her apron, puts it on the hook on the back of the kitchen door, and leaves the kitchen.

Sofia knows that her mother was pleased with the way the evening had gone, *judging by the look on her face*. She had a certain smile on her face, one Sofia had not seen in a long time. Shortly after Alexandra leaves, Sofia hears a quiet knock on the kitchen door. She opens the door to find Felix standing in front of her. His intense blue eyes and the hint of a smile on his lips draw her in immediately. Feeling he might think she is staring, she cast her eyes away respectfully.

"May I be of help to you, Fraulein Gunther? I am not much good in the kitchen, but I am an excellent student, and a quick learner."

Sofia, too embarrassed to answer, blushes, and brushes away a few loose strands of her long hair, which had come loose, falling out of the knotted braids twisted in circles above her ears. She hands Felix the dishtowel and asks nervously, "Perhaps you would like to dry?"

Felix takes the dishtowel, but not before stopping to hold her hand. Looking into her eyes, he says, "It would be my pleasure, Fraulein."

The two of them dry the dishes, one after another, putting them on the kitchen table. Felix fumbles with the towel, revealing that he had no idea what he was doing, confirming her belief that he was like most German men in that he had little experience in the kitchen. His lack of questioning about the task also told her that he had no interest in learning about drying dishes. Sofia did most of the work while he studied her and talked.

"Fraulein Gunther, may I call you, 'Sofia' . . . I hope you don't mind. I know we have just met."

"If you think it is proper, I don't mind."

"I do . . . think it is proper."

Sofia nodded.

"Well then, you must call me, 'Felix'. Now that we have been properly introduced, Officer Fuerst will not be appropriate, unless, of course, we are out in public."

"Yes, Officer Fuerst. I mean, Felix," she corrects herself.

"I understand you have just celebrated a birthday. I believe it was your eighteenth?"

"Yes."

"You must have been excited about that. All grown up now, are we?"

"I don't feel any different than I had at seventeen, or even at twelve for that matter."

"I suppose it had seemed you had grown up once your schooling had stopped?"

"No, I felt I grew up the day that my Oma had died."

"Why do you say that, Fraulein?"

"Well, it was true that I just stopped going to school when she had died. Vater wanted me to help him in the bakery. Vater doesn't believe in girls going to school, or in having any jobs outside of the home."

"Yes, I agree. However, it seems today that some women are taking on different roles in the workings of THE THIRD REICH."

"I wouldn't know anything about that. I don't even know any women in THE THIRD REICH. My only friend is Esther Rosenfeld and I haven't even seen her lately."

"You mean Esther Rosenfeld from the Rosenfeld Jewelry Store, Sofia?"

"Yes."

"She is a Jew, Sofia."

Sofia nodded in agreement. "Is that important?"

"Things aren't easy for the Jews now, Sofia."

"I have heard some others whispering about that and I have noticed the signs posted in the neighborhood. When I had asked Vater, he told me to forget about it and not ask questions."

"You should do exactly as your father has said, Sofia."

"I always do."

"Yes, I know you do. I've seen you in the bakery. You are a big help to your parents. They are very proud of you."

"I love them very much. I don't know what I would have done if I would have lost them as you had lost your parents."

"God gives us blessings and he takes them away too, Sofia. He doesn't give us crosses that are too difficult."

"I remember my Oma saying the same thing."

"She must have been a wise woman."

"Yes, Officer Fuerst . . . I mean, Felix . . .   She was very wise. I still miss her."

They continued their conversation while finishing the last of the chores. Sofia found that talking with Felix came easily. Felix asked questions about her childhood, school, and her activities in church and he seemed genuinely interested in her opinions. As she talked to him, she drew the comparison of talking to Esther. She started to feel comfortable around him and asked him a few questions as well. Hers were very mundane, but she thought that his replies were spontaneous and sincere.

"Would you grant me the privilege of your company at the Matinee next Saturday, Sofia? A documentary about Berlin is showing. I've already checked with your father and he has given his permission."

"If Vater approves, I accept."

"Perhaps we should go in the drawing room and confirm it with him?" Felix suggests.

"Yes. I must be sure that he approves."

*

Felix and Sofia spent time together after that.

It was always supervised and very public and always with her father's permission. Felix had always made it part of his daily police duties to stop in and check on the bakery. However, it had become obvious by his persistence, sometimes stopping more than once in one day, that he was really checking on Sofia and not the bakery business.

"Sofia, did you think Officer Fuerst was coming into the bakery just to buy sweets?" her father asked one day.

"What do you mean, Vater?"

"He's coming in to see you. I hope you know how very fond he is of you."

Sofia was glad that her father decided to share his thoughts because she wasn't sure how long she could continue harboring the strong feelings she seemed to be having.

"I look forward to seeing him each day, Vater."

Felix continued to see Sofia almost every day. One day, he kissed her.

It was just on her hand but the first one she had ever had. They were walking in a small park across the street from the cafe where he had taken her to dinner, the first time Sofia had ever eaten at a restaurant. They were standing in front of a large fountain surrounded by a bed of bright bronze-colored flowers, enjoying the sound of the splashing water and a light cool breeze of the late September afternoon. A large tree shielded them from view as the others filled the street, tending to their business. The couple seemed lost in their own little world. Sofia, off in thought about the matinee movie they had just seen, had only the theme song about Berlin on her mind. It was the first time she had seen a movie, also. When she looked up, she found Felix's lips moving down toward her.

"NOT ALLOWED," she thought as he took her hand in his and lifted it to his lips.

It was over.

In a split second, he was standing tall with his shoulders back, as if he just put his hand into the cookie jar, wanting to hide what he had done. Sofia felt her cheeks get warm and she was sure she was the same color of the red dress she was wearing, another one that had belonged to her mother.

It was at that moment that she decided she was in love with Felix. At least, that is what she called the unusual feeling, arising from the pit of her stomach.

In the weeks that followed, Sofia smiled more and she seemed to have a lift in her walk. Franz was the first to notice the difference in his sister and was the first to make comment. "Sofia walks around all day with a smile on her face," he teased. "She must be in love. She is in love. She is in love, love, love," he continued.

Sofia chased her brother around the table in playful fun. Franz had always loved to tease his older sister, which she had never really appreciated before, but this time she didn't mind in the least.

A few weeks later, Felix asked, "Fraulein Gunther, will you marry me?"

"Do you think Vater will approve?"

"Yes, I do. I've already asked him."

"Of course, if Vater says he approves, then I will," she replied without any hesitation. She thought Felix wasn't surprised with her answer. In fact, she thought that he seemed to have expected it.

Just as she thought she should continue sleeping, her mind flashed a bulletin to her:

This isn't any ordinary day – today Felix and I'll marry.

A knock at the door provides one last distraction.

"Sofia, are you still in bed? Today is your wedding day," her mother exclaimed as she burst through the door."

*

Sofia stops the story at that point and rings the bell for Clarissa.

"I hope you didn't think that I was prying earlier when I had asked about your personal life, Janene," she says.

"No . . . not at all. Most people think that I should be married by now or, at my age, at least in a relationship."

"It is just that I had never had the chance to be your grandmother and the thought of becoming a great grandmother overwhelms me . . . I guess I was really prying, now that I think about it."

"It will come in good time, if it is meant to be," Janene smiles.

"Indeed."

"You are very far ahead of your granddaughter with three husbands, Sofia."

"Yes, I guess I am. Obviously, Felix was my first husband and Randolph, Randy's father was my second. Of course, Jeffrey is my third."

Clarissa's knock on the door and entrance into the room interrupts them.

"The tea needs warmed, Clarissa."

"Yes, Ms. Sofia, I'll take care of it. Mr. Jeffrey also told me to remind you that he has planned a dinner out tonight."

"Thank you, I remember," Sofia says.

"He also said that I should tell you that he has made reservations at the restaurant on Mount Washington."

"Good. I am sure that you will like that restaurant, Janene. It has always been one of our favorites."

"That is nice of you. A visit to 'Mt. Washington' had been one of the sites on her recommended list. We were hoping that we would have some time for sightseeing. Dad is a big sports fan of Pittsburgh and he had been excited about visiting here for the first time."

"I'm sorry but I won't be joining you. I have discussed this with Jeffrey and we have decided it is best if I rest and have dinner here."

"I understand."

"I have just a bit more of my story to tell you before we can break and you can rest up and prepare for your dinner out tonight with Jeffrey and Bill. I was about to tell you about my wedding day.

*

The morning light shines on the tattered quilt as well as lighting Sofia's face, accentuating her beautiful features. A complexion as pure as fine china displays a small 'beauty spot', as her mother had called it, carefully placed on the right side of her check, close to her almost perfectly straight nose. Two dimples, one on her left cheek and the other on her chin, dot her face. She smiles, tickling the dimple, making it look as if it is jumping up to meet the morning light but then quickly disappearing into her cheek, dancing in and out with each movement of her jaw," Sofia continues before suddenly stopping and looking at Janene.

"I think you have the same dimples as Randy had, Janene."

"And I can see where he had gotten them," Janene smiles back looking at the same dimples in Sofia's cheeks, noting the family resemblance.

123

As Sofia continues the story, Janene feels a special connection to the storyteller and listens attentively as Sofia shares her wedding day:

"As she lay in the morning light, her long perfectly proportioned body shows its small hills and valleys beneath the lacy white night gown. Her graceful arms lay beside her, showing small muscles in her upper arms. They suggested she was somewhat of a tomboy but the truth was that her muscles had come from lifting the bakery trays, even though her delicate well-manicured hands belied all of their hard work. Last night's manicure now displays the beautiful antique ring that had belonged to Felix's mother.

Her eyes glistened like frost on a frozen lake; their icy-blue color warmed by a glistening, reminiscent of a warm Mediterranean Sea. A circle of gray-blue color outlined each eyeball, as if each had been set in an arrangement of blue glass. Her long eyelashes were several shades darker than her flaxen hair, held back by one pink ribbon with curls forming endless waves of shiny, blond hair, falling down to just past her waist.

She glances at Felix's picture sitting on the dresser, picking it up in her hand, pressing the gold frame against her lips, and whispering, "I love you, Felix Fuerst! Today I'll become Frau Sofia Fuerst. Today is the most important day of my life."

She reaches for her quilt, not finding it readily and panicking at the thought that she had misplaced it. She thinks it is odd that she had not realized until now just how important the quilt had become to her. She grabs it and wraps it tightly around her shoulders, dancing on her toes in circles.

"How can I ever leave you behind?" she asks as she presses it to her cheek.

Her heart races as she speculates on becoming a wife and mother. She squeezes the fibers of the quilt again and searches for some magic. She had been dreading asking her mother to allow the quilt to come with her when she married, apprehensive about what she would say, embarrassed that she still needed a security blanket. She shuddered at the prospect of acting like an adult and dealing with adult problems.

She had never understood the happenings outside of her world of the bakery, always depending upon her parents for guidance. Now, she knew she would have to depend on Felix, and on herself. "Until I had met Felix, I had been very unhappy but I had never realized it," she whispered under her breath.

"Now that I'll be the wife of a SOLDIER OF THE THIRD REICH, I'll be very happy – I just know it." However, some questions still nagged her.

"Why do people talk in whispers now?"

"Were the rumors true?"

She didn't like the whispers or the rumors, but she was happy the days of suffering in the Gunther household seemed to be part of the past. She believed what her father had said about the future because she saw that the customers seemed to have a better lifestyle now, too.

The fact that their lives had improved had given her the impression that everyone's life had gotten better, but rumors suggested it might not be the case. She didn't know what to believe. Her parents never answered any of her questions. They told her that it wasn't her business and not to worry. After talking to her father, she felt confident that their lives would continue to improve under the new Fuhrer and THE THIRD REICH, Sofia thought that he seemed happier than she had ever seen him. Suddenly, her mother brought her back to the present when she appeared in the doorway of her room. At first she thought she was still fantasizing, still seeing the images in the light, but another glance finds Alexandra holding her beautiful wedding dress. The sight immediately brings Sofia away from her daydreaming, back to reality.

Alexandra places the dress in front of her, directing her to look in the old oak mirror. Thoughts of her beauty and her German heritage make her think about the recent law requiring all citizens to declare and disclose their heritage. Her parents had to present papers to prove their bloodlines and those of their children. The new law was an example of one of the ways the Fuhrer planned to identify those of pure German ancestry. She may have gone on daydreaming if it had not been for the dress Alexandra held. "Oh!" she whispered. "It is the most beautiful dress I have ever seen."

Sofia examines the ivory-colored silk dress. Alexandra never takes her eyes from the dress as Sofia fingers the smooth cotton underskirt. Sofia notices the smile on her face and her look of pride as she stands in front of the mirror admiring her. She imagines how soft it will feel against her bare skin. She reaches for the gold locket, which now contains Felix's picture; placing it around her neck and admiring it as it will look gracing the bodice of the dress.

The locket had been a wedding gift from Felix. She was sure that it had to be the same one in the jewelry store window and she wondered how he had known. "This is a token of my devotion, Sofia," he had whispered to her.

She could still feel his hands on her neck as he had put it on her and his lips on her hand as he kissed it. "My picture is inside, Sofia," he had said as he closed the clasp. She feels aroused and her cheeks flush as she thinks about that moment, realizing that she shouldn't be thinking such things in front of her mother. She remembers thinking that it had probably been for the best when she had decided not to place a picture of Oma in the locket that her future husband had given her. Furthermore, she had hoped Alexandra would share some information about what to expect on her wedding night, but she never talked to her about such matters. Now, she says nothing, not seeming to notice Sofia's face flushing, but busily finding the loose threads on the hem of the dress.

Sofia turns her thoughts to the gold watch she had given Felix. It had belonged to her Opa. Gerhard had given it to her to give to Felix as a wedding present. She remembers the look on his face when she had presented it to him.

"Sofia, it gives me honor. I know how much it means to you and I'll treasure it . . . My hope is that, someday, I will give it to our son."

Her heart flutters again as she contemplates motherhood. Just the thought of what she would have to do on her wedding night frightens her.

I don't think I am ready to make a baby.

She places her hands on the fullness of the skirt, marveling at the artisanship that her mother had used. She is enthralled in her first experience with the dress of her dreams, but she doesn't want to miss the smile on her mother's face. "Thank you, Mutter. It is magnificent."

"How could it be anything less for my beautiful daughter? Today, you will start the beginning of your new life," she says putting her arms around her, kissing her cheek, and holding her tightly.

"Sofia, today our dreams are coming true. We are so happy you are marrying a good German man, one who will provide you with a good life. Felix is a good man and now that he is a member of THE THIRD REICH, God will bless you. You will not have to struggle the way we had. Come now, enough of this, we must get you ready for this afternoon."

As Alexandra places the dress back onto the hanger, Sofia's thoughts go to her grandmother's quilt. "Mutter, I must ask you something," she asks pulling the end of the quilt close to her, thinking, trying to make sure she uses just the right words.

"What is it, Sofia?"

"I have to ask you about the quilt," she hesitates. "May I take Oma's quilt with me?"

Alexandra looks surprised and glances at the quilt. "Sofia, surely you want a beautiful new bed covering to begin your life with Felix?"

"No, Mutter . . . I don't."

"I can't imagine why you would want this worn-out old piece of cloth to be part of your new life as the wife of a German Officer."

"On the contrary, this quilt is the only one I want. Only this one will do. I must have it. It will remind me of my life with you and Vater. It is Oma . . . I mean that it will remind me of Oma. I'll not forget this room, the chest, the mirror, and the curtains – anything about this room. I want to remember all of the stories Oma had shared. I need the quilt to help me do that, Mutter."

Alexandra smiles at her grown-up daughter as she holds onto the quilt, knowing it had always given Sofia a sense of security.

"Sofia, the quilt is something from your childhood. You are a woman now. I don't think Felix will appreciate your bringing your security blanket to his bed."

"Yes, I know, Mutter, and I don't intend on taking it to bed with me any longer. I'll put it in the chest and keep it for my own daughter. Felix doesn't even have to see it."

Alexandra smiles and takes the quilt in her hands, folding it neatly and carefully placing it into the old chest. "Very well, Sofia. I guess I couldn't live with myself if I didn't allow you to take your Oma's quilt. Promise me, you won't tell your father."

"I promise, Mutter," Sofia whispers.

Sofia watches with a renewed sense of confidence, content in the belief she is extremely ready to begin her new life with Felix. She knows now that the quilt would go with her, she would have all that was necessary.

"I am ready, Mutter," she said hugging her.

*

As she had made her final preparations to walk down the aisle, Sofia's thoughts had concentrated on Felix. When she thought about what he had shared with her concerning his work as a member of THE THIRD REICH, telling her of his induction, she had become confused. She had noticed that he had not shared the circumstances of the induction into the ranks of THE THIRD REICH with her parents. She wondered why he had told her but had neglected to share this important event with them – especially her father.

She recalls the conversation she had with Felix had shared with her concerning the changes in his role as a Police Officer of Berlin to a Soldier of THE THIRD REICH. "I had been called into Headquarters to discuss my 'situation'," he had told her. 'The Field Marshall had informed me that I had only one decision to make, Sofia. He said, 'Officer Fuerst, you will become a Soldier of THE THIRD REICH – or you will die' . . . Under the circumstances, I had decided to accept their invitation."

Sofia tries to digest what he had said but only becomes more confused.

*

That conversation never left her. She recalled it many times, as she often wondered about their future and about the many other choices Felix would make. Unable to focus on anything but the day ahead, she puts that conversation out of her mind and returns to the matters at hand.

She must decide how to wear her hair and what to pack in her suitcase. Her thoughts remained entangled in the moments of the anxiety of the day. With a renewed purpose, she decided she would make herself the most beautiful bride that Berlin had ever seen. "The wife of Feldwebel Felix Fuerst, member of THE THIRD REICH, will astound everyone," she decides. I'll not think about tomorrow or yesterday. I'll only think about today.

There would only be one headline for this special day:

'FRAULEIN SOFIA GUNTHER
MARRIES
FELDWEBEL FELIX FUERST
12 JUNE 1938.

She wasn't aware of anything happening in Germany or the world and she certainly wasn't aware of the fact that the German army had mobilized, or that the Fuhrer was casting his sights on the country's neighbors. In addition, she was completely oblivious to the simple fact that the new government had already begun to monopolize and dictate their lives and those of the entire country."

*

"Miss Sofia, Mr. McDeenon has arrived," Clarissa interrupts politely. "Mr. Jeffrey has greeted him. He has said to tell you that he would take care of getting him settled."

"Yes, Clarissa, thank you. Please show Janene to the guest suite."

"Yes, Miss Sofia."

"I'm anxious to meet Bill McDeenon," Sofia says with a smile, turning to Janene. "Perhaps we should stop now and meet in the drawing room before the chauffeur takes you to dinner.

"I'm sure he's looking forward to meeting you as well," Janene smiled.

"Clarissa, escort Janene to her room so that she can freshen up and get settled in."

"Yes, Miss Sofia."

Clarissa leads Janene up the broad staircase in the main hall to a room in the rear of the mansion, overlooking a beautiful garden, lined with neatly trimmed hedges and rows of chrysanthemums."

"Will there be anything else, Ms. McDeenon?"

"There is just one thing. Where is my father's room?"

"Just next door – the door in the far right corner adjoins his."

"Thank you, Clarissa. Please, call me 'Janene'."

"Yes, Miss Janene," Clarissa says giving a nod of her head as she exits the room.

After checking in with her father and sharing some of the particulars of how the meeting with Sofia had revealed her biological family, Janene collapses into the chaise lounge chair in front of the window, glad that Sofia had suggested a rest. Until then, she had not realized how exhausting the task of finding her biological family had been. She closes her eyes and finds that image of the beautiful woman on the cloud.

"I'll find you next, Mother," she thinks as she relaxes in the chair. "When I do, I hope that I'll also find out the truth about you and Sofia's son." She closes her eyes and sees the handsome American soldier kissing her mother as she holds her two baby girls in her arms." She enjoys the picture for only moments before she remembers that she must unpack her suitcase. She is surprised to find the empty suitcase and all of her things neatly placed in drawers or hung on hangers in the closet.

"It feels like home," she thinks as she undresses and looks forward to the hot bath, which someone has already drawn for her. After a much-needed soak in the bubbles, she dresses for dinner. A glance in the mirror this time doesn't make her turn away. "I wonder if my twin sister will look exactly like me," she asks as she studies the image in the mirror.

"Two surely are better than one – any time," she grins.

There is a little skip in her walk as she heads down the stairs.

* * * * *

CHAPTER 5
CHILDREN OF THE THIRD REICH

The next day, after a breakfast with Jeffrey and Bill, Janene and Sofia retire to the library for another session. "Janene, before I go on with my story, I want to tell you how pleased I had been to meet Bill. Last evening when you had returned from dinner, Jeffrey also shared with me that he had been impressed with him as well."

"I was very pleased to meet Jeffrey, also. My father and I both missed you at dinner. The view from Mt. Washington was extraordinary."

"It is my favorite part of this special city that I have come to call my 'home'. My first apartment was located on Mt. Washington. The view from my living room window had been one of the reasons I had leased it."

"Well, I can see why. The ride on the Incline had certainly impressed us."

"Randy would have liked Bill and I know he would be very grateful to him for caring for his lovely daughter. I'll always be grateful for the intervention of Corporal Robinson in your life. It had been truly a gift."

"Yes, without his help, who knows what would have happened to me," Janene says wondering about her mother and sister. "Do you think we will be able to find my sister and mother, Sofia?"

"I have the strongest hopes that my investigator will find an answer to what happened to them, Janene."

"I hope so. I have had the strangest feelings ever since you had told me about my twin. They were the same ones I had felt most of my life. I had always felt that someone was missing."

"Well I can see where you might have felt that way. You have lost many loved ones. I hope that after you have spent several days here getting to know Randy, you will come to love him as well. One of the things that life has taught me is that when it comes to love, the capacity of the human heart has no limits."

"I'm feeling closer to my roots already, Sofia . . . I mean, 'Oma'."

Sofia smiles broadly, obviously a reaction to Janene's use of the word, 'Oma. "Let me begin again where I had left off yesterday. I believe I was about to tell you about the birth of my children, Max and Ana. Since they are half brother and sister to Randy, they are your aunt and uncle.

*

It was April 12, 1942. Sofia is in the Medical Center of THE THIRD REICH in Berlin, thinking that the pain of childbirth with her second child will never end. The memory of giving birth to their first child suddenly becomes very vivid, causing her to conclude that she will not be able to withstand the current pain. To add to her anguish, she is worried about Felix and is unable to rest between the contractions. Trying to divert her attention from the pain, she concentrates on her son, three-year old, Max.

His little face with the large blue eyes and a crop of blonde hair had captured her heart from first sight. She remembers how the nurses had made a fuss over him when he had been born, almost exactly nine months after her wedding to Felix. "You should see Hauptman Fuerst's son! He's such a beautiful German baby," she had heard them say. The nursery had been filled to capacity with babies but baby Max had stood out among all the other babies in their little beds marked with swastikas and German surnames. "I wonder if we will have another boy. That would make Felix happy," she thinks as she pictures brushing a daughter's hair. "A girl would make me happy," she thinks as she braces for the next contraction.

"Where is my husband? Would you check to see if he has called yet? Are there any messages from Hauptman Fuerst?" she asks as the pain lessens.

"I have checked again for you, Frau Fuerst. There were no messages," she says trying to reassure her. Hoping to prepare for the next contraction, she drifts in and out of sleep. Her dream takes her to the day when she and Felix had been discussing names anticipating Max's birth. Felix had wanted to call the baby after his grandfather, his father, and himself.

"Maximilian Felix Fuerst IV! That sounds like a wonderful name for our son," Felix had told her.

"Felix, what if we have a girl? What shall we call her?"

"You will not have to concern yourself about that, Sofia. Our first child will not be a girl," he had declared.

At the time, she remembers laughing to herself a little thinking that it was just another example of her husband's strong will and determination, but she also recalls that she had been a little irritated with him because he wouldn't even discuss girl's names. Secretly, she had made up her mind that she would decide on the name for first-born child in the event that it was a girl, not allowing Felix any say in the decision; of course, she really had no confidence in her ability to do that since she had little experience in the process of making a decision.

After his declaration of the boy's name, she shared her decision with him but not without a great deal of anxiety. "Our daughter will be called 'Ana Alexandra'," she said waiting for his objection.

He smiled and said, "I think 'Ana Alexandra' is a fine name, Sofia. You have made a good choice."

Sofia looked at him in surprise but was pleased with his remark.

"I think Felix wanted me to make a decision on my own," she thinks as she recalls the look of pride on his face on March 24, 1939 when 'Maximilian Felix Fuerst IV' had been born.

*

Another contraction awakens her. She breathes deeply and concentrates on not thinking about the pain. Instead, she goes to worrying again about Felix. "It is some kind of an emergency," he had told her when they had first arrived at the hospital and he had to leave to return to Headquarters. "I'm sure I can take care of it quickly, Sofia. I'll be back as soon as possible."

Sofia couldn't hide her disappointment.

He always had some kind of an emergency lately. It seemed to her that she was always watching him come and go. He spent little time with her, not as he had when she had been pregnant with Max. She wanted him to be present for the birth of their second child, just as he had been for the first. She recalls the events that had happened earlier when her water had broken at home prematurely. This baby wasn't due for three more weeks.

She had immediately called Felix at Headquarters because he had told her to do so, but only in an emergency. She told the Desk Officer that she had an emergency, but the Officer said he couldn't locate Hauptman Fuerst. Finally, another Officer said that he would relay the message to him. She decided to call a cab and make the arrangements herself.

As planned, she called Helena to come and take Max. Helena Stein, her neighbor, who had also married an officer of THE THIRD REICH, came as they had arranged. The plan also included Helena calling Sofia's parents, who would take Max and care for him until Sofia came home with the new baby.

"Good-bye my darling, I'll be home soon. I promise to bring you a new baby brother or sister. You have to be a good boy for Frau Stein and for Oma Gunther," Sofia said after kissing him on both cheeks and sending him off with Helena.

She was still watching Helena walk hand in hand with Max toward her home when the cab had pulled up in front of the house. The driver came to the door and Sofia directed him to the vestibule where her suitcase waited. Just as the cab driver closed the front door behind her as he helped her to the curb, a military car arrived with Felix. Felix told the cab driver to put the bag in the military car and sent him away. He helped Sofia down the few steps in front of the house and into the back seat of the car. Sofia waited for him to say something.

Anything would be better than saying nothing.

He seemed preoccupied, as usual, and said nothing. He motioned to the driver to get going. Just as she was going to speak, a sharp pain made her scream. She glanced at the rear view mirror and noticed the driver's terrified look. She wanted to reassure him that they had plenty of time to get there, but she wouldn't dare speak directly to the military driver. She waited for Felix to speak to him but he said nothing, not even when he pulled away from the curb with a jerk and drove at a high speed, weaving in and out of traffic.

When she felt the next contraction, she screamed aloud again, "I have no intention of having this baby in the back seat of this car, Felix. Tell this driver to slow down!" The driver relaxed his shoulders, slowed the car, and looked into the rear view mirror, watching the back seat. Her scream and remark seemed to have brought Felix back to the reality of the moment.

"Try to be brave, Sofia. We will get you to the hospital as soon as possible," he whispered. "Hurry, Driver, please drive as fast as you can.

The driver again pushed the pedal to the floor; the car sped off, passing every other car. Sofia rolled from side to side as he switched lanes. Another strong contraction threw her into Felix's lap, screaming in pain. "Felix, tell the driver to slow down," she whispered to him between contractions. Felix ignored her request, but Sofia saw the driver's eyes appear in the rear view mirror again. The car seemed to slow a bit – at least Sofia stopped rolling around in the back seat.

When they had pulled into the emergency entrance of the hospital, Sofia had felt relieved for only a moment before another contraction doubled her over in pain. A nurse greeted her with a wheel chair. Several others hovered around her as they whisked the chair into the hospital. They took her to a room in the maternity ward but Felix had to leave before they had admitted her.

As Sofia labors, she thinks of how distant she and Felix had become. Now, when she needs him most, he isn't there again. If the clock on the wall is correct, she calculates that she has been in labor for four hours. It feels much longer to her and the contractions seem to be coming closer. "If one more person dressed in white tells me to breathe, I'll throw something," she thinks. Outside of worrying about Felix, all she can think about now is the pain.

"It is all coming back to me now," she thinks recalling giving birth to Max. As hard as she tries, she cannot figure out what was bothering Felix. At times, she didn't recognize him anymore. Headquarters had constantly called him away as soon as he had arrived home, *always one emergency after another.* He seems to be right in the middle of everything at THE THIRD REICH and Sofia thinks that *the business of THE THIRD REICH just never seems to end.* Another contraction comes fast and hard; the urge to push overcomes her, distracting her thought about Felix.

"We're going to take you to the delivery room, Frau Fuerst. Try not to push," the doctor instructs.

"That is easy for you to say," she thinks as they wheel her down the hallway on the gurney. The Interns transfer her onto the special bed in the delivery room. They quickly position her legs in the stirrups and cover her with sheets, all the while telling her, "Frau Fuerst, don't push."

Sofia lets out a scream just as the doctor starts shouting: "Push now, Sofia!"

She does and continues to push as two nurses hold her upright in the bed by her elbows.

"Felix," she shouts. "Felix!"

"Your husband has still not arrived back, Frau Fuerst," the nurse tells her in a calm voice.

She screams again and pushes one right after the other, and sometimes together. There seems to be no end in sight and there is no word about Felix. She pushes and pushes until she can't anymore, falling backward into the bed completely exhausted as the nurses let go of her elbows. Suddenly, she was in a deep sleep with the help of a gas mask. It was the last thing that she remembered before sleep takes over and her dreams occupy her mind. Now, flashes of the day they had married appear.

She remembers that Felix had taken care of all the necessary papers at the civil ceremony, one that was necessary the week before the church ceremony. The new government approved their marriage. After signing all the necessary papers, they had said their vows and then returned to their separate homes to await the ceremony at the church and the reception that

Gerhard and Alexandra had planned afterward. She sees herself walking down the aisle again in the beautiful ivory dress with the satin and lace veil. She had worn her hair up with small tendrils curling down around her neck and face. Small sprigs of baby's breath surrounded her gold tiara.

Alexandra wiped the tears on her cheek with a lacy handkerchief that had belonged to Oma. Her father had lifted her veil proudly; held her hand tightly, kissed her cheek and returned to his place in the pew beside his wife. Sofia started down the aisle, wondering if her legs would get her to the altar. When she saw Felix waiting for her at the end of the aisle, she found them, finding her strength by the look of pride on his face.

They had spent their wedding night in a Hotel Suite in Berlin. Felix had been kind and patient with her nervousness, guiding her through every motion, speaking softly to her and gently reassuring her. She had participated in the marital act by following Felix in complete submission. Despite his understanding, she had found no enjoyment in her first sexual experience, even though Felix had attracted her in a way she couldn't explain. She had called it 'love' but she wasn't sure what that meant. She felt as if she loved him – just as she loved her parents but she thought that she loved Oma and her quilt in a different way. Her thoughts left her confused.

Remembering the day they had taken their vows, she noticed that Felix had a look on his face, one that she had never seen. As he said his vows, she thought that maybe the strange look on his face reflected his deep feelings of pride but she worried that it was not one of *love*. She knew she was proud to be marrying him, but she wasn't sure what he was feeling – until then. She could only guess his feels. He had never actually said that he loved her.

Her thoughts take her beyond the ceremony to the day when they had arrived home from their wedding trip to the Baltic Sea. He had taken her to a house located on the outside of Berlin. In the taxi, he told her to close her eyes until he would give her permission to open them. "Now, open," he said excitedly after leading her through the door.

She opened her eyes to a spectacular home, filled with elegant furniture, expensive imported rugs, and regal drapes lining the tall windows. She was overwhelmed.

"What Sofia? Why are you crying? Aren't you pleased?" he asked when he saw her reaction.

"I'm crying tears of joy, Felix."

As he led her around the house, his faced beamed.

He took her from room to room. "I know that our first child will be a boy, Sofia," he said smiling as he showed her the smallest room. She was speechless, not able to believe he had done it all by himself.

*

Over the next few months, they were busy moving into the new house. The first item that Sofia brought into their first home was the chest that had been in her room, her dowry. She put it in the spare room because she needed some time to decide where she would put all the precious items that she knew were safely stored inside.

The only item that she chose not to use to furnish her new home was the quilt. It stayed safely tucked inside, knowing that the next time she would use it would be to wrap around their first child.

Happiness and excitement filled her days. They had a telephone installed upstairs and down. They attended parties, concerts, and affairs of THE THIRD REICH. Their associations were only with other officers and their wives. THE THIRD REICH encouraged the Officers to have a family, procreating pure Germans, so naturally the news of their anticipation of the birth of their first child had endeared Felix to the philosophies of the new government. Certainly, it seemed that their new life together was going to be perfect. She was deeply in love with her husband and now they were having a child together.

It seemed that costs didn't matter.

Felix never talked about money or finances. THE THIRD REICH seemed to provide for everything they needed or wanted. Sofia was so excited when she had missed her period when they had returned from their marriage trip to the Baltic. She had been hoping that she was pregnant, but she didn't want to say anything to Felix until she could have it confirmed by a visit to the doctor.

The day she found out that she was pregnant, she went immediately to the chest to hold her precious quilt. It lay folded neatly in the chest, just as her mother had left it on the morning of their wedding. She removed it from the chest and took it to the nursery, placing it carefully on the back of the rocker, which Felix had placed in the room. The rocker was an old one. It reminded Sofia of the one that her mother had told her father to burn in the stove. She was surprised that she had remembered the incidence when she had been only five years old.

*

The early days and months of their marriage had been special to her. Although Felix had never said that he loved her, except when he wanted sex, she thought that this child would surely be a symbol of their abiding love to their loved ones. When the doctor had confirmed her pregnancy a few months after their wedding trip, their time at the sea became a treasured memory. The thought of being pregnant, however, scared her to death. There were no signs of her pregnancy until after the fourth month and then just a little swelling in her abdomen. Even then, one had to look hard to notice the small bulge. Felix had demanded that they should wait until she had showed before they would announce it. They told Gerhard and Alexandra about the pregnancy first.

"Gerhard you are going to be an Opa," Felix had told him as he beamed with pride. Sofia was sure that the entire neighborhood must have heard his celebratory laughter. The only time he had seemed happier was the day he held his grandson, Max, in his arms for the first time in 1939.

*

The German Army was on the move but Sofia could only think of her children and her wonderful life as Frau Fuerst, the wife of a Captain in Germany's army. The first three years of her marriage had been glorious. She had wanted for nothing and she had been deliriously happy with her new motherhood. She hardly noticed the months were changing into years. Felix had risen in rank quickly, becoming a Lieutenant and then a Captain by the end of their first year of marriage. His duties included the position as a special guard assigned to headquarters. THE THIRD REICH had honored him for his service. His future was bright and promising. However, the more success he had attained, the less time he spent with Sofia and Max.

She had been so busy with the new house and baby that she had hardly noticed that he had not been coming home for dinner as often. She would feed Max and then spend the rest of the evening waiting for Felix to arrive home. Many times, she retired before he did. The gradual distance coming between them disturbed her.

Something is wrong! Felix isn't himself.

Her worries actually convinced her that she really didn't know her husband as well as she thought she had. He seemed preoccupied, always rushing in and out of the house, putting her off. "Not now, Sofia, I have too much on my mind to bother about that," was his usual response to any conversation she would initiate. Before Sofia knew it, the months had turned to a year and Max had celebrated his first birthday. Felix had almost missed the day when "pressing matters at headquarters" had called him away again.

The days became weeks, and weeks turned to months. Her knowledge of the war was limited to overhearing bits and pieces of conversations between others. Frau Helena Stein, her neighbor, had casually mentioned that the army had invaded another European county. One day, Felix came home very excited about the trip he had arranged that would take them back to the Baltic Sea for a holiday. He suggested that they take Max with them. He had hired a woman to travel with them to care for him so that he and Sofia could have private time together.

During the trip, she felt that Felix had seemed to be his old self again, except for the last two days when he had disappeared most of the day saying that he had to "'take care of business for the Reich." The time they had spent at the beach and making love at night, to the sounds of the waves and the light of the moon, seemed to Sofia to be just what their marriage had needed. She felt close to him, again. She felt for the first time since Max had been born that they were finally a family. However, despite how she had felt when they had first arrived home, it didn't last. Soon it was back to the same old schedule and the "same old Felix" disappearing again.

Sofia had been feeling out of sorts for several months and she thought that she may have been pregnant again, but she had hesitated to tell Felix the news until she was sure. The Doctor's confirmation prompted her to share the news with Felix. One evening, after she had put Max down for the night and she and Felix were having a quiet dinner, Sofia thought it would be a good time to break the news.

"I have wonderful news, Felix," she said as she removed the plate from in front of him. She waited for him to respond, but he seemed busy with lighting a cigarette. "Felix I'm going to have another baby," she said in a soft voice, not really being sure what his reaction would be.

He stopped and stared at her as if he had not been listening to her and then suddenly had heard her. "Are you sure, Sofia? Have you seen a doctor? Surely this can't be!" he said in a harsh tone of voice.

"Well, of course, I'm sure, Felix. I have seen a doctor. He's told me that I'm pregnant," she said. "I saw Dr. Hauptman, the same doctor who had delivered Max. He said to tell you how pleased it would make the Fuhrer to have another pure German child."

As if a magic wand waved in front of him, Felix changed his harsh questioning to soft remarks. "Oh, does he think it will be another son? Oh, I suppose he has no way of telling that, now would he? Perhaps, we will have another son. Max would be so happy to have a brother! The Homeland will be blessed with another German son," he rambled in a way Sofia had never seen him do before.

She was confused. When she had announced her pregnancy with Max, Felix had not been able to hide his enthusiasm. He spoke of his parents and his beloved grandfather. He said that they would be pleased to have a grandchild. He told her how happy this made him. This time, he didn't mention his family. He seemed troubled and only concerned with pleasing his country.

This incident and similar ones had caused her to think about Felix constantly. She felt that he had been changing before her eyes; not acting at all like the mild-mannered policeman who had come into her father's shop so long ago. She thought that it must have had something to do with her; thinking that she had not been the kind of wife that he had expected.

She blamed herself for the change in Felix; wanting things to be the way, they once had been. She tried to watch what she said so that she wouldn't upset him. Nothing worked. He would explode and then apologize. His behavior alarmed her and continued to cause her excessive worry.

She overheard someone at the market whispering that the German Army now occupied Paris. She had also heard about the German Air Force bombing England. It seemed to Sofia that some of her neighbors, like the Rosenfeld's, had disappeared. The rumors were flying. They hinted that THE THIRD REICH had forced some to leave but no one knew anything for sure, or if they did, they didn't share it with Sofia. She had heard that Esther and her family had left Berlin. Felix wouldn't comment on the matter to her when she had asked him. He put her off and said firmly, "Sofia, you must not talk or ask questions about this. It is imperative that you don't get involved. It is of the utmost necessity for your safety. Do you understand?"

He was so adamant about it that Sofia didn't pursue the matter again, going back to her role as the dutiful wife and mother. Time passed. Sofia became even more anxious. Worry consumed her. She was worried about their life, about Felix, about Max, and she was worried about the Homeland.

*

The sound of a loud wail, coming from her new baby daughter, Ana Alexandra Fuerst, awakened Sofia from the dream. Felix was standing by the bed, holding her. Dr. Hauptman stood beside him. The Doctor congratulated them both, again commenting on how their new daughter's birth would benefit Germany. Felix motioned to the nurse to take the baby. "She is beautiful, Sofia. Thank you for giving me another German child," he said. "I must get back to Headquarters now." Then, he left.

The nurse brought Ana to Sofia, placing her into her arms. Sofia looked down at the face of their child, marveling in wonderment at the magic of childbirth. She felt alone as she gazed at their beautiful little girl. It was April 12, 1942 and the war was in full swing. A few days later, the three of them went home to introduce Ana Alexandra to her big brother, three year-old, Max. Sofia wondered if the life that they had shared once would ever return.

A Few Weeks Later

Sofia is back on her feet, busy with the household and the children. This time she accepts Felix's suggestion for a nurse and a housekeeper. She wasn't too busy to notice the transformation in her husband. When home, Felix was withdrawn, doing little talking with her or the children. He lost his temper often, suddenly and without provocation. He was obviously out of control, displaying harshness, even in front of the children. Felix was now boisterous and demanding. She didn't recognize this man.

"Where did my husband go?" she asked herself constantly as she tried to make everything at home go smoothly so that he wouldn't become agitated or lose his temper. However, it seemed even the littlest thing would set him off. Since this seemed to be so out of character for him, she concluded at first that his work as an Officer of THE THIRD REICH must be to blame but couldn't dismiss her anxiety about her role as his wife. Worry and dark thoughts consumed her. She was losing sleep, weight, and feeling exhausted.

She withdrew into a life that revolved entirely around the children. Each passing day seemed the same as the one before. Felix was distant in every way. Their intimate moments had ceased. Sofia believed that his trips to Headquarters were to avoid being intimate with her. He didn't seem to be interested in her or the children. They stopped communicating.

Sofia wore fine clothes and dressed the children in the best that Berlin could offer. She looked stunning in her brown, wool coat and matching felt hat with the veil of lace. The silk stockings that other women yearned to own were hers. She wore them proudly with the seams straight as an arrow on her long slender legs. Her children were a sight to see, wearing clothes fit for royalty. However, the clothes didn't give her the self-confidence that she needed to deal with the prying eyes she perceived every time she went out in public. Days went into weeks and weeks into months and for all outward appearances, her life as a soldier's wife and mother would seem to be wonderful to anyone. However, it wasn't wonderful to Sofia.

*

Autumn 1943

Sofia had reconciled herself to the legitimacy of her fears and worries. She heard rumors telling stories about torture, rape, pillaging, and executions by the government. True, they always came in the form of whispers and gossip, too unbelievable to be true, but soon Sofia believed that they were and she worried about Felix's involvement in the suspected activities.

Once, she listened as her housekeeper whispered a story about a small child, who had watched as some officers had entered her home, beat her parents, stole all their belongings, and shipped them to work camps.

"What are their crimes?" she asks softly.

"They are Jews," the housekeeper replied.

Sofia's mouth dropped.

Her brain rattled as if someone had hit her in the head.

Where are Esther and her family, now?

What happened to Frau Shultz?

Her heart sunk.

She felt cold.

She feared for Esther's fate, but she dared not mention anything to Felix. However, she did talk to her parents several times. They said nothing that would either confirm or deny the rumors, but Sofia had noticed a change in them when she had asked their opinions about the new regime. "I don't know about such rumors Sofia and neither should you. Felix is an Officer; your brother is a soldier. For their sakes, we must be loyal citizens and remain true to the Fuhrer"

"But, Vater, how can we not ask questions."

"These are difficult times, we must be careful," her father had said in reply to her questions. She saw the same look in her parents' eyes as those of the patrons in the market. Recalling how their stares had caused her embarrassment and distress, she is confused again, wondering what had made them behave that way and what had precipitated the change in her parents.

"People walking in silence seem to have taken over Berlin, once such a boisterous bustling city," she decides not able to dismiss her concerns.

She fears for her children, no longer expecting a bright future for them. Her marriage seemed doomed. Her life seems doomed. Her children seemed doomed. These thoughts haunted her in silence, making her even quieter than she had been as the timid girl in the bakery, relieved that her father had introduced her to Felix.

Her thoughts were her only conversation, withdrawing into her own world, occupied by only the children. She turned her thoughts to fairy tales and nursery rhymes, while the war around her escalated, turning her mind away from it all, pretending it didn't exist. When the bombings began, she finally realized that the war had come home and the fear she had been experiencing turned to terror.

*

4 October 1943

In the early morning hours of a new day, the howling autumn wind disturbed the silence of the Fuerst home, blowing sheets of cold rain against the windows and pounding the rooftop. The children, tucked into their beds, dreamed of things that children do. Sofia Fuerst, watching the clock and missing her husband, waited in bed for him to return from his work at the Headquarters of THE THIRD REICH.

She checked the clock on the night table again – three o'clock.

She had not fallen asleep yet, wide-awake but with her eyes closed, waiting and worrying. When she hears the sound of the front door opening and closing, she breathes a sigh of relief.

"Felix is finally home," she thinks relieved that she can end the nightly ritual by retreating to the world of sleep.

When she had been a girl, she couldn't fall asleep without her quilt. Her attachment to it had become even more intense since her marriage to Felix. At bedtime, she would gravitate to it, but only secretly in the confines of her mind. The quilt was out of her sight because of her fear of embarrassment but it was never out of mind.

In order to keep it close now, she had given it a new function, elevating it to the status of protector for her children. She had used it as a carriage cover for their babies, first for Max and now for baby Ana.

She tried not to think about how tired she was or how long it had been since she had even seen her husband, yet alone felt him, smelt him or talked to him. Their lives had changed in the past several months. "We are like ships, passing in the night," she had decided as she looked to find ways to cope.

In addition, the stress of dealing with the daily activities of tending to their two small children had intensified when Felix had decided to let the last of the hired help go. For the first time in their short five-year marriage, Felix seemed concerned about money. He had always taken care of the financial matters, providing for everything, just as her father had always provided for her before her marriage.

She heard him come into the bedroom; relieved and believing that sleep wouldn't be far behind. She felt the frigid night air his entrance into their bed brought and she longed to hold him, feel him against her and to warm him, but she dared not move.

"Only Felix could initiate intimacy," she reminded herself. He had not done that in months. Besides, she was too tired. She squeezed her eyes closed, trying to hold in the wetness that had started to dribble down her cheeks. Soon, she went to the place where children played, sang, and where she felt safe.

*

The Next Morning

"Mutter I'm hungry," five-year-old Max says tugging on the sleeve of his mother's nightgown. Sofia looks into his wide eyes, remembering the first time she had seen them. He didn't have the tasseled crop of blond hair then, but his blue eyes had the same intensity as hers. Before she could offer Max a suggestion about his hunger, a loud wail came from the direction of the nursery.

"Ana's up! I'll go get her, Mutti," Max yells as he runs off to greet his adoring baby sister. The smiles of her two children greet her when she opens the bathroom door.

"She didn't want to come, Mutti. She wanted you. Her pants are wet," Max tells her as Ana runs over to her. Her chubby little knees hit each other as she toddles with her hands up in the air, reaching for her mother.

Sofia holds them close, squeezing them as if it would be the last time, petting the little blond braids and smoothing out the tussled hair. "Come, let's get Ana dry. Afterward, we will have some breakfast," she says leading them into the nursery.

"Eon, lwei, drei, vier, funf, sech, sieben, ach, neun," the Fuerst family sing in German as they descend the steps to the kitchen, counting in German as they march. They only know the numbers to nine and repeat the chant several times, but not in order, before reaching the bottom of the long staircase. The children are still singing when Sofia notices the folded sheet of paper with her name on it on the hall table. Since her only communication with her husband lately had been through notes, she anticipates Felix's latest would be telling her he would be coming home late again. A smile forms as she reads it.

"I'll be coming home early this evening," she reads aloud. "At last, maybe we will enjoy a day like the ones we used to have," she announces as she embraces her children.

She follows her gleeful children into the kitchen and prepares a hurried breakfast, thankful the children are content with just the oatmeal without the fruit. The huckster had not made his usual round yesterday because of the inclement weather. The pantry holds only one can of plums that she had been reserving for Felix's favorite dessert. "The plums had been delicious late last summer when Greta, one of the hired help, had canned them.

Her mind races to fix a menu for a special meal for Felix tonight, one that includes using the last of the plums. "We will be going to the fish market later, Max. Vater will be coming home early and I want to make a special supper for him," Sofia says plopping down on the chair between her children and then lifting a spoonful of oatmeal into her mouth. Her habit of taking a portion here and there sustains her as well as satisfying her diminishing appetite.

"Will Vater be home early enough to play with me?" Max asks. His wide eyes show his excitement at the prospect of having time with his father.

"I think so, Max."

"Will he tell us a bedtime story?"

"I'm sure if he is home early enough, he will play with you and tell you a story."

"I can't wait, Mutti. I want to hear a new story – not that one about that magical quilt."

"I thought you liked that story, Max?" Her narrowed brows searched her son's face.

"I like it, Mutti, but I like the ones Vater tells better."

"Tonight you will hear one of Vater's then. What about you, my little Princess?" Sofia asks tickling Ana's belly and making her laugh. A tickle made everything amusing and interesting to Ana. She went back to sitting quietly in her high chair, munching oatmeal from her fingers, licking them clean, and mumbling something only that Ana could understand. Sofia's plans for the day included a walk across town to the fish market, something they had not done in a long time.

It had also been a long time since she and Felix had enjoyed a mealtime together. She remembered their wonderful times at the Baltic, recalling Felix's insatiable appetite for the seafood, and for her. He had ordered fish for supper every day of the holiday, quenching his continued yearning for anything from the sea and, each evening, they had enjoyed each other. Tears formed in her eyes, but she brushed them away before curious little eyes could see.

"Let's go, we have a busy day, today," Sofia said. She picked up Ana, put her down on the floor, and directed them back upstairs. Getting the children prepared for an outing, as well as getting one's self ready at the same time had always been a feat for Sofia. She always wondered how other mothers who had no help could have possibly managed it. She found out when Felix had let Greta go. The tasks took most of the morning. By the early afternoon, she had washed the children, dressed and fed them their second meal of the day, and had dressed herself; they were ready for their walk across town.

*

It hadn't taken them long to make the walk to the fish market, a familiar one for Sofia, taking her back to the neighborhood where she had spent her girlhood. It was a beautiful, sunny afternoon. As evidenced by the small puddles on the uneven sidewalk, only remnants of yesterday's storm remained. Just to be on the safe side, and not wanting a mud bath, she cautioned Max about his behavior. Max had always enjoyed their walks, thinking of them as an adventure. He held onto the handle of the carriage as Sofia had instructed him. Ana stared at them from her 'throne' behind Sofia's heirloom quilt. Sofia periodically placed her hand firmly on top of Max's hand, just to remind him of the rules.

The fish store was visible from a block away as the new red awning with the name, "Wassermann Fish Market" shouted out the new establishment, replacing the previous one, "Goldberg's Seafood." When Sofia looked at the large awning, she recalled her childhood walks with her grandmother and she remembered 'Herr Goldberg' who had owned the store. He had a daughter named Louise, who had attended school with Esther at the private school across town.

Louise had never been very friendly.

Not like Esther.

Their last meeting was on her mind as she turned the carriage around, leaned her back against the door, and forced it open with the weight of her body. Max held tightly onto the handle as instructed. The noisy sounds of voices and smells of fresh food greeted her as soon as the door opened. Once inside, she was preoccupied with pulling the carriage forward far enough to allow the door to close by itself, turning the carriage around, and facing it toward the back of the store.

"Frau Fuerst . . . Frau Fuerst," the voices echoed, startling her.

The store went quiet.

Sofia shuddered.

Her eyes searched the market.

All eyes seemed to be on her.

She felt compelled to turn around and run.

A low hum from the voices of the patrons as they returned to their business extinguishes her urge. "Mutter, may I have a sweet today?" Max asks as his eyes find jars of candy lined up on the counter near the register. Obviously, the others in the market speaking softly about his mother's entrance don't bother young Max. However, the eyes of the patrons surveying her and the children disturb Sofia.

"Not today, Max. I'll have a special surprise for you and Ana with your supper tonight," Sofia said putting his hand back on the handle. "We must get our fish, Max. Come with me to the fish counter." All eyes seem to go back to their own business.

Sofia had noticed the difference in the market right away. As she walks toward the glass case displaying today's fresh fish, she surveys the patrons who were making their own selections. They mulled around the aisles, talked in whispers, and lined up in complete silence before the register.

She compares the Goldberg's Fish Market of her memory, recalling that it had been a hub of noise, laughter, and loud voices. The hush of the new market seems odd to her now but she identifies with the smell of fresh fruits and vegetables, piled neatly into bins, permeating the air. Known for their extraordinary line of fresh fish, the market also sold fresh fruits and vegetables.

As Sofia pushes the carriage over to the counter, she can't dismiss the voices calling out her name when she had arrived. "They really were not that loud," she decides as she tried to assess the situation and find reasons for her reactions. "It had been just the silence in the shop that had made them seem that way," she thinks as she looks to the far corner where she thought that the voices had originated. Two plain-looking matronly women glance at her while still making their selections of cabbage. Making eye contact with Sofia, one woman looks away, but the other stares at Sofia. Sofia stares back and the woman looks away, finding the cabbage.

Sofia decides to study the fish in the glass case, planning her purchase. The groups of black eyes fascinate Max. He put his fingers on the glass, trying to feel them. He squeezes his nostril with two fingers, expressing his dislike of the smells. "Do I have to eat fish tonight, Mutter?" The stillness in the market makes his little voice seem loud.

"Shush! You don't have to eat fish tonight. You must be quiet now, Max," she reprimands him. His eyes posed a question, but he decided to return his interest to the dead fish.

As the continuing aroma of fresh fish floats past her, black, wet, dead eyes stare up at her. Sofia returns her gaze to the fish, still searching for answers to what has now become an uncomfortable trip to the fish market for her.

"Why should they be noticing me?" she asks herself as she touches the fibers of her fur coat, which Felix had given her for her birthday in September. Her mind jumps to the image in the mirror that she had checked before she had left the house. The dark brown felt hat sets perfectly on the crown of her head, surrounded by the mounds of carefully rolled blond hair she had taken the time to do before rushing to get the children ready. Her hand reaches for her hat, making sure it was still where she had put it. She peeks through the dots of black on the veil making sure that her children are still in order.

"Maybe it is something about the children and not me," she wonders.

She recalls the shopping trip purchasing the beautiful and fashionable clothes that Felix had given her, and the special care with which she had fixed her hair as she had seen in the magazines. She had managed to get her figure back after having the babies. "Surely, this latest hairdo, rolling up and pinning around my face, wouldn't single me out," she considers as she checks the other patrons in the shop.

Most of the women have covered their heads in scarves tied securely under their chins. There are very few men in the store and she notices that there are no officers of THE THIRD REICH buying fish. The few men seem to be elderly ones dressed in dark coats and hats. Max and his baby sister ride royally in the best carriage available in Europe. "No children in Berlin are dressed as well," she thinks as she visualizes them in a portrait suitable for the cover of one of Berlin's society magazines entitled, "A portrait of a German Mother and Children of THE THIRD REICH."

Her thoughts dart to her menu for supper. The flounder looked to be the best choice, but she couldn't concentrate on her selection. She had spent her entire life, before marrying Felix, secluded from prying eyes. Her parents had worked diligently to keep her free of unwanted influences. She couldn't figure out why this was happening to her. She never had any attention before. Even when she had first married Felix, no one ever seemed aware of her at all. Now, it seems to her that all of Berlin is preoccupied with his wife and children.

She glances to the back wall of the market, hoping to get another look at the women whom she had heard call out her name. The women, wearing dark coats and triangular scarves, are now selecting potatoes, picking each one up and checking it carefully before putting any of them into their straw baskets. Nothing about them would give Sofia even a hint of the reason for their talking about her. She turns away again, avoiding their eyes, gazing at the flounder instead. A large woman ahead of her moves aside with her purchase, allowing the clerk to direct his attention to the next customer, Sofia. He nods his head and pauses, not greeting her but apparently waiting for Sofia to take the initiative.

"I'll have that large flounder, the one down in front," she says pointing her finger at the tray of fish. He replies, reaching inside the case for the tray holding the fish she had requested. While waiting, Sofia checks on the children, finding them waiting quietly. She ponders the fishmonger's behavior, wondering why he had not spoken to her. While he weighs and wraps the fish, her thoughts return to the two women who had seemed to be so interested in her. As she reviews Max standing in his fashionable little man's suit, overcoat, short trousers and knee high socks, and studies Ana in her white fur hat and coat, she concludes that envy is the only possible reason for their behavior.

"What else could it be?" she asks herself as she hashes all of the details of her life in her mind another time.

This incident had not been the first. Previous, similar ones had made her feel just as uncomfortable. The prior events had concerned her, but the ones today seem to have taken on a new dimension. She had the uncanny feeling that all of the eyes in the market were on her. As she watches the clerk wrap the fish in paper, she questions her own paranoia.

He calculates the cost of the fish, writes the total on top of the package, and places it on top of the counter above the glass case in front of her. Sofia, fumbling in her purse, finds the exact change and places the money on the counter. "Thank you" she says, reaching for the carefully wrapped package.

"You are welcome, Frau Fuerst," he says.

The market gets quiet again.

All eyes move to Sofia and her children.

"How did he know my name? I have never met him," she wonders as her heart begins to beat faster. Ana's soft whimpering is suddenly the only sound in the shop. Sofia feels her cheeks get warm. Her face turns red as her hand stops in midair with the package. She feels a compulsion to run but instead, she drops the package into her carriage, straightens Max's hat and straightens the quilt on top of Ana before pushing hard on the carriage, moving it toward the door, keeping her eyes down as she makes her way through the crowd.

The patrons move aside, making a special aisle for her.

Her mind races to make a quick escape.

A man steps up to open the door for her, making it an easier task than the one when she had entered. She acknowledges him with a whisper, "Thank you" as she passes through the doorway, but never looks at his face.

Once out of the market, she breathes a sigh of relief, still shaken by the strange shopping experience. Her heart races as she pushes the carriage in the direction of home.

Max tries to pull his hand away from the handle of the carriage. He had always been a very active, curious child, a fact that had been responsible for Sofia's obsession with keeping a strong hold on him. She couldn't bear the thoughts of ever losing him, or of any harm coming to him. She imagines Ana's reticent personality would make handling her easier. "Max, you must keep your hand on the handle. You must always walk with me, Max," she reprimands as they speed away.

"Yes," he said putting his head down and his hand back on the handle.

As the threesome continues their walk down the long wide boulevard of the busy market section, the event preoccupies her mind. She doesn't seem to be aware of the constant tapping sound of footsteps on the sidewalk behind her.

"Max! Max!" she shouts when he bolts toward the street in pursuit of a stray cat. She grabs his arm and pulls him away just as a speeding military car comes to a quick stop at the curb in front of her, Max, and the fleeing cat.

Max jumps back when he hears the squeal of the tires.

Several Officers with guns drawn surround the building in front of Sofia. Another military vehicle with two more soldiers stops behind the first. Before Sofia knows it, two of the soldiers whisk her and the children across the street.

"Excuse us, Frau Fuerst, but it isn't safe for you and the children here," Officer Reichman says.

Sofia relaxes, takes a deep breath, and tries to get enough wind to speak. A flash of the Officer and his wife at their dinner table comes to mind. "Are you all right, Frau Fuerst? Maybe you would like a car to take you home?"

"No, Officer Reichman, I'm fine. We are fine. We were coming from the fish market on our way home. We don't need a car. Thank you," Sofia says before starting down the sidewalk again.

The soldiers click their heels and raise their arms in unison. Sofia acknowledges with a nod and hurries away but her curiosity causes her to look back at the scene. The busy city street is now eerily quiet as the soldiers herd people out of a building at gunpoint and use their weapons to force the prisoners into the vehicle. The prisoners walk in silence, holding their hands above their heads, offering no resistance.

A big-eyed, boisterous soldier pushes a young woman carrying a small child. They both fall to the sidewalk. Sofia's mouth drops when she sees the soldier lower his gun, lift his boot, and kick the sobbing woman in the stomach. She covers her mouth with her hand, watching in horror. The woman screams for mercy as another soldier kicks the child and the child lets out a piercing wail that reverberates down the quiet street and joins the woman's sobs.

As the soldiers point their guns directly at them, the prisoners stand frozen, not able to assist the woman. A soldier orders the others in a gruff loud voice and they grab the woman and the child by their coats; throwing them into the back of the truck as if they were tossing away trash.

Sofia's stomach turns as she looks away and concentrates on her own children. Ana is sleeping but Max's eyes are big, glued to the scene of the soldiers who are wearing the same clothes as his own father. She turns his head, rushing them away from the scene, but her haste doesn't prevent her from hearing the sounds of the footsteps for the first time.

A quick look reveals a man in dark clothing behind her.

As they walk, she tries to regain her composure, but her thoughts keep going back to the incident in the market and the subsequent one on the street. She tries to remember the face of the man who had opened the door for her in the market but is unable to visualize him. She wonders if the man who seems to be following her now and the man in the market are the same.

She continues walking, pushing the carriage as she covers Max's hand with hers, pressing it tightly to the handle of the carriage. She looks into the carriage monitoring Ana, who is still sleeping soundly looking regal, safe, and secure under Oma's quilt. The more she thinks about the incident, the harder she presses on Max's hand.

"You are hurting me, Mutter," Max says looking up at her inquisitively, eyebrows raised.

"I'm sorry, Max," she says releasing her hand from his.

"Why did the soldiers treat that little boy like that, Mutti?"

"I don't know, darling. It isn't our business, Max. You must forget it," she warns looking into his curious eyes but she is convinced that her little boy wouldn't be able to forget the incident, nor would she.

They continue their journey along the wide city street, eventually turning on a cross street leading in the direction of home. As she crosses the avenue, another quick look brings another view of the same man still behind her. He is dressed in a dark overcoat and hat with a wide brim. For the first time, she concludes that the figure of the man who had helped her through the door and the man who seems to be following are indeed the same. Afraid, but mustering her courage, she looks back, trying to catch another glimpse but making it appear as if she is looking at something else. The man pulls down the brim of his hat and places the newspaper in front of his face as he darts into a doorway.

As she walks the remaining blocks, she busies herself with the children, keeping an eye on Ana, and trying to keep Max in hand while they crossed the cobblestone streets and concrete sidewalks before finally arriving at their house with the iron fence. She remembers, for only a fleeting moment, the day that Felix had brought her to their new home in the well-to-do neighborhood on the opposite side of town from where she had spent her childhood. Felix had told her then that the house had belonged to some wealthy Germans who had left, not even taking all of their belongings. At the time, she had wondered where Felix had gotten the money to buy all of the things that he had lavished on her. He had told her that everything had come to them when he had accepted his position in the new regime. Ana's cries distract her, interrupting the memory and the questions.

An iron gate marks the entrance into the yard with a bricked walk alongside a newly cut mat of grass. A wavy line of chrysanthemums, which Sofia had planted herself, follows the path leading to the front door. The sight of them, standing strong in all of their autumn glory, triggers a quick flash of a picture of Oma sharing stories, defining her love for the flowers. She lifts sleepy Ana out of the carriage and her head falls onto her shoulder, undisturbed by the transfer.

"Max, help me with the package," she says as she places the fish in his hands. We will leave the carriage until later, after I put Ana down."

"May I play outside for a while, Mutter?"

"No!" No, Max you may not." Her stomach flips at the thought of Max alone in his own yard. "Not now…maybe later."

Sofia gropes for her key, wiggles it into the lock, and pushes the door open with her side. She ushers Max inside while juggling Ana. As she closes the door, she sees the same man in the doorway across the street. Her heart pumps faster. Now, she realizes what she had seen on the faces of those in the market. It had been FEAR. She knows, because it is what she feels now. She closes the door and locks it.

*

Hours Later

Felix arrived home early as promised; the children greet him gleefully as he makes a fuss over them, picking up one at a time, kissing their cheeks and then carrying both of them into the drawing room. Max has his favorite toys ready and Ana sits on the divan next to him, showing him her dolly. While Felix plays with them, Sofia returns to the kitchen to put the final touches on their supper. When she comes back, she announces that it is time for Ana's bath. Max smiles knowing that he finally has some private time with his father.

Sofia loves to spend time with Ana alone, as much as Max yearns for time with his father. She loves to undo her braids and brush her hair with "a thousand strokes" as Oma had taught her, singing her silly songs while dressing her in the little night gown. Gathering Ana up in her arms, she takes her to the nursery and tucks her into her crib. She calls down the steps for Max to come for his turn in their nightly ritual. "Max won't get a bath tonight. He will have more time to spend with his Father," she thinks as she helps him with his pajamas and toothbrush.

Max barely has the rinse out of his mouth before he shouts down to his father that he is ready. After Felix had appeared at the bedroom door,

Sofia kissed the children goodnight and made her exit downstairs to put the final changes on the dinner. She set the table with the fine china that had belonged to her Oma and the crocheted tablecloth that had belonged to her great grandmother, Oma Kraus. A chilled bottle of wine sat in the ice bucket engraved with the letter, 'S'. Sofia remembered that the former owners had left it in the house. She thought it was odd that she had never wondered about the initial before now.

Why would they leave without taking all of their beautiful things?

"Where could they have gone that they wouldn't take their belongings with them?" she wondered but, before she could draw any conclusions, she heard Felix coming down the steps. She struck the matches to light the candles and placed the small crystal dishes of raw cabbage salad on the chargers just as Felix flopped down into his chair. The drawn look on his face and the deep shadows under his eyes concerns her.

"I must be getting old, Sofia. I don't have the energy I used to have," he said never looking up.

"You work hard, Felix. You haven't been getting your rest or your nourishment."

He sipped the wine, running his tongue on his lower lip. "Is this a new bottle of wine, Sofia?"

"It is the bottle you told me to save. Do you remember? We brought it home with us when we last visited the Baltic Sea," she said waiting to see if the mention of the Baltic Sea would get a reaction from him.

"Ah, yes," he said taking another drink. "I wonder if we will ever do that again." His eyes were small and his lips stiff. His reaction wasn't the one Sofia had expected.

"Try the salad, Felix. I got the cabbage fresh from the huckster this morning. He said he won't be making any more rounds because the weather is changing." She wished she had not mentioned the Baltic Sea since he had apparently not remembered their intimate times there. He took a bite, but made no comment.

Sofia waited anxiously but stopped after he had taken several more, still not offering any comment. "It isn't like Felix. He usually makes comments about the food, unless he doesn't like it," she thought as she got up to go back to the kitchen. She brought the main dish, the flounder drenched in butter with boiled potatoes.

Felix sat in silence.

His lack of talking continued to disturb her.

He ate the flounder, ignoring the potatoes and never speaking to Sofia. She felt a pang of disappointment that her husband hadn't seemed pleased with the dinner she had gone to such lengths to prepare. She continued to wonder if she should tell him about the happenings at the market and on the street. She waited, hoping she would get a sign for the right opportunity. Her usually enthusiastic husband at mealtime had again disappeared.

Even the plums and crème don't impress him, she concludes as they finish their dinner in silence. She wants to initiate a conversation, sharing her worries with him, but she can't find the right moment. She doesn't want to upset him as she had the last time when she had approached him, but finally, she just can't hold back any longer. She has to talk to someone who can explain to her what is happening. Her face tightens and she stiffens in her chair. She fiddles with her fork, finally putting it down, and blurting, "I need to talk to you about something, Felix."

Felix stopped and looked at her, crumpling his napkin. "What is it, Sofia? You aren't sick, are you?" he asked as his face softened a bit.

"No, Felix. I'm not sick. I am worried. I have been worried since the last time I had talked to you about this."

"You mean about people embarrassing you and staring at you?" he asked with a stiff lip and narrowed brows.

"Yes, but what happened today has me very worried, Felix," Sofia responded in almost a whisper.

"What exactly happened today, Sofia?"

She told him every detail of her trip to the market.

Felix sat silently listening to her every word. His face tensed. His lips remained straight and his eyebrows wrinkled.

She waited for him to say something as she told each part of the day's events. He said nothing. When she had finished, he started to get up and move away from the table. "Felix, what could those people have possibly done to deserve such treatment?"

"They must be enemies of THE THIRD REICH, Sofia," Felix said without any hesitation. It appears that some of our fellow citizens have decided to hide some of the enemies of the State and are suffering the consequences.

"Surely, little children aren't the government's enemies?"

"THE THIRD REICH decides who their enemies are, Sofia."

"Do they imprison children?"

"You aren't to shop in that part of town anymore," he ordered avoiding an answer to her question.

"That is where I grew up Felix. Vater's bakery is still there."

"That was then. This is now. You must not go to that part of town again. I forbid it. You are the wife of a Soldier of THE THIRD REICH. You don't belong there."

"You are frightening me, Felix."

"Maybe you need to be frightened, Sofia. Do what I tell you."

"What about the man who seemed to be following me?"

"It is just your imagination. There are many men in dark clothing on the streets of Berlin."

"Felix, this isn't the first time this has happened. I told you about the other times."

"I am sure he was just someone looking for a particular address."

"I am certain he was interested in me."

"What could he possibly want with you, Sofia?"

"I have no idea. That is just the point. It frightened me then and it is terrifying me now."

"Forget it, Sofia. It is best for you to forget it," he said as he gets up quickly. "I'm returning to Headquarters immediately. You need not wait up for me," he said as he left the dining room. He dresses in his uniform overcoat and cap, opens the door, and leaves.

As Sofia cleared the table, she thought about what Felix had said. "I can't forget what I don't understand," she thought as she washed and dried the dishes. "How can I forget something that has scared me to death?"

As hard as she tried, Sofia couldn't rationalize Felix's reaction. The pictures of the day's events kept flashing in her mind as she tidied the kitchen, turned out the light, and went upstairs to bed where she lay awake again, waiting for her husband to return. She wasn't alone. "I have worry, confusion, and gloom to keep me company."

*

"She couldn't forget the experience in the fish market, Neeny," Sofia continues as her eyelids droop and her voice wavers. Janene becomes alarmed, noticing the change in Sofia and fears that this second day of storytelling is beginning to take its toll on her. "She has deep shadows under her eyes and her voice seems weaker than yesterday," Janene thinks. Despite the signs of stress, Sofia's ability to recite the story from memory amazes her, but she worries that her desire to find her roots has placed too much stress on Sofia. Just as Janene was about to suggest another time for the storytelling, Sofia began again, apparently energized by a deep breath.

*

"This experience and similar ones play repeatedly in her mind. She is glad that her duties for the children, running the household, and being a good wife occupy her mind. However, despite them, at times her fears become so intense they soon consume her thoughts, interrupting her during the day, and causing her to lose sleep at night. The more she concentrates on the fear, the more she tries to analyze and draw conclusions. She decides that she no longer suspects danger, but now knows that it is eminent.

As she ponders the events, she compares how her life is now to how it had been when they had first married and moved to this house. She is sure that the entire city seems to be changing, fading away, and giving way to a 'new Berlin', not the one of her childhood. The new one seems dominated by the politics of the new government. She thinks of the rumors she has heard, ones too horrible to comprehend, and wonders if they are true. She has always doubted Felix's involvement, but now finds it increasingly hard to do so.

How could Felix do such things?

She had concluded many years ago that he was an Officer of THE THIRD REICH and he had to obey orders but the answer to the question and the question itself bring her instant panic. She remembered the day when they had ordered him to "become a Soldier of THE THIRD REICH – or die." The horrible recognition that Felix may actually be a part of their plans for this 'new' Germany makes her heart flutter.

Could they force him?

She couldn't deny the possibility, remembering that they had forced him to join. *If they had ever doubted his loyalty, it would mean certain death for him, for the children, and me.* She considered the possibility that the residents of the old neighborhood who had known him and loved him when he had been the neighborhood police officer might be second-guessing him now. "Maybe that was the reason for their stares," she contemplated again making herself sick with worry.

"It isn't my imagination," she said to no one but herself.

She can't condone the racist behavior of the new government – *even if it is my own husband*, she decides. She had a fear so intense it paralyzed her. She felt like a trapped animal. Like the animal, she thinks that she must freeze in her tracks, blend in with her surroundings, and look only to survival. She feels alone. After months of worry, she knows what she had to do.

I must get away from Berlin and I must do it now.

She could see no way out for Felix and decided that she must protect the children. "How can I possibly run away with two little children?" She has no answer but she knows she must find one and that for the first time in her life, this will be one decision that she will make completely on her own.

*

The next afternoon, Sofia visits Helena. The two women had become friends when Helena and her husband, Hans, had moved into the house several doors away. She and Helena had a lot in common. Both of them had married Officers of THE THIRD REICH, and their children were about the same ages. They had provided the children with mutual play times and come to interact with each other. They had recently discussed a play date in the near future, giving Max and Helena's son another playtime. Helena had an older daughter who enjoyed playing with Ana. Recently, Helena also had given birth to their third child, Herman.

Sofia hoped Helena would give her some more information that might allay her fears and help her to arrive at a different conclusion. Helena's husband was serving in Africa but she also knew that she should be careful of what she said to Helena. In the past, Sofia had noticed that Helena had shared gossip about the neighborhood and had seemed to know about everyone and everything.

She walked the short distance to her house and the two of them got the children settled in the drawing room. It wasn't long before the children were busy with toys; they moved into the dining room within eyesight and hearing of them. Helena served some tea and started to make some small talk.

"I'm glad you and I can talk, Sofia. I don't get to talk to anybody anymore, especially another adult. I'm very worried about Hans. I've not heard from him for a while. I've heard rumors about how the war is going but that isn't all," she rattled on in a whisper, her hand over her mouth, trying to make sure her children didn't hear her.

"I'm worried too, Helena. The other day, I had thought that I was being followed."

"Me, too, and I have had the feeling several times in the last month. I can't imagine why anyone would want to follow me. I told Felix about it, but he claims it is just coincidental." Sofia said.

"I heard a woman at the library talking in whispers the other day, Sofia. She said she heard they had set up work camps. They had herded those whom they considered their enemies into a ghetto, then relocated them to the camps. Eventually, they say, they become death camps. The woman whispered that she had heard that the government had some system of methodically killing their enemies."

"Are you sure? Helena, surely, it is a mistake – just a rumor."

"I thought so at first, too. My house cleaner told my cook that she had heard the rumors but she also had proof that they were true."

"What proof?"

"I don't know. I'm not sure. I'm so confused; I don't know what to believe. Sofia, I'm frightened."

"Share your toys with Max," Helena shouts turning her attention to the children.

Sofia looks to Max, pleased that her son is the one waiting patiently for his friend to share the toys he is clutching in his arms. She notices Helena's older daughter is still playing with Ana, keeping her contented. She again listens to Helena, now whispering about all of the things she had heard and about more abuses enacted by the soldiers. She hesitates for a moment and stares at Sofia. "I don't know if I should tell you the rest, Sofia."

"What? What is it, Helena. Tell me.?"

"It may concern Felix, Sofia."

"I need to know, Helena. Please, tell me."

"You must remember I can't prove it."

"I understand."

"It is about a form of 'selective breeding' designed to produce a new generation of pure babies."

"What do they mean 'Pure babies'?"

"They only have German blood in their veins."

"How do they propose to do that?"

"It would mean the eradication of thousands, those whom the government deems inferior, all those who aren't pure German." She hesitates, trying to catch her breath while Sofia does the same.

"I can't believe this, Helena. Surely it's false."

"I thought the same thing until I had gone to the medical center to have the baby. After they delivered Herman and I was feeling better, I decided to go to the nursery. If I had not seen it with my own eyes, I wouldn't have believed it. I must have made a wrong turn because I came upon an entirely different nursery," she whispers still keeping an eye out for the children and for anyone to overhear her.

"I was curious, so I went in. There were rows of baby beds and every one of them had one thing in common – each bed had been marked with the word, 'Officer.' Quickly, I hid behind a door and listened as two nurses talked about the babies. I overheard one nurse speaking to the other about how overworked she had been because of the extra load of taking on several shifts to care for the 'large number of illegitimate babies of the officers born that week.'"

"Are you sure you heard her correctly? Did you hear them call the children 'illegitimate'?"

"Yes, Sofia, I'm positive. Apparently, they are using the Officers in the military to produce a new generation of children who will take over when they are victorious. The mothers are women screened for their pure German heritage."

"Why would you think it would involve Felix? It has to be a mistake. I can't believe it, Helena." As Helena talked, she kept watching over her shoulder to make sure that no one was hearing any of the conversation. Sofia listened as Helena continued to tell her about the plan to conquer the entire world. She got a sick feeling in her stomach.

It had surprised Sofia when Helena had brought up her experiences, especially the one when she also thought someone had followed her. Both of the women spoke in whispers. Sofia listened as Helena told her of her fears for her husband. "I have heard rumors and have talked to others who have told me of the terrible things they are doing. They suspect everyone, even their own – even going so far as to execute them for treason by firing squad or by hanging. That is why it seems that all of Berlin is talking in whispers, Sofia. Most are scared to death. Who can you trust?"

"This is incredible. How can this be?" Sofia said sitting very still with a shocked look on her face.

"Hans says the war isn't going well. There is fear that Germany will be defeated again."

"If this is all true, what will happen to us?"

"I don't know, Sofia. I don't know," said Helena shaking her head. "Why would I be followed? Sofia, do you feel as if you are being watched?"

Sofia remembered Felix telling her to be careful what she shared with Helena. She feels as if she might be 'pumping' her to get information. She remained tight-lipped and offered no agreement or disagreement as she tried to change the subject back to talking about the children. However, her pale face announced her feelings and she was glad that the children interrupted them. The boys wanted the same toy again. She thought how simple it was to settle their disagreement. All she had to do was tell Max he should share.

"Well I suppose the children have had enough time together, Helena. I better go," Sofia told Helena as she got up and separated the children from the same toy.

"Oh, don't go yet, Sofia. Stay a while longer. Let's have some more tea. We can talk about something else . . . besides all of these worrisome things. I never get to visit with another adult."

Sofia smiled and agreed to stay a little while longer, and they talked about other things while enjoying their tea. Soon the children showed signs of tiring with their toys and Sofia decided to go home, promising that they would set up another play date.

"Sofia, I'm not going to mention our conversation to Hans and I don't think you should say anything to Felix . . . No one can be trusted," Helena said as she helped Sofia dress the children in their coats.

"I think you are right, Helena," Sofia said wondering if she could even trust Helena. "Thanks for everything."

*

Later that night, after they had shared what had become a rare occasion, a dinner together, Sofia told Felix about the play date with Helena and the children. "I feel so badly for Helena, Felix. She misses Hans so much. You know she hasn't had any word from him or about him in three months."

Felix seems distracted and doesn't comment.

"Helena told me about the rumors that she has heard, Felix."

"What rumors, Sofia?"

" . . . That the war isn't going well for Germany," she says pausing for his response. He offers none.

"Some are saying we will lose the war," she continues. "I was not aware that so many of the cities have been bombed – not just Berlin."

"Frau Stein is just a nervous woman, Sofia. She has little to do but stir up rumors and cause trouble. I forbid you to have any further contact with her," he shouts.

Sofia shudders at Felix's loud and harsh tone. She turns away, moves to clear the table, and drops the conversation, not daring to mention the rumor about the pure illegitimate children of the officers.

"Now, Sofia, what did Dr. Wolfe have to say about Max and Ana when you had taken them for their physicals?" he asked changing the subject and his tone of voice, going from anger to just a mild agitation.

Sofia shared the doctor's report, making sure that she reassures Felix that the doctor had confirmed that they are "fine examples of healthy German children." She hoped this would make Felix happy but, if it had, his face didn't show it.

After their conversation, he immediately leaves for headquarters for another emergency. She goes to bed that night with a deep fear in her heart of an impending doom that would envelope not just the country but also all of Europe. At three o'clock in the morning, she hears Felix come to bed.

*

The next morning, Sofia decides to take the children for a visit to their grandparents. Preparing, she rings her parents.

"I just wanted to tell you I plan to bring the children over for a visit today, Mutter. They are anxious to see their Oma and Opa again and I want to talk to both of you about something important."

"Good. We are anxious to see you," Alexandra says.

160

"Would ten o'clock be good for you?"

"See you then."

*

Sofia walks from her house to the other side of town, pushing Ana in her carriage and watching Max as he walks beside it. As they walk, she thinks about what she is going to tell them. She is defying her husband's orders by returning to the north end of town and by the time she reaches Pappelstrasse, she still has not made up her mind as to how she should approach them with her plan to leave Berlin.

Max opens the door and holds it for her and the carriage before running over to his Opa, throwing his little arms around his legs, giving him one of his famous hugs.

"Max, my boy, how is Opa's big boy?" Gerhard asks picking him up and hugging him hard.

"My, goodness, Ana is so beautiful and she is so big!" Alexandra says. Max starts to fiddle with the first button on his coat, trying to remove it.

"Max, don't take off your coat . . . not just yet. Winifred is going to take you to the park for a little while," Gerhard says as he puts him down. Winifred, a clerk who works in the bakery, walks into the store from the back room, dressed in her coat and hat.

"Come, Max. We will have a good time in the park," she says, leading the children out the door as Gerhard holds it open.

Sofia's face shows her surprise at her parents sending the children to the park with the hired help. As soon as they are gone, her father explains, "Sofia, we need to talk to you. We should go into the kitchen. Come."

He puts the 'CLOSED' sign on the door and ushers Sofia into the kitchen. Sofia follows her parents through the bakery, behind the counter, and into the back room. She notices that her father checks the store several times to make sure no one else had entered. He keeps looking over his shoulder as they follow him to the kitchen and he locks the back door. "We're glad you called, Sofia. We were going to call you. It is safer to talk here than in your house," he whispers.

"You are scaring me. What is it? Are you ill? Mutter, are you all right?"

"We're fine, Sofia, but we have some disturbing things to tell you," Alexandra said.

"What?"

"Sofia, it involves Felix. It's dreadful information. We know it will upset you, even more than it has upset us," Alexandra said.

161

"I'll tell her, Alexandra. I'll be the one to speak of these horrible things. I just don't know where to begin," her father said.

"It is about the soldiers, Sofia," Alexandra said.

"Vater, I came to talk to you about the soldiers. I have heard some terrible things from Helena. I also think someone is following me. I think people are talking behind my back. I'm frightened, Vater. I'm worried about Max and Ana."

"I've heard some things too, Sofia. I've been hearing rumors for a long time. However, I know that these things are not rumors. In addition, they are very disturbing. You know I have been supportive of the new regime, but now I'll no longer believe in that man," he said shaking his head from side to side.

"He is truly a monster, Sofia," he whispered looking to the left and right to make sure no one could hear him. "There is no doubt, Sofia, he and all his henchmen are murderous monsters," he said his face turning stark white.

Tears filled Alexandra eyes as she listened to her husband.

"The things that have been done to our neighbors are too horrible to even imagine," he whispered. They starve them and work them in camps. If they don't die from starvation, they kill them by gassing them." He tried to regain composure by taking a deep breath. Sofia put her hand up to her face, covering her mouth and her scream. "What about Esther, Vater?"

"I don't know about Esther and her family, Sofia," he said. "I don't know about any of them. The only thing I know for sure is that they are all gone. Their homes and businesses are now occupied by the soldiers, or they have been ransacked and emptied," he said continuing to shake his head slowly from side to side, leading Sofia to a chair.

"You must be strong, Sofia. These things were difficult for us to hear too, but they are the truth," Alexandra said, her voice cracking.

"Your husband is one of them, Sofia. Oh, my God, Felix is one of these monsters."

"Now, Alexandra, be strong. We need to tell Sofia. Come sit down. Sit next to Sofia," he said, moving the chair and helping her.

"They are herding hundreds of Jewish people and any others they deem unfit: men, woman, children, the old and the young, the sick – herding them like animals into cattle cars and transporting them to camps under the pretense they are being 'relocated'."

Sofia gasps and places her hand over mouth.

"I know, Sofia. It's too horrible to comprehend, but you must listen. I can't believe what I'm saying is true either, but it is true. God help us! It is true," he exclaimed taking a deep breath and allowing his body to slide into the chair.

Sofia and Alexandra lifted themselves higher in their seats, wiped their tears, and turned their eyes toward Gerhard. "People are sent to chambers where they are gassed; they are all gassed! They kill them, doing it very systematically. It is a horror of unbelievable proportions. I spent two years in the trenches and I have never experienced anything like this. This is unbelievable. I can't even imagine anything as horrible as this," he said focusing his eyes directly into theirs.

"There are beatings, rapes, robberies, and incidents of vandalism occurring every day. These are happening all around us, before our very noses. No one dares to speak up against the Fuhrer. None dares to help anyone. To do so is to sign your own death warrant."

"Vater," Sofia interrupted, "You told me such wonderful things about the new government. You told me that under their leadership, Germany would become great again. You believed in them. You told Franz to believe in them and you were so happy when I'd married Felix because you said the soldiers would make our life wonderful. You said we wouldn't have the hardships you and Mutter had."

"I was wrong, Sofia. I was so wrong," he lamented, his voice cracking. "I wanted it to be true. I'm ashamed."

"We misjudged him, darling. We believed in the things he had said. We wanted to believe them. We were desperate. We turned our heads away from what was rumored, not willing to believe it," Alexandra said adding to her husband's confession.

"Sofia, in 1932, we really believed what he had said. He was very convincing and we needed to believe that someone would make a change for the better after all that had happened since the war. Since then, we have learned the terrible truth," he whispered trying to explain. He got up from the table, moved closer, and whispered. "The tales are so abominable. The truth is too unbelievable. Our country has become a murderous state of hoodlums and thugs."

"Vater, how do you know this?"

"I know because of what your Uncle Adam has told me."

"Uncle Adam? What does he have to do with this?"

"Yes. He has confirmed these and other things."

"What other things?"

"In this government's grand plan, they will dominate the entire world. They have even gone so far as to arrange the births of children who are pure Aryan. These children are the bastards of the officers. They are part of the plan to preserve the power they have gained and continue their reign into the next generations. Sofia sat speechless thinking that her father had corroborated what Helena had already told her.

Felix!

Her face drained of blood. "I can't imagine Felix impregnating another woman, Vater." She felt sick, faint, as she remembered that they had granted Felix a promotion to a higher rank and he was now one of those officers. She waited for her vater to tell her more and confirm that this practice didn't include her husband.

"Why did I ever tell Franz to join his Army?" he asks losing his composure. In a sudden fury, his face red and sweat pouring from his brow, he blurted, "I should never have arranged your marriage to him."

Sofia's mouth dropped and her eyes popped open wide. Her mind raced. *Vater had arranged my marriage to Felix!* She felt so naive, never dreaming that her vater had made the arrangement. For the first time, she questioned her husband's love for her.

Drips of perspiration run down Gerhard's forehead. "Franz, Franz, oh, what have I done, Franz?" he asks, catching himself from falling and gasping for air. Sofia rushed to the sink for water, fearing he was having a heart attack.

"Vater, take a deep breath. Vater, try to relax" Sofia instructed, as if he were a child. "Take a drink, Vater."

"I'm so worried about Franz," he cried.

Alexandra came over to her husband's side, put her arms around his shoulders, and held the glass steady for him. Gerhard bowed his head into his hands and sobbed. Sofia and her mother began sobbing.

"Sofia, we don't know where Franz is. We don't know if he is dead or alive. We can only imagine the worst in this army of mad men. Adam said he thinks he may be in a prison camp in Russia," Alexandra cried breaking the silence.

"Franz, oh my son!" she wailed.

"Come, Mutter, you must sit down too," Sofia said. She put her arms on her mother's shoulders and moved her to the chair. She sat down beside her. Suddenly, Gerhard stood up, raised his head high, put his arm high in the air, and shouted as if he was going to salute.

"No! We must not let them destroy us. We must do something. We must do something, now," he shouted as he brought his arm down and pounded his fist on the table.

"Vater, what can we do?"

"Sofia, I have never felt this kind of fear before. It will not be long before the world knows about this. I am sure if the world survives this, it will wonder how an entire country had allowed this to happen. However, I can't allow my fear and shame to dictate my actions any longer. I am afraid for us. I am afraid for you. I'm afraid for Max and Ana," he said regaining his composure. "I'm afraid to act and I'm afraid not to. It is in God's hands, now."

"I'm afraid too, Vater. That is why I came here today. I'm afraid for the children."

"Sofia, we are leaving; we must leave immediately. We must run for our lives while we still may have the time. We think you should do the same," he said taking a deep breath. "The tide of the war may be changing. The Allies are stronger; the target will be here in Berlin to bring him down. If we don't leave now, I don't think we will get another chance. I can't imagine what Berlin will be like when it falls and I can't imagine what it will be like if it doesn't. I fear the Berlin we have known and the country that we have loved will never exist again. We all must leave. We must go."

"Vater, where will you go? How will you and Mutter survive? Where will I go? How can I leave with two small children? Surely, if we flee, we will die. And if we stay, what happens then?"

"We have no choice, Sofia. If we stay, the chances are we will all die just the same. Even if Germany wins the war, we could never live here any longer; this isn't the country of my father," Alexandra added.

"I have talked to Adam about this and he has a plan. He will help us. We can only concern ourselves with survival. I have put my confidence in Adam to get us to a new place. He thinks he can get us to safety – wherever that might be. We can't do it alone but we have a chance if we let Adam help us.

"Uncle Adam? Vater, we have not heard from him in a long time. At least, you haven't told me anything about hearing from him?"

"He has been in contact with us for some time, Sofia. He told us not to say anything to anyone, including you. He said the only way to protect ourselves was through absolute secrecy."

"Adam contacted us and told us he was working underground. I can't say anymore, Sofia, for his safety as well as ours."

"I understand, Vater," Sofia said, feeling her voice getting stronger.

"Adam no longer supports Germany. He has not since Oma died and he went back to France. He believes in the destruction of the present government. Thoughts like that are treasonous. Adam is in grave danger. His life is in danger, no matter what the outcome of the war. If Germany loses the war, it will not be safe for any German who had supported THE THIRD REICH. If Germany wins the war, it will not be safe for us either, because we will never support them now that we know what they are capable of doing. My Faith will not let me turn my head to them any longer and neither will my conscience. If it means that I'll die in the process, then it will be God's Will but I'll no longer sit by idly and watch them take over my life with evil of such proportion. You are in grave danger. Your husband and your brother are Soldiers of THE THIRD REICH.

"I agree with Uncle Adam, Vater. I want to leave Berlin and I want to leave Felix. He isn't the same man I married."

Gerhard seemed relieved, nodding his head in agreement and continuing in a strong voice. "We are preparing as we speak, Sofia. Don't talk to Felix about this plan. They can't suspect him of having a family of traitors. If they do, they will arrest all of us. Just wait for the next word to come. It will come from Adam. Don't say anything to the children. Take nothing with you except the clothes on your back. Leave anything that could connect you to Felix."

"Vater, how can I not talk to Felix? He is my husband. How can I leave with his children without telling him?"

"You have no choice now. You must leave Felix. It is too dangerous to confide in him. You must sever all of your connections with him. You must not be linked to them in any way," he said. His whole body seemed to melt into the chair. "Sofia, I would never tell you to do this, but these things they're doing are never going to be justified, and the world will never forget this. I don't want to live in this kind of world. I would rather die first. There is never going to be forgiveness for those who have committed these horrible crimes – nor should there be."

His mood became quiet. He sat perfectly still, shaking his head slowly from side to side. Then, suddenly, as if in a rage, he stood up and shouted: "You must go . . . . You must for the sake of the children." They should never be labeled with this stigma." He pounded his fist on the table.

"God help them and all of us."

Sofia felt the pain of her father's words. It made her stomach flip and she felt nauseous. She thought she would faint as she continued listening to her father, trying to comprehend what he was proposing, but not able to understand. Her thoughts stayed on Felix. She felt betrayed by the man she had loved with all of her heart, the father of her children. Now, she feels childlike, wanting her quilt, but suddenly a feeling of strength overcame her. She lifted her head high and asked her father, "What should we do, Vater?"

"First, we have to have confidence that everything will work out, Sofia. There are some hard times ahead for all of us but we have had hard times before. Have faith in God and in yourself. We can no longer believe in Germany."

He got up from the table and embraced her and Alexandra.

She thought of how she had felt when her father had held her on his shoulders, when she had been a child. She realizes now that he wasn't ten feet tall, but rather, he seemed small in her arms. They hugged and held each other close for a brief moment. Tears welled and streamed down their faces. Finally, Gerhard pulled away from his wife and daughter and wiped his cheek.

"We must be strong. We should say no more. From this moment on, we will be united in complete silence." As he stared at their blank faces, the bell on the bakery door rang.

"Opa, may I have a treat now? We had fun at the park, Opa," Max said bursting into the bakery.

Sofia and her parents started back into the shop from the kitchen, wiping the tears from their eyes and making a fuss over the children. Opa and Oma gave the treats to their grandchildren and visited with them. Sofia noticed the time.

"It is time for us to go, Max. Give Oma and Opa a hug," she told him as she started to ready Ana.

"I'll come again, Opa. Maybe the next time, you can come to the park with me," Max suggested.

"Yes, Max. That would be good. Next time, we will go together. Just you and I," he said, hugging his only grandson. He hugged him harder than usual. Alexandra lifted Ana, holding her in her arms, kissing her on both cheeks and then handed her to Gerhard. Wiping her eyes, she hid her tears from the children. There was only time for one more whisper for Sofia from her father.

"Sofia, remember only one word. Remember the word, 'Escape'. Someone will only say one word to you and you should go with him."

"God go with you, Sofia," Alexandra whispered in her ear and kissed her cheeks.

"I'll pray for both of you," she said pushing the carriage through the door.

The bell on the door clanged. Sofia waved good-bye one more time, and prayed that it wouldn't be their last time together.

* * * * *

CHAPTER 6
ESCAPE

"After that last kiss good-bye, I wondered if I would ever see my parents again. From the moment that I had left the bakery, my stomach had been in knots, wondering if I had made the right decision. As it had turned out, I didn't have much time to fret, word had come that same night," said Sofia. "It had been the first time in my life that I had made a decision on my own and I had no idea of its magnitude."

"I can't image making a decision like that," says Janene. "You must have been terrified to leave everything that you had ever known behind."

"Indeed, for years I had wondered if I had done the right thing, but I am getting ahead of myself. Before my own thoughts distract me again, I'll continue with telling you about the night that had changed my life."

*

14 January 1944

Felix was at Headquarters on urgent business. A knock came at Sofia's back door. She opened it to a man who said only one word, 'Escape.' He motioned with his hands to hurry. She nodded and then grabbed her coat and hat, putting them on as she led the man upstairs to the where the children slept. As she was running up the steps, she removed her locket and wedding ring and placed them on the chest in Max's room. The man picked up Max, wrapped him in the blanket from his bed, and headed downstairs with him. Sofia went into Ana's room, picked her up, wrapping her in the pink blanket with the lambs on it, and carried her downstairs. Remembering her father's instructions, she collected their shoes, coats, and hats as she left, following the man into the frigid January night air.

The man said nothing; made no eye contact with her. He opened the door, putting Max into the back seat of the car. Then he motioned to Sofia to get in beside Max, closed the door and ran around to the driver's side of the car, got in, and started it. He looked into the rear view mirror and then, in a flash, he drove away.

Sofia dressed the children in their warm clothes trying not to wake them. Max opened his eyes several times but sleep overtook him and he decided against it, his head falling back down onto Sofia's right knee. Ana never stirred as Sofia put her coat and hat on over the little gown she was wearing and then wrapped her in the blanket, and placed her head on her left knee.

There was frost on the window from their breaths and it occluded her view of the outside. From her limited view in the rear seat, she peered through the front windshield. It appeared to her as if they were traveling west. She closed her eyes and took a deep breath. Looking down at her sleeping children brought a sense of anxiety as she began to question her decision to leave. She wondered what would become of them. Ana lay sleeping peacefully with the pink blanket pulled up over her head, and Max was sound asleep on the other side of her lap. As Sofia gazed down at them, she thought that she had everything in the world that was important to her in her lap – until she remembered the one thing that had always been the most important thing in her life – her quilt.

She had made a mental note to take the quilt with her – even though her father had told her to take "only the clothes on your back," but somehow in the haste and anxiety, she had left it safely tucked into Ana's carriage. "How could I have forgotten it?" she questions, still feeling her body shaking. Despite the circumstances and the quick exit, she can't excuse her incredible carelessness and just the thought of it sends her into a panic, bringing on doubts as to whether someone so careless could possibly be successful in the undertaking she has begun.

She rehashes the event in her mind, remembering how she had thought about what to take and what to leave and had begun a plan for the time when the first messenger would come. She recalled that she had planned to get the quilt from its place on Ana's carriage. She thought that the plan would come to fruition tomorrow – maybe next week, *but never tonight*.

The booming sounds of what seems to be gunfire interrupt her remorseful thinking about leaving the quilt behind. "They sound like they are close," she thinks as she feels the car lunge forward faster and notes the driver turns off the headlights, driving blindly in the darkness down the deserted country road.

Her heart ached as she asked herself, "Why did I leave you behind?" She longed for it—to feel it and hold it close. Her body felt limp and she felt powerless, her strength drained. She felt like she had left a part of herself back in Berlin. "The quilt was supposed to be for Ana," she thought as she remembered her intentions of giving it to her when she was old enough to understand the story behind it."

She had not felt this way since Oma had died, not able to imagine a life without her quilt and without Oma, too. Her thoughts go to Felix and her life with him that she has left behind. Her heart beats faster and she feels her stomach flip as she tried to overcome her terror. At that moment, she hated Felix. *How could you do this to us?* She pictured him and heard his words warning her not to return to her old neighborhood and not to talk to anyone about the workings of THE THIRD REICH. She tried to make sense of what was happening now and questioned her decision to leave. "We are all going to die anyway," she thought. "I can't imagine my life any other way than with Felix."

What have I done?

She had so many questions with no answers. They were questions she continued to ask herself as the car sped away into the dark. She pondered the situation, beginning for the first time to conclude that she wasn't alone. Many others would be asking the same questions and would have no answers. She looked down at her two children, sleeping peacefully; very unaware of what was happening, trusting completely in their parents, as she had always trusted in Gerhard and Alexandra. She knew that someday they would be asking her the same questions—*If we live that long.*

She also doubted her ability to answer the questions in any way that would make sense to them. The magnitude of her decision struck her for the first time. She concluded that she would never be able to go back to the life she had once had. *That life doesn't exist anymore – not for me or for any other German.* "I won't think about the past. I'll not think about the future. I'll only think about the present and how to get us away from the madness," she decided as the car sped away into the cold darkness of the unknown.

Twenty-three year old Sofia felt like she was five years old again and at the same time, she felt like an old woman who had lost all of her strength. As her eyes start to close, she reaches for her quilt, but the emptiness reminds her that she can't sleep. Her mind floods with one depressing thought after another and her head feels like it will burst. *The children need me.* It takes every ounce of will power, but she focuses, organizing her thoughts as she looks for some semblance of sanity and something to validate the decision she has made. It seems to her that the whole world has gone insane, at least the world that she had once known.

"What was I thinking? How could I have decided to leave Felix? What will he think? I know I don't have my quilt, but I do have my Oma . . . Yes, she is right here in my heart and I must be as strong as she was. I have to be strong . . . for Max and Ana," she says with a prayer to God asking for strength.

The Soviet Troops had advanced into Poland and the Americans were planning a massive invasion of Europe, one coordinated with the English and Canadians, but Sofia knew nothing of that. Nor, did she know that the escape plan, arranged by Adam, would take them into France, where the Allies were planning a surprise assault on Normandy— her 'Destination'.

*

Sofia awoke when she heard Max crying. His crying woke up Ana. Soon, they were both wailing. She felt like crying too, but no tears would come. She knew why they were crying; they did not.

They were frightened, hungry, and confused, and so was she.

She gathered them into her arms, kissing them, trying to comfort them. She had no food to give them; their clothes were of little help in the cold room. She wrapped them in the blanket covering her. Realizing she needed to get herself under control before she could possibly care for the children, she took a deep breath, straightened her body, and tightened her grip on them.

Her mind swirled, reviewing what had happened so far, and worrying about what was going to happen next. "How could I do this to them?" she asked again, recalling how she had taken them out of their beds in the middle of the night – *their beds where they were safe and secure with their father to protect them.*

"Surely, this is a dream; I'll wake up soon," she screamed, but it was only in her mind. Tears flowed down her cheeks and she began to sob.

"Mutter, you are crying," Max said as he stopped his own crying and studied her face.

"No, Max. I am not. Everything is fine," she said wiping her face with her hand.

"I'm hungry, Mutti and I am cold. I have to go to the bathroom. May I get out of my night clothes?"

"Me. Me," Ana shouted with tears running down her cheeks. Sofia couldn't find words of explanation, not able to give her children what they needed.

I can't take care of my children.

Panic struck her.

Her heart raced and she pulled the children close. A soft knock on the door intensified her fear. She pulled the children tighter to her and froze. The children followed her lead. The three of them sat watching the doorknob turn and the door open.

A tall, brown-haired woman entered the room carrying a tray of bottled milk, bread, butter, cheese and some fruit. As she set the tray down on the small table beside them, she smiled at the children and spoke in a soft voice in German, telling them not to be afraid.

"Do you speak French?"

"Yes," Sofia acknowledged.

"It is necessary for you to speak French now. From this moment on, you should speak only in French, or you shouldn't speak at all," the woman told her in French. "Come with me," she said pointing to the door.

The woman directed them out into the hallway toward a small bathroom. The children were attentive to Sofia and seemed curious about the woman who was no longer speaking in German. When they came back from the bathroom, they found the woman busy setting up the refreshments on the table and starting a fire in the fireplace. Sofia led them to the table and seated them. Their eyes were big as they surveyed the food and drinks. Sofia nodded and gave them permission to begin eating.

"You should eat something also, Madame," the woman said in a soft voice.

"I'll eat after my children have finished."

"You will only be here a short time. Later this evening, some others will take you to a new destination. You are safe here, but you must be quiet."

"Where will we be going?" Sofia asked.

"You must never ask questions," the woman said moving toward the door.

"I'll return in a little while."

The children ate almost everything on the tray, leaving only a few crusts of bread and a little milk for Sofia.

"You should teach the children as much French as you can," the woman said when she returned to the room. By that time, Sofia was playing with the children. Now that their stomachs were no longer empty, they laughed and sang as they engaged in one of the games, which Sofia had always played with them in the past.

"Yes, of course" Sofia said turning away from her interaction with the children and giving her attention to the woman. The children continued playing the little clapping game.

"I must leave now. I'll return later with your papers. The papers will identify you as 'Madame Adeline Debauch' and the children are 'Michel and Jacqueline Debauch'. You must never use your German names. The Germans are looking for you and you can trust no one. You should call the children by their new French names. You will have to teach them. Do you understand?"

"Yes."

"Perhaps, you could play a game with your son about his name change. The little girl will make no difference."

"Max likes games."

"Michel seems like a bright boy."

"Yes, he is."

"The papers indicate that you are a French women, widowed, age 23, traveling with your son, age five and a daughter, age three. Your home was Alsace Lorraine, a town on the French German border, which has always been in controversy over its ownership by the French and Germans. You are the widow of Maurice Debauch, a farmer. The Germans had killed him in 1942. Recently, shelling had destroyed your house. You are refugees. You should only give this information – nothing more. Don't volunteer any information. Only answer what they ask. If you are unsure, you must act as if you are dumb. Instruct your son not to speak unless you are alone."

"I understand."

"I must leave now. I'll return later. Farewell, Madame Adeline Debauch."

Sofia thought about the task of teaching the children to speak in French, deciding it would be best to start immediately as the women had suggested. However, even German words were not coming easily to her right now. She felt as if she was dreaming, hoping soon she would wake up from the nightmare. She let the children play as she tried to finish what was left of the refreshments, moving them back and forth on the tray, finally forcing herself to eat the few crumbs of bread and small piece of cheese.

As she ate, she contemplated what she would have to do next. She thought a language change would be easy for Ana. Most of her vocabulary was babble. *Max is a different story*. His larger-than-normal German vocabulary might be difficult for him to dismiss. She realized she had no comprehension of the magnitude of Uncle Adam's plan when she had agreed to it. Reminding herself of the danger they were in, she decided to talk to Max about what was happening, reassuring herself at the same time.

"Max, come here, darling," she said as she motioned to him to come sit beside her on the bed next to Ana.

"We're on a holiday. You and Ana and I are on a holiday," Sofia said in a soft firm voice.

"Will Vater be coming with us on holiday, Mutter," Max asked.

"No, Max. Vater isn't coming with us on this holiday. He couldn't get away from his work," Sofia lied to him, but then she reminded herself that *Felix really couldn't get away from his work, so it isn't really a lie.* Her stomach flipped. She had never lied to anyone, especially Max. "This is a special holiday for just you, Ana and me," she said waiting for him to respond. Max said nothing, seemingly satisfied with the answer Sofia had offered.

"We will be leaving later today to continue on our holiday, but until then, were going to play a game. This game has special rules, just like the other games I have taught you. Do you understand, Max?"

"Yes, Mutter."

"Good. In this game, we will call you, Michel. We will never call you Max, or we will break the rules."

"Mutter, how will Vater know what to call me?"

"He already knows the rules of this game. He will know what to call you," she lied again. Max looked at her, swallowed hard, and seemed to accept the rules.

"Alright, Max. Here is the first rule; you must never speak to any strangers until I give you permission."

"Mutti, you have always taught me to not talk to strangers."

"Well, yes, I know but this game is different, you must not talk at all when we are in the company of strangers . . . not even to me. Do you understand?"

"Yes . . . Mutti."

"Good. Now, here is the second rule, once you have learned all of the new words that I am going to teach you, you must never use the old ones. For example, you must never call me 'Mutter' or 'Mutti'. Call me by this new word, 'Mère'," she says. "Do you understand?"

"Yes. I understand."

My name will no longer be Frau Sofia Fuerst. It is now Madame Adeline Debauch. Do you understand?"

"Yes, I understand, Mutti."

"No Max, I am not Mutti. I am 'Mère' . . . you should say 'Ma Mère'."

"Yes . . . Ma Mère."

"Good, Max. I think you will be good at this game."

"This game seems like fun."

"Yes. I think so, too. Now, we will not call you Max any longer. You are now 'Michel' and we must call Ana, 'Jacqueline'. You and Ana are now 'Michel and Jacqueline Debauch', the children of Madame Adeline Debauch."

"Are we still your children, Mutter?"

"Yes, my darling, 'Michel' . . . You and Jacqueline will always be my children," she said hugging them tightly.

Tears formed in her eyes, despite her efforts to hold them back so that the children wouldn't see them.

"Do you think that you are smart enough to play this game?" she asks Max placing her arms around them.

"Yes, Mutti, Vater has told me that I am very smart."

"No . . . You must not say 'Mutti'. You must say, "Yes, 'ma Mère'. Remember from now on, I am 'ma Mère' to you."

"Yes, ma Mère, I will."

Sofia smiled at him.

She has a renewed sense of confidence as she explained the rest of the game to him. "Michel, we will start playing the game now," she said with enthusiasm. She thought that Max seemed very interested in playing the game, thinking that he thought it was fun. As they began to play the new game, she changed them into the clothes the woman had given them. Sofia thought about her reading primer of German to French, hoping it would come back to her, and was surprised when it did. Calling each item of clothing by its French name, she sang a little song about each one in French as she dressed them. The song always included their new names. Soon, Max was singing the song about Michel too. They played the game all day as she taught him the French name for everything in the room. She was surprised that he was able to recall all of the new words so quickly, much quicker than she had remembered learning French.

It seemed to Sofia that Max had actually been relieved when she had explained what was happening. He listened intensely. His large blue eyes, wide with interest, reminded her of Felix. They spent the rest of the day in the room, playing and learning new words. "Michel, we will continue playing the game. It will be our little secret. No one else may know we are playing a game. This is very important. Do you understand?"

"I thought you told me we should never keep secrets?"

"This is special. This is an important one and it is just one between you, me, and Jacqueline."

"I like this game . . . ma Mère," he said waiting for her reaction to his calling her the French name.

"I do too, Michel," she smiled back. "However, Jacqueline is still too little to understand the rules. Maybe, we should help her . . . Do you think you can help me with Jacqueline?"

"Yes, Ana . . . I mean 'Jacqueline' loves to play with me."

"Yes, I know. However, for this game we have to play very quietly," she said putting her finger in front of her lips, signaling. "Remember, you must not talk unless you are told to talk, or you will break the rules."

She and Max continued to play the game all afternoon and into early evening. She told the children some stories and played some games with them, all of them in French. By the time, the tall buxom woman had returned, they were very hungry and very happy to see the tray with some more food and drinks. The woman spoke to the children in French and it seemed like Max understood her *or maybe he was just hungry,* she considered. The woman presented her with her new traveling papers, going over them with her several times to make sure she understood them. By nightfall, the children were back in their nightclothes. The woman said good-bye and left them alone. "Au revoir, Michel and Jacqueline," she said making a point of saying a special good-bye to the children in French.

Sofia and the children got comfortable on the day bed again. The children had just closed their eyes and were about to fall asleep when a knock came to the door. The door swung open. The man standing in the hall said, "Adam sent me," speaking in French. He moved toward them, motioning Sofia to come with him. Max sat up on the bed, cuddling close to his mother; Ana started crying.

"Enfuis," he whispered.

Sofia replaced the German code word for "Escape" in her mind and repeated the French, "Enfuis."

"It is all right, Michel," Adeline said as she picked up Jacqueline and wrapped her in a blanket.

The man's eyes went to the pile of clothing on the floor. He pulled a gunnysack from his pocket, stuffing the clothes into it. He wrapped a blanket around Max's shoulders and helped him with his shoes.

Sofia took his hand and let him outside, following behind the stranger to an automobile parked outside. The man ushered them into the back seat of his car and sped off into the cold darkness with its headlights off. Sofia watched through the window, seeing only one dark shadow after another as the car made its way down the dirt road, its destination unknown. She closed her eyes, but sleep wouldn't come.

*

Adeline and the children repeat the same activities day after day. Each new destination brings the same routine. She loses track of the number of destinations and becomes weary from the large number of them. At first, it seems they move every night; then, they move every few days. She even loses track of the places, all seeming to blur in her memory. She begins to think that they are traveling in circles. She still has not discounted the notion that it is all a dream, a full-fledged nightmare.

"Perhaps, we're still in Berlin," she thinks as they arrive at the newest destination. The many farmhouses, barns, and lofts are all the same. The people who usher them from place to place say nothing, nor do those who provide them with supplies.

It doesn't take the children long before weariness shows on their faces, too. Sofia is long past exhaustion, but she pushes forward, knowing she must remain strong for them. She is sleep deprived and the children are showing signs of fatigue and poor nourishment. They, at least, get some sleep while traveling in the cars or trucks moving them around the countryside. However, she finds it impossible.

The anxiety of each move doesn't allow her even one moment to relax enough to fall asleep. During the day, the children need her. All of her efforts to establish any kind of routine with the children fail because of the constant changing of situations. Any kind of normalcy seems impossible to her. At times, she thinks she is losing her mind.

The long days grew even longer.

Each time she had arrived at a new destination, it would take a while to adjust and then they would leave, sometimes in a day, a few times a little longer. Through all of the uncertainty, she continued playing the game with the children. Maxi's ability to sustain the game surprised her but she worried someone would approach them, putting him to the test, praying that his first five years as a German, or that Ana's babbling, in her limited German vocabulary, wouldn't give them away.

She congratulated herself on her ability to continue the game. In fact, she actually believed it when she said, "My name is Madame Adeline Debauch," wondering if she would ever reclaim her birthright or if there would ever be a time when they could stop playing the game. The stress turned her from a slightly protective mother into an overly possessive one, guarding his or her every movements, not trusting anyone, sometimes not even herself. She detached herself from the dangerous world she had found herself in, talking only to the children and in French. She longed to talk to an adult again in her native German tongue. Upon arriving at one particular destination, her wish came true.

A knock at the door causes her to jump, leaving the children sleeping on the day bed. The door opens before she can reach it and she sees the form of a man with full facial hair and a beard, dressed in a dark overcoat and hat. Without a word, he tiptoes into the room. Her heart stops as her mind remembers *the man who was following me*.

"Bon jour, Adeline" he says in a soft quiet voice, removing his hat and taking a few steps toward her. Reaching out with both arms, he moves to embrace her. Her heart thumps and her stomach falls as his arms surround her.

"Hello, Sofia" he whispers in German.

She collapses in his arms and he lifts her up to him, pressing his mouth into her neck. She didn't need to see his face to recognize him. His voice had given him away.

"Uncle Adam," she breathes in his ear.

He holds her tightly and kisses her cheek, caressing her hair. She hugs him back very hard not wanting to let go of him.

"You are even a more beautiful woman than the girl I remember, Sofia," he says.

"I am so glad to see you."

He glances at Max and Ana, still sleeping, and smiles as he places Sofia's feet down on the floor. He takes a few steps toward them, being quiet so not to disturb them. Looking at the little face of his sleeping nephew, he says, "He reminds me of me at that age." He looks at Ana; his eyes glued to her, and whispers, "Alexandra." He quickly wipes the tears from his eyes.

"She looks like your mutter, Sofia. She's lovely."

Sofia, visibly taken by his sweetness and charm, thought about her parents and the last time that they had seen the children, feeling as if it had been years ago instead of only weeks. It had been almost fourteen years since she had seen her uncle. She almost had forgotten his sweet, gentle nature. She looked at his full beard and mustache, tinged with gray, trying to see the former man who had always been like a second father to her. Suddenly, she remembered about the fish market.

"It was you who was following me from the fish market that day. Wasn't it Uncle Adam?"

"Yes, Sofia I had to make sure you really wanted to leave Berlin. Your parents were not sure you would leave Felix."

"Felix isn't the same man that I had married, Uncle Adam."

"None of us are who we once were, Sofia."

"I was afraid to stay and afraid to leave. When my father had said he had decided to leave, I knew I must make the same decision. I did it because of the children," Sofia said.

"I made the same decision many years ago. I have been traveling all over Europe since Oma's death. Mostly, I stayed in France. I have learned and done many things in my travels. However, through them all, I have never stopped loving Germany, but I don't love what Germany is up to right now. I'll always love the country of my birth," he said as his eyes glazed with moisture. ". . . It is difficult to be that kind of a German now, Sofia. THE THIRD REICH has changed Germany into a different country, one which our ancestors wouldn't recognize," he whispered as he moved away from the sleeping children.

"I'll always be a German, Sofia. At least, in my heart," he said cupping his hand over his chest. "No matter where I go or what I do, I'll always love Germany. She will always be the country of my heart, the country that had made our ancestors proud but, sadly, that isn't the case now."

"I feel the same way, Uncle Adam."

"The actions of THE THIRD REICH are despicable. History will mark this time as Germany's darkest hour. The situation is very serious, Sofia. The outcome of the war is tenuous. It appears that Germany will be victorious, but there are no guarantees. Since America has entered into the war, the Allies have gained strength. I pray that Germany will lose the war. That is the only way to destroy THE THIRD REICH. The world will know them as the murderous, racist group of criminals that they are and there will be consequences. It is the time after the war, when we will have to pick up the pieces of our former lives that will be the most difficult. Our futures, if we live to see them, depend on Germany's victory – or her defeat."

"I'm married to a soldier, Uncle Adam."

"I know. Felix's advancement in rank had created a very dangerous situation for you. I've been working underground for some time. I have followed the politics since losing the farm and coming to live with you. I watched from France, growing increasingly concerned, powerless to do anything about it. When I had found the underground, I found a way to become involved. I have been worried about Alexandra and Gerhard, but I had been hesitant to approach them. I knew your father had developed an allegiance to them, thinking their policies were improving the country. I had to bide my time until I was certain that he had come to know the truth about them. I could trust no one. I knew if your father came to realize the truth, he would never support them. However, when Franz had joined the ranks, I became even more discouraged."

"I feel as if I have been living a hermit's life, Uncle Adam."

"Sofia, you shouldn't blame yourself for your ignorance. Oma had never understood why the farm had been lost and she blamed herself too. Don't do that, Sofia. If any blame should fall on anyone, it should rest solely with those who are the leaders."

"I am so worried about Vater and Mutter." Vater was so upset when he realized how he had misjudged them and he is worried sick about Franz."

'I know. All I can tell you is that I have used every resource to get you and them out of Berlin. I followed you from the fish market that day and afterward, I talked to your mutter and vater. I had talked to them previously about the plan to get you all away from Germany, but they couldn't tell me what your feelings would be. I needed to know if you were ready to commit to a plan, to leave not only Berlin, but also Felix. They were frantic to get you and the children away from Berlin, even if it meant having you wander the French countryside, pretending to be French refugees. Germany will never be the same, no matter who wins this war. I wanted to get you and the children out now because, in the coming months, it will be extremely dangerous to stay and probably next to impossible to leave. Time is running out."

"What about Franz, Uncle Adam? Do you know anything about him?"

"The only information that I have is that his unit is making its way to the Russian Front."

"What about Mutter and Vater?"

"I can only tell you that they aren't in Berlin. I didn't feel it safe to have all of you traveling together. The plan for their exodus took them in a different direction, at least for the time being. A few hours after they had left, the soldiers raided the bakery. It no longer exists. They confiscated everything, looking for a connection to you and the family. What they had not looted, the bombs destroyed the next day. There is very little left on the street that you had loved so much, Sofia."

She listened as Adam told her about the fate of her family. She wanted to ask him more about Felix, but she hoped that he would volunteer because she was afraid to ask. Her heart dropped when Adam finally mentioned his name.

"Felix is in grave danger now that you and the children are gone. He will have to prove his loyalty and that will not be easy, Sofia. They can be very persuasive. I can only anticipate that they will arrest him, if they have not already. The good thing for Felix is that he can tell them that your family had arranged your marriage. Maybe he can convince them that he was unaware of your father's betrayal of them. In any case, it is best that you and the children don't concern yourself about Felix. You must not tell anyone about your connection to him. He is an Officer and he has obligations. No one could possibly predict what will happen now. The Allies seem to be making progress. I pray this government will fall, one-way or another. If that happens, the courts of the world will hold the guilty parties responsible, including Felix."

Sofia's heart fell.

Adam's words brought the reality of her future before her. She loved Felix and hated him at the same time. She hated the man who had become a soldier, but she still loved the man who had taken her heart away. He was the man to whom she had made eternal vows of love and devotion, and the man who had fathered her children. She thought of the arrangement of her marriage. "Felix never loved me. He only wanted a wife whose pedigree pleased them," she concluded as a lump appeared in her throat.

She swallowed hard several times. A strong feeling of determination replaced it as she coughed, dispelling the lump, and looked into her Uncle's eyes. "What now, Uncle Adam?"

"There will be more destinations for you and the children. I can't give you any details. At least you have different identities now. You are no longer Germans. That is good as long as you are not in the company of Germans. There is always the possibility they will stop you. You must forget everything I have said today and you must be prepared to convince them that you are a French refugee and not the wife of one of their officers. The less you know, the safer it will be for you and for anyone who is helping you."

"I'm glad Oma drilled me in French," Sofia said managing a smile.

"Be brave, Sofia. Be brave for the children," he smiled. "Oma would have been proud of you. Remember no matter where you go or what happens, you will always be a German and that is something to be proud of, but not now. Now, it is something no one must know. You must abandon everything that is German." He kissed her cheek and then her other cheek, hugged her, and then he left. The next transfer for 'Madame Debauch and her children' came later that evening.

Adeline and her children stayed almost a month at that destination, the home of a French couple whose farm was in a secluded countryside. The older couple, who only gave their names as 'Rene and Gwen', took them into their home and treated them well. They showed interest in the children and the children returned the attention with smiles and laughter. Sofia had almost forgotten how wonderful it had felt to hear her children laugh. Max learned more French and Ana learned about keeping her panties dry.

After traveling for over a month, it was a relief to be in one location, but it was also a worry someone would find them. Because they were there so long, she wondered if Uncle Adam had set this location up after his visit at the last destination. Then one night a knock came at the door. They were moving again. This destination brought them back to their first destination, the farmhouse, and the tall, dark haired, French woman. She was much warmer and receptive this time. She spoke only in French.

"My name is Margo. It isn't safe for you to travel anymore. You will stay here with my husband and me. His name is Peter. We are doing this because of your uncle. We owe him a great deal."

"When will it be safe to travel again?"

"Nobody knows."

*

They were there three weeks. During that time, the children played with Margo's young children, seeming to enjoy this visit and they were unhappy when they had to move to yet another place. The new destination was a deserted farmhouse. They had arrived under the cover of darkness and didn't dare light a candle or lamp that would call attention to them. She was surprised by the morning light when she looked out the window to see that the little farmhouse set in a green valley surrounded by trees. It appeared as if the owners had just stepped out leaving dishes still on the table and cold food in a pot on the stove.

The house was clean and tidy. Sofia guessed at their location, thinking that they may be somewhere in the north of France, close to the Normandy Coast. She sensed that the soldiers were close-by when she had heard the sound of tanks in the distance and some airplanes overhead. Sometimes, the smell of gun smoke replaced the sweet aroma of lavender as the gentle breezes of the French countryside carried the pungent odors past the house. She wondered about the owners of the farm and the circumstances that had caused them to leave their home in such haste, leaving things behind.

She felt a chill.

* * * * *

CHAPTER 7
THE JOURNEY

"Somewhere on the Atlantic Ocean, Madame Adeline Debauch sits dazed on a long bench in the congested cabin below the main deck. Her face is blank, except for a stare into space. Rows and rows of benches line the room, each one occupied by a passenger who shares Adeline's same expression of terror, fatigue, and sadness, but Adeline stands out from the masses. She speaks to no one but herself, except for occasionally when she carries on a brief conversation with the empty seats beside her. Her eyes survey the room continually, checking each corner and then returning to stare into space.

Round windows, portholes, looking out onto an endless sea of water, line the interior walls. "We must be on a ship," she says to no one, her language indescribable, maybe French, part German, or some unknown tongue that only she knew. The room is strangely quiet, despite the large number of people aboard the large ocean vessel. Most of them speak in whispers, their faces displaying total weariness, disguising their ages. The young are unusually quiet; the old are stoic, almost in a stupor. Each face tells a different story, one with the same commonality, the depravity of war.

She rises from the bench and finds her way to the restroom, walking with her hands out to the side, as if she is holding hands with a person on each side of her. Once she is inside the restroom, she looks into the mirror, jumping back in surprise at the sight of the old woman in the mirror, a sight that frightens her.

"Who is this woman?" she screams at herself in a shrilled voice that echoes in the room, startling the others. Her dull and sunken eyes, once bright and glistening, now stare back at her, reminding her of the dead fish in Goldberg's Fish Market. She moves her face closer to the mirror, checking to see if the image before her is her own. She places her hand on her face, running her fingers over the valleys of her hollow cheeks and the deep dark recessions under her eyes. She smoothed her hair and brushed the tangled strands away from her face with her fingers. She fiddles with them, trying to secure them back into the braids that had been holding them in place behind her ears.

She looks in disbelief, her mouth dropping in surprise, as her eyebrows arch. Not able to recognize the image in the mirror as her own, she forces a closer look into the mirror. The once beautiful young woman now looks like a very sick middle-aged one. She tries to remember her name or the circumstances that had brought her there, but she can't recall anything that would answer her questions. She squeezes her eyes shut, trying to remember even one detail, but the harder she tries, the more she can't. Terror strikes her. She looks to the left and to the right, searching as if she has lost something. "My children, where are my children?" she screeches.

Thinking she has left the children in the cabin, sitting on the bench, she turns away from the mirror and hurries out of the rest room. She runs down the long hallway leading back to the cabin, searching for the place she had left them. Others now occupy the bench where she thinks she had left her children. She looks to the next bench and to all of those surrounding it, but can't find them. She wanders around in the large room, dazed and confused. Finally, she collapses into a seat at the end of an empty bench.

"I remember walking up the steps to get on the ship," she says aloud. "I had the children with me . . . I think that I did. The woman beside me said that the next destination is America. We must be going to America," she says aloud again.

At least she thinks it is aloud, but only her lips are moving. She looks to the right of her, studying the woman sitting next to her. "Are we going to America?" she asks in French.

"Yes. America. We go America," the woman answers in some form of broken English. Sofia quickly turns away from her, not daring to repeat the question in German.

She settles down onto the bench again, listening to a voice in her mind questioning what is happening.

She has no answers.

She chooses to divert her mind away from all of it, too weary to think. Her lips move in a silent prayer. "Dear God, please let us get to the next destination safely. Please, dear God." Overcome with fatigue, she closes her eyes, hangs her head, and rests it on her chest. She wants to sleep, to escape to that special place where her quilt had taken her. She reaches for it but her hand comes back empty. Looking at her bare hand, she speaks aloud. "If it were not for Max and Ana, I would want to die."

The thoughts of death bring an image of Oma into her mind. She is dressed in the beautiful gown and she is smiling. "No, Sofia. You must not come. The children need you. I am here now. You're safe," she hears Oma say.

She looks to the empty bench, seeing her children sitting beside her. They are silent, sitting as if they are in a trance. "I can't take care of them anymore," she whispers to no one, hoping the children will not hear and become frightened. "I am so tired, so very tired." She closes her eyes, slouches down onto the bench, and gives in to her fatigue.

The calm voice of a man who is standing in front of her, looking down at her, interrupts her dream or perhaps nightmare might describe it better. Frightened, she opens her eyes and studies the tall blond haired man. His soft blue-gray eyes stare down at her, reminding her of Felix. She thinks he might be German but she can't be sure. He is speaking English. "Are you all right? " He asks.

She stares at his lips, trying to concentrate on what he is saying, but she doesn't understand much English. His voice and eyes reassure her that he means no harm but she can't be sure of that either. He repeats his question in several languages, including French. Even though she understands, she doesn't respond, not trusting him. She sits motionless, confused, and with a look of bewilderment on her face.

"I want to help you, if you'll let me?" he whispers in German.

Her body freezes, only her eyes move, lit with a renewed intensity. She draws back and searches his face again, and then turns to her left and right checking the faces of those nearby, not wanting to react until she knew she could trust him. The gleam in his eyes and his lips that turn up at the corners in a sweet smile remind her of Felix.

"Felix," she says softly, almost inaudibly.

"Yes, Adeline. I'll take you to Felix," he says in French.

"He likes plums. Mutter will prepare him plums," she replies in French, *as Uncle Adam had instructed me.*

"Allow me to assist you, Adeline," he says lifting her by the elbow. She offers no resistance, allowing him to lead her out of the room, not really knowing why she is placing her trust in a perfect stranger who seems to know Felix, but too weak to care.

I can't play the game anymore.

"I am Frau Sofia Fuerst and I am German!" she screams at him in German.

The area around them goes silent.

Just like it had in the fish market.

Her heart falls and her stomach flips as she recalls her discussion with Uncle Adam telling her to keep her German ancestry a secret for her protection. She recognizes the expression on the faces of the other passengers.

FEAR

"Will you allow me to help you, Frau Fuerst?" he whispers.

She searches his eyes.

"How does he know my name?" she asks herself but unbeknownst to her, her voice asks him.

"Adam Schmidt," he answers. "He sent me to help you."

The mention of Uncle Adam's name gives her permission to let him help her. She willingly allows the man with the reassuring voice who had said her uncle's name lead her, placing her fate in his hands.

"I am so tired. I need my quilt," she murmurs to him in a language that sounds like German, mixed with French and a great deal of gibberish.

"I know. I know, dear. Take my hand."

She follows him with her eyes closed, holding onto his arm but they are not out of the room before her legs buckle underneath her. He catches her in his arms, lifts her limp body, and carries her to a cabin where he places her on the bed, takes off her sweater and shoes, and places a blanket on top of her.

Her eyes open for just a moment before she gathers up the blanket, presses it to her nose, trying to smell the familiar aroma of her quilt. In a moment, she goes to that special place where children play and laugh, and no one is hungry, cold, tired, or frightened. Her dreams take her back to her little room over the bakery in Berlin. Although sound asleep, her finger moves on the blanket in a circular motion, stroking the same spot that she had once stroked on her quilt.

*

The Next Morning

Oma is there holding Sofia in her arms; she feels safe. Suddenly, just as Oma is about to pull her closer, she awakens. "The quilt isn't here. It's a dream," she says to no one.

Her stomach aches.

"I'm not back in my room above Vater's bakery," she thinks as panic overcomes her.

"Where am I? Max? Ana?"

She jumps out of the bed, searches the room, and calls out their names repeatedly until, in total frustration and near hysteria, she runs into the long hall, shouting their names.

"Max! Ana! Jacqueline. Michel. Max. Ana. My children!" she screams in French and then in German and then in her own language.

The hall is desolate.

Every door on both sides is closed.

No one responds to her pounding on the doors. She runs down the corridor, up the steps, and onto the open deck of the ocean liner, shaking with fear and confusion.

"MAX. ANA. JACQUELINE. MICHEL. MAX. ANA . . . What have I done? How could I lose my children? I have lost my children . . . Where are my children?"

She pushes open the doors leading to the huge outdoor deck. The bright light of the morning sun, shining in the blue sky, greets her, blinding her. She squints and tries to focus. "Where am I? Where are Max and Ana?" she shouts in German, or was it French?

"MAX! ANA! JACQUELINE! MICHEL! MAX! MAX! ANA!"

Her eyes dart to the left, to the right, and then right to left, and back again. She searches the crowds of passengers. They are standing in a long line, seemingly moving toward a common place. She tries to see around them, looking under them and over them as she continues calling out the names of her children and asking anyone who would listen if they had seen them. She is oblivious to the fact that the ship was no longer moving. It has docked at its destination, Ellis Island, in New York Harbor.

"Have you seen my children? Have I lost my children?" she asks a man who stands before her with an incredulous look on his face. He shrugs his shoulders and looks away.

"Max. Ana. Jacqueline. Michel," she calls as she checks the benches lining the walls of the deck, now all empty. She looks under the tarps covering parts of the ship, under and inside the lifeboats, and everywhere else. She grabs hold of a woman's sleeve and starts asking her about the children. She is speaking in German and then French but the woman just shakes her head and turns away.

Undaunted she searches for the children. The throng of passengers who had lined up to exit the ship sweeps her along with them as they move toward the exit gate. A sea of humanity, all hoping to pass through the identification center, wraps around her like a swarm of bees. She has no idea where she is going or what to expect when she gets there, she just hopes that wherever it is, Max and Ana will be there safe.

An unknown force pushes her along the ship's deck, down the ramp, onto the open dock, and into a large warehouse. Thoughts of her children and pictures of their faces flash in her mind as she moves behind the crowd of passengers toward one of the lines of patrons standing in front of long tables. The two figures in front of her move to the side, revealing the faces of two women who were sitting behind one of the tables. "Do you speak English?" one of the women asks her while displaying the same question, printed in many different languages on a large card displayed in front of her.

Sofia moves her lips to speak but collapses on the floor, falling in a heap, escaping again to another destination looking for her children. She dreams of that place again, the one where her children could play, dance, sing, and not be afraid.

*

Several Days Later

"Welcome back to the world, Frau Fuerst," the woman says in German when she sees Sofia open her eyes. Sofia doesn't reply. She closes her eyes and blinks, opens them again and watches as the woman, dressed in white with a nurse's cap on her head, takes her wrist in her hand and checks her pulse. She closes her eyes and returns to that special place only she can go.

Several days later, she opens her eyes again. A woman in white with soft brown eyes and a sweet smile speaks to her in a low voice. "You've been sleeping for a long time, Sofia. We've been worried about you," the nurse says in German. This time Sofia wants to talk but her lips can't form the words. The nurse offers her a drink of water from a straw. Sofia studies the woman constantly while she sips on the straw, wondering about the nurse who speaks German, but isn't dressed in the uniform of the German nurses.

"Where am I?" she finally whispers – brave enough to speak in German.

"You are in the United States of America," the woman answers.

"Am I in prison?"

"No, of course not . . . You are in a hospital in New York City . . . You have been here for a long time."

"Escape," Sofia says in German but it sounds a little like French.

It is Sofia's own language.

She closes her eyes, again, too tired to speak.

*

Hours Later

When she awakens the next time, a man is standing beside her bed, next to the nurse. He looks familiar, but she is confused as to how she might know him, or where and when she might have met him. "Do I know you?" she whispers.

"My name is Wilhelm Miller, Frau Fuerst. I hope I can help you," he says in German as he pulls a chair close to the side of her bed.

"I do know you."

"We met on the ship."

"Yes."

"I work for an organization to help refugees, bringing them to safety in the United States. Do you remember? I helped you when we were still on the ship."

"Yes."

"I apologize for leaving you alone in the cabin. I had intended on escorting you to the admissions desk, but you had left the cabin before I had returned. When the ship was about to dock, I searched for you, but I couldn't find you. I decided to wait at admissions for you. I was there when you collapsed."

"Yes," she murmurs not really remembering what had happened.

"You are going to be fine. You have suffered a concussion and extreme exhaustion, but the doctors say you will recover. You are a very strong woman, Sofia."

"Yes," she whispers.

"The organization that helped you escape Berlin has ties here in America and there are many German Americans who want to help. They have arranged your passage to America with information supplied by your Uncle Adam. I watched you on the ship, but I did not want to call attention to you unless it would be necessary because you are German and many of those on the ship don't look favorably on that. I saw you on the bench the day before we were to dock at Ellis Island and I knew that you needed help then, and I couldn't wait any longer."

"Yes."

Once you are feeling better, you will go to a rehabilitation hospital. This process helps refugees who are fleeing from Europe become citizens of the United States. Would you like that, Sofia?"

She gives him a silent stare.

"You should get some rest now, Sofia."

She gets a faraway look in her eyes but suddenly her brows narrow and wrinkles appear in her forehead.

"Max! Ana! Where are my children?" she cries.

Startled, Miller looks at her with a confused and shocked face.

"Michel! Jacqueline!" she yells before he can speak.

His face drops as he hesitates, trying to find words. "I'm sorry to tell you, but, your children, they are dead, Frau Fuerst."

Sofia's face blends into the stark white of the sheets.

Her stomach turns upside down.

She bolts upright, tearing at the tubes, screaming at the top of her weak voice.

"Max! Max! Ana!"

She continues screaming as she tries to get out of the bed, pulling on the side rails. Miller jumps up; he runs toward the door. "Nurse, come quick," he hollers as he runs down the hallway toward the nurse's station.

A doctor and two nurses follow the distraught Miller back toward Sofia's room. Miller watches as the nurses hold her down and the doctor fills a syringe with some medication, tests it with a quick squirt, and gives her the injection.

"I'm so sorry. I thought they had told her about the loss of her children in France?"

Sofia's thrashings stop; her eyes roll back into her head.

Max and Ana's faces flash in her mind for only a moment before everything goes black. She lapses into a deep, drug-induced sleep where her mind remains blank.

At last, her journey to escape Berlin finally ends – or maybe it has just begun."

*

Sofia stops speaking, overcome with emotion, unable to tell any more of her story. Tears flow down her cheeks. Hers are not the only ones. "I'm so very sorry, Sofia," Janene chokes through her tears. She is thankful when Clarissa enters the room.

"I'm sorry, Miss Sofia. Mr. Jeffrey has asked me to check on you."

"Tell him our meeting is done for now," Sofia says in a soft voice.

"Yes, Miss. Sofia," Clarissa confirms.

"I'm tired, Janene. I would like to finish telling you my story after I have had a chance to rest and collect my thoughts. If you don't mind, Clarissa will show you to your room."

"I understand, Sofia. I'm tired myself," Janene says getting up and following Clarissa back to her room.

*

Twenty Minutes Later

She hears a knock. "I'm sorry to disturb you, Janene," Jeffrey apologizes.

"Oh, you aren't disturbing me, Jeffrey."

"Bill is waiting downstairs, but I would like to talk to you first before we go down."

"Of course, what is it, Jeffrey."

"I'm concerned about Sofia. She isn't in good health. This is proving to be a real ordeal for her, although she would never admit it," Jeffrey says. "Perhaps, this will make it easier for you and Sofia," he says, handing her a copy of the biography he had written about Sofia.

Janene looks at the title, A NEW BEGINNING and looks back to Jeffrey for an explanation.

"It is the story of her life as I had written it when I had first met her. That was shortly after her first book about the magical quilt had become a best seller and the first film a box office hit. I placed a bookmark on the part of the story where Sofia had left off today. She has read the story so many times that she has it memorized. Sometimes, it is particularly hard for her to discuss her life, especially the loss of her children.

When she had told me that she wanted to tell you the story of her life by reciting every word of my book, I feared that she wasn't up to the task, but she insisted and, in case you haven't noticed, Sofia can be very stubborn."

"Of course, thank you, Jeffrey. I was getting worried about Sofia, as well. She seemed so upset after she had told me the story of losing Max and Ana."

""Yes. Well, actually she has been upset for some time. She worries that her life will end before she has had the opportunity to accomplish everything."

"I am surprised. She has accomplished so much already."

"Sofia had never really gotten over what had happened to her children. The only thing that had helped to get her through the ordeal was her belief in the traditional upbringing her family had taught her. However, when she had run away, she denounced her German heritage, finding that she could no longer embrace it after what had happened. She looked to her quilt, her childhood security blanket, to restore some of the faith she had always had in her family and country. She had always harbored guilt over her decision to run away with the children but once she had started a new life in America, she wanted to put her past behind her and raise her son in a free country."

"When she had lost Randy, she had just about given up. She had lost everyone she had ever loved. I think that the only thing that kept her going

193

was a kind of intuition, or feeling that his daughter had not really died. For years, she had harbored that feeling, at least privately. When you had contacted her about finding information for your article, as well as your own biological family, and she had realized that you were Vietnamese, she told me that she thought it was Randy, reaching out to her from the grave."

"I'll always be grateful that I had made that internet search."

"As I said, Sofia had decided that she had her own special way planned for telling you about Randy and your biological family. Maybe we should call it a day?" Jeffrey asks.

Janene nods her head in agreement.

"I'll persuade her that you are tired and need some time to reflect on what she has told you so far."

"Yes, of course."

"I thought maybe you and your father would like to see a little of Pittsburgh. Sofia thinks of it as her second home now. She loves it so. I have arranged for you to have a tour and dinner. I'll join you, but Sofia must rest."

"Thank you so much, Jeffrey."

"You are very welcome . . . and thank you."

* * * * *

CHAPTER 8
AN AMERICAN FAMILY

Hours Later

Following their tour of Pittsburgh and dinner in an exclusive restaurant in the downtown area of the city, at the top of one of the tallest buildings, and overlooking the point of the confluence of the three rivers, Jeffrey, Bill, and Janene return to the mansion. After saying goodnight, the three retire to their rooms. Unable to think of sleep, Janene dresses in her nightclothes, and curls up on the chaise lounge with Jeffrey's book in hand. She is pleased that he has left a bookmark on the section beginning with Sofia's arrival in Pittsburgh as a refugee, exactly where Sofia had left off telling her story. As she begins reading, she understands now why Sofia had never used the word 'I' as she had told the story. The fact that she had memorized every word of A NEW BEGINNING, Jeffrey's biography of her, totally amazes her. She begins to read, but she hears Sofia's voice in her mind, reciting each word.

*

10 October 1944, Pittsburgh

Annie Schneider stops one more time to adjust the crocheted doily that is covering the top of the table located near the front door of her home in Pittsburgh, Pennsylvania. She is in a nervous tizzy to make everything just perfect before leaving for the airport, wanting it to be that way when they return with the newest refugee they had agreed to sponsor. For Annie, everything about her modest home in the predominantly German American neighborhood where they live has to be perfect.

"I have an odd feeling about this one, Hal," she had said to her husband last evening when they had received the call from Bill Miller.

"You always have those odd feelings, Annie. Every time they have asked us to sponsor someone, you say the same thing. This one isn't any different."

Now, she could hear Hal shouting from his position outside, holding the door of the cab. "Annie, I have the keys. Remember to put the lock on the door," he yelled from the curb. The cab driver put their suitcases in the trunk as he checked his watch. "Come on, Annie, we are on the clock now. We will miss our flight if we don't hurry."

As she walked down the long flight of steps of her century old home on the north side of the city, she reviewed her checklist one more time, hoping that she had packed everything they would need for their trip to New York. She thought of their conversation with Bill from the relief organization last evening, telling them about a young German woman who had needed help. Bill is an old friend of theirs. Actually, his real name was 'Wilhelm Mueller' at one time but he had changed it. He wanted to hide the fact that he was German because of the rising anti-German sentiments in the United States, and the fear of reprisals.

"This woman is in pretty bad shape, Hal," Bill had told them during the phone conversation. Hal held the phone away from his ear so that Annie, nestled into his shoulder, could hear the conversation, too. "I first saw her on the ship. She seemed to be in a stupor, suffering from extreme exhaustion. She could hardly speak. Records had indicated she was French and that is how she boarded without any difficulties, but a ship to shore telegram from her sponsor, a man named Adam Schmidt, also known as, Adam Dupree, confirmed that she was German. She talked in some language that was a mixture of German, French and hysteria."

"What makes you think she'll be a good match for us, Bill?"

"I don't know. She looks so childlike. I thought of Annie immediately and then the fact that she was German, of course. You and Annie seemed like the best match for this poor woman. She needs a lot of emotional support. She has sustained great losses. Her sheltered upbringing in a very traditional German home and the war in Europe has shattered her life."

"So, you think she will bond with us?"

"You never know, Hal. In this case, I think Annie will be the deciding factor. She keeps talking about her Oma and some kind of a security blanket. The Doctors have determined that she might be suffering from Amnesia."

"This woman may have more problems than we can handle."

"Well you might be right. However, she really has no other place to go, at least right now. Helping a German isn't on the list of priorities for this country, or many others for that matter. If you and Annie don't take her, she will just stay in the mental hospital and rot. I hate to see that happen. She looks like a little girl. I want to find out some more information about her husband. He is a German officer. From what I know and as far as anyone is concerned now, she is a refugee from Alsace Lorraine going by the name of Adeline Debauch. I don't think there are any security problems to concern anyone. Dupree said that he could guarantee that her husband wouldn't be looking for her."

"Okay, Annie and I'll fly out tomorrow. We will bring her home, if she will come, and then we will just have to take it day by day."

"Good. I was hoping you would say that. I'll see you at the hospital tomorrow afternoon."

"Good. See you then. Bye."

Annie and Hal had volunteered to help the refugees, but it seems to them that Sofia's story was more severe than the others had been. Each time they would travel to New York City and arrange to bring the refugee back to their home in Pittsburgh. All of their prior refugees had some other contacts to find in the United States. This refugee was the first German they would try to help. When they realized that this one apparently was very alone, they didn't hesitate, reacting immediately by making all the necessary arrangements.

This process of helping the victims of the war had worked well in the past. The sponsors would meet with the refugee, talk with counselors, and then bring the refugee back to their home, where he or she waited for further processing. It wasn't a permanent arrangement, but rather a temporary transition for the refugee.

Annie and Hal's previous experiences had all been positive. Although they had been through the routine before on several occasions, they were still apprehensive about what to expect with each particular situation. Since both she and her husband were of Germanic descent, both raised in bi-lingual homes with German as the primary language, matching Annie and Hal to Sofia seemed like a good idea to Miller. They also had strong ties to local German organizations, which had offered additional resources.

Of course, each of the immigrants went through the strictest of security checks. However, there was a decisive negative feeling tone for anything "German" because of the war. It had started during WWI and had escalated into a serious problem for German Americans and the Japanese Americans. The government had ordered the Japanese Americans into camps, treating them more severely than the German Americans. Americans with obvious German ancestry found it difficult as well. Many wouldn't even admit to their German heritage, often changing their names to avoid any connection.

The taxi driver held the door while she and her husband entered the cab. In a few moments, they were on their way down the steep hill that took them into the Downtown section of Pittsburgh. Annie noticed the skyline of the golden triangle that was the keystone for the city. She couldn't help but think about the city's rich history, beginning as a settlement, known as Fort Pitt, for the early settlers of Pennsylvania. She thought it was ironic that the city located at the jointures of three rivers would again be the site of a group of new "settlers," who were fleeing Europe yet another time.

The cab driver found his way through the streets easily. He cruised onto the route that signaled their exit out of the city. Soon they were on a plane with others who had also volunteered to help in this relief effort. It was a private plane; everyone on the plane was involved in the program to help people displaced by the war. They had gone through the strictest of military security checks. It proved to be a good system that helped those who needed help desperately.

However, thoughts of the system and its success couldn't take the feelings away that Annie harbored. She had a premonition about this case. She couldn't put her finger on it, but she knew this woman was going to be significant to them in some way. From the moment the word had come, she felt a twinge. Of course, she didn't mention the twinge to Harold, knowing he would just tease her.

She and Harold Schneider had been married for twenty years. Harold had always told everyone "his Annie" was "the love of his life." She felt the same about him. They had met when Harold had been in the hospital, recovering from pneumonia. Annie had been his nurse. Harold was a Professor of Psychology at the University. When Harold saw Annie for the first time, he knew it was "love at first sight."

They had similar backgrounds and seemed perfectly suited to one another. Both born and raised in Pittsburgh and of first generation Germanic descent, they had met each other through their membership in local German organizations, but had never made a connection until Annie had nursed Harold through his pneumonia. It had always been Harold's dream to get his Doctorate in Psychology and Annie dreamed of becoming a nurse while they both hoped to have a large family. However, after many years of trying to conceive, they had accepted the fact they would never have children of their own.

It had been the heartbreak of their lives, but Harold had caught his dream eventually and earned a Doctorate degree. Annie continued nursing, getting a Master's Degree and teaching Nursing Skills at the University.

When the war had come along, they both were in a position to help with the war effort because of their now reduced schedules. They were in their early fifties; they had the means and ambition to help in any way. Harold had lost his older brother in WWI. The fact that the world was now engaged in another war with Germany disturbed him greatly.

When the Japanese had bombed Pearl Harbor in 1941, bringing the United States into the war, Harold was frustrated. Despite his age, he yearned to become involved. Through their church, Annie volunteered to work for a Relief Organization. At a time when German Americans feared revealing their German heritage, Harold and Annie Schneider felt compelled to embrace their German culture, despite the growing animosity toward anyone Japanese or German. As the war had progressed, German Americans had become very concerned for their loved ones in Europe. However, most got little support from a world that was rapidly developing a hatred for the country that had destroyed their lives. Annie was praying for an end to the war as the plane set down in New York City.

"The victory must be an Allied one," she prayed.

*

New York City

When Annie and Harold had met Sofia for the first time, they felt Sofia was probably the saddest person they had ever met. Dressed in a hospital gown that hung on her small, emaciated body and her blond hair tied into a long braid down her back, she waited in the Psychiatric Ward of the Rehabilitation Hospital. She sat hunched in a chair, her arms wrapped around her knees. The young doctor introduced them but she sat motionless, looking at them with her piercing, sad eyes. Her face was chalky and as white as the hospital gown.

The Doctor made a point of introducing Harold and Annie again. "Sofia, I want you to meet some people who want to help you," he said. She didn't speak or acknowledge him, but her eyes fixed on the two of them, and then settled on Annie.

"Sofia, Annie, and Hal would like you to come to their home for a visit," the doctor said to her in French. Previously, he had explained to Hal and Annie that Sofia wouldn't respond to anything said to her in German.

Sofia looked away from the doctor, her eyes focusing on Annie.

"Would you like to leave the hospital, Sofia?" Annie smiles at her. Sofia still doesn't move. Shall we go to the cafeteria? We can have some tea."

Sofia makes no response.

"Would you like to have some tea with Annie, Sofia?" the doctor suggests when he notices Sofia's apparent connection to Annie. However, Sofia still showed no response. Finally, the doctor took the initiative, encouraging Sofia by lifting her elbow, and helping her to her feet. Annie made the next move.

"Come, dear," said Annie in German, placing her hand on Sofia's elbow.

Sofia looked directly at Annie when Annie spoke in German, her body relaxing as she studied Annie's eyes. She allowed Annie to lead her down the hall to the Cafeteria. Hal and the doctor followed.

"She walks like she is in some kind of catatonic trance," Hal whispered to the doctor.

"Yes, but she is much better than when she had first arrived."

"Perhaps, we are biting off more than we can chew."

"The fact that she had even allowed Annie to take her by the arm is a major accomplishment."

Later That Evening

Annie and Harold discussed their first meeting with Sofia, both expressing concerns and reservations about taking on the responsibility for the latest refugee. "Annie, do you really think this is a good idea? I'm not sure we can be of any help to this young woman."

"I told you before we came, Harold, I have a premonition about this one. Now that I have met her, there is no doubt in my mind. I want to take her home with us," she said with a strong determined voice.

"What makes you so sure?"

"It was her eyes, Hal. I saw something in those eyes."

*

December 1944

In the early days of Sofia's coming to stay with the Schneider's, each day seemed to blend into the next. Harold and Annie bonded very quickly with her, caring for her as if she was their own daughter. To them, it had seemed as natural as if she *was* their own daughter. However, for Sofia, it wasn't going to be that easy. Her physical injuries were healing. However, her psychological and emotional ones posed a long road to recovery. She suffered from amnesia and depression from the physical and emotional shock brought on by traumatic events she had experienced. The doctors cautioned Hal and Annie not to expect much.

The war had started to turn when the Allies made strides into Europe on their way to Berlin. The War in the Pacific worked in their favor as well. There had been credible reports of assassination attempts against the Fuhrer. Europe was in turmoil, brought on by the air raids from both sides. Harold and Annie had made every effort to protect Sofia from all news about the war, thinking that she wasn't up to handling it.

The refugee center had provided a short description of Sofia's history, revealing that she had fled her husband and that all of her family was either dead or missing. Sofia's two small children were dead, although Sofia had no apparent recollection of them. The doctors in New York had told them that, because of her age, she most likely would recover from all the physical problems. However, her psychological problems were another story. He emphasized her fragility, recommending professional treatment. Harold and Annie arranged for an appointment with a renowned psychiatrist in Pittsburgh, Dr. Isaac Simons, a friend and colleague of Harold's. He began treatment by making a house visit to their home soon after Sofia had arrived. He confirmed the diagnosis made in New York, not giving a prognosis until after he had some time to work with Sofia. Harold and Annie arranged for that to happen.

It was easy for Hal and Annie to like Sofia. She was very childlike, speaking little in a strange language, never smiling, and withdrawing into her own special place. Annie's nursing background   and her motherly instincts drew her out, a slow process, not an easy one. She started by including Sofia in some simple food preparations in her kitchen. Annie did all of the talking, trying to picture what it might have been like for Sofia in Germany. She thought the familiarity of a kitchen would bring Sofia into reality.

Sofia let Annie brush her hair and fix it in two long braids and Annie thought this was a positive sign that she was bonding with her. She had the appearance of a teen-age girl. Her periods had stopped and her chest was flat. Sofia showed no signs of bonding with Hal in those early days.

They were persistent. The more they did for her, the healthier she became. Annie liked making some favorite German dishes. She helped Sofia in the kitchen and Annie noticed her special talents for baking, seeming to have the recipes stored in her head. However, she couldn't really communicate them to anyone; even her native German seemed to have disappeared.

Annie and Harold constantly translated everything from German to English and from English to German and occasionally they translated French to English, or German. Sofia responded. She started to smile. Once she even giggled. Annie thought they would take any little sign as progress. They allowed her to sit in the parlor, listening to instrumental music on the phonograph, never on the radio, for fear something would upset her. She sat for hours, just listening.

One day, Hal gave her a pencil and a notebook. He suggested she start writing down some of her thoughts or even drawing some pictures. Surprisingly, Sofia accepted the idea readily, but the marks on the paper were more like the rudimentary drawings of a young child. Sofia was very protective of her entries, not wanting to share them, and keeping the book hidden under her pillow. The entries were very confusing, impossible to understand, and were only decipherable by her.

The doctor said this was good, showing signs of progress. He suggested Annie give Sofia a special blanket. He shared that during her stay in the psychiatric ward, she had cried for her 'quilt'. Annie found an old quilt in the attic. Sofia looked at the old blanket and looked confused. Annie left the blanket with her. Soon, Sofia showed signs of attachment, keeping it on her bed at all times. Sometimes, Annie would find her curled up in the corner of the room with the quilt wrapped around her. Her entries in the diary improved. French words started to pop into the fragmented entries, occasionally a few German ones, too.

In only a few months, Sofia was writing almost totally in French. However, she still did not speak. The doctor encouraged other activities to increase communications. Harold purchased some art materials and gave them to Sofia, who drew while listening to the phonograph. They decided to give her a special room in the attic for her art activities. Sofia seemed pleased to retreat to this special place. The attic had a small window, which overlooked the street. Harold placed a small chair in front of the window. The subject of all of her work was always the same: pictures of children. Soon, Sofia seemed to be comfortable enough that Harold took her to museums and the library, always very selective about what he showed her.

The program called for Sofia to stay with the Schneider's six months. After that, they would evaluate her situation. In late March, the evaluation was completed and the paperwork submitted to the organization. The organization approved Sofia's staying with Hal and Annie if they wanted to continue. They agreed to keep Sofia, providing extended care for her. Harold made sure the papers were legal by contacting immigration and hiring a lawyer for her. He knew the process of getting an American Citizenship would be difficult because of the war. However, Harold put everything in place so that, one day, Sofia could become an American citizen.

A name change seemed appropriate, if Sofia was to become an American, especially with the feeling against anything German. Changing her name from German to English amounted to just a translation. The German surname 'Fuerst' translated to 'Prince' in English. 'Frau Sofia

Fuerst' became 'Miss Sofia Prince.' By April 1945, the three of them were living as a family. Harold and Annie had no other family and they had become so fond of Sofia, they had decided to change their 'Last Will and Testament', making her their sole heir. Of course, they never revealed this to Sofia. She wouldn't have understood anyway. They were proud when Sofia suddenly started calling them, 'Annie' and 'Hal.'

Annie and Harold tried to protect Sofia from any news of the war, fearing a relapse, but Harold knew that in order for Sofia to move forward, she would ultimately have to face her past. He watched for some signs from her. The first event occurred at a session with the doctor at the psychiatric hospital.

During that session, while talking to the doctor as they had been doing for the previous year, suddenly and without any provocation, Sofia sat up from her prone position on the couch, looking bewildered and startled. Whatever the thought was that had prompted that response lasted only a second and then it was gone. Those moments started to happen more often after that and they lasted longer, happening at home as well. An incident happened again in a therapy session when Sofia sat up, appearing very startled. This time she spoke, but only one word, "Max!"

The doctor suggested Sofia enter the hospital for inpatient care. They admitted her to the psychiatric ward of the hospital on Oct. 13, 1945, almost a year since she had come to live with them in Pittsburgh. It was a little over a month since the United States had dropped the first atomic bomb on Hiroshima, Japan. While she was there, some news came about Sofia's family.

Hal had learned that Sofia's parents had died in Switzerland in their flight out of Berlin. They had also learned that her brother, Franz, had died at the hands of a Russian firing squad, and that the Germans had hung Uncle Adam. The last piece of the puzzle came with news about her husband. Felix Fuerst was dead, killed during the bombing. It was now official – Sofia Prince had no living relatives.

After a month of not seeing or talking to Sofia, they visited her. They were pleased with her condition. She was extremely happy to see them and remembered them with perfect accuracy, wanting to come home with them. The Doctor told them she was responding to treatment, and although her memory was beginning to return, she was still not ready to go home. They visited her twice weekly. Each week of the visits, Sofia showed improvement, remaining in the hospital for three months. The doctor told them that he thought that they should become a part of her final therapy sessions.

Sofia had come a long way. She spoke of her childhood and her dear Oma, and of her beloved quilt. She described her parents, her brother, her uncle, and her husband. She talked of her marriage and the birth of her children. She remembered that a bomb had exploded on the farmhouse and then she asked questions about the children. The doctor told her about their fate.

Annie held one of Sofia's hands as the three sat together on the doctor's couch. Hal held the other. They watched the doctor's lips as he told Sofia the news her family was all gone. Sofia collapsed, crying uncontrollably. Hal and Annie held her tight and supported her body, as if it she was a rag doll.

The doctor reassured them Sofia understood everything. He had already told her the details in therapy, but he wanted to reiterate it all again in the presence of Annie and Hal. Sofia had agreed to this. He suggested that she stay a few more days explaining that he wanted to make sure she was ready for discharge. When, Sofia had protested, expressing her strong desire to leave, Hal convinced the doctor to discharge her. They took her home.

'Frau Sofia Fuerst' no longer existed. In her place was Miss Sofia Prince, an American, not by birth, but by choice. She had no living relatives. The only people in her life were Harold and Annie Schneider, whom she now thought of as her adoptive parents. Sofia celebrated the New Year's arrival with Hal and Annie in March instead of January that year. They toasted with champagne to the beginning of a New Year for 'Miss Sofia Prince."

"To a new beginning," Harold said, raising his glass. It was truly a "new beginning" for Sofia in 1946.

*

In the days and months after Sofia had come home from the hospital, she grew stronger, both physically and mentally. She mentioned her life in Germany infrequently, each time carefully avoiding those subjects that were particularly emotional for her. When the time for an evaluation had come, she asked the agency to allow her to continue living with Harold and Annie Schneider. She had come a long way since they had first found her in New York, but she still had a long way to go. They willingly offered her all the support she needed. Harold's many contacts with the university helped Sofia to start anew.

Harold was particularly concerned that Sofia should make some new acquaintances. He felt it extremely important and necessary for her to socialize in order for her to get better. Her ability to adopt English as her first language amazed him. She spoke with only the slightest of an accent, not easily detected. It was a plus, because of the continued hatred for anything German, an aftermath of the war. In addition, Sofia shared her writings and drawings with them, revealing a special talent for the creative fields.

"Harold, I have something I would like to share with you," she greeted him one day. He had just returned from a workshop at the university.

"That's wonderful, Sofia, just wait until I hang-up my coat and hat, and I'll read it" he said. Sofia brought the diary over to him, anxiously holding her journal in her hand. She acted like a little girl, excited about her homework, plopping down on the sofa beside him.

"This is wonderful, Sofia," he said, reading it to himself. I really think you have some writing talents. I have been thinking, maybe you should take some writing classes?"

"You mean go back to school? Harold, I haven't been in school since I was twelve!"

"I know Sofia, but age doesn't have to be a factor. You can go to school at any age. I think you would love it."

"Well, if you think I could do it, Harold. I could try."

"Good! I'll arrange it tomorrow. I know an English/Writing professor whose class I think you would like."

Sofia was apprehensive at first about attending the classes. Her fears soon abated after the first class; she found an overwhelming love for the subject matter. Harold also was instrumental in enrolling her in English Language classes. She loved them all and she did extremely well. She consumed her time with learning the language, writing, and reading books. She astounded the professors.

Annie gave Sofia a typewriter. She and Hal watched for her reaction and thought she would burst with excitement. Hal enrolled her in a typing class. From then on, she spent every free minute in front of the typewriter. She wrote short stories, essays, and poetry for the variety of classes at the university. She made new friends, some of whom she invited to the house to meet Annie and Hal. However, as much as Sofia loved writing, she wouldn't save any of her writings. She only shared the writings that had been her assignments. She never wrote about her life or her experiences. When she finished an assignment, she trashed it. The professor encouraged the students to 'write about things you know.' She couldn't bring herself to write about her life before Hal and Annie. The thought of ever having to write about her past panicked her. Pleasant things, at least those that did not cause her pain, found their ways into her writings. She never referred to the past in any capacity, or to the future. She could only write about the present.

*

1 January 1947

The world was trying to forget the war but finding it hard to ignore the role of Germany in creating widespread horror. Sofia never talked about her German background. Not even an accent would give her away. Harold and Annie relinquished some of their protectiveness, believing Sofia needed to become independent of them. The independence would be her impetus to begin a new life as an American, which they thought would be the best course of therapy she could have. "Sofia, we've been thinking; we want to talk to you about something," Annie said to her one morning, as they had finished their breakfast.

"Did I do something wrong?"

"No. You did not do anything wrong, Sofia. Don't be silly. We've been thinking about your future and we thought maybe you would like to get a job," Harold says.

"Did I hear you say that you wanted me to get a job?"

"Well, not exactly, not at first. That is what we wanted to talk to you about," Annie says.

"We've noticed how much you love children. We are thinking you have a gift, a special aptitude. Would you like to become a teacher?" Hal asks.

"I don't know, Harold. Do you really think I'm qualified to become a teacher in the United States?"

"I guess you wouldn't think you were qualified, Sofia. However, that is just the point. You could be made to feel qualified," Annie added.

"There's a need at the Relief Organization for volunteers to work at the Children's Center. We thought of you right away. You would love working with the children, and you would be perfect with them," Hal said.

"Hal and I thought that if you tried working at the Children's Center and liked it, perhaps you would like to continue your studies at the university. You could get the qualifications necessary to teach children and get paid to do it," Annie said.

"Do you mean it? Do you think I could do that? I love working with children and the idea that someone will pay me surprises me. That would be wonderful."

"Good. Then you will start tomorrow. We have arranged for you to go to the Center. I'll take you there and I'll come to pick you up. It isn't far from the University," Harold said.

The next morning, Harold took Sofia to the Center. It was the first of many days to come where she worked with the children. Harold enrolled her in classes at the university. He also started the process for her to become an American citizen. He would act as her sponsor and the classes she took at the university would help in the process. She needed the certification of achievement of a high school diploma. That would lead to University and earning a Degree. Sofia worked hard. She loved the classes, and especially loved working with the children.

She talked at great length with Harold about her activities at the Center and her classes at the university. A special program allowed her to start working with the children while she was still attending the university. She worked with children at the university's campus school. The school population included children from many different backgrounds.

Sofia became totally involved and infatuated with her role as a teacher. She found that teaching the 'Three R's': Reading, Writing, and Arithmetic, as they were called, was completely fulfilling. Miss Prince, as the children called her, felt comfortable in her role as their teacher.

"Sometimes, I have to remind myself I had been born in Germany," she confided to Annie one day. It was shortly after she had succeeded in getting the papers for American citizenship.

"You may have been born in Germany, but you are an American now, Sofia," Annie reminded her. "America is a country of immigrants. That is why they call it 'The Melting Pot' of the world."

"Annie, when I think about what is happening in Germany now that the war is over, I feel like I'm living in a dream. It doesn't seem real to me. I can't believe how my life has changed," she told Annie. "It is as if my former life had belonged to someone else."

"Sofia, when I think of when we had found you in New York, I can't believe how far you have come. You are a very strong person. I know you will have a wonderful future and the United States will be proud to call you one of their own," Annie said giving her a hug and holding her tight.

*

September 1949

At the beginning of the school year, a unique opportunity presented itself to 'Ms. Sofia Prince'. It was a new student-teaching program, beginning with an apprenticeship. If she completed the program successfully, perhaps she could win a teaching position.

The opportunity proved to be the single most important thing that could have happened to Sofia. She excelled; by early January 1950, she had her own classroom of first graders.

"This is the very first time I have ever been given any money," she told Hal and Annie on the day she had brought home her first paycheck.

"I bet you are excited, Sofia. Maybe you shouldn't cash it; maybe you should frame it," Harold teased.

"Oh no, Harold, I'm going to cash it and then I'm going to spend it," Sofia said laughing. "I have never had my own money to spend."

"What are you going to spend it on, Sofia?" Annie asked.

"I don't know, Annie. Now that you mention it, I really don't need anything. You and Harold have been so good to me. You have provided me with everything I could have ever needed or wanted. Maybe, I could spend it on you. May I buy you something?"

"That's ridiculous, Sofia. We don't need a thing." Harold said.

"Then, what will I do with it?

"Maybe you should frame it," Hal teased.

"Do you really think that?"

"I was just kidding you . . . Of course, you shouldn't frame it. You should put it in the bank," Harold said.

"I should? Oh . . . Will you help me with that?"

"Tomorrow, we will take you to the bank to get you set up with a bank account. You start saving your paychecks. Then, when you need something, you will have the money to buy it. The bank will even give you some money for letting them hold your money for you."

"It is called 'Interest'," Annie said.

"Maybe, it is best if I find my own place. I mean to live on my own?" she asked looking toward Annie and suddenly becoming very thoughtful.

"Where would you ever get that idea? Of course, we don't want you to live anywhere else. We love you, Sofia. You are like a daughter to us," Harold replied.

"This is, and always will be, your home," Annie said.

"I'm so glad. I am so happy here with you. I am happier than I have ever been in my life. Well, except when I had Max and Ana" she said with a sudden sadness in her voice. They noted that this is the first time she had mentioned the children since she had left the hospital.

"Now, Sofia, don't think about the sad times of the past. Don't ruin this wonderful day that is yours alone. Think about how wonderful your life will be now," Annie said. Sofia remembered Uncle Adam had said that when he had reminded Oma about not "thinking about things that make you sad." The next day, Annie and Harold helped Sofia set up a checking account and taught her how to use it. She continued to live with Hal and Annie and work as a teacher.

*

Sofia loved living in Pittsburgh. It seemed to her that the little community where they lived reminded her of the old neighborhood. Pittsburgh, like Berlin, was a big city, but she felt they both shared the markings of a small town with all of their neighborhoods. Sofia thought that Pittsburgh epitomized the idea of America as a 'melting pot' because of its large number of ethnic neighborhoods. Her work had provided the perfect opportunity to learn about the city and grow to appreciate each of the communities for its unique flavor as per its ethnicity. Sofia thought of the children in her classrooms as a mirror of the world with a wealth of culture and diversity.

Slowly, she seemed to put her past behind her, embarking on a new and exciting future. She met many new people, bonding with the university family and school families. However, more than anything, she held a special place in her heart for each of her students. Every one burned a special place, right next to Max and Ana. One day, her students surprised her with a large decorated cake. Several of the mothers from the Parent Teacher Association told her about their custom of presenting the teacher with a cake on her birthday.

"Happy Birthday, Miss Prince," the children shouted as the "PTA Mother" brought the cake into her classroom. They burst out in song, singing the traditional birthday song.

"Oh my, today isn't my birthday," she admitted.

"We didn't know the correct day and nobody else seemed to know either, Miss Prince. We just picked a day at random. Today is your adopted birthday," Mrs. Sloan, the 'Homeroom Mother' said.

"Well, that's wonderful. From now on, today will be my birthday!" Sofia said, thanking them again. *In Germany, the birthday person throws the party,"* Sofia remembered wondering why she would suddenly recall a German tradition.

"My birthday was September 6, 1919," she thought to herself.

Later, Sofia shared her day with Hal and Annie. "Do you believe I wasn't able to remember my birthday until today? I was so embarrassed in front of the children. I told them today would now be my new birthday even though I remembered the real one.

"Don't give it another thought, Sofia. Many people forget their birthdays – on purpose," Harold, laughed. "Do you want to celebrate your birthday on your real day or today, March 21st?"

"I think you should celebrate one on September sixth and one today, March twenty first," Annie grinned.

"Does it sound silly of me to say that I like the idea of celebrating it on two days?"

"Not at all but, just for curiosity's sake, why are you saying that?"

"Because I feel as if the September date will honor my German heritage and the March date will honor my love for my new country, America."

"Then it is settled. We will celebrate your birthday twice every year, beginning today. Come on Annie, get your coat, and hat. We're taking Sofia to get ice cream."

* * * * *

CHAPTER 9
RANDOLPH ROBERT BLACKBURN II

The school year went by quickly. In the spring of 1950, Sofia talked to Harold and Annie about taking a holiday during the summer break. Harold and Annie agreed it was a good idea. "Have you thought about where you would like to spend the vacation, Sofia?"

Sofia immediately thought of her holidays with Felix to the Baltic Sea, especially remembering the one when they had taken Max and she had gotten pregnant with Ana. "I would love to see the ocean again. I have always been happy there. Could we go on a holiday to the ocean?"

"Here in the United States, we call it a 'vacation'. Yes, we can do that easily. Annie's folks have a place at the ocean. It is located off the coast of the Atlantic, in Delaware."

They decided to make plans; Harold starting making some calls. Sofia thought of the last time she had seen the ocean with Felix. As hard as she tried, she couldn't remember seeing the Atlantic when she had fled France, but remembering the Baltic Sea had a special significance to her. The Atlantic Ocean had brought her to this new life and to the realization that she had lost her children. She still felt the pain of losing them, completely accepting the fact they were dead. Mental pictures as they lay helpless in the farmhouse haunted her.

Lately, the role she had played as their mother had dominated her thoughts. She decided that it was because of her work as a teacher and the fact that she had begun to think of her students as her own children, bringing back memories of Max and Ana. She could never forget them but she hoped that she had come to some acceptance of the fact that they were gone forever, but her preoccupation with memories of them worried her.

She looked forward to spending some time at the beach cottage. Harold and Annie had decided to spend the summer there with her.

Sofia was awe stricken when they had arrived at the Fenwick Island cottage on the beach. The Atlantic Ocean was as beautiful as she had imagined. The beautiful sunrises and sunsets demanded her attention every day. She was relaxed and contented by merely sitting on the oceanfront porch and writing. Harold and Annie had a group of friends with whom they had enjoyed previous summers. They were mostly the same age and they had a lot in common, connected through the university. Several couples also owned homes in the area. The group shared invitations to visit their homes.

Sofia was pleased that Hal and Annie's University friends received her so graciously. One couple, Robert and Regina Blackburn, had impressed her. She liked them from their first meeting, impressed by their warmth and sincerity. Robert, now retired from the military, had been a high-ranking officer of a unit of all Negro soldiers during the war. One evening, they brought their only son, Randolph, to dinner with them. Once a pilot, named after his father, his family had decided to call Randolph by his middle name of 'Robert'. When his son was born, they called him Randolph. .

Randolph and Sofia were about the same age and they seemed to immediately drawn to each other.

*

"Hello, Sofia" he said to her the next day when she answered his knock on her door.

"Hello, Randolph. It is nice to see you again. Come in."

"Thanks. I hope I am not intruding. I just had a thought. If you have not had lunch yet, maybe you would like to join me?"

"I haven't had lunch yet, and I would love to join you. What did you have in mind?"

"There's an out-of-the-way place not far from here. They serve a nice lunch – nothing fancy, and the atmosphere is good, but I must warn you, the stares may make you feel uncomfortable."

"What do you mean, Randolph . . . stares?"

"The ones on their faces . . . That is, when a beautiful white girl walks in on the arm of a Negro."

"I'll get my purse."

*

After their luncheon date, they spent almost every day together. Sofia noticed the looks they got when out in public. They reminded her of those directed at her and the children at the fish market so long ago. Going out in public with Randolph did not make her as uncomfortable as it had seemed to make Randolph, but she agreed with him to go to "out-of-the-way places," away from the icy stares of so many. The day before he was to go back to duty, he told her he wanted to keep in touch with her. Three days later, when Sofia arrived back in Pittsburgh, a large bouquet of yellow roses awaited her. The card said simply, "I am thinking about you, Randolph."

Harold and Annie were happy that Sofia and Randolph seemed to have become friends. They were extremely fond of Randolph. They had known the Blackburn family, both socially and professionally, for many years. Harold and Robert had once been classmates and professors at the university. Ten years younger than Hal, Robert had enlisted during the war and had seen action in the Pacific, decorated for his heroism. They had known Randolph since he had been a little boy. However, despite their close ties to Robert and Regina, Hal and Annie worried about the cultural differences, recognizing the great strains on the relationship of a mixed race couple in America. They knew that racism was a prominent force in America, and Sofia's emotional health was very fragile after all the tragedies that she had endured.

They feared for Sofia's reactions and worried about how she would handle, not only a new relationship with a man, but with the inevitable problems that would befall them as a mixed race couple in a racist America. The advent of yet another war, this one in Korea, and Randolph's role as a pilot had also given them pause to think, concerned for Sofia's emotional state after what she had gone through with Felix.

They didn't want her to be hurt again. They talked to Sofia about it when she had first started to see him in Delmarva, but they decided it would have to be her decision. Although she wasn't their daughter by blood, they felt she held that title by love. They felt that she had come a long way since her days as a young refugee, but her past wasn't something that would just go away either. Despite their concerns, they didn't want to overstep their boundaries. After all, Sofia was a grown woman.

They returned to Pittsburgh, putting their concerns away after Sofia had shared that Randolph had returned to duty and she was anxious to open her classroom for a new school year. However, the look on Sofia's face when she had read Randolph's card with the bouquet of roses had told them that Sofia had opened her heart to the handsome young officer. Concluding that there was little for them to do, they decided to keep their concerns and opinions to themselves.

"I think it is best if we just let things take their course," Hal had said to Annie.

"That's what I'm worried about, Hal. You know me and my premonitions."

*

Janene turns to the next chapter in the book Jeffrey had given her. She is surprised to find a handwritten marker in the book. As she reads it, she smiles:

"Janene, Jeffrey is a worry-wart. I am fine. I am looking forward to telling you the rest of my story. Jeffrey thought that if he would give you his biography of me, it would be easier on me, but I am enjoying the story telling sessions. I am much stronger than he thinks. Let me know where you stop reading tomorrow at breakfast. I'll proceed from there – just to make Jeffrey happy! Love, Oma."

"I think Jeffrey had a good idea in giving me the book to read. It will take some of the stress away from Sofia. She is looking rather frail. I hope someday my husband or 'significant other' is as thoughtful as Jeffrey," she thinks as she begins reading again.

*

September 1950

Sofia was back into the routines of teaching elementary school, hardly having time to think about Randolph and the wonderful, but few weeks, that they had shared at the beach. However, in her quiet times, she remembered the special meetings they had shared. She knew she had become attracted to Randolph physically. It had been a long time since she had experienced that kind of relationship. From the moment they had met, she had felt drawn to him, comparing him to Felix, noticing similarities, as well as the differences between them right away. "Felix was interested in my thoughts and my ideas, at least that was the way our relationship had started," Sofia thought. She had blamed herself for not being a good wife to him, when he had stopped showing interest in her physically. She wondered about Randolph and, if they had a relationship, how it would turn out.

Randolph was easy to talk to, taking control of the conversation. The same way Felix had been. Their conversations never lulled, nor were they boring. They could talk for hours and never discuss the same thing twice. Sofia thought the biggest difference between the two men were the physical ones. Felix was fair skinned and blond. Randolph had dark skin and dark hair, and just as Harold and Annie had been the first Americans whom she had ever met, the Blackburn Family had been the first African-Americans.

She hated the racist philosophies. A picture of Esther flashes in her mind and her memories of Esther bring more sad recollections of her family. She knew her parents wouldn't have approved of anyone but a 'good, solid German man' for her. Her thoughts about what comprised a 'good' man had come a long way since her experience with the arranged marriage to Felix. He had let her down and she didn't want to go down the same road again. Sofia thought of Felix often when she was with Randolph. The thoughts alarmed her. She felt that she was falling in love with him. A relationship such as the one she had with Felix terrified her. The disappointment in finding out that Felix had never really loved her, but was more interested in his ambitions, had devastated her.

She and Randolph spent countless hours together at the beautiful beach area of Delaware, off the beaten path, out of the way, avoiding the eyes of others. The atmosphere was ripe to take her back to her memories of the Baltic Sea, where she and Felix shared the most intimate times and had conceived Max and Ana. The time that she had once cherished is far too painful to remember now. Pictures of Max and Ana still burn in her memory, surrounded by feelings of guilt. With the help of the doctors and time, the intense pain lessened, but she had never stopped blaming herself for the death of her children. However, since meeting Randolph, many of the feelings have resurfaced.

However, as much as she rationalized, she couldn't stop herself from heading fully into a relationship with Randolph. She felt a connection so strong it was as if a magnet was pulling on her. She couldn't let all the flashing memories of Felix interfere with the beautiful new relationship that was growing with Randolph. They became very close, in a very short time.

They found a "little world of their own" where they easily retreated. None of the secrets of the past and the problems of the present existed there. Nothing mattered to them except they were together. Sofia knew she was falling in love again. There was little she could do about it, or even wanted to do about it. Even if she wanted to stop her feelings, she knew she couldn't, and she felt that Randolph felt the same way. The two were oblivious to all their similarities, differences, likes, dislikes and backgrounds. The 'moment' was the only thing that mattered. They spent the rest of the summer enjoying each other, hoping it would never end.

However, their relationship was a purely platonic one. The thought of having sex again intimidated her. She knew she wasn't ready for those intense emotions. She thought Randolph must have known this somehow, because he never pressed her for a sexual relationship. "An intimate relationship was reserved for marriage only. That's what my parents taught me," Sofia told Randolph. However, when they were together, she longed for that closeness she had had with Felix after their marriage.

Randolph respected her wishes. When they separated in Delaware, they both agreed to remain friends. "I'm going to war, Sofia. I don't think it is fair to you to change our relationship with a one night stand."

"Randy, I'm not ready for such a relationship. I don't think you are, either."

*

Sofia had only been back to work a few weeks when Randolph contacted her again. Her heart fluttered when she answered his phone call.

"Sofia, I have been going crazy. I can't stop thinking about you. I wake, and there you are. I go to sleep, and there you are. Sofia, I have fallen in love with you. I know it sounds crazy. We have only known each other a couple of weeks. I know that we come from two very different worlds and we don't have a whole lot in common, but, Sofia, I have fallen in love with you. Will you marry me? Marry me, Sofia. Please, marry me."

"Randolph, I feel the same way. I know it is crazy, too. I can answer your question honestly. "Yes, Randolph, I'll marry you. I'll go to ends of the world with you."

They made plans to marry, selecting the weekend of the Thanksgiving Holiday in November 1950. They wanted a simple wedding, easily accomplished because Sofia had no family, although she considered Hal and Annie her family, and Randolph's was limited to his aging parents and a few aunts and uncles. Between the two of them, the guest list amounted to about twenty-five people. Sofia accepted Annie's offer to make all the arrangements.

They held the ceremony at an old German Church where several generations of the Schneider family had worshiped. They held a small reception in a ballroom of a downtown hotel, overlooking the 'Golden Triangle' of Pittsburgh. Sofia had to return to the classroom after the Thanksgiving Holidays, and Randolph was leaving for a new assignment overseas. Although Sofia had rented a small apartment for them, they decided to consummate their marriage in one of the Honeymoon Suites at the Hotel after the reception.

*

Her first intimate experience with Randolph had proved to be a very special one for Sofia. She was nervous and apprehensive and feared that she would do or say the wrong thing. Randolph took the lead offering her tenderness and patience. She tried to concentrate on her love for him but her thoughts kept returning to Felix. Finally, not able to relax, her body tensed, she confided her fears to Randolph.

"Randolph, I love you so very much. I want to remember this time as the most wonderful moment in my life, but I can't stop thinking about Felix," she confided as they lay in bed together.

"Sofia, it is only natural for you to think about your first husband. Don't feel guilty. Please don't do that to yourself. We are making our own memories now, darling – just let me make love to you. Let me show you how much I love you," he said pulling her close.

"I do love you, Randolph, and I don't want to think of Felix."

"Sofia, I'm not trying to make love to your memories right now. Just relax, please, just let me love *you*, Mrs. Blackburn," he said. "I love you no matter what or who you are thinking about, Sofia," he said as he kissed her neck and found his way to her lips. His touch took away all of the memories. "He is right," she thought. "I need to make some new ones," she decided as she relaxed in his arms and let him make love to her.

Afterward, the two lay together in silence, neither of them wanting to move, nor to lose one moment of their precious time together. "I resolve, from today forward, never to talk about the past or the future, just to concentrate on the moment and how much I love you," Randolph said breaking their silence. "I hope that you will do the same."

"I love you, Randolph. I love you for who you are; I'll always love you. Please don't leave me. Come back to me."

"No matter what happens, Sofia, I'll never leave you. I'll be right here," he says as he places his hand on her heart."

Her heart skips a beat. "That is what Oma had said."

*

The Next Morning

Sofia accompanied Randolph to the airport; they said their farewells in the cab because Sofia couldn't bear to see him get on the plane. Earlier, they had decided they wouldn't say good-bye. It was much too permanent for the new, 'Mr. and Mrs. Randolph Blackburn II'.

"I love you, Mrs. Blackburn," Randolph whispered before kissing her.

"I love you with all heart. God be with you, my darling," Sofia replied releasing him and watching him as he walked away.

"Felix never said that he loved me. He never kissed me like Randolph does," she thought after telling the cab driver to take her home. She felt a chill. She had promised herself that she would never compare her two husbands, but after the experience on her wedding night with Randolph, it seemed impossible. "Please, dear God, let him come back to me," she prayed.

*

1 December 1950

Sofia was living alone for the first time in her life. Even though she and Randolph had never spent a night together in their new apartment, Sofia was very happy there preparing for the time when he would come home to her. Perhaps then, they would buy a house in Pittsburgh. She awaited any communication from him, worried the war would change their lives as it had changed hers after marrying Felix. She spent every minute when she wasn't teaching, trying to find information about the war in Korea. She looked forward to the upcoming 'Winter Break' and the holidays, longing to be with Randolph. On Christmas Eve, she got a telegram from the Air Force. She sat down in a chair before she read it. As the words appeared on the page, she hung her head and cried.

"Randolph Blackburn II . . . Missing in Action . . . No further information is available.

The words pierced her heart.

"No, please, not him too."

The news about Randolph brought Harold and Annie to the realization of their worst fear – Sofia would relapse into the catatonic state in which they had originally found her. They were particularly concerned when Sofia told Annie she had missed a period. They hoped that she wasn't pregnant and yet were overjoyed at the same time. They encouraged her to see a doctor and he confirmed that she was, indeed, pregnant.

Sofia was delighted with the idea of having another child but the news about Randolph had curbed her enthusiasm. She waited anxiously with mixed emotions. She was overwhelmed with joy at the thought of having Randolph's baby. However, her joy faded as her despair grew over the fact that Randolph was still missing. The diagnosis of a pregnancy at high risk only added more anxiety. The doctors had advised not returning to work. The policy of the school district was that a woman couldn't teach after she had started to 'show'. Harold and Annie urged Sofia to stop working immediately and take it easy. They also wanted her to give up the apartment she and Randolph had rented, and return to living with them.

However, they respected her right to make her own decisions and supported her when she decided to continue teaching, staying in her own apartment.

*

A Few Months Later

Word arrived; Randolph was no longer missing in action. They had found his remains with his downed plane. The news crushed Sofia. The next few weeks were a blur for her. She went through the motions necessary for Randolph's funeral, contacting his parents in North Carolina and traveling by train with Hal and Annie for the full military funeral.

As she watched and clutched the American flag close to her, they lowered Randolph's coffin into the ground. Tears streamed down her face as she thought of Randolph and the child she was carrying. She looked at the folded flag pressed against her belly holding the new life growing inside her, and she thought of Felix, Max, Ana, her parents, Uncle Adam, Franz, Esther, and the Nazi flag that had driven her from Europe and taken them all away from her. She felt completely and utterly alone.

After the funeral, they returned to Randolph's childhood home where his relatives and friends greeted her and offered her sympathy. She told his grieving parents they could expect a grandchild, and they hugged and kissed her as their sad faces showed smiles. She took the train back home with Hal and Annie. They wanted her to come and stay with them rather than go to the apartment, but Sofia insisted on going to "her home."

The next day, Hal got a call from a frantic Sofia.

"I'm bleeding, Harold."

Hal called an ambulance and they met Sofia at the emergency room. The bleeding stopped but the doctors warned that the stress would jeopardize her pregnancy, possibly taking her into a miscarriage. They discharged her to the care of Hal and Annie and advised her to take it easy.

She decided that it was best to give up the apartment as well as working. This seemed to heighten the impact of Randolph's death, making it even more real for her. She grieved for Randolph and concentrated on the new life she was carrying, but the grief grew deeper and deeper as it now included the loss of her whole family and everyone she had ever loved, except for Hal and Annie.

* * * * *

CHAPTER 10
RANDY

The first day of September in 1951, Randolph Robert Blackburn III was born. Sofia decided to call her new son, 'Randy'.

Her emotions were up and down like a rollercoaster. When she had held the baby for the first time; her heart skipped a beat, overcome with joy and sorrow at the same time. Her thoughts went to Max and Ana, imagining what they would look like now and what they would think of their new stepbrother. She remembered how happy Max had been when she had brought home a new baby sister to him. It saddened her to think that the little baby boy looking into her eyes for the first time was her only living relative.

"I can't tell you what will happen, darling. However, I know one thing for sure; I'll do everything I can to make sure you are safe. You will not suffer the same fate as your brother and sister. You are completely dependent on me, just as Max and Ana had been. That thought terrifies me, Randy," she said, looking down on his little face. "When I had Max and Ana, I had Felix with me and I had my parents. Then, I had no one. Thank God, I have Hal and Annie, but how will I ever do this?" she asked herself, but talking to her newborn son.

"I don't know how, but I promise you, Randy. I will."

When she thought of the task ahead, raising a bi-racial child in America as a single mother, without his African-American father, she felt completely overwhelmed. Already, she had noticed the reactions of others. *The nurses seemed surprised when they had realized that he belonged to me.* She recalled that she and Randolph had discussed the problems they might encounter if they had children. He was certainly aware of the wide spread prejudices and he knew she wasn't. "I have spent my whole life dealing with prejudice, Sofia. I am still dealing with the hatred of some people. It is hatred that has no explanation and can cause so much pain," he had told her.

"I'm not sure I am strong enough to be your wife, Randolph," Sofia said quietly.

"Sofia, we will deal with it. We will deal with it together," Randolph had promised when they discussed their racial differences.

"I guess I'll have to figure this out on my own, Randy," she said to her infant son. "I guess we will have to deal with it together – just you and me."

She thought of how the nurses had raved about Max when he was born. *He is 'too pretty' to be a boy.* To the Reich's delight, he was the perfect example of an Aryan child. His blue eyes and crop of blond hair boasted his pure German heritage. Randy's dark eyes and crop of curly brown hair announced his heritage too.

"When I look into his eyes, I see you, Randolph. I miss you so much," she whispers as if Randolph is there with her. She looked at the sweet face of her newborn son, thinking how unfair it was that Randolph would never know his son and his son would never know him.

"Randolph wouldn't want me to dwell on his death. He wants me to move on," she thought, remembering how Oma used to talk to herself and answer herself, too. From somewhere deep in her despair, a flash of a bright light showed her the courage she needed. "I have faced devastating losses in the past and I'll overcome this one too."

Randy depends on me – just as Max and Ana had.

"You will be safe with me, Randy. It will not be like what had happened to Max and Ana. I promise that you won't have their fate," she whispers in his ear. She felt an energy she had not felt in a long time. Every moment that she spent with her son, she gained an added sense of strength and empowerment. *Raising Randolph's son will be my mission in life!* She knew that all of her experiences in life thus far would be the catalyst for her to do just that. She embarked on her new role as an American mother with trepidation, but also with enthusiasm. She knew she would have a great deal to learn, but she felt Randolph would be helping her, not in person, but in spirit."

*

11 September 2008

The bright morning sun brings a beam of light into the room as Clarissa opens the drapes of the guest room.

222

"Good morning, Miss Janene," Clarissa says. "Miss Sofia has given me instructions to wake you and invite you to join her for breakfast on the patio. Your father is already there, having his morning coffee with Mr. Jeffrey."

"Thank you, Clarissa. Tell them I'll be right down."

*

Two Hours Later

"Let me begin again, Janene," Sofia says as she again makes herself comfortable under her quilt in the library. Jeffrey had arranged to take Bill to the sports stadiums on the North Side of town and they are in route.

"I have turned the recorder on, Sofia," Janene says. In addition, I wanted to make sure I told you that I am enjoying reading Jeffrey's biography, but listening to you tell the story personally is my first choice. However, I'm worried about you."

"I appreciate your concern. Please don't give it another thought. I loved the biography and I wanted to share it personally with you when I had discovered that you were Randy's daughter. I have read it so many times that I have it memorized. During the time when Jeffrey was writing it, it was a very special time for us. Until then, I had not come to any reconciliation about what had happened. It had been a long process for me to accept everything and move on with my life. Sharing it all with Jeffrey as I had fallen in love with him had proved to be the turning point in my life, another new beginning. "

"I'm glad that you had decided to share your story with me and I'm also impressed with the way you have decided to do that. Your hospitality to my father and me has been outstanding. We are very grateful."

"You are family and are welcome here any time, as is Bill and your brothers. In fact, I would like to invite you, Bill, and your family back to spend the upcoming holidays in November. We have a great deal to be thankful for this year."

"That is very kind of you and, of course, we will accept the invitation."

"I always seem to be starting anew but, I must say that this 'new beginning' is making me very happy. Oh, but I do digress; let me refresh your memory. You said at breakfast that you had read the biography up until the time that Randy had been born?"

"Yes. I'm anxious to hear more about him."

"I am anxious to tell you, Neeny."

Their eyes lock at the same time as their smiles begin.

"I've been looking forward to telling you this part of my story. I can never tire of talking about Randy. It was July 1957 and we were vacationing in Rehoboth Beach, Delaware.

*

Sofia is exhausted when she arrives at the seashore. The 1956-57 School Year had been a long one. She loved her work as an elementary teacher in the public schools, but it was challenging and difficult work. She was always very involved with each of her students and this year was no exception. Her students' academic successes were paramount and she put a great deal of pressure on herself, making sure each one of them reached his or her potential.

Despite the stress, this had been an extremely rewarding year for her. All of the students in her class had made grade level or above. The tests results were spectacular, delighting her. "The reward for the highest achieving homeroom goes to Mrs. Blackburn's third grade, Room 207," the Principal, Mr. Harris, had announced. Sofia felt a rush. All of the trials and difficulties of the year vanished as she looked at the faces of her young students.

The year had been an eventful one for her in another way. Randy had entered Kindergarten. She could hardly believe he was old enough to attend school. She enrolled him in a class in her building, glad that she would still be able to be close to him. He did extremely well academically. She never had any doubts. He was already reading when he had entered school. However, she was more concerned about his socialization skills.

There were no children in the neighborhood. Harold and Annie were getting up in years. Robert and Regina Blackburn lived in North Carolina. He had little contact with children his own age and no interaction with any mixed race children. Sofia hoped his Kindergarten would give him the social skills he needed but it didn't turn out the way she would have wanted. Randy was the only bi-racial child in the class. There were other African-American children and there were other Caucasian children, but Randy was the only child of mixed race. He found it difficult to bond with either of the two groups and often went off by himself.

She remembered the first time that her students had found out that "Randy is Mrs. Blackburn's son." Each of their faces had shown surprise and Randy had noticed. She had explained to Randy as best as she could, telling him that they were reacting to her "as their teacher" in their school, surprised that one of their teachers had a child in the same building. Despite what she had told him, Sofia knew the real reason that she couldn't address the issue of prejudice with him, especially when she didn't understand it herself?

His first school experience had confused him as he tried to figure out why the students seem to reject him, and Sofia had been equally as confused as to how to handle it. He was one of the few students in the school of mixed race. She looked forward to the end of his school year because she planned to take him to Delmarva where she had met his father. It would be Randy's first visit to the ocean, and Harold and Annie had expressed their desire to come as well.

*

When they had arrived in Delaware, Sofia was still reminiscing, enjoying mental images of the smiling faces of her students. On the last day of school, every one of her students had hugged her and thanked her. "Good-bye, Mrs. Blackburn. Have a great summer! See you in September," her students had said as they had filed out of the classroom. Sofia handed each one of them an envelope containing a report card, knowing that their good grades would please their parents. That was one of the rewards for a teacher's year of hard work and dedication.

Randy carried her suitcases upstairs as she beamed with pride. "Randy, you are such a big boy. Such muscles you must have to lift that case all the way up the steps," she told him. As he brought the case into the room, he smiled broadly showing his teeth, reminding her of Randolph. Once in the room, he found the big bed and started to jump up and down.

"This is a big bed, Mommy. Will you be sleeping here alone?"

"Yes, it is a big bed, Honey. And yes, I'll be sleeping here alone, unless you are going to be frightened again and will want to curl up in it with me?"

"Well, I'm not sure. Maybe I can sleep with Hal and Annie. Which bed is theirs?"

"I thought we had settled this at home, Randy. You are too big to still want to sleep in our beds."

"I know, but that was at home, Mommy. I'm not sure about this house."

"Come on, I'll show you your room," she said taking him across the hall to the room with a wallpaper border of boats floating around the ceiling above a set of bunk beds.

"Wow. This is really cool."

"Is 'cool' good or bad?"

"Oh, it is good. Cool is good. Can I sleep on the top bunk?"

"I think we can arrange that" she said hoping he would change his mind by bedtime and not fall out of bed. As they continued to unpack, he came in and out of her room several times, stopping to jump on the bed each time. Sofia cautioned him about falling and he decided to try a few jumps on his own bed. Before she knew it, making one last jump, he closed his eyes, and fell asleep. Knowing that the long trip had worn him out, she decided to let him sleep.

Her room had always impressed her with its bright, airy qualities. Simple, white lace curtains covered the windows, reminding her of the ones Oma had made for her room at the bakery. A small wicker chest with a mirror was on the other wall. Some framed prints of ocean themes hung in a grouping on the wall above the bed and a cotton throw rug lay positioned carefully in front of it. The nightstand held a small wicker lamp with a crisp, lacy, white shade and a doily underneath. The doily matched those at Hal and Annie's house in Pittsburgh and she pictured Annie bringing them to the beach house.

Sofia remembered the linens from the first day she had arrived in Pittsburgh, so many years earlier. They reminded her of the ones tucked away in the trunk she had to leave behind in Germany. Annie had told her they had special significance because her grandmother and mother had made them. Thoughts of the ones her mother had placed in the chest in her room made her feel sad, knowing that she had no idea what had happened to them, and feared that they had been victims of the war as well. For a fleeting moment, she thought of Oma's quilt, but she quickly shook off her sad feelings, not wanting to feel the pain of leaving it behind again. She diverted her attention away from thoughts of the past. "I won't spend one moment thinking about my life in Berlin," she thought. Feeling at home and glad she had come, she smiled remembering the summer she had met Randolph. The double poster bed pushed into the corner of the room, covered with bright white linens and piles of pillows proved to be too inviting. Soon she was asleep.

*

Several Hours Later

A knock on the door awakened Sofia. "Sofia, it is dinner time," said Harold.

"Oh, Harold, I must have fallen asleep. When did you arrive?"

"Several hours ago . . . We decided to let you and Randy sleep."

"Are we going to eat dinner now?" asked Randy, wide-awake, as he followed Hal to the doorway. "I am hungry."

"Yes, but we must get ready quickly. We don't want to miss the early bird."

"What kind of bird, Pap Hal?"

"We will explain later, Randy. Hurry and change your clothes."

"My friends from the university have shared that there is a new seafood restaurant on Rt. 1, Sofia. Annie and I thought we would try it, or would you rather go to 'The Fish House,' as we had done in the past?"

"I think whatever you and Annie decide will be fine with us, Hal."

"Well then, we all better get ready. Come on, Randy, I'll help you pick out something to wear to dinner," said Harold. "I think those new Bermuda shorts your mom bought for you in Pittsburgh will be just fine."

"Are you sure, Pap Hal? None of the boys at home wear them."

"Trust me. I am sure. You will fit right in here at the beach."

Sofia got out of bed and started to rummage through her suitcase. She knew she didn't have time to shower. A quick sponge bath, the application of some make-up, a quick change of clothes, and she was ready. She took one final look in the mirror, checking the simple beach dress and sandals, and joined them downstairs. A flood of memories surfaced, but she fought them off. "We better get a move on it, Sofia. If we leave now, we will be able to beat the crowds and get the early bird menu," Harold hollered up to her.

"We're coming, Pap Harold," Randy yelled back. Sofia was still explaining the meaning of the 'early bird' as they walked out to Harold's car. Soon, they were on their way to Bethany Beach. As they pulled away from the house, her memories roll by again. The coastal area had always struck her, reminding her of the times she had spent with Felix. The house was an older one, reminding her of the older homes in Europe. The structure of the house exemplified the character one would expect of a house at the beach. Its many windows, balconies, and decks for viewing the ocean were Sofia's favorite parts of the house. She took a deep breath and inhaled the salty air, allowing the sounds and smells of the sea to captivate her. The feeling brought thoughts of Randolph and Felix, followed by thoughts of Max and Ana. "Now, I'll have new memories, ones of Randy." Time had not helped to lessen the pain of losing her little boy's father and she forced herself to think about the gift of having his son in her life. As she recalls the joyous times with both of her husbands at the beach, she decided that she had absolutely no desire to meet another man. *Randy is all I need.*

It was a lovely evening in late June. A beautiful sun was setting in the western sky over the bay. She had always thought that the Atlantic Coast boasted the most beautiful sunrises and sunsets in the world. "Where does the ocean end?" Randy asked as he gazed out of the car window at the Ocean.

"This ocean ends on the shores of another continent," Annie told him. "It is the continent on which your mother was born."

"When we get back to Pittsburgh, I'll show you on the globe in my study, Randy," Hal interjected.

Randy was full of questions. Sofia was glad she had Hal and Annie, and she feared the day when they wouldn't be there to help her explain the many things he would need to know. They had become a replacement for her parents, and grandparents to Randy. She knew she needed all of the help she could get to raise Randy. She looked lovingly at Randy's innocent little face, feeling a pang of nostalgia for his father. She saw so many faces in his. He had his father's deep brown eyes, curly dark hair and dark complexion, but outside of the colors of his skin and hair, he was the image of Max and Ana. Although his complexion was much lighter, his appearance announced his heritage.

Once Randy had gotten to be of school age, she had found out just how difficult the task of raising a bi-racial child in America would be, especially as a single mother. As they pulled into the parking lot of the new restaurant, Sofia was lost in thought, worried about his future and her ability to raise him.

They entered the restaurant and a host directed them to a table. Sofia had become accustomed to the constant stares from others; however, she still resented them. She knew Randy was now getting old enough to notice and she anticipated giving him explanations, though not really being able to explain it herself. After sitting down at their table, they noticed a couple at a table nearby who were flashing steely glances their way, whispering under their breaths. Even though Sofia had experienced the reactions of others to her appearing with an African-American child many times in the past, each new instance hurt her. However, the unrelenting stares of this couple became disturbing, causing embarrassment to not only her, but also Hal and Annie. Randy didn't seem to notice. Instead, impulsively, he started a conversation with the small boy who sat with the couple.

"Do you want to play with me?" he said taking a small metal car from his pocket. The little boy smiled and started to say something, until the woman interrupted.

"You turn around here and mind your own business, Theodore," the woman said in a harsh voice as she placed her hands on his shoulders.

"Mother, I just wanted to play with him," the little boy replied.

"You aren't allowed to play with that kind," the woman continued sending an icy stare in Sofia's direction.

228

"Theodore, do what your mother says. You aren't allowed to play with that little boy," his father added. By now, several tables of diners had stopped to look at the exchange and the restaurant had gone silent. Randy's mouth dropped. Tears filled his eyes as he hung his head down. Sofia thought of the fish market.

"Randy, let's see if we can read the menu," Annie said trying to divert his attention and ease his disappointment.

"I think you will find something good to eat on this early bird menu," Hal said as he put the menu in front of him.

"Does the bird have things for children, Pap Hal?"

"Yes, Randy, lots of things for you to choose," Sofia finished casting her eyes from the family, losing her appetite for dinner.

*

On the return home, Randy asked questions about the boy in the restaurant. They tried to explain to him why his mother had refused to allow her son to play with him. However, they provided little that would help Randy. It was difficult enough for them to explain it to themselves.

"There are some people in the world that dislike other people for no good reason," Hal tried to explain. "They are just afraid of anybody who they think is different from them."

"What do you mean by 'different', Pap Hal?"

"Well, it means things that aren't the same," he said struggling to define the word.

"Am I 'different' than that little boy?"

"No, you are no different. It was just that his parents thought so and they are ignorant people," Annie interrupted. "That little boy in the restaurant doesn't dislike you. His parents are some of those people who don't like others who are not the same as they are," Annie said. "You know how you like broccoli but you don't like carrots. Well, it is sort of like that."

"I have a reason for not liking carrots, Nana."

"You do?"

"They taste awful."

"The little boy's parents have no reason for disliking you or anybody else. They are wrong to teach their son to be mean to you, or to anyone else," Sofia smiles.

"Some of the kids in my school are like that. They don't like me."

"They don't even know you, Randy. You must not let them hurt you. There isn't anything about you not to like."

They pulled up in front of the house and continued their conversation as they walked up the path. A loud "Hello" from their neighbor, Vivian Long, interrupted them.

Harold was a bit relieved that he no longer had to explain the subject of 'Prejudice' to six-year-old Randy. Happily, he introduced his neighbor Vivian Long, to Randy. Hal knew that Vivian had only seen pictures of him and that she had only met Sofia once, a very long time ago. She smiled and shook Randy's hand. They talked small talk and made plans to get together at the beach the next day.

"Come on, Pap Hal. Let's go down to the beach and watch the kites," Randy shouted. He seemed unaffected by his dinnertime experience. Hal took him by the hand and led him toward the beach, commenting on all of the bright colored kites in the evening sky.

*

Later that evening

The incident with the little boy at the restaurant had bothered Sofia, Harold, and Annie for the rest of the evening, but none of them would bring it up. Later, after Sofia had tucked Randy into bed, she joined Harold and Annie on the deck overlooking the ocean. They continued to avoid a discussion about what had happened at the restaurant, talking about other things, each thinking about bringing up the issue but not daring to do so, concluding it was just not a subject they had wanted to discuss. "Maybe, it was just one that was undeserving of discussion," Sofia thought as she said goodnight and considered the incident one more time before retiring for the evening.

She looked out at the bright, star-lit sky over the ocean, focusing on the horizon, knowing that she was looking east. She knew that her homeland, the one of her Oma and all of her family was just beyond the horizon. She considered how far she had come – not calculating the distance in miles but in losses, wondering if she would ever return to Germany.

She felt her stomach drop anticipating the enormous task of raising a son in a country of which she knew little and without the family traditions from both sides of his family. She hoped that the incident they had experienced tonight was a random one, but somehow she knew that it wouldn't be the last time racism would raise its ugly face toward Randy. For the first time in a long time, she thought of Esther, remembering that she had no idea what had made Esther so frightened when Franz had put on the Nazi Youth Uniform. Since the war had ended, she had decided that she would renounce her German heritage, not able to imagine that her country's leaders had been capable of such horror. Now, as she attempts to embrace a new country, she fears that the prejudice she had seen in her homeland has permeated this side of the Atlantic.

Her thoughts center on Randy and his first year in school. She wanted Randy to have an experience in school where he interacted with students of many nationalities and cultures, learning to accept people for their differences as well as their similarities. She wouldn't allow him to be embarrassed or ridiculed. She wanted to teach him to embrace his uniqueness and respect others. During one of their many conversations, Harold had mentioned that he had wanted Randy to attend the University School, a private school within the University.

She decided to investigate this school because she wanted to make sure Randy would grew up feeling proud of his ethnicity. She thought the University School might be the place to get him started on that goal of wanting him to become a kind, sensitive and tolerant man, who believed in the value of all people regardless of race, color of skin, religion, or gender, just as Randolph had. She wanted him to be happy, free of the ignorance of racism she had left behind in Germany. She was disappointed to find it, apparently, alive and well in the United States of America.

*

I had hoped his father would have been pleased," Sofia said looking up inquisitively at Janene.

"I am also hoping that you didn't experience the kinds of prejudice growing up that Randy had endured, Janene," Sofia says.

"Well, I can say that I had my share," Janene replied.

"I think my decision to enroll him in the University School had helped. He had Hal and Annie as well as Randolph's parents. They all proved to be a blessing. I don't know what I would have done without them, or how I would have managed to bring him up alone."

"I had never felt that I didn't belong in the McDeenon home, however, it was a different story outside of my home. I had no contact with any African-Americans or Vietnamese. From what you have said, I think that I had much the same kind of childhood that you had, Sofia. When I think back on it, it had been a very sheltered one. Even now, Bill is very protective of me. I don't think that he would ever approve of any man wanting to marry me," Janene said with a smile.

"If he could arrange my marriage as your father had done, he would jump at the chance. Although, I don't know where he would find a man that he thought was good enough for me."

"I guess that was the way my father had felt when he had arranged my marriage to Felix. It isn't that I feel Bill and Madeline haven't been a good influence on your lives, but it makes me very sad to know Randy didn't have a place in it, nor did I. He would have been a very good role model for you and your sister."

"You talk as if you believe that my sister is still alive."

"I have never felt comfortable with the story that you and your mother had been killed. Now, that I know that there were two babies, not one, I have the feeling that she will surface just as you have."

"I hope you are right. When I get back to Atlanta, I plan on beginning a search of my own."

"I have an investigator working on it and I have alerted my center in South Vietnam. As soon as he discovers any more information, I'll let you know. I'll arrange everything."

"Thank you," Janene replied hoping that Sofia's display of confidence would be a good predictor of the outcome. She smiles enthusiastically as she waits for Sofia to begin her story again.

*

"It is the fifteenth day in May of 1969. The fact that Randy had enlisted in the Army, when he could have kept his status as a student and avoided military service, had upset Sofia. Her heart had sunk when he had told her that he had signed the papers the day after graduation from high school.

With the war in South Vietnam in full swing, she couldn't believe another person she loved would be involved in yet another war. She knew her son well enough to know why he wanted to join the military, but she still regretted that she was unable to change his mind.

He had always been infatuated with anything about the military, and the knowledge that his father had been an Army pilot had made him want to become one just like him. The news of his enlistment had brought a feeling of impending doom just like the one she had felt in Berlin.

She knew Randy had a deep admiration for his dead father, respecting him for his devotion to the country by giving his life. His father's career in the military had been a magical story for him when he had been a little boy growing up. He had often talked about the fact that he wanted to help people who were not as fortunate as he was.

Sofia had begged him not to get involved in this war, as his father had done in Korea, but she knew by the look on his face when he had broken the news to her, that all of her pleading and praying was in vain – she could never talk him out of it. Randolph Robert Blackburn III was going to Vietnam to fight for his country; she was powerless to do anything about it.

She felt only pain as she kissed him goodbye at the train station. An inexplicable feeling of finality had come over her. She hated her pessimism. All she could think about was leaving Berlin with Max and Ana, traveling around France from one abandoned farmhouse or barn to another, and never seeing them again.

*

Sofia's depression started the day Randy had left for Vietnam. Along with the dreaded sense of doom, came flashbacks of her life in Germany. She felt like a giant sinkhole had swallowed her. She continued to work, but only going through the motions; her mind was always somewhere else. She was in Berlin; she was in France; she was on the Atlantic Ocean; she was in New York; she was everywhere, but where she was. She recognized only one common thread in her life – those connected with memories of her quilt. She reached for it in her daydreams; she reached for it in her dreams and in her nightmares. The loneliness was unbearable.

Harold and Annie had both passed away before Randy had left for the military. First, Harold had battled cancer unsuccessfully for about a year, then, only a few weeks later, Annie had suffered a fatal heart attack. Sofia had only Randy.

"It had been his decision," she reminded herself once again.

She was proud of Randy, but she never gave herself any credit for the way he had turned out. He grew up to be a caring, kind, and wonderful man. She thought his close relationships to Hal, Annie, Robert, and Regina had been the biggest factors in his life, not her. When Hal had died, Randy had been devastated.

It seemed to Sofia that Randy's desire for a career in the military grew stronger after his beloved father figure had passed away. With her prompting, she and Randy started to make application to universities. The replies came in, but Randy showed no enthusiasm. Even the offers of scholarships to the Ivy League Colleges didn't impress him. All he could think about was "going to Vietnam and making his country proud of him." Sofia hoped he would change his mind, but she worried. She didn't know he had been secretly planning to enlist when he had turned eighteen, knowing he wouldn't need a parent's signature to join once he was of age.

Sofia had absolutely refused to hear of his going to the service, but it did her no good to protest. The more she fought with him to attend the university, the more he resisted. In addition, he said that he wanted to become a pilot. He didn't want to keep his student deferment. When other young men were trying desperately to get out of the Draft, Randy was trying to convince his mother that he shouldn't go to one of the Ivy League schools that had offered him full scholarships. Shortly after his eighteenth birthday, he enlisted and was on his way, training as a helicopter pilot headed to South Vietnam.

The fact that he was the only relative left in Sofia's life made his decision to go all the harder for Sofia. The Vietnam War was in full escalation. Protests against the war had occurred on every campus. She couldn't help but think about her past and the times when war had affected her. She watched the progress of the war everyday on the television. Like millions of other mothers, fathers, wives, sons and daughters, she stayed glued to the television set, listening to the news reports. Americans watched and listened for any news about their loved ones, fearing the worst. Randy had signed for another term, and another tour to Vietnam had begun. The nightmare continued. He had a brief leave and came home, but all he could talk about was going back. When two soldiers arrived at her door on September 2, in 1972, her heart had sunk.

"We regret to inform you that his helicopter has been shot down over Cambodia."

Sofia collapsed into their arms, retreating to the same place that she had after the shelling of the farmhouse in Normandy. This time she didn't have Annie and Harold. She remained in the hole for months. After a while, she found comfort there and little reason to leave it. It protected her the same way her childhood quilt had. She considered suicide.

However, in the midst of her depression, a glimmer of light gave her motivation, compelling her to keep on living. A strange energy gave her the will to live. The force took her away from the notion of taking her life. She knew she had to do something before she died, something that would affirm the reason that her life had continued while the lives of everyone she had ever loved, except for Oma, had their lives taken. That thought made continuing her life without Randy, Max, and Ana, Oma and her quilt, meaningful for her. It became important that she continue living to fulfill the promise she had made to make Germany proud.

For the first time, she realized that she was indeed responsible for Randy's death as well. She had shared her story with him from the time he was little, telling him to do something in his life to make his country proud. "That something was going to Vietnam and giving his life for his country." *Germany no longer exists for me. Now, neither does Randy.* Suddenly, she realized that what Oma had told her about not losing her when she had died was true for Max, Ana, and now Randy. She had always felt helpless because she didn't have Oma's quilt but now she realizes the error in her thinking. "The children will always be with me, right here in my heart, just as Oma had said, and so will the quilt."

All I have to do is remember.

She knew that she must accomplish something good to make up for all the wrongs of her world if she was ever to enjoy any peace. She understood the guilt that Oma had taken on when her beloved farm was lost and she had to do something to help her family. Sofia feels guilty for the terrible crimes that her country had perpetrated on the world and reflects on the promise she had made to Oma. She had vowed to her grandmother to use her quilt to help needy people and the fact that she had lost her quilt had made her believe that she could never accomplish that promise or anything important. Now, she realizes that she still has the essence of the quilt within her, stored in her memory. She decides that she will get on with the task of helping all of those needy children, the ones who have been haunting her. Each had cried out for help in her mind – ever since that day in the farmhouse when the beam had fallen and she could do nothing to help her own children.

*

One day, she found herself getting on a bus and going to the Pennsylvania Railroad Station in Pittsburgh. She went into the station, walked right up to the tracks and stood in the middle of them, directly in front of the train. "Simon! Simon!" she shouted as she walked down the train tracks. "I know he is in one of these cars. Which one is it?" She walked up and down the tracks, trying to open the doors of the train cars, all locked. "Simon, Simon!" she shouted. "I'm coming, Simon. I'm coming." Crowds formed around her, watching, wondering. "He won't last much longer. He has been in there too long. He needs some food and water. I have to get him some help. I can't get in the car unless someone helps," she thought as she turned to one of the patrons.

"Can you help me, please? I must find Simon."

The man looked at her helplessly and turned away. She ran over to the uniformed man standing beside the platform. "You have to help me. You have to help. A boy is in that cargo car. His name is Simon. He is in that car, all alone. He has no food or water. He will die if you don't help me. We must get him out. We must. We must get him out now," she screamed, tugging feverishly on his shirt.

"Hold on, 'Lady', there is nobody in that car. The only thing in that car is coal. What in the world makes you think there is a kid in there?"

"We have no time to delay! I'm telling you, he will die."

"Okay, I'll help you, but you have to get off the tracks. You can't stand there. There are trains coming in. It is dangerous."

"I'm not leaving until you get Simon out of the car," she ordered and ran back to the train. "I'll stay here until I know you have opened that car and taken Simon out," she said as she positioned herself in the middle of the tracks.

By now, a larger crowd of people had gathered around the conductor, all of them staring at the woman standing on the tracks where the next train passes by the station. Sofia put her hands over her ears, shook her head back and forth, and shouted at the conductor, "I'm not listening to you anymore. You go get the door opened and you get Simon out. You do it now."

The conductor took his Walkie-Talkie Radio out of his pocket and called his supervisor. A whistle blew, indicating the possibility of an approaching train. The crowd started screaming. The conductor tried to keep them away from the tracks, pushing them back.

"Okay, I have called. They are going to open the car and get the kid out of there. Come on now. Give me your hand. I'll help you across the tracks," he said, trying to persuade her.

"No, not until you get Simon, not until he is safe," Sofia said holding her ground in the middle of the tracks.

An emergency vehicle squealed into the station. A police officer ran across the platform and stood in front of Sofia, now standing in the middle of the tracks. "I understand you are worried about a little boy, Miss? Well, you need not worry anymore. We have rescued the little boy. He is safe. He was just where you said he was in the coal car," he lied. "What is his name?" the young police officer asked. "He was much too frightened to tell us."

"He has gentle eyes just like Felix's and the same as Randolph's," she thought as she contemplated telling him.

"His name is Simon," she said softly.

"Simon . . . Okay . . . good. If you will allow me, I'll help you off of the tracks and I'll take you to see the boy," the Officer continued moving toward Sofia who backed away from him. "You needn't be afraid. Simon needs both of us to help him. He is asking for you."

"Yes, I need to make sure Simon is okay," she agrees. I must make sure that you have released him from that car," she says, allowing the man to take hold of her arm, guiding her away from the tracks. The Officer leads her to an awaiting ambulance. They take her to the Psychiatric Ward of the Hospital.

*

The deep despair and depression swallowed her once again. Dr. Eva Shermansky, a thirty-eight year old Psychiatrist from the Hospital, began weeks of intense therapy, helping Sofia to release the terrible visions that had tortured her, causing her to lose touch with reality.

Dr. Eva, as Sofia came to call her, was able to diagnose her and offer her treatment. She realized the only way Sofia would become well again was by bringing these visions to reality and having Sofia face them. She thought that the key to her therapy lay in the fact that Sofia had never accepted the death of her two children, Max and Ana, and further, the crisis had escalated with Randy's death. As the therapy had unfolded, it became evident that Sofia's breakdown had been the result of her inability to come to grips with the death of her children. She had never accepted their deaths, believing that were still lying on the floor of a farmhouse in Normandy, bruised, bleeding, and crying for her. She had never released her feelings of guilt over their deaths. She had assumed responsibility for the death of the children, including Randy's, placing blame on herself for sharing her life stories with him, causing him to want to take on the cause of seeking out evil and doing something meaningful to right the wrongs of the world.

In her detachment from reality, Sofia had visions of imaginary children, who were in various states of desperation, confusion, and peril. The visions became real for her, forcing her to detach from reality by her complete inability to help any of them. With months of therapy, Dr. Eva was able to identify the children and pull their stories from Sofia's mind, allowing Sofia the opportunity to intercede with each child, and help them.

Each child in Sofia's visions suffered torment and Sofia blamed herself for it. She had to be the one to release them, one by one. After months of treatment, she began to recover. The therapist made progress soon after she had persuaded Sofia to begin writing in a diary. The task was a familiar one for her, having done so much of it when she had first arrived into the United States. At first, Sofia could only find a few words for each page. As the therapy continued, she filled a page, and then another, and another.

She had taken on the task of helping each child as her personal challenge. She released the vision of twelve-year-old Simon, locked in a freight car, six-year-old Carmen, hiding in an attic, four-year-old Henrietta, lying at the bottom of a well, nine-year-old Steven, lost in the woods, and countless others. It took almost a year of treatment before she realized that she couldn't help five-year-old Maximilian Franz Fuerst and his three-year-old sister, Ana Alexandra Fuerst, lying under a fallen ceiling beam in an unknown farmhouse in France. They were dead.

*

Sofia Blackburn rejoined the living. The deep hole that had gripped her once was now gone. In its place, she experienced a myriad of creative energy. She began to write and found it impossible to stop. The stories came, one after another, all about children. This time she saved them, every one of them. The doctor thought that she needed more time to share her experiences further, but she wanted to leave the hospital. Dr. Shermansky, now more of a friend than a physician, discharged her from the hospital. Sofia returned to the beach house, the closest she could get to the Atlantic Ocean and the country of her birth, which she had denounced.

As she had prepared to make the trip, she received a letter in the mail from a relief organization in Vietnam. The contents had shocked her. Randy had fathered a child in Vietnam with a Vietnamese woman. The letter went on to explain that the Vietcong had killed both the woman and her child, a little girl, in a raid on the village. Randy had never said anything to her about the woman or the child. Sofia thought that if Randy had felt comfortable enough to tell her, maybe she could have spared the lives of the little girl and her mother by arranging their exits from Vietnam. She knew that she would have done anything, at any cost, to get them out of harm's way.

She also thought that, if she had received the news about her granddaughter before her breakdown, she would have held herself responsible for her death as well. However, because of her treatment and therapy, she held no visions of an African-American-Vietnamese child, abandoned, and calling for help.

This time she buried the memory of the granddaughter she never knew with the memory of her beloved son. However, deep in her heart, she always had a strange feeling about the validity of the story. Despite the fact that she was dealing with reality now, she couldn't help but wonder what it was about her life that had prevented her from having anyone in it. Randy's death and the death of his child was yet another tragedy, another loss, heartache of unbearable proportions. When she had arrived in Delaware, she was still questioning why her life had turned out the way it had.

There must be some kind of shadow over me. Maybe, it is a curse.

"Why is my life so full of sorrow and grief?"

Expecting to spend her time in Delaware alone, she was surprised to make a new acquaintance, the daughter of the next-door neighbor. Her name was 'Mary Long'.

Mary had recently been divorced and she was spending the summer there, trying to begin a new life. The two women found that they had much in common and became friends quickly. Sofia had not spoken about her past to anyone but Dr. Eva. However, she found that she and Mary could talk about anything, each sharing her life willingly. One way they had interacted with each other, getting to know one another was by touring the Delmarva Coastline on their many outings. On one of these excursions, Mary, very familiar with the area since she had grown up spending summers there, took Sofia to the site of some observation towers along the coastline, remnants from World War II.

Mary explained that the military had used them to guard the Atlantic shoreline, searching for German ships. Sofia became very emotional and broke down, confiding in Mary the details of her life. For the first time, she told a perfect stranger her story. Likewise, Mary shared the details of her life. They concluded that it was ironic that they would actually meet and share their lives because, if they had met as children, they would have been enemies. They formed a unique bond, one that neither had known before. She remembered her only friendship with Esther Rosenfeld and shared her thoughts with Mary about Esther and how, for the first time, she had realized why Esther had run away when Franz had appeared in his soldier uniform. They became friends and confidants. Mary had just embarked on a new career as a publisher. After Sofia had shared her newly found passion, writing stories for children, Mary encouraged her to continue writing.

One day, she asked Sofia if she would like to have her stories published. Sofia's agreement put Mary into full gear. Sofia wasn't sure she was ready for the publicity of having her work published. Mary suggested she use a pen name. Sofia agreed and she came up with the pen name, 'Sophie Simon'. 'Sophie' was the nickname Mary coined for her and "Simon" was the first child, since Max and Ana, who had demanded so much of her attention that she had been willing to die for him.

It didn't take Mary long before she had Sofia's stories in print. One, in particular, was an immediate success. It was the story of a Prince and Princess and their Magical Quilt. Soon after publication, a producer contacted Mary about making an animated movie.

It was an instant box office hit, bringing Sofia instantaneous fame and wealth. By the end of the year, Sofia had become famous for the movie and the book. The royalties started to pour in and Sophie Simon published her second book and then her third. Soon, the movies about the magical quilt were part of the childhood experience of millions of children around the world. Sofia's life changed after her first book had brought her wealth and fame. Although Mary Long was the publisher of Sofia's books, she also became her best friend. She and Sofia traveled the world; promoting Sofia's books, now 'Best Sellers'.

Everywhere they went, the news media and photographers followed, including the Opening of the animated movie, 'The Magical Quilt', an instant hit." She had hundreds of book signing sessions around the world, one at a bookstore in Berlin. The thought of going back to her hometown had made Sofia very apprehensive and Mary was anxious about even suggesting it or scheduling it. When she talked to Sofia, her response surprised her.

"It's time for me to go back, Mary."

*

1973 Berlin

Almost thirty years had passed since Sofia had made her secret exit out of Germany. As she sat in the airplane, crossing the Atlantic Ocean, her thoughts return to the Germany of her childhood, when she had lived in her little room above the bakery. She was quiet on the trip, lost in thought. The Allied bombs had destroyed Berlin. Over the course of time and from the ashes of the former city, a new one had emerged. After the Allied Forces had arrived when Berlin fell, the city was in a state of chaos, as were most of the European cities. The allied forces arrived in the defeated city and divided it into two sections, the East and the West; eventually a wall divided the two.

The book signing session was in the western section known as West Berlin. Naturally, coming home was disturbing to Sofia who found little that resembled the city of her memories. Shortly after her arrival, she asked Mary to accompany her back to Pappelstrasse – or what was left of it. The cab driver took them to the location where her home at once been but, of course, nothing was the same – only her memories, revealing ghosts of times past. Her heart ached. She sat in the cab, looking through the window at the place where her father's bakery once was and cried. She remembered Oma's words and her crooked finger pointing to her heart.

"Take us back to the hotel," she said to the cab driver as she took her diary from her brief case and began to write. By the time the driver had arrived at the hotel, she had written several pages of the beginning of her next book. It would become the next bestseller, another book for children titled, THE LITTLE DOE'S SECRET. It was a story about a baby doe that runs away from home.

The next day, she and Mary Long had their first book signing session at a large well-known bookstore across town. For the three days previously, they had traveled to every section of Berlin signing autographs for the many people who had come out to meet the famous author. At this session, one surprised her. When she looked up after signing a book for a male patron, a familiar face greeted her. It was as if she had seen a ghost from times past. *Esther Rosenthal.* She immediately got up from her chair and embraced her.

Forty years had passed for Esther and Sofia but they were unaware of time and place . . . They were still the same little girls who had played together in front of their fathers' shops. With tears in their eyes, streaming down their faces, they held each other and let time stand still. Sofia became very emotional and immediately asked Mary to stop the signing and give them privacy.

The manager of the bookstore took them to a room in the back of the store where their reunion proved to be a very emotional one for both of them. They shared how they had often thought of each other and the fact that neither of them had known the fate of the other. The signing session for Sofia's book wasn't a place to catch up on the past. They decided to meet the following afternoon.

*

The next day, Sofia and Esther met at Esther's home in West Berlin. Esther told Sofia that she had been living there since 1946, when she had returned to find her family. She confided in Sofia the details of her life under the Nazi government. She wept as she told Sofia that most of her extended family had died in the concentration camps. Only her parents and her brother had managed to escape into Switzerland.

"It had only been through the efforts of your husband, Sofia that my parents had escaped. He had befriended my father when he was a young police officer in Berlin before the Nazis. Felix had worked secretly to get as many people out as he could. It had been extremely dangerous. If he they had discovered him, they would have killed him and all of you. We hid in the woods in the countryside with others who had escaped. We knew that some wouldn't live through the harsh winters, but we would have rather died than stayed.

The revelations stunned Sofia. She shook all over. The more she mulled the information in her mind, the harder it was for her to understand. "If it were not for Felix's secret interventions, Esther would be dead," she thought sobbing, tears running down her cheeks. She listened as Esther continued her story.

"It had been early in 1946 by the time I had been able to finally return. It wasn't the city of our childhood, Sofia. I had met a man while I was in Switzerland. We married. We also became very active in organizations to locate the victims and to help them find their relatives. It was through this organization that we had discovered information about Felix," Esther said.

"Felix?"

"Felix had fought his own personal battle with THE THIRD REICH from the time he had joined their ranks after they had forced him under the threat of death. He had to become one of them, but secretly, he had initiated his own single-handed battle. There were many that Felix couldn't help and that fact had bothered him greatly. Shortly before the Allied forces had invaded Berlin, they found out the truth about Felix. Word came they had executed him by firing squad after discovering that he had helped the wife of one of the other officers, your neighbor, Helena Stein. Rumors also said that when they had learned that Felix's family was no longer in Berlin, they had become suspicious of him and his wife's family who had owned the bakery on Pappelstrasse. After Helena's husband had died in Africa, and you were gone, she must have had some contact with Felix, or maybe your uncle, because we had heard that he had arranged for her to leave Berlin with the help of a contact person named Herr Adam Schmidt.

Uncle Adam?

The revelations left Sofia's head swimming, but things did start to make sense to her. "Felix had arranged the entire escape with Uncle Adam," she thought. "The information that he had been instrumental in getting her and the children away from the Nazis shocked her. *I should have had more faith in Felix.* She realized now that he had tried to protect them and he had ultimately given his life for them. She wondered if he had known of the death of the children, or that she had survived, and had been smuggled into the United States. Her heart fell when she thought of the firing squad. When she thought of all the negative thoughts about him, she had then and since, she felt humiliated.

I wish he had told me. If I had only known, then maybe I could have helped Felix.

"He knew that I would never leave without him if I had known," she answered her own question. She knew in her heart of hearts that Felix did the only thing he could. He tried to save them from an enemy that was so fierce it had the entire world by the throat. As Sofia sat stunned with a blank look on her face, Esther continued.

"Sofia, Helena is still alive and she is living in West Berlin," Esther said. The women arranged for a meeting.

*

The Next Day

When they had stopped crying and hugging each other, Sofia and Helena shared their stories. Helena cried as she told Sofia about the deaths of her two older children when they had encountered a German patrol during their flight.

242

Sofia begins crying, remembering her own flight with the children. "When I had received word of my husband's death and you had disappeared, I could only think of one thing – get out of Germany. Felix and I had talked privately several times after you had left. Once Hans was dead, I found no reason to stay but I was scared to leave. You see, Sofia, Hans had doctored my papers in order for me to stay with him. I have Jewish blood in my family. Felix knew about it but he never disclosed it. On the contrary, he had offered to help me, arranging for our secret flight to Switzerland. On the second day, a patrol confronted us, firing at us before asking any questions. I had been shot and fell down on the baby during the gunfire. Herman lived but our other children did not. "

"Oh, my God, Helena, I can't believe it."

"Sofia, there's more," she said. "I had wrapped the baby in a blanket that Felix had given me." She went to the closet and pulled out a large cardboard box, placing it on a table in front of Sofia.

"Open it, Sofia."

Sofia lifted the lid. Her mouth dropped. Tears rolled down her cheeks. "It is just as I remember it," she said as she looked inside, her eyes finding her quilt, folded neatly and wrapped in tissue. She ran her fingers over the quilt, lost in thought, while Helena continued with the story.

"The night that Felix had arranged for us to leave Berlin, he came to our house after dark, and he told me to wrap the baby in the quilt. He told me that the quilt was 'magical' and that it had belonged to you. He said that it would protect the baby and that someday when the insanity was over, I should give it back to Sofia." She looked to the blanket, her eyes getting wet with tears. "It had done just that," Helena said. "I held onto the quilt all of these years, knowing that someday, I would give it back to its rightful owner. I searched for news about, 'Sofia Gunther,' or 'Sofia Fuerst,' never hearing a word. I was surprised to find out that, "Sophie Simon" was you."

Sofia lifted her quilt to her face, smelled it, and caressed it against her cheek. She returned to that special place in her memory where only she could go. She was sure, at that moment, that all of her deceased family was standing in the room with her. She saw all of their faces, one by one. Only Helena's reassuring voice and gentle embrace brought her back to reality.

She had a *sense of empowerment*, knowing that she had a mission.

She wasn't sure what that meant exactly, but she felt a powerful force energizing her with a power of determination. She couldn't speak of it, nor did she understand it. She knew it had something to do with 'being German' and that she had something to accomplish in her life.

She remembered her promise to her Oma. "I'll use the quilt to help people, just like the prince and the princess in Oma's story and like Frau

Schultz. I am rich now. I'll help those who are in need," she vowed to herself.

She and Mary returned to the United States. She had an extra piece of luggage on the return trip, one holding her quilt. In addition, within her heart, she held an enormous plan for fulfilling her promise to her Oma and to herself.

*

Sofia was still reacting to the news that she had learned about Felix, not able to fully digest it all. She went directly to the phone and dialed Mary's number. As the connection was going through, she thought about the last time that they had talked when they had been on the airplane.

She remembered that Mary had been excited about Sofia's reunion with the quilt and she had told her about a plan to use the reunion of the quilt for a promotion for her books. She was still thinking about the trip home from Berlin and the conversation that she had with Mary when she heard Mary's voice on the other end of the phone.

"Hello, Sophie, I have been thinking of you. You must have ESP," she said. She was in her office, up to her ears in work that had piled up while she was traveling in Europe with Sofia. "I'm so glad you called. I have a fabulous idea to run by you."

As she listened, Sofia thought that the events of their trip had started Mary thinking. *When Mary's mind started to work, anything could happen.*

"I've been thinking – you should write your own autobiography."

"Mary, I don't think I'm ready for that."

"I just knew you would say that. Let me tell you my second idea."

Sofia, knowing that something would brew quickly when Mary's creative juices stirred, thought about proposing her own idea to her, but decided to hear out Mary's idea first.

"Look, Sophie, getting that quilt back couldn't have been planned better if we had tried. This could be just what your books need to send you over the top as one of the most celebrated authors of children books. This is just a natural consequence of this event. We have to get the news about the quilt out to the public. I thought the perfect way was to hear the story from you. That is why I thought of the autobiography, but I knew you would say that you were not ready to dig up your past. Therefore, I thought we could hire a writer – a special one to write your biography. What do you think?"

"Oh, I don't know, Mary."

"I have the perfect writer in mind – and he's single."

Sofia laughed a little before starting to protest, but Mary put her off in her usual way. "Sophie . . . this will be the best thing that could happen.

Please, just meet him, talk to him. What do you think, Sophie? Come on – just say it is okay."

"I never can say 'No' to you . . . now can I, Mary?"

"I take it that is a 'Yes'?

"Okay . . . Yes, I will meet him."

"Good . . . You won't regret it . . . I promise . . . His name is 'Jeffrey Anderson' . . . I'll arrange everything."

"You always do!"

* * * * *

CHAPTER 11
JEFFREY ANDERSON

Sofia's agenda called for her to spend the next month relaxing at the Schneider's home in Rehoboth Beach, Delaware. Mary arranged for her to meet Jeffrey Anderson there. Sofia knew Mary well enough not to protest too loudly. "So now, she is going to play matchmaker," she considered. A smile formed on her lips when she thought of the intentions of her friend. Perhaps, it would be yet another "new beginning," she thought as she planned her next contact with Mary.

She had thought that she should have mentioned the reason for her call to Mary when she had last talked to her, but Mary's excitement about the biography project had prompted her to decide against it.

"I didn't want to burst your bubble before when I had agreed to this biography thing but . . . What did you say his name was?"

"Jeffrey Anderson."

"Oh. Well I have been thinking . . ."

"Now, Sophie, not to worry. I told you I'll make all the arrangements."

"It's not that, Mary. I think I am getting cold feet."

"Come on, Sophie, trust me. This is the best thing that could happen. It is an opportunity that is just too perfect to ignore."

"I do trust you, Mary. You are my best friend."

"Well, just sit back and let this happen. You won't regret it. You know how I feel about our friendship, Sophie. We are best friends for life and I would never do anything to hurt you. I have complete faith in Jeffrey . . . Just meet him . . . you will know why when you meet him . . . Oh, by the way, why did you call me?"

"Oh, never mind. It is just something that I am considering. I'll talk about it to you another time."

"Okay, Sophie. Take care."

"Maybe I should have told Mary about my plans," she thought the minute she had hung up with her. She knew that she still had some plans to formulate before she shared her idea with Mary or anyone else. She reassured herself that she had done the right thing by keeping it concealed. She had been thinking about it ever since she had returned with her quilt, but her idea, still in its infancy, needed some refinement. She went over it in her mind.

"I want to create centers for needy children. I want to do something for all of the children of the world who are suffering. Maybe those of us who have denied our heritage, as I have, may once again lay claim to it, holding up our heads in pride, instead of shame because of our good deeds. I know I can never erase the evil that was forced upon the whole world in Germany's name, but I also know that I have to do something for no one else but myself." As her mind raced, she pictured replicas of her quilt hanging on flag poles on the newly opened centers around the world. She decided on the name for the centers, the World Organization of Quilts or W.O.O.Q. "One day, I'll open one in Berlin," she thought deciding to keep her plan to herself a while longer.

She thought that her decision to wait and meet Jeffrey Anderson first was a good one. The research for the biography would connect her to her past again and help her to formulate plans to initiate the centers for the world's children. She shivered when she thought of it all. She didn't want to share the idea with anyone yet, not even Mary. At least not until she knew that her plans were strong enough that no one would be able to talk her out of them. "I don't care what the costs are . . . I'll find a way."

She felt empowered for the first time in her life, and she knew that the reunion with the quilt was responsible. She decided that she would hold onto the powers of the quilt for just a few more weeks. Then, she would share them with the world. "After all, Oma would want nothing less than that," she thought as she pulled the quilt around her and enjoyed its warmth again.

*

13 May 1973

Sofia needs the peace and quiet of the beach house now more than ever. The information revealed to her by Helena and Esther had overwhelmed her. She was still reeling from all of it, needing time to reflect, and hoping that the information about Felix wouldn't send her into another deep depression. To her surprise, her new sense of empowerment energized her in a way that she had never known before.

She knew that Mary had the best of intentions by suggesting the writing of the biography. Yet, she was still wishing that she had managed to say "No" to the project so that she could take this newly found energy and direct it to her cause. She wasn't sure that this was the best time to be rehashing her life. It seemed to her that she had spent the better part of the last twenty years putting the memories away. Bringing them back to life now didn't seem like the best idea, but taking them and directing them to the accomplishment of her new passion did.

"However, I have agreed and I can't get out of it now," she concluded. The only thing consoling her was that the meeting with Jeffrey Anderson wasn't until the day after tomorrow. That would give her some time to just relax and reflect. She was glad of that. She had some things to do to prepare for the meeting. Mostly, she wanted to gather her thoughts. A warm bath would be the place to start, knowing that in the past, the warm waters and the relaxing atmosphere of isolationism would allow her to do just that. With that in mind, she headed upstairs and sunk herself into the large tub. Soon, all of the stress seemed to fade away.

She settled into the tub, leaned back, and took a deep breath. Her mind started to dart back to Germany, but she stopped herself abruptly. She wouldn't let herself think about anything. She learned this technique in therapy. She knew that relaxation could only come if she made her mind become completely blank. She needed to enjoy the nothingness that she could find in the total process. Soon, she was off to that place where her mind had been before, the one that she knew she needed. She lost track of time. The skin on her legs turning to prune prompted a quick exit from the tub. She toweled off and got dressed.

She decided afterward to take a short trip to the market. She walked down the road, past her house and onto the sidewalk of the next street. That street led her to the business area of the resort. She passed several boutiques and shops and did some window-shopping. Dressed in her favorite sundress, bonnet, and sandals, she thought she looked more like a local than a tourist. She shifted the straw basket she brought to the other arm, and entered her favorite market, owned by the same family for as long as she could remember coming to the resort. She thought of Berlin, remembering how she had loved to walk the streets, looking in the windows of the stores on Pappelstrasse. After an exchange of greetings with the owner, she put a few items in the basket and headed back to the house.

She made a salad for a late dinner, opened a bottle of wine, and then found the soft lounge on the balcony, wrapping herself in her newly reclaimed quilt. The sounds of the waves crashing against the shore soon took her to a place of complete relaxation.

The morning sunrise over the ocean woke her with a bright jolt of light. It was a pleasant awakening and Sofia found herself thinking what a wonderful way to wake up – the way she had remembered waking up in Germany. She reached down and felt for her quilt. Lost in time, she flashed back to the little room above the bakery. All she could think about was sharing the magical feeling that the quilt had given her. Thoughts of providing the same sense of security that she had derived from the quilt to the many children in the world who were suffering, added fuel to her plan to open children centers.

She felt a strong sense of resolution. It was an awesome mission, but her determination formulated an action plan. She couldn't imagine allowing one more day to go by without offering some help to the children who needed it. She knew she would never reach every child, but she was hopeful that she would reach some. The quilt had always seemed magical to her. It had given her the power to conquer her fears and the strength she had needed to endure her childhood. However, at that moment she recognized that strength and courage had not come from the quilt.

Instead, she knew that it had come from within her and that she had become stronger by realizing the wisdom of those who had raised her and loved her. The quilt was merely the catalyst, and its return to her had provided her with an inspiration. The quilt wasn't just a relic of a past life, but it would be the catharsis for the beginning of something wonderful. It had empowered her with a plan and she knew exactly what she had to do to fulfill the promise she had made to Oma and herself.

Her heart was heavy as she thought of the thousands of children who might be going to bed hungry, or those who were cold and homeless. She would use her fame and fortune to reach them. The idea of marketing the feelings of security and warmth that she had grown up with back in Germany, directing them toward needy children seemed very possible to her. She thought that it would be costly, but that it was possible with the help of contributions and donations from those who share her dedication and desire to help. She was determined to set up relief organizations across the world that would identify and help all children suffering from poverty, war, natural disasters or personal ones, or any other circumstances. She knew that in order to bring her idea to fruition, she had to pull together all of her resources and it would never happen unless she made it happen.

Her first step was to talk to Mary Long.

"I want Mary to funnel my royalties into this project," she thought. She jumped up from the lounge, wrapped herself in the quilt, and danced.

A smile came on her face as she remembered doing the exact same thing the morning of her wedding to Felix. This time when she looked in the mirror, she saw the faces of countless children smiling back at her.

Each one had a broad grin. Their smiles generated a sense of power and conveyed to her that her plan would become a reality. Then, she saw one face after another appear on the patches of her quilt. The faces were of children from every corner of the globe. "My quilt truly is magical," she said aloud, taking it in her arms and embracing it tightly.

She knew what she had to do.

Her quilt was back.

It is as if it had never left.

She knew that the future was going to be bright, not only for her, but for countless children. "I have so much to do and so little time," she whispered. She would use the next few weeks at the beach home in Delaware to set the plan in motion. She picked up the phone to call Mary, but stopped and hung it up quickly. The plans buzzed in her brain with a sea of details as she considered what to do about Jeffrey Anderson and disappointing Mary. She finally concluded that there was no need to call it off. She thought she could do both. She knew one thing for sure.

Nothing, nor no one, would stop her.

*

Months Later

After spending only days with Sofia, interviewing her and getting to know her, Jeffrey Anderson, falling deeply in love, asked Sofia to marry him. She turned him down. After hearing her reasons, which had centered on her great motivation to establish the childcare centers and her passion to accomplish a childhood promise to her dead grandmother, he had said that he understood her decision and that he realized that he had no choice but to help her with it, if he ever wanted her to change her mind.

The quilt had been so important to her during her lifetime, taking on so many dimensions, that it seemed natural that her reunion with it would take her into the future. It had made her rich and famous, and she believed that now that she had it back, it would help her to fulfill her promise to her grandmother – and to herself.

Actually, she believed that the Princess in the story, who had used the magical powers of the quilt, was actually her. Her feelings of making the children centers a reality were not superficial. She felt an overwhelming need to make this story a reality and the idea of creating the W.O.O.Q. centers would do just that. She saw the centers as places where they would provide services to needy children. To her, it wasn't the question of 'If' the centers would open, but 'When' and she felt an urgency, the same as the one she felt when she wanted to get Simon out of the train car.

Sofia knew that Jeffrey was amazed at the magnitude of the proposal that she had developed. She could tell that by the surprised look on his face. She listened as he tried to present some negatives for comparison that might prohibit her from accomplishing her lofty ideas. However, she wouldn't hear of any of it. She reminded him that opening the centers had become her "mission in life." Nothing, nor no one, was more important to her now. After a few minutes of discussion, Jeffrey's decisions became evident when he declared, "Will you allow me to be your, 'Prince', Sofia?"

*

The two became a pair. Their determination and convictions put the plan into motion. They called Mary Long together to share the plan with her. They were delighted to hear that Mary would do everything to help them. With Sofia's creative energy, Jeffrey's devotion, and Mary's business sense, success for the new project seemed promising. It wasn't long before the legal and financial plans were set in motion.

Sofia hired a lawyer and an architect to design the site for the first W.O.O.Q. in West Virginia. They worked diligently and looked forward to the Grand Opening, inviting all of the news media. They promoted the Centers by commercials on television, radio announcements, and magazine articles, announcing the new idea. Famous movie stars, writers, and media people offered contributions for the new project. So much 'hype' developed with the opening of just one center, they feared that they might have generated too many needy children, and hoped that they would be able to help them all.

During the time of construction on the first site, they found a second site and then the third. The expanded projects quickly attracted the support of celebrities, politicians, dignitaries, and organizations for charitable donations to fund the growing number of centers. In a short time, a dozen sites opened.

Sofia was pleased to see her visions realized, but rejected the notoriety that had come with the fame. Mary Long took on the role of her 'Ambassador of Good Will' and Jeffrey helped with the business side. The work of the centers became well known. However, Sofia didn't want to divulge her identity; she used her pen name, Sophie Simon, as the founder of the centers. The four letters W.O.O.Q., with the two O's set as the shape of a pair of eyes made up the logo. The eyes represented those of the children whom the centers would help. A background of a swirling quilt was set behind the painted letters. Pictures of children's faces covered the surface of the quilt. They represented all races, ages, genders, and nationalities.

The Logo generated interest worldwide. Soon there was a demand for more centers in different locations around the world, servicing thousands of children with never a cost to any child. The donations became investments, and the interest and dividends funded each center. Each center had a board of directors and each of those ultimately reported to the main office of Sophie Simon.

With the large volume of children served, the centers expanded their services. It seemed to be a natural outgrowth for the centers to become adoption agencies for some of the needy-orphaned children. Hundreds of families received assistance, and thousands of children experienced the warmth and love of an adoptive family, because of the establishment of the centers.

*

Sofia and Jeffrey were proud of the centers, working together tirelessly for three years, making each idea for a center a reality. One evening, as they sat in New York at a quiet restaurant, Jeffrey asked Sofia to marry him again, telling her of his undying love for a 'certain Princess'.

"I think that if you will marry me, Sofia, then your Fairytale will have a happy ending. Will you marry me, my beautiful Princess?"

She remembered the first time that he had asked her to marry him. She had put him off, saying that she had too much to do before she could think about herself. She noted that he was waiting now, very anxiously, for her answer. "I thought you would never ask, my handsome Prince. Yes. Yes. I'll marry you."

Shortly after that, they were married in a private ceremony while on a trip to Florida to be present for the opening of yet another center. They had a whirlwind honeymoon that took them all over the world, visiting all of the centers.

Sofia decided that every child connected to the centers should receive his or her very own quilt. Needy children received thousands of replicas of the quilt. The smiles on the childcare's faces told the story of a beautiful Princess and handsome Prince who had found happiness and had lived happily ever after. Not long afterward, a toy manufacturer designed dolls of the Prince and Princess and replicas of their magical quilt. The revenues poured in and the centers became a huge success all around the world. "

*

"I suppose you would think that is the end of the story, Janene. In a way, it was. It is the end of Jeffrey's biography, but in my usual fashion, it is only another 'new beginning'. I am going to share with you my autobiography. I had never really felt confident writing it until much later in my life. However, now, I think of it as one of my best personal accomplishments because recalling my life had been very painful, and writing about it had proved to be very therapeutic for me. In 1979, I traveled to New York City and I wrote about that time in the autobiography. I would like to share the story with you, if you don't mind indulging me a bit longer."

"Not at all; it is my pleasure," Janene smiles.

"Then let me begin anew," she smiled back.

*

14 February 1979

"Jeffrey stood smiling, thinking about the event and the fact that the theater had sold out. The ceremony for the awarding the best-selling Book of the year, ANOTHER NEW BEGINNING, written by Jeffrey Anderson was about to begin. All of the profits from the ticket sales went to my adoption centers. They displayed a replica of the Logo design for the W.O.O.Q. on the center stage and surrounded it with patches from the quilt, each one imprinted with a picture of one of the children. Lights, cameras, and microphones dotted the large theater. An orchestra played the theme song from the first animated movie of the magical quilt. The animated characters, represented by costumed actors, sat on the stage with props from the movie.

The guest of honor, Sophie Simon, sat on the stage to the right of the podium. Next to her sat Mary Long, the publisher of the book and master of ceremony.

"Good evening! I am pleased to be the Hostess for this evening. I'm especially honored to be here, because the Author of the Best Selling Book of 1978 is a very good friend of mine," Mary began. "Please put your hands together and welcome the author of the bestselling book of 1978, Mr. Jeffrey Anderson."

The orchestra played another piece from the movie about the prince who had fallen in love with the beautiful princess as Jeffrey came onto the stage. A loud burst of applause echoed through the theater and continued. Spotlights followed him onto the stage, to the center near Mary who offered him a gold trophy of an opened book, engraved with his name.

Jeffrey smiled and bowed. The audience roared. They stood and gave him another round of applause. A group of other writers, as well as the judges, stood and applauded with the others. Jeffrey's cheeks turned a deep pink.

The audience returned to their seats after they offered several minutes of unrelenting applause and Jeffrey encouraged them to sit down. He stood silently in front of the microphone for several moments before beginning. "The first light, of the early morning sunrise, burst through the lacy pattern of the curtains on the opened window of Fraulein Sofia Gunther's bedroom.

The audience listened in silence. An immediate loud applause interrupted him as soon as the audience recognized the first sentence of Jeffrey's Biography of Sofia, entitled, "A New Beginning." Jeffrey thanked the audience again and they followed with another round of applause. He began again.

"In the summer of 1973, a friend of mine had asked me to write the biography of a special friend of hers. I accepted that offer and began a journey that would be the turning point in my life. I began to write her life story, but I began something else as well. I began to fall in love with her. Recently, that journey finally completed, I married that 'special friend of a friend'."

The applause stopped him. The audience showed their surprise and approval with another long round of applause. Jeffrey paused and allowed the audience to applaud, obviously enjoying the moment with them. He looked intently at Sofia, who sat blushing on a chair next to Mary.

"When I had begun to gather information about Sofia, I was amazed by the particulars of her life. Her story had captivated me from the beginning. I admired her courage and determination to bring herself from harsh beginnings and terrible hardships to fame and fortune. However, it was her strong generosity and desires to fulfill a promise that she had made to her grandmother about helping others that had given me inspiration. Life had dealt her some strong lessons in tragedy, but she had managed to overcome them and become a stronger and better person, for having had to endure them. She came to the United States as a twenty-three year old widow of a Nazi Officer and mother of their two dead babies. She couldn't speak or understand English. Her entire family was gone. The only thing that she had brought with her had been the memory of a dear grandmother and her 'magical quilt'. However, I suppose I am telling too much of the story. For the rest of the story, you will need to read the book. It is an honor for me to accept this award for writing a book which, for me, had been purely a 'labor of love'."

Another round of applause interrupted him.

"Sofia has dedicated her life to helping needy children around the world. In a relatively short time, her books and movies have reached every corner of the world. However, her philanthropy continues to touch the lives of children personally. I'm honored to accept this award, but I must acknowledge that this award belongs more to her than it does to me," he said looking to his right and finding the eyes of his new bride.

Jeffrey raised his arm, motioning for Sophie Simon to join him at the microphone. "Ladies and Gentlemen, My Princess," he announced. They embraced and kissed as the audience applauded. He placed the trophy in her hands. The orchestra began playing again and a long line of children marched up onto the stage, each one carrying his or her miniature quilt. Several ovations later, the curtain came down and Mr. & Mrs. Jeffrey Anderson lived happily ever after.

*

Janene reaches for the recorder. "What a beautiful ending, Sofia," she smiles. "You must have been so very happy."

"Not quite, there is more to my story, Neeny," Sofia says noticing that she is about to turn off the recorder. "I think you might want to leave it on for a while. The conclusion of my story is one you will not want to miss.

"Don't stop now," Janene encourages as she withdraws her hand and settles back into her chair.

* * * * *

CHAPTER 12
THE STERN FAMILY

"It was October, 1983 in Paris, France," Sofia says.

"A woman named Jacqueline Stern is working at her design studio on the latest fashions for women. The schedule that her secretary places in front of her overwhelms her. She checks each day of the next month, not able to imagine how she would fulfill all her obligations. "It just seemed so much busier than usual," she thought and when she had mentioned the schedule to Antoinette, her secretary, she remembered the reason. This season she had sold twice as many designs.

The success of her business, "Fashions by Jacqueline Stern" pleased her, especially after working so hard to gain recognition in the design industry, but she had not anticipated that the biggest price she would pay for fame would be her time. Ordinarily, she could handle the stress but, since finding out about her pregnancy, she noticed that her endless supply of energy had limits.

She knows that fatigue is natural in the first trimester and she looks forward to it lessening, but she wonders if that isn't just another 'old wives tale'. After discussing it with Stephen, her husband, she had deliberately not told anyone but her brother Michael about this pregnancy. She had already had two miscarriages and felt that she wasn't up to the pain of announcing another. This time, she had decided to keep it to herself for as long as she could. She thought that she could deal with the loss, if it happened again, a little better that way. It sounded like a very pessimistic way to begin a pregnancy, but she felt it was the best.

As she and Antoinette discussed the schedule for the next month, she had almost blurted it out to her, but she caught herself, deciding to keep the news a secret a little longer. As she examined the schedule, she decided that her decision not to go to the New York show was probably a good one. She would send her assistant, Raphael, in her place. She noticed the look of surprise on Antoinette's face and almost slipped when she had told her of her decision. "It will be a great experience for Raphael to go," Antoinette had said.

Jacqueline had held her tongue and had never shared the reason for the decision. Now, as she looks over the schedule one more time, she notices that her appointment with the gynecologist isn't on the schedule. "Good,   there are no conflicts at that time. I can steal away easily," she thought as the intercom interrupted her planning.

"Stephen is on your private line, Jacqueline," Antoinette says.

His call surprises her because she had had breakfast with him only hours before and he never called her at work at the beginning of the day.

"Hi," she says into the phone.

Stephen replied, "Hi yourself." He told her how he knew that they had just seen one another, but he couldn't wait to tell her again that he loved her. She reacted to that statement with happiness, etched with a great deal of skepticism.

"Now, tell me again, darling, why is it that you are calling me?"

"Well, I just thought that I would prepare you. I have to fly to London later today. I wish I could get out of it but I can't. I have to represent that client I had told you about last week. I'm sorry."

"I understand, Stephen. I'll miss you, but don't worry. We will be fine."

"I'll call you when I get there. I love you, Jacqueline."

She said good-bye in the same way that the two of them had always closed out their phone conversations.

"Me, too," she says, hanging up and returning to her scheduling, welcoming the privacy. She pictures Stephen in her mind, remembering the first time that they had met. A mutual friend had introduced them at a party in New York. In addition to his fantastic looks, his warm smile had impressed her immediately. They had danced together all evening, exchanging all the niceties. Their friends had introduced her as a "promising fashion designer" and him as "an established trial lawyer, working for a distinguished law firm." Both living in New York City at the time, it had been coincidental that his law practice would bring him to

Paris and her design business needed to have the Paris market. After several months of dating in Paris, they returned to Pittsburgh for their posh wedding and then moved to Paris permanently.

They had decided to try to get pregnant right after getting married, but it didn't happen for another year. She had lost the baby in the second month. They had been very disappointed but were optimistic that they could try again. When they couldn't get pregnant again, they went to fertility doctors. After several years of trying unsuccessfully, they were frustrated and decided to put their desire to have a family on the back burner for a while. Soon after that decision, she was pregnant again, only to lose that baby in the second trimester.

That was three years ago. Since then, they had explored the options of adoption, filling out applications, and investigating the various agencies in Europe and in America. Not long after making application for adoption, Jacqueline became pregnant again. The doctors cautioned her: "Because of your history and your age, you should take it easy."

Antoinette interrupted her thoughts when she delivered another memo for her to review with the daily mail. Jacqueline declined her offer to get her some coffee, hoping that Antoinette wouldn't draw any conclusions by her refusal because of the many times before that she had avoided caffeine. The two women had become close friends, as well as sharing a business relationship. She took the pile of mail and started to sort through it. Antoinette let herself back out of the office.

The first several pieces of mail were just routine invoices and correspondences about the new designs. However, an unmarked white envelope labeled "PRIVATE" and addressed to 'Mrs. Jacqueline Mansfield' caught her eye. The envelope caught her attention immediately since she had not taken Stephen's surname, 'Mansfield', when they had married. She had never wanted to relinquish her maiden name for professional reasons. She opened the envelope; shocked to find that the letter was a pasted letter of words cut out of print from a magazine or newspaper. The letter alarmed her immediately and even more so as she read the pasted words:

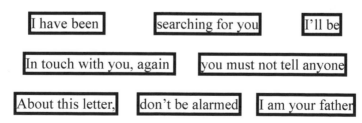

Jacqueline sat dazed, confused by the letter. "Who sent this letter?" she asked herself, not expecting an answer. She knows perfectly well that her father wouldn't send her such a letter – *not even as a joke*. "Surely, it is a mistake." She looked closely at the name and address on the envelope once again. She couldn't understand how it could be a mistake when the envelope displayed her married name and the company's address clearly on the front of the envelope. She had a sudden sick feeling in the pit of her stomach as she read the letter again, not being able to make any sense of it. She began to think that she might be over-reacting.

She thought of the pregnancy and cautioned herself to remain calm and not to let the letter upset her. However, she couldn't help but have it upset her. She wanted to call Stephen back immediately, but she read the part about not telling anyone. She wondered what would happen if she told anyone about the letter. She wondered what would happen if she didn't tell anyone about the letter.

She sat motionless, not able to concentrate on any of the other mail. Finally, thinking it through, she picked up the phone and dialed the one other person in the world that she knows will tell her exactly what she should do about this mysterious letter – *Michael*. She wasn't sure what she was going to say to him when she dialed his number, but she was sure that she had to share this with her brother. "Michael will know what I should think or do about this odd letter," she thought as she listened for his voice at the end of the other line. She was shaking and not able to believe that she was allowing the letter to upset her. She tried to formulate the words to tell her older brother about this letter when she heard his secretary answer the phone.

"Irene, this is Jacqueline. Is Michael there?"

"Hello, Jacqueline. No, I am sorry but Michael had an appointment early this morning. He wasn't sure when he would get back to the office."

"Okay, Irene. Would you give him a message? Ask him to call me and tell him it is important."

"Sure, Jacqueline, take care."

She hung up, looked at the letter, and then stuffed it into her briefcase. She thought that she would just have to deal with it later, when Michael called her back. It was upsetting her too much and she was sure that there was some logical reason for the letter.

"Maybe it is just someone's idea of a sick joke," she considered. She was sure that she was getting herself too upset; it wasn't good for her or the baby. Antoinette entered her office again with another pile of memos that needed her attention. This time she was glad to have the diversion, needing to be very busy right now . . . extremely busy. That way, she wouldn't be able to think about the letter.

*

3 November 1983, Pittsburgh

Michael Stern called his office from the pay phone in the hotel where he had been meeting with his client. The meeting had gone well and he was in a good mood. When his secretary told him about a phone call from his sister, Jacqueline, saying that it was important for him to call her back, his curiosity peeked. He and Jacqueline were extremely close. He knows that she is pregnant again and he prays that her phone call wasn't about the pregnancy, hoping that she is able to carry this baby to full term.

"I'll be back in the office later on this afternoon, Irene," he said into the phone, trying to put one arm into his overcoat at the same time. "I have a few things to do at home and I think it will take the rest of the afternoon. If Jacqueline calls again, tell her I'll call her later," he said, before saying his good-bye.

He put his other arm into his overcoat, picked up his briefcase and walked toward the elevator. The elevator took him to the parking garage. He headed out of the city, to the suburban neighborhood where he and his family lived. He was thinking of the file he had left at home in his home office as he drove the familiar route home.

The file pertained to a complicated custody case that he was working on, which made him think of his own adoption. He had lived in Pittsburgh since he was a little boy. His adoptive father, Marcus Stern, told him that he and his sister had been orphaned, French Jews whose parents had been killed in World War II.

The Sterns were Jewish Americans who had lost all of their immediate families in the Holocaust. Their families had been rounded up in Germany, sent to concentration camps and had perished. Marcus and Harriet Stern had met in the United States where they were attending graduate school. They were both German born students who had come to study and get their degrees in the late 1920's. They had loved the United States, deciding to stay and get their U.S. Citizenship and eventually go into law practice. Their families, back in Germany, had encouraged them to stay in the United States, as the growing Anti-Semitism that the new regime in Germany had put in place had disturbed them. They had become involved with a unique program to help orphaned refugee children

Michael remembered that his parents had told him that as soon as they had seen him and his sister, sitting huddled together at the children's center, they knew that they would adopt them. He described them as, "pitiful, sitting completely silent, just clinging to each other and looking terrified." They didn't seem to understand much said to them in French and they understood no English. Their hearts went out to them. For some strange reason, Marcus spoke to them in German. For the first time, they smiled and he was compelled to make sure he adopted them.

Michael had forgotten everything from his early childhood. He only knew what Marcus had told him . . ." It was probably the best thing that could have happened to you, in light of what you had endured." He and Jacqueline grew up as the children of Marcus and Harriet Stern, who had raised them as their own, teaching them their Jewish religion and customs, sending them to private schools and to the best colleges and graduate schools.

Michael joined his father's law firm when he had graduated from Law School, and when he had met "Elise Morris," a medical student; he fell in love almost immediately and asked her to marry him. Elise had just completed her Residency at a Pediatric Hospital, and contemplated joining a group of established pediatricians. Because of a kidney problem presenting in childhood, she could probably never bear children. She and Michael decided that they would seek adoption.

Jacqueline had studied fashion design in New York where she had met her husband, Steven Mansfield. They married and moved to Paris shortly afterward, satisfying his new position with a law firm involved in international matters. Her new fashion design business had taken off, making her one of the up and coming fashion designers in Paris. They had been trying to have a family but had suffered several miscarriages.

Michael pulled into the driveway of his suburban home in Pittsburgh, PA. He knew that he had several memos to review before he could return to the office. He reminded himself to call Jacqueline, and went to the office to place the over-seas, long-distant call. He was pleasantly surprised when Jacqueline had answered the phone.

"Hi, Jackie, it is good to hear your voice again. Irene said that I had missed your call earlier. Is everything okay?" he asked.

"Yes, Michael...well no, I'm not sure," she replied.

He had grown up being very protective of his baby sister, and was missing her since she had gone abroad. When he heard the tone of her voice, he became alarmed. He listened as she told him about the mysterious letter which she had received.

At first, he thought that perhaps it was someone's idea of a sick joke. However, as he thought about the facts about their adoptions, as well as the fact that he knew very little about the details, he was confused. He also knew that Marcus and Harriet had never told Jacqueline about her adoption. *The letter indicated that the author of the letter was Jacqueline's father.* He mulled the idea in his head, not able to figure out what that meant. He knew that Marcus would never send a letter of that nature, especially to Jacqueline, but since he knew nothing about his biological family, he didn't know how to handle the situation.

"Don't worry about this, Jackie. It is probably some sick person's idea of a joke, or it is just a big mistake. It happens all the time....case of mistaken identity or something," he said. He was trying to convince himself, as well as her. "I'll talk to Father and see what he thinks. It isn't good for the baby. So don't worry. I'll call you later, as soon as I figure it all out," he told her in a gentle voice, trying to reassure her.

"Okay, Michael, if you say so. Please don't tell Mother or Father about the baby." Sounding very excited, she says," I want to be the one to tell them."

"Don't worry; I won't spill the beans. Take care. I love you," he said as he hung up the phone.

"I love you too, Michael."

Michael decided that he wouldn't call his parents. Instead, he would go to their home in a well-to-do, eastern neighborhood of the city known as 'Squirrel Hill', an easy stop on his way back to the office in downtown Pittsburgh. "This isn't something to discuss on the phone," he thought, as he quickly reviewed the two memos that had brought him home and placed them in his briefcase. He walked out to the car, threw his briefcase onto the front seat, and moved to get in. Then, he remembered the mail; he was surprised to find a large white envelope, marked with the word 'PRIVATE', and addressed to him.

He opened the envelope while walking back to the car. Since he had talked to Jacqueline earlier, he wasn't at all surprised to see that the envelope was an exact duplicate of what his sister had told him that she had received. He read the message and read it again. He decided that he would definitely not tell his parents about the letters, not until he could get some answers.

He sat behind the wheel of his car for a long time, looking over the letter.

He read every word several times, trying to think clearly. He tried to remember anything from his childhood that would give him a clue as to what this all might mean. He read the note again, concentrating on the part to tell no one, wondering why whoever had written the notes would want to keep everything so mysterious.

If the person, who had written the letter, were actually their biological father, why would he choose to contact them like this?

"Did Marcus and Harriet know this person? Why was this person contacting them, now? Where had he been all these years?" he asked himself.

He tried to concentrate on his childhood, trying to recall anything that would help him to solve this mystery. Finally, he decided that he needed to talk to his father about his adoption. "It is best if I don't tell him about the letter until I get more information," he decided as he put it with the memos in his briefcase.

He got into his car and headed to his parents' home.

*

The Stern Family Home

"Michael, what a nice surprise," Marcus said opening the door. "It isn't like you to stop by on a week-day. Come in. Let me take your coat."

"I'm on my way back to the office, Father. I have something to ask you and I didn't want to do it on the phone. I don't have a lot of time."

"Let's go into the study. Your mother will be sorry that she has missed you. She is at a meeting for some charity fundraiser," he said ushering him into his study. "Lily, get us some coffee," he said to his housekeeper.

"No, none for me, Father. Thanks. I had several cups earlier at a breakfast meeting." He sat down in front of his father, who was sitting in his big leather chair behind the large oak desk. He felt as if he was sixteen years old again, about to ask his father for the keys to his car. He had always had a good relationship with his father, learning to respect and love him as a very little boy. He remembered when Marcus had told him that he had adopted him, and how "special" he was to them because they had "picked him." He also remembered that he had started to call Marcus by the name of "Father" soon afterward

Marcus had never told Jacqueline about the adoption and he had asked Michael to keep the secret until he had told her, but that had never happened. Now, Michael had anxiety about bringing up the subject of his adoption with his father again. Since he had always been straightforward with his father, never mincing words, he began by getting to the point of his visit. "I need to know about my adoption, Father. We are trying to get pregnant – going to some specialists because of Elise's medical problems. We think that it is important that we know as much about our genetic background as possible," he said, carefully avoiding the mention of the letters sent to Jackie and him.

Marcus moves to the family portrait of the four of them that hangs on the wall behind his desk. Michael was about ten in the portrait and Jacqueline was about eight. Michael remembers the day when he and his sister had sat for the portrait. He recalls his happiness and suddenly feels the same joy now. He recalls the exact moment and feels the same

264

happiness now as he had then. He watches as his father pulls back the portrait and reaches his hand onto the dial of the lock on a safe, hidden behind it. He had never known about the wall safe hidden behind the portrait. Marcus put the combination into the lock; the door of the safe opened easily. He reached into the safe and pulled out a large manila envelope.

"This file will tell you everything that I know, Michael."

He walks over to the cabinet holding his collection of liquor and pours two drinks, not saying a word while Michael opens the file. Marcus takes a sip of brandy, watching his son intently as he reads. Michael's facial expression changes as he read the file further, a look of surprise shows on his face. He accepts the glass of brandy Marcus offers him.

Michael had always been very animated; anyone could read his mind just by looking at his face. He reads the file, starting with the heading on the first document: "Michel and Jacqueline Debauch."

A French Underground Organization had sent the information to a German American Relief Organization in the United States. The information concerned two children who were German orphans, named 'Maximilian Franz Fuerst' and 'Ana Alexandra Fuerst'." He takes a drink of brandy and sits the glass down on his father's desk. His mouth drops as he continues to read that their father was "Captain Felix Fuerst," a German Officer in Berlin. He continued to read that their mother was 'Sofia Gunther Fuerst' and that she had fled her husband and THE THIRD REICH in 1944 with the help of an undisclosed underground organization.

Their new names were 'Adeline Debauch', Michel, and Jacqueline Debauch, her children, in order that they could be smuggled out of Germany. Their flight out of Berlin led them to Normandy, staying in a farmhouse near the Normandy coast exactly at the time when the Allies had made their surprise invasion. Shells hit the farmhouse, killing Adeline. The French freedom fighters had found them, took Michel and Jacqueline to an organization that offered help to the war refugees. Michael, moved by the document, sat staring at it. Without looking up, or saying anything to his father, he scanned the document again.

There was no information about the fate of their biological father. The file said that he had been a police officer in Berlin and that he had become a soldier of THE THIRD REICH, primed for a place in the hierarchy of THE THIRD REICH. A document confirmed that the Sterns had taken custody of the children on August 1, 1944. The Organization verified that their parents, Felix and Sofia Fuerst were dead. The official document of adoption, issued in January 1946, states that Marcus and Harriet Stern of Pittsburgh, Pennsylvania, U.S.A. had adopted the children, and changed their names to Michael and Jacqueline Stern. The document confirmed the deaths of Captain Fuerst and his wife. Michael reads the papers again, sitting quietly, lost in thought.

"I'm sorry, Michael. Maybe, I should have told you. I thought that it was better for you if you didn't know about your German connection," Marcus said putting his hand on his son's shoulder.

"It wasn't easy after the war for anyone, and those who were German or Japanese had it particularly hard." Michael sat silently, listening, and hoping that his father would offer further explanations.

"To be honest, Michael, I believed that Felix Fuerst was still alive and I pulled some strings to make sure that your file had indicated that he was dead. I didn't want you or your sister brought up by the likes of him. I could never let that happen – not after what they had done to my family and so many others."

Michael looked at his father's face, noticing that talking about the war brought out the deep grooves in his forehead and the circles under his eyes. "I understand, Father. I understand."

"If it had been known that one parent was still alive, it would have complicated the adoption process. Michael, when I heard of your background and the facts about your parents, I could never allow him to raise you. The documentation had been proven and consistent about your mother stating that she was dead– killed in the act of leaving her husband. There was little doubt in my mind what I had to do."

"I understand, Father," Michael said again remembering the story that Marcus had shared with him many years later when Michael had joined his law firm.

"I did everything that I could think of to make sure that you and Jacqueline would be two children who wouldn't be harmed any further. I didn't care what your heritage was," he said firmly. "When I saw you both for the first time, I thought that you had suffered enough." Michael shifted his body in his chair and reached for the brandy. "I fabricated everything about your biological father's death, because I didn't want him to find you and try to take you away. I wouldn't allow that, Michael."

"You never had any other contact with him over the years, Father?"

"No, Michael, I have never heard another word. This is the first time that this file has been out of the safe. We had thought about sharing the file with you, from time to time. Frankly, we could never find the appropriate time. Since you are here today asking questions, then today is the day. We have been very negligent in telling Jacqueline. We could never find the words to tell her. I guess we should, especially now that she is having so much trouble conceiving. Maybe it is something in her genetic background. She still believes that your mother and I are her biological parents."

"I completely understand, Father. Until today, I never really questioned my background," he said, thinking about the mysterious letters that he and Jackie had just received. He thought quickly, deciding that he shouldn't tell his father about them, at least not until he has had a chance to investigate their validity.

"Your mother and I had just talked about booking a flight to Paris, to talk to Jackie. I think that we should do that as soon as possible."

"Yes, Father. Maybe it would be good to show Stephen the file first. Perhaps he could find out some more information about our biological background and then share it with both of us."

"Please don't say anything to her, Michael. We want to be the ones to tell her."

"Of course, Father. I won't say anything to her until you have talked to her," Michael said thinking that it may be difficult now because of the letters. "If the letters are legitimate, then our biological father, Felix Fuerst, may have written them," he thought as he confirmed his decision not to share them with his father as a good one. He knows he will share them with him, but not now.

"May I have this file, Father?"

"I have no use for it now, Michael. I hope that it will help you find the answers that you and Elise are looking for." They embraced. Michael held on just a little longer than usual.

"Give Mother my love, Father? I'll talk to both of you again soon." He put on his coat and walked to the door.

*

Michael has a great deal to think about as he drives the remaining miles into the city to his law office he shares with his father. He isn't sure how he will handle the events. He knows that he had to get back to Jacqueline, uncertain as to what he would tell her, but certain that he wouldn't tell her about her adoption. He also recognized that he must find out about the letters, and who had sent them, and why.

"Jacqueline is on line one," Irene announced as he had entered his office. He thought quickly as he picked up the phone and started to talk. He listened as she again expressed her concern over the letter.

"Listen, Jacqueline, I talked to Father about the letter. He thinks it must be a hoax. It must be some kind of a mistake. He suggested that it could possibly have been sent to the wrong person by someone who had been given the wrong information," Michael lied.

He had never lied to Jackie before. He didn't tell her that he also received the same letter. He decided that he would investigate the letter and tell her to, "Go on with business, as usual."

"If the letter is legitimate, in some crazy way, then the person will contact you again. However, I am sure that it is some kind of a mistake. Don't worry, Jacqueline."

"Okay, Michael, if you think I should, I'll just forget about it."

"I think it is best, Jackie. I love you."

"I love you, too, Michael. Bye."

After they had hung up, he thought more about the letter and the mysterious author. "I especially don't want to upset Jacqueline any further. It might jeopardize this pregnancy if she thinks she is dealing with some kind of a 'nut'," he thought pushing the intercom button.

"Irene, get Richard Saunter on the phone."

Richard Saunter, Michael's friend but also a Private Investigator, had helped Michael on some previous cases. Michael decided that he needed to find out everything he could about a man named 'Felix Fuerst'. He had a funny premonition about the whole thing.

*

Several days later

Richard Saunter had easily found the information that his friend Michael Stern had hired him to discover. He only had to make several phone calls to a few of his contacts and he was able to find the man named 'Felix Fuerst'. It took his contacts only a few days to track down the information, discovering that Fuerst was living in West Berlin. He called Michael and shared the information with him. Michael's tone of voice had indicated that he was pleased. That was yesterday. Now, his secretary told him that Michael Stern was on the phone, wishing to speak to him again. He picked up the phone and began the conversation with his friend.

Michael didn't delay telling him the reason for his call. The first words out of him mouth were that he needed to arrange a meeting with the man as soon as possible. Richard said that he would do that and get back to him. Richard contacted Fuerst and arranged a meeting with Michael and Fuerst in West Berlin, explaining to Michael that Fuerst was in poor health and not able to come to Pittsburgh. He also shared that he actually had spoken to Fuerst's son, who told Richard that his father had asked him to try to find Michael for him.

Michael told Richard that he was very pleased and thankful that he had been was able to locate Fuerst, but he didn't divulge any other information to him. He made plans to fly to West Berlin according to the arrangements that Richard had made. Michael didn't tell anyone about the meeting with his biological father in West Berlin. He didn't even tell Elise the nature of his trip to West Berlin. He told her that "business" was taking him to W. Germany. He planned on stopping in Paris to see Jacqueline. When he arrived in West Berlin, he checked into the hotel and made contact with the man who had said that he was Felix's son. His name was Frederick and he spoke very good English. They arranged that Michael would come to visit his father in the nursing home the next morning.

Michael caught a cab and traveled across town to the nursing home. He was met there by a man who appeared to be somewhere in his early forties, identifying himself as "Frederick Fuerst." He was a handsome man with dark blonde hair, blue eyes, and a warm friendly smile. Michael was somewhat taken aback by the man, thinking that he looked a lot like Jacqueline and himself. That was his first clue to unraveling the mysteries of his adoption. He thought that the mild-mannered German man might indeed be a connection to their past life.

*

Frederick and Michael sat in the lobby of the nursing home, carrying on a conversation that would give Michael some answers to his questions. Frederick explained to him that recently his father had been in contact with a man from his past life, a man named 'Adam Schmidt'.

"Adam Schmidt was your great uncle, Michael. He and your grandmother, Alexandra Schmidt Gunther, had been brother and sister, twins actually. Alexandra had married a man named Gerhard Gunther, a baker; they had two children, Sofia and Franz. Sofia, born in 1919, was your mother. Gerhard had arranged her marriage to the neighborhood police officer, Felix Fuerst, who was your father." Michael listened, remembering the file that his father had given him.

"My father is your father, Michael . . . I guess that makes us step-brothers," Frederick said.

Michael felt uncomfortable; not sure if he liked finding out the information that Frederick had just shared. Frederick continued to explain what he knew. Seeming to understand Michael's discomfort, he spoke in a quiet, deliberate manner, keeping his eyes on Michael.

"Felix and Sofia were born and raised in Berlin. Felix was a police officer, but when THE THIRD REICH had risen to power, they forced him to become a Nazi. He never sanctioned the policies of THE THIRD REICH; he had secretly worked to help the oppressed Jews, and eventually some of the Germans, the very few who had stood up against them and had lived to tell about it. He worked with a secret underground organization of which your Uncle Adam was a member. In early 1944, he and Adam devised a plan to get Sofia and their two children out of Berlin. He couldn't tell Sofia, or anyone, about his workings with the secret organizations, nor could he tell anyone that his contact with them was Adam Schmidt.

When the Allies had occupied Berlin in 1945 and the regime had fallen, our father had secretly escaped to East Berlin and had managed to establish a new identity before finally escaping to the west just as they had constructed the Wall. Later he learned that Sofia and the children had not survived their flight out of Berlin and he stopped looking for them. He had become instrumental in the reconstruction of Germany, working for organizations whose missions had been to reunite those displaced by war. Felix had worked his whole life helping others."

"This is unbelievable, Frederick."

"He had never forgotten his children, or Sofia; he had assumed total responsibility for their deaths, blaming himself for everything. He had thought that he might have acted too hastily in sending them away. Perhaps, if he had not arranged to send them, they may have survived. He worked his entire life to right all the wrongs through work with the reconstruction and relief organizations. It had taken him by total surprise when Adam had found him and told him that he believed that Sofia was dead, but that the children had actually survived. Father asked me to find his children for him. It is the wish of a dying man; he has terminal cancer. He won't live much longer."

"Then, it was you who had sent the letters to Jacqueline and me?"

"Yes, my father wanted it that way. He didn't want to disrupt your life but he didn't know what information you might already know about your parents, or if you had known about your own adoption at all. He had learned that a Jewish American family had adopted you. He didn't want to cause more heartache in your lives by revealing the truth that your father had been a Nazi. He thought that when you received the letter, it might be enough to get you to act, to find him or the person writing the letter. He wanted to see you one more time before he died, but he was uncertain if the wish would be mutual. He thought that you would either dismiss the entire thing or come searching for him. As it turned out, you found him."

"Thank you for telling me the story of my parents. I feel like I should tell you what I know. It makes more sense to me, now."

Michael told Frederick about the file. After talking to each other and sharing the details of their lives, both men realized that they shared a bond. Michael shared his life as an American, after being born German. Frederick shared his life as a German, living in post-World War II Germany. Finally, Frederick asked Michael if he would like to meet his father. Michael affirmed that he would.

Felix Fuerst's Hospital Room

Michael could never have prepared for the meeting with his biological father. He looked at the man who was lying in the bed, trying to force memories. Something came over him. He felt a connection. Flashes of his childhood appeared. He couldn't identify the flashes, but sensed that they were real.

As he looked at Felix, studying him, he couldn't find any memories of the time before he had come to America. He thought that he was sleepwalking and that he would wake up from this dream. He walked slowly to the side of the bed, stared at the man, and wondered why he wasn't able to remember him. However, he felt an uncanny link to him, one that didn't fit. Frederick walked to the side of the bed and took his father's hand to wake him. Felix opened his eyes and looked at his son. His eyes went to the man who was with him.

Frederick didn't have to introduce Michael.

Felix looked at Michael and whispered, "Max."

As soon as Michael heard the man say, "Max," a vision flashed in his mind, showing him as a little boy, playing with the man.

"Max …. Max …. Max …" Felix repeated.

Each time he heard his name, Michael saw another vision of him and the man together. Felix smiled as he said the name, recognizing the man standing beside him as his little boy, Max. He reached his hand out slowly to touch Michael's with tears in his eyes. Michael offered his hand and smiled.

"Ana?" Felix asked looking into Michael's eyes.

"Ana is fine, Vater. She is still in Paris," Frederick said in German.

When Michael heard Felix speak in German, it shook him. He remembered his voice and he thought that he even understood some of the German words. The three of them spoke back and forth in English and German with Frederick acting as a translator. He told the entire story. It seemed to give Felix satisfaction because he had a smile on his face when they had finished.

"I have never forgotten you, Max, or Ana, or your mutter. Please, tell me what happened to you."

Michael told Felix (through Frederick) that a Jewish American family had adopted him and his sister and that America had been their new home, providing them with a good life as the children of Marcus and Harriet Stern. He told of his Law practice and of his sister's Fashion Design business. He told Felix that Marcus Stern had raised them as Jews. He also told him that Marcus would never allow a Nazi to raise them and that he had done everything possible to hide them from their biological father because he was a Nazi.

Felix sighed.

"I'm glad you grew up in America and that you didn't know about your German heritage. You never had to experience the guilt of saying, "I am German" to all of those who had been harmed," he said to Michael tears coming into his eyes. "But, it saddens me that you had no knowledge of your German heritage. Before the war, it had been an honor to be German."

"Close your eyes, Vater. It will be all right. We will come back, again. You are tired now," Frederick said noticing how the visit had weakened him. The two of them filed out of the room.

"Would you like to come to my home and meet my wife, Michael?" Frederick asked as they boarded the elevator.

"Oh, thanks, Frederick, but I can't. I have a plane to catch. I'm on my way to Paris to meet with Jacqueline."

*

On his flight to Paris, Michael had much to ponder. He had decided not to tell Frederick about Jacqueline's condition. He wanted to tell Jacqueline about her adoption, but he remembered his promise to Marcus not to do that. He needed to call Marcus and tell him what had just occurred, but he wasn't sure just how the news would affect Jacqueline or if she would also want to meet her biological father. Michael had received a phone call from Stephen just before he had left for the airport. He told Michael that Jacqueline had just had another miscarriage.

"I'm on my way to Paris, Stephen," Michael told him.

*

Paris, France

During his traveling, Michael had time to digest all that had happened in the last several days. He also had some time to think about whether or not he should tell Jacqueline about their adoption. Felix had expressed his desire to see her but Michael knew that Jacqueline would be depressed after having yet another miscarriage. He knew what having a baby meant to her and he knew that losing another child was going to be devastating.

He didn't know how he could possibly tell his sister about Felix or about her adoption. He decided that he should call his father and tell him what had happened. As soon as he had arrived in Paris, he called them from the airport and shared the news.

"We will take the next flight to Paris, Michael," Marcus told him.

Stephen met Michael at the airport and took him back to his home. Michael greeted Jacqueline with a kiss and a hug and expressed his deep sympathy as he held her close.

"I'm so happy that you could come, Michael. I hope that you didn't cut your business trip short."

"Well, actually, something important had brought me to see you besides my wishing to support you at this time, Jackie. I won't say any more until Father gets here."

"Father is coming to Paris?"

"I've talked to Mother and Father, Jacqueline. They're coming tomorrow."

Jacqueline looked surprised.

She had thought that he was acting very mysteriously, but she was glad to have him and her parents with her, and she asked no further questions.

*

The next afternoon, Stephen and Michael went to the airport to pick up Marcus and Harriet and the five of them sat down in the living room of Jacqueline's home, giving Marcus the opportunity to talk to her for the first time about her adoption.

"Michael was older and I thought that he would have memories of his early life. It seemed best to tell Michael at the time. I told him that he was 'special' and that we had 'picked' him above many others to become our son. You were so young. We knew that you wouldn't have memories of a past life. As it had turned out, Michael's memories seemed to disappear as well. We decided that it was best to not tell you of the past but some things that have come up now demand that we do."

He began by telling her that she was indeed as special to them as if she had been their own biological child. He apologized to them both again for not telling the truth about their heritage, but he qualified the apology by again saying that he had done everything he could to prevent their biological father from ever coming to take them away. He confessed that he had arranged to have the adoption secured by falsifying the records to show that their father was actually dead. He also had taken steps to show that the two of them were dead, just in case their father would ever search for them.

"I made up my mind that you would never be raised by a Nazi."

Jacqueline listened as Michael told her about his trip to West Berlin and meeting their biological father. He explained that he had also received a letter, the same as hers, and that he had hired Richard to track down Felix Fuerst from the information that Marcus' file had provided.

Jacqueline sat still, obviously stunned by all the information.

"We love both of you as if you are our biological children. We have never thought of you in any other way," Harriet said.

Jacqueline and Michael hugged their parents and hugged each other.

"You will always be my mother and father – no matter what," Jacqueline said, choking back her tears.

The Stern Family was still intact. Nothing could ever break the bonds that held this family together, simply because it wasn't blood, but love.

*

Several days later, after the Stern family had time to think about all that had happened, Jacqueline expressed the desire to meet Felix Fuerst. They all decided that they would go to Berlin to meet with him, again. "We will have to do it quickly," Michael said.

"Felix is on his deathbed."

They all thought that the meeting was essential for the family to move on with their lives. Marcus and Harriet had expressed their opinion that their children needed to have closure. They needed to make it possible for their children to come to grips with the secrets of their births and their heritage. They also needed closure.

Jacqueline met the father and stepbrother that she had never known. Again, Michael met with their father, the one whom he had learned to forget, but was now trying to remember. Marcus and Harriet met the man whom they had hated because he was a Nazi. They told the dying man "raising his two children had been the most important thing that had ever happened" to them.

Felix cried.

Later, Jacqueline and Stephen returned to Paris and Michael and his parents returned to Pittsburgh. They promised Frederick that they would keep in touch and asked him to do the same.

*

Several weeks later, Jacqueline was back to work at the office shortly after losing her third pregnancy. She was still trying to digest the information revealed to her. In a strange way, the revelations had made her feel whole. She had no recollections of her biological parents and only remembered

Marcus and Harriet. However, for the first time in her life she really appreciated her adoptive parents, realizing their depth of love for her.

She hoped that she and Stephen would someday be able to share the same sense of family by having their own child but with all of the problems they had experienced, she wondered about her inability to carry a pregnancy to full term. She often thought it might be genetic, but there wasn't anything in Harriet's history that would suggest that it was. Now, with this new set of information, everything seemed to change.

"If nothing else comes from these new revelations, maybe, I can find some answers to my inability to have a child," she thought.

She was acutely aware that the stress of getting pregnant, only to lose the baby within the first three months, had taken a toll on her both physically and emotionally. She and Stephen talked again about the possibility of adoption. Stephen felt that the idea of adoption was the best course; he expressed his desire to proceed with the process.

Jacqueline couldn't accept the fact that they would be childless. She was tired after the ordeal with the latest miscarriage and the news of her own adoption and reunion with her biological father. She persuaded Stephen to put everything on hold. They decided not to make any decisions either way.

Her business was doing very well and she thought that perhaps it might be time to move back to the States. She was missing home; the news about her own adoption had made her even more homesick and she was still finding it hard to believe that she wasn't the biological daughter of Marcus and Harriet Stern. She knew that no matter what ever happened they would always be her parents. However, the events had aroused her curiosity about her biological parents and their German background.

"It certainly is a strange situation. One day you wake up and find out that you aren't who you think you are."

Antoinette interrupted her day dreaming with another phone call. It was Michael.

"Felix is dead, Jacqueline. Frederick said that he had passed peacefully in his sleep last evening. The service will be a simple one, to take place in several days. I told him that I would fly to Berlin; I have already begun to make the arrangements. Elise will be coming, too."

"Michael, I want to come too."

She was pleased that Stephen said that he would go with her to West Berlin, and glad that he said he would make all of the arrangements.

*

They attended the service at the church and then went to the cemetery. Afterward, there was a reception for the mourners at a hotel. It was an equally strange experience for Jacqueline and Michael. At the funeral, others referred to them as 'Felix's children'. They met other family and friends, including Adam Schmidt. Frederick helped as a translator for Adam and the other family members who didn't speak English.

"You are as beautiful as your mother, Jacqueline; to me you will always be 'Ana.' I loved my twin sister very much. I know that she would be very proud of you and Max," Adam said in fluent French.

"I'm sorry that I never had the opportunity to know my biological mother, Adam. I'm glad that I have met you," Jacqueline replied in her very strong command of the French language, recently developed even further since she had become a resident of Paris.

"The last time that I had seen you and Max, you were sleeping on a bed in a farmhouse somewhere on the outskirts of Paris. Your mother was worried. She had questions about whether she had done the right thing by leaving Berlin and your father. After the invasion of Europe, my heart ached when I found out that you had all been killed," he said, choking back tears. After the war, I worked with a group of patriots who were determined to restore France. I eventually became involved in the restoration of Germany. It had become somewhat complicated once the Berlin Wall went up. We established many databases to help those who were looking for displaced relatives. I never came across anything about you, your mother, or Felix until recently, confirming my belief that all of you had perished."

"I often questioned my decision to help Felix. He was so determined, much like your great grandmother 'Frieda'. She was a very strong woman, determined, and strong willed. You come from a long line of very strong men and women," he said tears rolling down his cheeks. "I have never gotten over losing my twin sister, Alexandra. I blame myself for her death," he said putting his head down, and then gently shaking it from side to side. "I should never have sent them to Switzerland."

"Perhaps, you shouldn't talk anymore about it, Uncle Adam," she said. "It is much too painful for you."

Adam sighed, surprised to hear the word 'Uncle' attached to his name. He closed his eyes and dropped his head, his chin resting on his chest.

On the return trip to Paris, Jacqueline was very quiet. Stephen noticed it and commented to her about it. "I'm fine. I just have an enormous amount to digest." They never discussed their plans for parenthood, feeling that it was something they would discuss another day.

One morning and a few days later, Jacqueline looked into the mirror and decided that she would be too old to be a mother unless she acted immediately. At forty-two years old, she thought that it was time for them to try to adopt a child. After talking it over with Stephen, he agreed. Since then, she has thought of nothing else.

Stephen said that he would use his legal contacts to see what he could find out about the process. In the meantime, she made phone calls and sent out applications to every agency that she could find, both in Europe and in the United States. In the process of searching, a contact told him about childcare's organization called the "World Organization of Quilts" or W.O.O.Q. The Organization had started out as a relief organization to help needy children, branching into worldwide adoption agencies. The first center had opened in West Virginia. An American woman, a well-known author, Sophie Simon, had started the Organization. She had written several best-selling books for children. Made into animated films about a magical quilt, they had become box office hits. Jacqueline remembered seeing them with Harriet when she had been a little girl.

As far as Stephen could find out, there were no centers in Paris. He mentioned it to Jacqueline and they decided to plan a trip back home to visit the center in West Virginia. They were excited about this center because they had felt that their chances of adopting a child were good. They flew home to Pittsburgh and stayed with Marcus and Harriet. It surprised them when Marcus shared that he had heard something about these centers. "I think that the woman who started these centers actually lives in Pittsburgh," he had said. "And, Michael has promised to investigate further for you while you make your first visit to West Virginia."

*

A Month Later

From their very first look at the WOOQ facility, they had been impressed with what they had seen. When they had pulled the car up to the entrance, the first thing they had noticed was a large metal structure arched over the paved driveway. An array of patchwork squares, each engraved with a child's face, covered the surface of the arch. Stephen stopped the car in front of the arch and they spent several minutes looking at the structure before crossing under it and pulling up in front of the front door. A Director greeted them and then guided them to each section of the complex, offering explanations and answering their questions.

In each section of the complex, they observed children engaged in various activities, depending upon their ages. There was a large cafeteria where the children ate meals family style. There were many adults interacting with them. The director told them that some of the children would only spend a few days with them and others would spend a month or more. Others would be there longer, but the goal was always to return the children to their families as soon as the families could take them. In some cases, that was impossible and they turned to providing adoption services.

Every case received individual treatment. There were no charges for the services, although there was a strict review process to make sure that the children admitted were indeed needy. The mission statement came down from the founder: 'No child will be turned away.'

Each center was responsible for finding charitable organizations that would fund them. This was the first center and it had become a model for all the others. Recently, they had found a need for a family of six children, orphaned by the death of their parents. The organization worked to find suitable families for the children, but wanted to keep them together. Through diligence and persistence, they found a childless couple who wanted all six of them. Impressed by what they had seen and heard, Jacqueline and Stephen told the director that they would like to make application.

On the way back to Pittsburgh, they discussed the experience hoping that it would bring them a child, but exercising some guarded enthusiasm, not wanting to be disappointed. When they arrived at her parents' home, they couldn't wait to share everything with Marcus and Harriet. After discussing the process with them, they were pleased that Marcus offered his encouragement, recalling that adopting Michael and Jacqueline had been the most rewarding part of their lives. Jacqueline also discussed with them that she and Stephen wanted to move back to the United States. They also visited Michael and Elise to tell them the good news.

*

Michael was happy to hear his sister and her husband were coming back to live in the United States. He was also happy to hear that they had decided to try to adopt a child. *That will make it easier for me to tell Jackie that Elise is pregnant.* He knew Jacqueline would have mixed emotions in light of her miscarriages, but he thought that maybe her enthusiasm about adoption would make the news a little more bearable for her. When he heard about the organization that they had visited, he promised to investigate it and make sure that there were no legal problems.

The next few months were busy ones for everyone. Jacqueline and Stephen had to coordinate the move home. Michael and Elise were busy getting ready for the birth of their first child. Each day seemed to fly by for both couples. They were absorbed in their lives and all the changes that were taking place.

Elise started a practice in pediatrics. She had some contacts with some parents who had told her about the W.O.O.Q., and she mentioned it to Michael. Michael remembered that it was the same organization impressing Jacqueline and Stephen. When the discussion came up with Elise, he remembered that he had promised to investigate the centers.

The next day, he made some phone calls and found out more information about the center in West Virginia. He also decided to ask his friend, Richard Saunter, to investigate them to make sure that there were no improprieties. He knew that his sister and her husband suffered enough disappointment in their desire to have a family.

He didn't want this to become another one.

Richard Saunter called him several days later and told him he had accumulated quite a bit of information about the centers, and about the woman who had established them. He told Michael that he would gladly share everything that he had found. He also told him that the woman had become quite wealthy and quite famous for her work as a writer of children books and that she had made her home in Pittsburgh.

He said a writer named 'Jeffery Anderson, who coincidentally happened to be her husband, had written a bestselling book about her life. The book, A NEW BEGINNING, had received rewards. The woman who had started the centers also had released a best seller, called ONCE UPON A TIME, followed by three others, that had made it to the top of the charts too.

Michael told him that he would like to get a copy of both of these books. He also said that he wanted to go over the contents of the file that Richard was sending him. Michael was surprised to hear from his parents that his sister and her husband planned a move back to Pittsburgh at the end of the month. He was even more surprised to get a phone call from Jacqueline.

"I just couldn't wait one more moment. I have to tell you. I'm pregnant again."

"I'm so excited for you. I can't wait for you to come home. This is great news!"

Not long after, in November 1984, the entire Stern Family sat down for Thanksgiving dinner in the Stern's family home in Pittsburgh. They felt that the events of the past year had been blessings. They had revealed the secret of their children's heritage and they were now expecting two grandchildren in the next year. In addition, they were all together again. It was a great day for giving thanks and looking forward to the future in the Stern household.

*

21 May 1985

Michael called his parents with the news that he had just become a father. He was so excited that he could barely get the words out. "It is a boy," he shouted into the phone. "It's a beautiful, baby boy." He heard the joy in Marcus' voice on the other end of the line, shouting to Harriet.

He went back to the waiting room, joining Stephen and Jacqueline who were present with him during the long labor. Elise and the baby were resting, and the nurse told him his son would be in the nursery soon for them to see him.

As they stood in front of the crib in the nursery window, the three of them couldn't take their eyes off Michael's new son. Stephen and Jacqueline held hands and hoped that, soon, they would be looking at their own baby in the nursery window.

Jacqueline's pregnancy was progressing well. She was in the third trimester and had not had any of the problems like those that had plagued her with the other pregnancies. The doctors had just told her at her last checkup that everything was fine. They were very optimistic she would carry this baby to full term. They had not heard anything about the adoption. They thought that it must have been a good omen because they had found out that they were pregnant shortly after they had made application to the W.O.O.Q. That had been seven months ago, and they had not heard a word since then.

The next two months flew by for Michael and Elise. They were totally enthralled in this new adventure called, "parenthood." They decided to call their son, 'David Michael Stern'. He was a beautiful addition to the Stern Family, and one that everyone cherished.

*

July 1985

Jacqueline thought the days and weeks couldn't go by fast enough. Each day, she was one more step toward the end of the pregnancy and the birth of their child. She was still worried that something would happen to spoil this pregnancy. She was especially concerned when she remembered what Uncle Adam had told her about his mother, Frieda and the difficulties she had delivering her children.

One day, she got a phone call that took her by surprise. It was from the Adoption Agency, the W.O.O.Q, telling her that they had a child for them to adopt. The Agency asked her if she and her husband could come to the center to discuss the adoption of a little, four-year old boy. She told them that she would call her husband and get back to them.

When she called Stephen, she was surprised to hear some hesitancy in his voice. He told her that he wasn't sure if they should go ahead with the adoption now. Stephen's reaction stopped Jacqueline's enthusiasm. She had been so excited when the woman told her about the little boy for adoption that she had not even thought about her pregnancy. She thought that it should make no difference. That evening, she decided to tell Stephen that she wanted to go ahead with the adoption anyway, and that she wanted to meet with the agency. He agreed and they called the agency back to make the appointment.

A few days later, when they visited the center, the director was surprised to hear about Jacqueline's pregnancy. She asked if this fact would change their desire to adopt a child. They assured her that this new turn of events wouldn't change their desire to adopt. They felt that since this child was older, it was perfect for their plans to have more than one child and they asked about going forward with the adoption. As it turned out, the center granted them permission to bring the little boy home within a week of the phone call. Although the final adoption would happen in six months, they released the child to them. Suddenly, they became parents of one and expecting another.

The little boy had lost both of his parents in an automobile crash and had no other living relative. He had survived the crash without a scratch physically but not emotionally. He was a special little boy who had a sweet personality and easy disposition, and the counselors were optimistic that he would make a good adjustment, after he worked through the grief of losing his parents. He needed the tender loving care of a devoted couple who could replace his mother and father. His name was Raymond.

When they told Michael about the little boy and the pending adoption, Michael remembered that he had promised to investigate the agency. He still had the file in his office that Richard had accumulated for him. When he went to the file and began to read the contents, the information surprised him. He read the information several times to make sure that he had read it correctly. He was completely stuck on the first line of the text about the organization, known as the 'World Organization of Quilts.' The founder of the Organization is 'Sofia Gunther Fuerst Blackburn', he read.

He couldn't believe his eyes. Unless there were two people in the world with the same name, it appeared that their biological mother, Sofia Gunther Fuerst, was the founder of the Agency. He read on further and then read a synopsis of the bestselling book written about her life by Jeffrey Anderson.

He sat at his desk completely dumfounded. "My mother isn't dead," he whispered to himself. Shocked, he sat motionless, completely frozen in time and trying to remember. As he read about Sofia and her life, he noted the picture of the quilt shown on one of the pages describing the reason for the logo.

The quilt . . . Mother . . . I remember.

"Our mother isn't dead and I must tell Ana."

* * * * *

CHAPTER 13
A MIRACLE

"Since the publication of my latest book and the subsequent three bestselling books, the name 'Sophie Simon' had become well known," Sofia, continued. "The significance of coming to fame as a writer had produced a welcomed side effect for me. The centers became even more productive, allowing for the establishment of an additional five centers. My life had become complicated with signing sessions and interviews. All of the proceeds went to the Centers, but something else happened – something I could never even imagine yet alone think it possible.

One day in March of 1985, Jeffrey received a letter from a man named, 'Frederick Fuerst.' In the letter, Frederick told Jeffrey that my Uncle Adam was alive. He had to read the letter several times before he actually comprehended it and shared it with me. The publication of my books had brought attention to me; they had brought about things that proved to be nothing short of a miracle for me.

A thirty-minute conversation with Frederick informed him of the details. The news shocked him and he knew what it would mean to me. He told me later that he had thought that it was ironic that my obsessions with my quilt had become the catalyst for what would become the most important event in my life. However, he worried about the shock it would bring to me and he carefully planned the reunion with my uncle. He arranged his travel to Pittsburgh, rented a suite of rooms at a downtown hotel, and set the reunion for two days later. Before he shared the news with me, he asked me to sit down first.

"Jeffrey, you are scaring me," I said as my heart beat faster. "What happened? Is it Mary? Did something happen to the twins?"

"No, my Darling, this is good news. However, it is also shocking news. It is about your Uncle Adam. It seems that the Nazis had not killed him. He is alive. He will come to Pittsburgh for a meeting. It will be the day after tomorrow at a hotel downtown," he said taking her hand in his. "There is more. The Nazi's had not killed Felix. He lived and had a son named, Frederick. Felix died in a nursing home in Berlin only last year. Frederick is the one who had contacted me by letter and asked me to make the arrangements for you to meet them," he said squeezing my hand.

"What? Felix was alive and just died? Are you sure, Jeffrey?"

"I'm positive, Sofia. There is no doubt."

"I sat motionless staring into Jeffrey's eyes, searching them for answers. He put his arm on my shoulder and said, "Sofia did you hear what I've said? Are you okay? Do you understand what I've said?"

"Yes, I understand what you have said. I just can't believe it. Are you sure? There is no mistake? Adam is alive?"

"Adam is indeed alive. He is a very old man and not in great health, but he is alive and he and Frederick want to see you. They will be arriving the day after tomorrow. All of the arrangements have been made."

*

Two Days Later

Jeffrey and I arrived at the hotel for the reunion with Adam and Frederick. It had been a stressful two days for me. I had anticipated the meeting and had gotten myself into quite a state of anxiety. Jeffrey wanted me to see a doctor but I refused. I remember wondering about the ballroom he had rented. Why would he rent a ballroom, even a small one, for a meeting with two other people? I just figured it was Jeffrey's way of adding drama to the meeting. When I stepped off the elevator and looked through the glass windows down onto the Golden Triangle below, I felt a sense of nostalgia, remembering the first time I had come to Pittsburgh . . . flashes of my first time in America . . . all intermixed with all my memories of Berlin.

"I can't believe that Felix has been alive all these years. It is too unbelievable to be true. He was living a very different life and so was I. If I had only known, that Felix had been alive. Oh, I don't know, Jeffrey. To think that he just died only a year ago. At least, he was able to see Adam one more time. I just don't know how I am going to handle seeing Adam, Jeffrey. It has been so long," I said shaking my head.

"Darling, don't do this. You will meet your uncle in due time. You resolved your past many years ago. The past is the past. Remember?"

"I know you are right, but when I think of the person that I was then and who I am now. I don't recognize myself. I hope that I'll recognize Adam. Do you think he will recognize me? I have changed a lot since the last time I saw him."

"You haven't changed a bit, Sofia. You are still as beautiful as you were when you had lived in Germany."

"What would I ever do without you? I bless the day I met you, Jeffrey Anderson."

"No, Sofia. I am thankful. Thank God for Mary Long."

"I know, Jeffrey. God has been good to me and I'll always be grateful."

"Mmm, I smell something good Jeffrey. What have you done?"

"I have arranged for dinner after you meet Adam and Frederick."

"Is that sauerkraut I smell?"

"Yes, you smell the aroma of a German dinner with all of the trimmings, including the German beer."

"You think of everything Jeffrey. I love you," I said pulling him close.

When I walked into the room, I couldn't feel the floor under my feet. Ever since Jeffrey had told me the news, my anxiety level had reached monumental proportions. I had tried to imagine his face, trying to picture an older version of the man I remembered. As I entered the room on Jeffrey's arm, I saw an old man standing in front of a couch, waiting, supported by a cane. I recognized him at once. His balding head with a fringe of gray hair couldn't disguise the man whom I had loved. I moved toward him and whispered 'Uncle Adam' as I extended my arms out and embraced him. I shook as he tightened his grip on me. I thought that his body seemed so frail and small, not at all, as I had remembered. Tears streamed down our faces as we held each other.

"Am I actually holding one of my relatives?" I thought as I held on to him tightly, hoping it wasn't a dream. I had faced the realization that I had no living blood relatives many years earlier and holding onto him felt like a miracle had happened. Adam took the lead and braced himself with one hand on his cane, putting his other on my elbow and leading me to the couch.

"Sofia! Sofia! Sofia!" he repeated softly as he stroked my hand. I wanted to remember some German words so that I could speak to him but as I was trying, another man approached us. I was shocked. He looked just like Felix. My body froze as Adam squeezed my hand.

"Hello, Sofia, my name is Frederick Felix Fuerst. I'm Felix's son."

My mouth dropped and I looked at him as if he was a ghost. He spoke in English but with a strong German accent. "I have a story to tell you, Sofia. You will be shocked, but I think it will make you very happy. Adam wanted to tell you the story himself, but he didn't feel comfortable telling you the story in English and he wasn't sure if you still understood German or French. If you are ready, I'll begin."

I think I must have nodded in agreement. The rest is a blur but I'll tell you what I remember.

Frederick sat down on a chair beside the couch and turned to face Adam and me. "My father never forgot you, Sofia. He told me the story of how he had to send you and your children out of Berlin, fearing that the Soldiers of THE THIRD REICH would find him out and kill you and the children. The guilt of sending you away haunted him his entire life. You see, he had survived the reign of terror, and had been living in West Germany. They had arrested him and imprisoned him but not before torturing him trying to get him to divulge his accomplices. Among some other patriots, he had been working with Adam and eventually your father. He knew that there would come a time when they would discover his treasonous acts and execute him and everyone involved, including you and the children. He devised a plan to get you and the children out of Germany to a safe place, but he knew that you would never leave him willingly. He worried that he wouldn't be able to withstand the Nazi torture and that he would reveal Adam, your father and you if he had confided in you. As it turned out, he had escaped from prison before they could break him down or inflict the final blows. He left Berlin the same day that the world learned of Hitler's suicide. He wanted to find you, the children, and me. I am his illegitimate son, born of a woman designated as 'pure German' and part of their plan to foster a new generation of Germans who would take over the reign. They had chosen Felix to become a high-ranking officer in the police and had granted him rank accordingly. Part of his indoctrination was to impregnate one of these designated women. He did what they ordered and I am the result. The woman who was my mother died giving birth to me. They had become suspicious of him, but they had discovered that you and your parents were gone and looked to Felix, eventually arresting him. Felix searched for me and then took me to some friends of his in France while he went to look for you and your mother. He searched for you for years, hoping to reunite his shattered family. He never married again, saying that he 'would never have another Sofia.' It wasn't until last year that he had discovered Adam was still alive. He met with Adam shortly before he had passed away. Sofia, there is more. I have more to tell you."

I looked to Jeffrey for reassurance. He smiled and nodded back.

"There are still some others from your past who would like to meet you. Adam wanted to tell you that when he had read your autobiography, he realized that you were alive and he knew that you would want to know that he thought that your children also had survived," he said pausing and looking toward the door. "Max and Ana aren't dead," he whispered trying to keep his composure. "They are very much alive and are living in the same city where you live. They live here in Pittsburgh, Sofia." Just as planned, a middle-aged couple entered the room. My mind shouted out their names as flashes of them as children appeared in my mind. Some unknown force picked me up and moved me toward them.

Time stood still.

Jeffrey came to my side and reached under my arm to hold me up.

My legs collapsed under me. Jeffrey caught me as the couples stood in front of me, staring at me as if they knew me.

"My God . . . Max . . . Ana!"

We stood crying and holding on to one another until others, ones I didn't know, joined us. "Sofia, darling, there are some children who want to meet their Oma," Jeffrey whispered in my ear.

Michael Stern took his baby son from his wife's arms and brought him over to me, placing him in my arms. When I looked at his beautiful little face, I saw Max.

Stephen Mansfield, holding his adopted son's hand and carrying his newborn son, walked toward Jacqueline and put the baby into his mother's awaiting arms. When I saw her holding her newborn baby, I thought she looked like me when I had held her. Raymond trailed behind, holding the quilt that he had received at the W.O.O.Q center. I stood surrounded by my children and grandchildren, all forming around me, a ring of love, reuniting our shattered family.

An abundance of tears flowed in the room that day, tears of joy tinged with sorrow.

*

The next day, Sofia and Jeffrey hosted a reunion of Sofia's family in order for them to meet Janene and Bill. It was a day of getting to know one another and sharing their pasts, as well as making plans for the future. Later that day, Janene and Bill returned to Atlanta. As Janene exited the "Fort Pitt Tunnel" going south, the woman on the cloud appeared again. As she gazed at the beautiful woman, her heart skipped a beat.

"I'll find you, Mother. I promise."

* * * * *

CHAPTER 14
JANENE'S STORY

19 September 2008

As she walks from the elevator of the parking garage of the company where she works, Janene is lost in thought, remembering all of the conversations she had had with Sofia during their first meeting just over a week earlier. She mulls the details of what she had learned over in her mind, one by one, deciding that the meeting had provided her with some pieces to the puzzle of her heritage, but not all of them. As she recalls the details of each story, she pictures Sofia's face and sees her stroking the patches on the quilt.

It was as if she was stroking the head of one of her own children, lying quietly in her lap.

Sofia's stories, as well as the storyteller herself, had captivated her then and for days afterward. She reaches into her purse, pulls out the picture that Sofia had given her, and studies it.

"So, you are my father," she says staring at the soldier's eyes.

"If only you could talk," she smiles.

The soldier smiles back. It is a warm smile, much as the one Bill McDeenon wears every time he looks at her. Suddenly, a plan for her future emerges in her mind. Even though her adoption experience had been a wonderful one, seeing her biological father's picture and hearing his life story had filled a gap, one she had never recognized before. For the first time in her life, she feels complete. "Except for one branch of my family tree – the Vietnamese one," she thinks. Now that she has information about it, she promises herself that she will find out what happened to them and what the circumstances had been that had led to her birth.

Things fit. A deep feeling of closure fills the place where some of her questions once had been, but the new revelations have opened up new mysteries. She had always felt as if something or someone was missing in her life but she had never given into it, but rather had allowed others to divert her attention away from finding information about her roots. They had offered a whole host of negative ramifications, reasons for not beginning a search for her biological family. For the first time, she realizes that the reason she had never wanted to search for her biological family had been due to her own insecurities.

She had never really wanted to confront the possible truths, afraid of the story of the actions of a soldier in the jungle that had led to her conception. From what she had learned about the Vietnam War, she felt that the particulars of her mother's pregnancy would be emotionally upsetting to her, satisfied to leave the questions unanswered – until Madeline's death. "I miss you so much, Mum," she mourns as her mind races with images of what she should have done or might have done. As she runs to the elevator and glances at the clock on the wall, she realizes that she is early for the first time. She exits the elevator, walks down the long hall, and bursts into the office where she has been working for over two years. *Everything looks the same as when I had left it.* She knows that the office might look the same, but nothing will ever be the same for her.

"Good-morning, Janene," smiles Alison Tyler, a co-editor of the magazine.

"Morning, Allie, and such a great morning it is," she replies as she hangs her coat on the rack, not noticing the look of surprise on Allie's face.

"What kind of weekend did you have, Neeny?"

"You won't believe it, Allie."

"I thought you seemed to have a little bounce in your walk this morning. What happened? Did you meet a new hunk?"

"Well, yes and no. I did meet a new person in my life – actually several of them, but I'm not sure you would describe my father as a 'new hunk'."

"What in the world are you talking about?"

"I actually found this man," she says pulling out the picture and showing it to Allie.

"He's my biological father. His name is or I suppose I should say was -- 'Randolph Robert Blackburn III'."

"Was?"

"Yes, he's dead. He was killed in South Vietnam."

"Wow, you really did have an interesting week end, didn't you?"

"I did. I met my grandmother – my German grandmother or my 'Oma' as I have come to call her. It's even hard for me to believe, so I know you won't believe it, but 'Sophie Simon' is my biological grandmother!"

"You're kidding!"

"No, I'm not. She told me about my father and his whole family, for that matter," she said stopping to breathe. "Her story is incredible."

"Do you mean THE 'Sophie Simon?'?"

"None other . . . Can you believe it, Allie? I feel as if I've been reborn."

"Wow," she says shaking her head.

"Now, all I have to do is find my mother and my . . ." Stopped in the middle of a sentence by the sight of her boss standing in the doorway in front of her, she quickly moves to her chair in front of her desk and sits down. Allie busies herself with the papers on her desk. "Time is wasting, you two!" Mr. Corcoran prods as he moves further into the room.

"We have a deadline to meet."

"You can say that again, Mr. Corcoran. I've wasted too much time already," Janene answers as she touches the button to boot up her computer. "Actually, I have a great deal of work to do today. I'm beginning what I should've started a long time ago," she says as she clicks open the Word processing program.

"Is that so, McDeenon?"

"As soon as I put the finishing touches on the article I've written for my assignment in Pittsburgh, I'm going to write a story that will astound you, Mr. Corcoran."

"Now, what would that be?"

"I'm going to surprise you," she answers as she starts tapping the keys. She doesn't notice the shrug of his head as he leaves the room. She is preoccupied with a last minute check of the story she had written for the assignment. She wants to make sure it is perfect before she submits it.

*

A Few Hours Later:

"Hey, McDeenon, get busy on that surprise you had promised me," shouts Mr. Corcoran as Janene leaves his office.

"I already have, Mr. Corcoran."

The article she had just submitted to him buzzes in her mind. After a mental scan of it, she concluded that he had not seemed too impressed by his first glance. "He never commits himself until he has had a chance to review it several times," she reassures herself as she hurries back to her desk and puts the article out of her mind. Armed with the recording that she had made of Sofia, she feels equipped to tackle writing a story of her own.

She begins by writing about the meeting of an African-American-Vietnamese orphan who is searching for her roots and an old German woman who wants to find closure for her life after three wars on three different continents had shattered it. She decides that writing a story about how a Vietnamese orphan had found her roots would be a timely article and one that her boss would approve. She places the recorder next to her keyboard, puts on her set of headphones, and listens to Sofia's voice telling her the stories all over again, another time.

With the headphones still on her ears, she types. Soon, the first page appears on the screen. She hits the SAVE command. She still has the headphones covering her ears listening again to Sofia's voice, almost missing the ring of her cell phone.

"Hello?"

"Hi, Janene," says Bill McDeenon.

"What's up?" she asks wondering why he would call her at work.

"I think you had better come home right away, Neeny. Jeffrey Anderson called. You may want to go to Pittsburgh again. Sofia has had a stroke. It looks very serious."

"My God, I'm on my way."

*

On the way to the suburbs, Janene thinks of Sofia. She tries not to think the worst, but the memory of Madeline's funeral keeps spinning through her mind. She recalls Sofia's remarks after she had revealed her reasons for starting the centers. Her devotion to her family and country, despite her great losses, had impressed her.

"At my age, Janene, one needs to tie up the loose ends in life," Sofia had said before kissing her on the cheek and saying "I'll never say 'Good-bye' to you, Janene. That would be far too permanent. Now that I have found you, you won't get rid of me."

"Don't worry, Oma. I'll be back just as I had promised."

Picturing her last days with Madeline before she had died, she feels cold. The memories force her to consider the dreadful fact that she may have seen her new grandmother for the first and last time. The fact that Sofia had thought that she was dead gnaws at her, bringing her sadness. *One of the last things that Sofia may have done was sharing her life with the granddaughter she had never known.* It occurs to her that it was only because of Sofia's intervention that her life is starting anew and that, now, Sofia's may be ending. She hopes that, when she is Sofia's age, she can look back on her life and think that her 'loose ends' have had as much importance as Sofia's.

She thinks of the new project she has started, motivated by meeting Sofia and hearing about her life and the promise to Mr. Corcoran to write another article for the magazine. Perhaps, my efforts to find my Vietnamese family will help others who are searching for theirs. As she presses her foot to the pedal, following the freeway home, the article and the text develop. Her mind drifts to the time before she had even met Sofia.

"I think I have just started to write my first book," she decides. "I never thought it would be an autobiography, but then I never knew that I had such a wonderful story to share. The first chapter will begin with the time before I had even met Sofia – when I had been contemplating it – with a great amount of anxiety.

*

"Her mind jumps from the words of the title of the article she will write, 'The New Adoption Trends in the United States' to the word 'curiosity'. The word stares back at her after she had entered it into the dictionary function on the Word Program, an invaluable resource for an aspiring editor of a woman's magazine at the H.H.H. Publishing Company in Atlanta, Georgia. Her calendar shows tomorrow's date, ninth of September 2008, circled in red marker. The circle serves as a reminder of her interview with 'Sofia Blackburn-Anderson', also known by her pen name of 'Sophie Simon', world-renowned author, but little known founder of the international chain of adoption centers. However, despite her enthusiasm for meeting a famous person, she can't stop thinking about 'Curio', a stray cat who had found his way into their hearts.

'Curiosity', or 'Curio' as Janene had nicknamed him, has a unique penchant for sticking his nose in where it doesn't belong. The name had been a natural extension of the behavior, seeming to fit the gray and white animal perfectly. His numerous pranks had soon endeared him to the McDeenon family, who had never given a thought as to where he had come from – or why.

She decides that it had been the same with her. Bill and Madeline McDeenon had never demonstrated any concern for where she had come from. She supposes that they knew the answer to 'why' because they had lived through the war, but that they were not privy to the details identifying her background. "The name fits me as well as the cat," she thinks as she recalls the first time she had quizzed her adoptive father about the particulars of her adoption, hoping to get answers to the questions she had never raised until after her adoptive mother had died.

"You know I'll help you anyway I can, Neeny, but we never had much information about your birth," Bill replies. Madeline had just passed away after her long battle with breast cancer. Janene was missing her, trying to deal with the emptiness of losing her mother as well as her best friend. "I have this overwhelming need to know more about me, Dad. Before Mum died, I never thought much about it."

"Your mother and I always wondered if you would ask one day. When you didn't, we thought it best to just let it follow its course."

"What do you know about me?"

"Mum had a friend from college who was serving in Vietnam. They had exchanged letters. In one of his, he mentioned a little girl in an orphanage outside of Saigon. Your mother and I had been married several years and having no luck getting pregnant. The War in Vietnam had generated a lot of interest by American couples wishing to adopt the Asian children of the American soldiers. Madeline and I had decided that we wanted to adopt as well. She decided to take the necessary steps to find the little one who had impressed her friend so much. The next thing we knew, we were picking you up and bringing you home."

"Do you know how old I was?"

"No. The orphanage had estimated your age, saying you looked to be less than two years old. You were so tiny and not in very good health. They hospitalized you here in the States, delaying the adoption for a month or so. We had always celebrated your birthday on the day we had gotten you, February 2, 1973."

"Do you know the name of the soldier who was my father?"

"No. There was never any information other than your father was African-American and your mother was Vietnamese."

"Do you know where I was born?"

"We only knew that a Vietnamese woman had abandoned you and that some American soldiers had taken you to an orphanage run by a religious group."

"I have to find out more. Maybe, it is because I just want to thank them for giving me up. My life as Janene McDeenon has been wonderful," she says reaching for his hand, wrapping her small fingers around his huge ones, and squeezing them.

"No matter what happens, you and Mum will always be my parents."

"We've been the lucky ones. Who would've ever guessed that scrawny little tot would turn out to be you?" he asks with a shy grin.

"I know you are my biggest fan, but, come on – enough of that 'Daddy stuff'."

"What do you mean?"

"Stop teasing me. Where do I start?"

"I may have the perfect starting place, Neeny. I think you should start with the military, the Department of the Army. That's where we first got word of you."

"Who should I ask for?"

"A soldier named 'Corporal James Robinson'. He was the one who had told Mum about you," he says pausing with a raised eyebrow. "He had designs on marrying your mother but I came along – swept her off her feet," he smiles.

"I never knew there was anybody but you in Mum's life."

"There are a few things you just might not know, Miss Know-it-all," he teases. "Robinson might be the key to finding your answers. Maybe he can give you some information about the persons who had abandoned you. He might also be able to tell you the name of the orphanage that had held so many of the children of the American soldiers. In particular, he may shed some light on the one little orphan who had captured his heart, as she has captured mine," he says giving her a hug and kissing her cheek."

*

As thoughts of her adoptive parents flood her mind, Janene exits the freeway and heads toward the small suburban neighborhood on the outskirts of Atlanta where she had spent her childhood. Her mind goes back to the day before she and her father had made the trip to Pittsburgh. Her thoughts center on a beginning for the story as she travels the familiar trip back home.

*

"When her work has ended each day, she hurries away from her desk, dashes out of the door and runs down the hallway as if she had been a newly fired cannonball. She times her jaunts so that she will not waste time waiting on the elevator, thinking that each minute lost would keep her longer on the freeway, the worst part of her day. As she glances at the clock on her desk again, she hopes that her quick looks will make the time go faster. *Three fifty-six, four minutes to quitting time, I am one day closer to finding my parents.*

Today's excursion brings her to the elevator door just as the door is about to close. Her extended foot keeps her from falling into it, but she can't escape the penetrating eyes of her former colleague, Simone Lawrence, whose face brings her instant panic.

295

Simone had left a lasting impression. *Nothing in my life could ever be interesting enough to share with the over-confident, conceited Simone.* She dreads any further contact with her because she knows that anything she says will fly back to the small group of insecure writers who had never accepted her. Trying to weigh her words, she blurts, "Long-time, no see, Simone."

"Hey, long-time, no see," Simone says simultaneously.

She takes a deep breath, not at all confident of what to say next.

"Hey back, Simone. It has been a long time," she says trying to plan an attack. "So what's up with you?" she stammers, hoping Simone will be inspired to talk about Simone – *something she always does quite well.*

"Well, let me think. Oh, Howard and I are married now," Simone, says pausing to see if Janene reacts.

"Congratulations," she says with a straight face.

"We just purchased a condominium in that new high-end building across town. Oh, yes, the article about the Senator – I mean the new President Elect – earned me a promotion after it had been selected for syndication," she says with a pause.

"Let me see, what else? Did I mention that I think I may be pregnant?"

"You have been a busy, little girl, haven't you?" Janene sighs trying to be sincere, but not trying very hard.

"I guess so. What have you been up to?"

"Not much," Janene replies wanting to take the remark back. The humble feeling is all too familiar. Hesitating, she tries to think of something that will merit sharing it with Simone. Nothing comes to mind. Feeling she may have run out of time, she offers a desperate statement about the only thing on her mind.

"I just have to tell you about what happened to me the other day," she says immediately wishing that she had not brought up the subject.

"What? You didn't have another one of your, 'Day-jay-vu-thingies', did you?"

"No," she answers looking into Simone's eyes while holding her tongue before saying anything else she will regret.

She remembers sharing some of her uncanny experiences with the odd sensations with Simone, revealing her decision to begin a search for her roots. Simone, pretending to tease her, had mocked her in front of the entire staff. Now, she tries to push the memory of her terrible embarrassment out of her mind while continuing the conversation.

"Remember when I had told you that I had been adopted and I wanted to research my biological family?"

"I remember. Wasn't that last year's big project?"

"Yes, but I think that I'll find my family this time."

"That's great. I hope you will not be disappointed. You know what they say about 'picking your friends and not your relatives'," Simone says using that same silly little giggle that she had used when she had been caught passing the rumors. Her gossip had accused Janene of having her father use his influence to get Janene moved up the ladder to the position of Junior Editor.

"All I have is a name. I have to drive up to Pittsburgh."

"Pennsylvania?"

"Yeah, that's the one."

She decides that she will not tell Simone that she is meeting with the famous author. Just thinking the name 'Sophie Simon' gives her an inexplicable rush, one she will not share with Simone. "Simone will just have to read the story when I publish it," she thinks as she gazes at the blinking buttons marking the passing of each floor. She hopes that someone will get on and prays that Simone's stop isn't the 'GARAGE' where she had planned to get off.

The light stops on the ninth floor.

The doors open to no one.

Simone pushes the button to the next floor. The elevator is silent.

The doors open again and Simone steps out. As she watches, Simone's hips move back and forth down the hallway. She sees a scene in her mind of Simone as she shares the latest news about her with the others. She hears Simone's squeaky voice saying: *"She is trying to find another father who can pave her way to the top of the company."*

As she makes her way from the elevator to the garage, she remembers the time when she had first shown interest in finding her biological family and had made the dreadful mistake of sharing it with Simone. From those depressing feelings, her mind jumps to the embarrassing moments when Simone had made fun of her in front of the others, calling her *the company's little orphan.* Depression accompanies her on her walk to her parking space.

She had had a difficult time liking the other young writers in her former department because of the demeaning way they had treated her as the newest member. However, it had not taken her long to realize Simone had convinced the others that she had used her father's influence to gain status in the company. The falsehoods fueled talk among the small group of writers who had dished out a heavy dose of subtle ridicule, sometimes even making innuendos with racial overtones. The hurt had lingered as she had felt that there wasn't another person in the department to befriend.

The fact that she was the only employee of mixed race in the company contributed to her loneliness. She knew that the rumors were false, but that didn't help. Her adoptive father had never been involved with the company in any capacity. His career had been in the Department of the Army as a 'Special Investigator'. She found the situation with her colleagues painful, feeling that it was just one more rejection in a long line of ones that had surfaced early in her childhood.

She bore little resemblance to her Caucasian adoptive parents or siblings. The McDeenons eventually had two biological sons after they had adopted Janene. Both of the boys had inherited their father's blue eyes and mother's light hair. Despite appearances, she had never felt that she had not belonged. On the contrary, it was the only place she felt secure. In her mind, she was the big sister of the family, the only girl, and "Daddy's little girl" for sure. However, her school experience had been the opposite.

*

She had always felt "different" from the other children, never fitting in with the many groups. She was the only student of mixed racial background and she had little contact with any African-Americans and no contact with any Asians, remaining a loner through school. She had only one girlfriend whose military parents had moved, leaving her feeling a great loss. She had little social involvement, just with the church group, but she had graduated high school with honors and attended a local college, earning a degree in Journalism.

At thirty-something, she was still living at home with her father – with 'no significant other' in her life. She viewed her job at the publishing company as her most important accomplishment. However, more than wanting her peers to view her work fairly, she wanted them to like her, and she felt that Simone's vicious rumors had taken any hope of that away. As it had turned out, she had earned a promotion out of the department to Senior Editor with a hefty raise – which had just seemed to make things worse. She felt like she was back in grade school where she had spent her childhood trying to prove one thing or another to her peers, meeting with one rejection after another or, worse yet, reliving her high school years. Her senior year presented the final embarrassment when one of the McDeenon cousins, Jeremy, was kind enough to volunteer to take her to her senior prom because no one else had offered.

As she stands in front of the car door, trying to get her mind cleared of the depression that would always grip her, she recalls her background while fumbling for her keys buried in the bottom of her purse. After a bit of trouble, she finds the keys, opens the door lock, and throws her purse across the seat to the passenger side where it lands upside down, spilling its contents onto the seat and floor. The site of the spilled items, scattered about, reminds her of the state of her life. It seems to her that she has never been able to get things on track. "My life is one big train wreck," she thinks as she makes a half-halfhearted attempt to gather up a few of her things. "Damn it. Why is my life so disorganized?" she shouts closing the car door with a thud. A woman getting into her own car parked beside hers issues an icy stare. Their eyes meet. She looks away – casting her gaze toward the dashboard. Feeling a flush, she hides her face, turns the key in the ignition, and moves the car toward the exit. She passes her employee-parking card into the machine, makes a couple of right turns, and exits the downtown area.

Thoughts of the anticipated trip to Pittsburgh and the joy its success might bring distract her and her driving goes to a form of automatic pilot. The expert skills she had learned in the Student Driving course in high school are now rote, allowing her thoughts to dart back and forth between driving the familiar trip home and her decision to find her birth family. She recalls the many searches she had done on the Internet and the disappointment when she had found that Corporal Robinson had passed away. She returned to the Internet, searching for orphanages in Vietnam, becoming optimistic after finding an on-line agency. A counselor for the agency had provided her with some answers to her questions. For the first time, there seemed to be a glimmer of hope. After following up on the lead, she received a surprise call from the author herself, inviting her to come to her home for an interview.

She coasts the car down the exit ramp to the intersection with a glaring red light. Waiting for the light to change, she wants to look in the visor mirror to check her lipstick, but she feels anxious at the prospect of seeing herself in the mirror. She wonders if she will ever become self-confident, something she has longed to achieve. She takes a quick glance into the mirror and looks away.

"How can I find my family when I seem to have come from three different continents? Who am I anyway?" she asks looking at her reflection in the rear view mirror again studying her face.

She notes her mixed racial features, comparing herself to a person who is looking at a wrapped package, wondering what is inside, confused by the wrapper. When the light turns green, she makes the familiar right turn onto the boulevard with the rows of Magnolia trees lining the midsection. A quick glance at the trees brings her mind back to the previous spring when the trees had been in full bloom and had discarded their petals after only a few days. The magnificent flowers had fallen to the ground, covering it with a burst of pink, reminding her of a layer of cotton candy. The sight causes her to conclude that the flowers' short-lived-magnificent display may have been a waste, but the splendorous green foliage had endured and had served as a superb replacement, a memory marker. The images make her wonder if her biological parents had discarded her.

At that moment, she realizes that curiosity had nothing to do with her wish to find her family. She knew it had more to do with her innate desire to know about her roots, revealing information that would lead to a discovery of her own self. Up until this time, she has had no direction in life. However, what she does know is that she wants to become as magnificent as the flowers on the Magnolia trees and as enduring as the tree itself. She decides that she must study the branches first, comparing them to the branches of her family tree. "Just as they defined the Magnolia tree, finding them will give me the answer," she decides as she passes the last group of Magnolias and turns left onto Maple Avenue.

Sophie Simon's name comes to mind, not able to believe that tomorrow she will meet her and that she may have knowledge of her roots. Her only hope is that any new people in her life will be half the parents that her adoptive ones had been. She smiles, thinking about her adoptive father's willingness to help her with the search by becoming her chauffeur another time. She turns the wheel to the left at the second street, "Mulberry Drive," pulls into the driveway of #2314 and breathes her usual sigh of relief. "Sort of like a warrior coming home," she says aloud. She thinks she understands, for the first time, why she had never really felt comfortable in the world outside of the McDeenon home. She turns the key again, bringing the engine to a stop. One by one, she throws the contents of her purse back into their safe hiding places. A sense of organization comes over her.

Sophie Simon.

"What's her real name, again?" she giggles to herself. Talking aloud when there had been no apparent person around was something her adoptive mother had always done and she had found the habit amusing. A teacher, she had told her: "When you are a Kindergarten Teacher, 'talking to yourself' is an occupational hazard." She smiles and laughs aloud when she remembers her finishing statement: 'You might just as well talk to yourself – the kids aren't listening to you anyway.'

As she crosses the front lawn of the only home that she has ever known, she thinks she must look silly with the big 'Cheshire Cat Grin' on her face. As she pulls the handle of one of the two doors of the restored plantation home, a huge smile lingers. For a moment, she thinks that she hears her mother's usual greeting, 'Is that you, Neeny?'

"Mum is listening," she thinks as she enters the house. It still contains her mother's scents. Curio comes out from behind the divan, purring, and circling her leg. When she puts her hand onto his head and strokes his fur, she recalls the word 'curiosity' one more time, satisfied that tomorrow her own curiosity may bring the answers she wants. Sophie Simon's real name appears in her mind.

Sofia Blackburn-Anderson. Her mind jumps, bringing her back to her search for her 'first mother', as she had come to call her. *Now, what is it they say about people who talk to themselves and then answer themselves?* She falls down in her favorite chair, kicks off her shoes, and lets out a deep sigh. Curio jumps onto her lap, licking her hand. She closes her eyes and lets her mind take her to unknown places. Her heart takes her to South Vietnam."

*

Janene pulls into her driveway after rushing home after she had heard the news about Sofia's stroke. She reviews the plans for making the trip to Pittsburgh again. Unlike the last trip when she had traveled by automobile with Bill, this time she will fly. Rushing to get her bag packed, she prays, "Dear God, please don't let Oma die before I get there."

* * * * *

CHAPTER 15

MR. CORCORAN'S SURPRISE

It is 21 September, less than two weeks since Janene had traveled to Pittsburgh with Bill to meet with Sophie Simon. She sits in the airplane on the flight from Atlanta to Pittsburgh, anticipating her next visit with Sofia – in the hospital. "It just seems so unfair; I have just found my birth grandmother, now I may be losing her," she thinks as she buckles her seat belt, preparing for lift-off in the airplane leaving Atlanta on a non-stop flight to Pittsburgh. She closes her eyes and lets her mind drift back to the days surrounding Madeline's death.

Although the agonizing weeks of daily visits to Madeline as she had fought off death had been two years earlier, the memory of watching her suffer is as real as if it had been yesterday. She feels the plane level off as it meets the clouds, but she doesn't open her eyes, preferring to stay with the visions of her adoptive mother, cherishing every moment she had with her. The treat is short-lived when she realizes that she needs to get busy on the project that she had started before learning of Sofia's stroke. She pulls out her laptop, puts on her headphones to the recorder, and starts tapping out the next chapter on her keyboard, feeling a sense of urgency she has never known.

As she listens to the recording, she recalls the meeting with Sofia and begins to write. The words of her book ignite a fire under her fingers as they pound the keyboard, recounting the recent events in her life to include in her book. The first two chapters had developed in record time. "Must be a family trait," she concludes as she inserts a page break and begins the next chapter:

"If you are diligent and extremely lucky, when you least expect it, a person comes into your life, changing it so profoundly that you don't recognize the person you had been and, for the first time, you can see the person you want to become. " I may not have been diligent, but I think my luck has just changed," she thinks as she travels to downtown Atlanta from her home in its suburban neighborhood. It is the morning after her visit to Pittsburgh and she thinks the drive seems shorter than usual. The words of her next chapter come with little effort on her part. Writing had always come easy to her, but, now, with her grandmother's words echoing in her mind, the book takes shape.

The process brings to mind every detail of her visit with Sofia. As she turns into the parking garage, her mind is still in Pittsburgh, still overcome with emotion, but she remembers the first time she had parked in the garage on the first day of her employment by the publishing company almost three years earlier. As she guides her car into the spot marked RESERVED, she feels as if someone else is parking her car. So much has happened in such little time, she thinks as she hurries across the garage to the elevator, something she has done by rote every other morning.

Everything seems so different now.

She pictures Sofia's arthritic hands as she fingered the patches of the tattered quilt, telling her tale, remembering every phase of her life as if it had been yesterday. However, she still can't erase the memories of the experience nor the lingering doubts. *Is she really my grandmother?* The pictures of her handsome son blaze in her mind. "Is he really my father?" she asks as she sees his smiling eyes, looking at her while she had listened to Sofia's words. They reverberate in her mind. Since the day she and her father had left, a movie has played in her mind, repeating dozens of times, each time making her relive the meeting."

*

City General Hospital of Pittsburgh

Janene takes a deep breath. The sight of Sofia in the hospital bed reminds her immediately of the long days of vigilance by Madeline's deathbed. Still formulating her own story in her mind, she is lost in thought as she sits by her bed praying that it will not be her death bed. Remembering how Sofia had learned of her children's deaths, emotions overcome her. Recalling Sofia's words, she formulates her thoughts into a story in her mind:

"It would take some time for Oma to comprehend everything that had taken place in that room that day. The mysteries of her past, the people whom she had thought were gone and the things that she had tried to forget were now part of her present, real world. She would enjoy being part of the lives of the grandchildren, something that she had never expected.

However, as fate would have it, another twenty-three years would pass before she would discover that the story of the "shattered seeds" of her family wasn't complete. The shattered seeds had been scattered farther than she could have ever imagined. Her son's Vietnamese daughter had not died. She had survived after someone abandoned her at an Army base outside of Saigon, placing her into the hands of a young soldier who would take an interest in her and arrange for his friends, a couple in Atlanta, to adopt her.

Janene's mouth dropped when her new Oma told her about her birth family. Her dream was coming true and as much as she had prepared for the moment, she felt unprepared. Her eyes went to the picture on the piano of the handsome young soldier who had captured her curiosity.

"Then, he is my father?" she asked, moving toward the piano.

"Yes, he's your father," Oma said, slowly rising from her chair and joining her in front of the pictures. I am your grandmother – or as you would call me in Germany, I am 'Oma'. I would be pleased if you would call me 'Oma', she said, picking up a picture of her son, showing him as he looked before going to Vietnam.

"I would love to call you 'Oma.' I can't believe I have actually found my father, and my grandmother," she says, tears running down her cheeks.

"It is true. You have not only found your father, but his entire family," Oma said, holding out her arms to embrace her. The two hugged each other and stayed locked together for a few moments, both finding it difficult to comprehend the moment and not wanting to separate."

*

City General Hospital of Pittsburgh

The sight of Sofia lying so still and looking completely helpless in the intensive care unit of the hospital in Pittsburgh moves Janene. "She looks so frail," she whispers to Jeffrey Anderson, recalling the first time she had met him at the meeting with Sofia. "They had seemed so happy," she thinks noticing how much older he seems now.

"She is frail, Janene. She has been sleeping around the clock. Of course, the medications have been keeping her sedated," he says through blood shot eyes.

"Have the doctors given you a prognosis?"

"No. Because of her age, they say there is no way to predict what will happen." Tears moisten the corners of Janene's eyes.

"She would want us to be strong, Janene," he says putting his hand on her shoulder.

"I know. Thanks, Jeffrey. It is hard. I have just met her and, now, it seems that I am losing her. It makes me wonder why there has to be so many losses in my life."

"Sofia had always said the same thing. All we can do now is to pray. Miracles do happen. At least that was what she had said when she had found you and had realized that you were the granddaughter that she thought had died, Randy's child. She has been failing for some time but the moment that she had uncovered the truth about you, she felt energized."

"I just wish I had made an effort to search for my biological family sooner."

"If we all just had crystal balls, maybe life would be different. Well, we don't, unfortunately, so I suppose that we have only the one option. Sofia had great faith in the power of prayer."

"I've already started."

"She would appreciate that, Janene. She always was a very spiritual person."

"Yes. I got that during our many conversations."

"I think you are a lot like her, Janene," he smiles. "I want to make a few more phone calls. Do you mind staying with her for a while?"

"I'm not going anywhere, Jeffrey," she answers glad to have some time alone with Sofia.

"Thanks," he whispers kissing Sofia's cheek and leaving the room.

Janene pulls up the straight back chair, bringing it closer to Sofia's bedside. The machines helping her breathe and the drip of the liquid in the IV bottles are the only sounds in the room.

She glances around the room, finding Sofia's quilt sitting on a chair, bringing back the memory of Sofia stroking it. She places the quilt over the sterile, white sheet covering Sofia, and then carefully lifts Sofia's hand and presses it down onto it. Sofia's fingers don't move and they are icy cold. She moves them for her, making them curl into the fibers of the old, tattered blanket that she loves so much, and being careful to position them on the cluster of pink squares.

She sits for a while, looking at Sofia and lost in thought before reaching for the recorder again and setting it up on the bedside hospital table. With earphones on, she listens to the tape, concentrating on every word Sofia had said.

*

Jeffrey comes back into Sofia's room, interrupting Janene's train of thought. "I'm sorry, Janene; I didn't mean to break in on your writing. Is there any change?"

"Sorry, Jeffrey but she is no different than fifteen minutes ago when you were here."

"I talked to the Doctor, Janene. He said that the machines are the only thing that is keeping Sofia alive right now. He suggested that I make a decision. Sofia signed a 'Living Will'."

"I'm so sorry, Jeffrey."

"I promised Sofia that I would honor her wishes. I know what I have to do, but I don't have to make the decision right now. Actually, your being here gives me a reason to delay it. I know that this is important to you; we can give you all of the time you need to finish up your writing. Is there any way I can help?"

"As a matter of fact, Jeffery, would you mind sharing some of the details of your meeting Sofia? That was one part of the story that Sofia seemed to gloss over."

"I'm not surprised, Janene. Sofia tends to be very private about some things. It would be a pleasure for me to vocalize what was the most important time in my life. Let me begin by telling you that I have my friend, 'Mary Long', to thank."

"It was 1973," Jeffrey began. "I had just packed my bag and drove down to the Delmarva Peninsula from New York, where I had been living at the time. I had promised Mary that I would meet Sofia in order for her to decide if I was the one who should write her biography. Mary and I had been associates as young rookies in the field. When she called me, I hesitated, until she said, "When you meet Sofia, you will know exactly why I have asked you to do this assignment, Jeffrey." She added that she and Sofia were close friends and she expected Sofia to be very "choosy" in her selection of a writer.

After having spent a half hour talking to Mary about her, viewing her picture on the inside of a book cover and reading several chapters from her acclaimed book, "THE MAGICAL QUILT", I felt that there was more to this writer than would seem from her perfect appearance. I couldn't wait to begin.

"It wasn't difficult to pick her out of the crowded restaurant. The host gestured to where she had seated her earlier, but it wasn't necessary. I spotted her immediately upon entering the dining room. She was sitting beside a window, overlooking the ocean. The sunlight cast highlights on her hair, falling softly onto her shoulders. The reflections of the ocean sky in the windowpane accentuated the brilliance of her blue eyes. She seemed to be lost in thought as she gazed at the rolling waves of the Atlantic

Ocean. Her picture didn't do her justice. She was remarkably beautiful. I hated to interrupt her and I could have just stood watching her, but I called out her name.

"Mrs. Blackburn?" I asked, feeling nervous.

She looked up, nodded, and smiled before quickly casting her eyes shyly away. "You must be 'Mr. Anderson'. Please sit down," she said with a gesture to the chair across from her, and her eyes again finding mine.

As I sat down, my preoccupation with her caused me to fumble with the chair, making a considerable amount of noise, drawing attention to the table. The moment of awkwardness seemed to embarrass her; her face flushed slightly; she lowered her head and fiddled with the silverware. "I'm sorry to be late, Mrs. Blackburn. The traffic on Route 1 was unbelievable. I thought those kinds of jams were only reserved for Washington," I said, trying to cover up my clumsiness.

"That's all right, Mr. Anderson. Actually, I just got here. I had to deal with it as well. The traffic always gets crazy on a cloudy day at the beach. When the tourists don't have a beach day, everyone just seems to get in their cars looking for a substitution," she said as her cheeks blushed again to a soft pink color. I hoped that it wasn't a result of my intense staring. The appearance of a waiter took us away from the nervousness that both of us seemed to be having. At least I knew I was feeling jittery, and I interpreted that my behavior might have caused some embarrassment to her. Perhaps I might have just been letting my male ego get the best of me. I could understand her embarrassment because Mary prepped me about her shyness. However, I was having a difficult time explaining mine.

We began with the simple niceties of ordering drinks. A mannerly, young waiter guided us through the wine list and suggested the house wine. It seemed like only a few minutes before he returned with the glasses. He poured some into my glass and allowed me to sample it. I gave my approval. I couldn't help notice her lips as she sipped hers. I couldn't focus on anything, but kissing them.

The dinner menu in front of my nose interrupted my fantasies. I had to shake off the urge and make a selection from the long list of Italian Cuisine. She ordered an Antipasto salad and I ordered the shrimp pesto. During the course of dinner, we exchanged some non-personal information about each other. She was definitely shy; her body language was a dead giveaway. I am not sure what my problem was, except that I couldn't take my eyes, or my mind, from her.

She readily answered my questions with simple direct responses, not volunteering any extras. I found it difficult to select questions that wouldn't appear to be too personal for an initial meeting. I thought that I wanted to know everything there was to know about her, immediately, but I didn't want to scare her away. All of my questions seemed so stupid to me. I just wanted to find out everything I could for my own personal knowledge.

The book was the furthest thing from my mind. All I could think of was how much I was attracted to her. I had not enjoyed that feeling accompanying an introduction to a woman since I had met "Victoria Spencer" on a blind date in college. That relationship, unfortunately, had the same ending as all of my encounters with women, including my last, a failed marriage after ten years. I tried to make small talk. She responded with even smaller talk, in the sense that the conversation almost went to nil.

However, overall it proved to be a pleasant first encounter. The food was delicious and so was the atmosphere. I thought the company was superb. I could only hope that she did also. I had met my promise to Mary to, "keep it business like," but I wondered if I might have overdone it a bit. I declined dessert but suggested an after dinner brandy. I thought that perhaps I was overstepping my limits by going to a social mode. However, I proceeded dangerously.

"Mrs. Blackburn, if you don't mind my asking I have a question for you: "Where is Mr. Blackburn?"

She seemed startled. I wanted to take back the question immediately.

"Mr. Blackburn is dead, Mr. Anderson."

"Oh, I'm sorry, my mistake. I didn't know."

"It is all right, Mr. Anderson. I have been a widow for a long time."

"It was stupid of me to ask. I'm sorry," I continued, feeling like a real ass.

"Please, don't apologize. It is a perfectly logical question. Is there a 'Mrs. Anderson?'" she asked, remembering that Mary had told her that he was a bachelor.

"Yes. There is one. Perhaps I should say 'there was one.' We are divorced," I answered, thinking that I deserved the question.

"I'm sorry," she said softly.

"No need to be sorry. That was a long time ago."

"Well, Mrs. Blackburn, I think that we've accomplished quite a bit in our initial visit," I said. I closed my napkin, trying to give her a clue that I thought our meeting was finished.

"May I walk you to your car?"

"Yes. Thank you, Mr. Anderson."

I walked her to the parking lot, noticing that all eyes focused on her as we exited the restaurant. I knew that because I knew that they were not staring at me. At her car, I finalized the arrangement for the following day, saying that I would be at her house around noon.

It was a pleasant experience for me, and I thought that it seemed to be the same for her. We had accomplished the goals of our first visit to meet and establish a business relationship that would culminate with my writing her biography. Her accomplishments as a writer seemed evident and the task seemed to be an easy one for me.

I left the parking lot and drove back to my hotel room, feeling good about this new assignment. Based upon what I knew about Sofia Blackburn, I thought that writing a biography about Sofia's life would be quite benign. She was the writer of children books and had become famous for her work, writing about a quilt that had magical powers. It had captivated the imaginations of thousands of children worldwide. The animated movie that followed, "The Magical Quilt" had been a blockbuster, making millions. The name of "Sophie Simon" gained notoriety overnight, especially among families with young children. The books, and the related toys, brought in additional revenues in the millions.

The opportunity to begin my task began the following afternoon when I arrived at her beautiful waterfront. She answered the door, dressed in a long, white, sleeveless dress and beach sandals. Her flaxen-colored hair, tied up in soft, yellow ribbons, allowed strands to fall into tendrils around her face and neck. She greeted me with a smile and ushered me into her home.

I followed her into a room, meticulously decorated in a beach theme. It faced out to the ocean, with large floor to ceiling windows that allowed full view of the private beach. A large desk and chair sat in front of the window, looking as if someone had placed them there just for me. She seated herself on a comfortable chair nearby, telling me that I should use the desk and chair. I set my typewriter on the desk, took out my pen and notebook from my briefcase, and placed the audio equipment and camera nearby.

"I'm ready if you are, Mrs. Blackburn," I said.

"Yes, Mr. Anderson. I'm ready," she said, nodding shyly, waiting for me to make the next move.

"I suppose we should start at the beginning -- a logical place?" I said to her.

She smiled. "The beginning may be difficult to determine, Mr. Anderson. I have had many "beginnings" over my lifetime," she said.

It was at that moment that I formulated the title of the work. I intended on calling the biography, "A New Beginning." I kept that title to myself, however. Instead, I said simply, "Then should I have said, 'The first of the new beginnings.'"

She laughed and said, "I guess that would be the day that I was born."

She began by telling me about the birth of "Sofia Gunther" in Berlin, Germany in 1919. Her expressions and usage of words exemplified her natural gifts as a writer, with every sentence.

We spent several hours just delving into her birth and early childhood. She went on to explain that she had an unusually close relationship to her grandmother, a very sheltered childhood, and that she felt that her grandmother's death had taken her childhood away. She told me about the quilt that her grandmother had made, and about how her attachment to it had helped her through the difficult times in Germany after World War I and during the Great Depression. It was a lesson in history, as the story seemed to revolve around the events of the times. It was apparent that history shaped her life as if it were a sculptor's chisel.

She looked drained after talking about her childhood during the rise of the Nazi's. I suggested that we stop and pick up where we left off on the following day. She looked relieved. I thought that we had covered a lot of ground in our first session. I felt extremely comfortable with her and I guess I was even a little presumptuous, but I asked her if she would like to dine with me that evening. To my surprise, she accepted the invitation.

I returned to the hotel, shaved and took a hot shower but I couldn't get her out of my mind. I went down to the beachfront bar, had a cocktail, and watched as the waves rolled into shore. I felt as if I was beginning a new chapter in my life, and not one in a new book I was about to write. Actually, I felt a little giddy much as I had on my first date in high school – without the anxiety of having to ask my father for the car.

When I arrived at the beach house later, she greeted me at the door, looking refreshed and very beautiful, dressed in a long, pink gown. If Mary had not told me her age, I would have guessed her to be much younger than her fifty-four years. She definitely would pass for my younger sister, even though she was almost ten years older than I was. The only evidence of age, were the fine laugh lines at the edge of each eye. The dimple on her cheek moved when she smiled. She led me into the foyer and she began to apologize for her appearance. I wondered why she had found it necessary to apologize.

"Obviously" she explained, "the dress I am wearing isn't meant to be worn out in public."

She couldn't prove it by me and she certainly didn't have to apologize for her appearance. On the contrary, she astounded me.

"I hope you don't mind, but I decided to prepare dinner for us here."

She hoped that I would find it acceptable to dine at the house rather than at a restaurant. I was pleasantly surprised, actually telling her, "that will be just fine with me, Mrs. Blackburn."

"Well, I'm afraid if you are to dine with me this evening, Mr. Anderson, you will have to abandon one thing." she said, getting very serious, making me very nervous.

"Oh. What would that be Mrs. Blackburn?"

"You will have to lose the, "Mrs. Blackburn" and call me "Sofia," Mr. Anderson."

"Of course, Mrs. Blackburn…err…Sofia, I mean," I stuttered.

"However, you will have to call me Jeffrey then."

"That won't be a problem, Jeffrey."

With that, she led me into the dining area and asked me if I would like a drink. The bottle of wine that she had left sitting in the wine cooler was perfect. We proceeded to the living area where we sat down and began some small talk. She explained to me that she loved to cook and thought that tonight would be a wonderful opportunity for her to try out a new recipe. The wonderful chicken dish was one she had found while traveling in Europe. She was able to "bribe" the recipe from the cook.

The dinner she prepared was marvelous. It was a chicken dish that she had found particularly appealing. I thought it best not to ask her how she had, "bribed the cook." I was impressed with the thoughtfulness of her actions of making our dinner, rather than dining out at the restaurant. I assured her that I still "owed" her dinner out, and hoped that she would give me the opportunity to take her out again at another time.

We ate by candlelight on the balcony, overlooking the Atlantic Ocean. It was obvious that she had really worked hard to make this dinner a very special occasion. I made certain to tell her that I was appreciative of her efforts. I was thankful that she had changed her mind, and just thrilled to be having a home cooked meal. We talked over a few more glasses of the wine. Conversation was easy with Sofia. Her thoughts were melodies in words. She was also an extremely good listener. We set the ground rules for the evening early, to exclude all talk about the biography. We decided that we would only talk about the present. Although, she did say that she wanted to know more about my life, if I didn't mind and hoped that she wasn't prying. I gave her a brief synopsis of my boring life. I spoke only briefly of my disastrous attempt at marriage and subsequent divorce. I told her that I had one child, a daughter. She was the best thing about the marriage. My daughter married and I was the proud grandfather of twin boys!

"I envy you having a family, Jeffrey," she said getting misty-eyed. I changed the subject to my relationship with Mary when I saw that she seemed to be getting upset. I told her how Mary and I had worked together and that we had become friends, but not in a romantic way. Since we agreed on the rules of conversation, including only our present lives, I made it brief.

Presently, I told her I was working as a freelance writer for a nationally syndicated newspaper. It was easy to reveal my inner most secrets to her about life, love, career, likes, and dislikes. I noticed that it was late and I mentioned that we made plans to meet again tomorrow afternoon, for the second session on the book. She agreed that we should end this evening, seeming as reluctant as I was. On the way back to my hotel, the fact struck me that I had just spent an entire day with a stranger, and that I felt that I had known her my entire life. I had an overwhelming feeling that this beautiful stranger would become an important part of my life.

The next afternoon, I met with Sofia again, and the next afternoon, and the next, until we had met for two weeks. Each session was a new trip, back down memory lane, a road that wasn't exactly comfortable for Sofia. However, as the sessions went on, Sofia found a level of comfort with me that was inspiring. She was able to tell me the most intimate details of her marriage at eighteen to Felix, and of her life as a Nazi wife. She told me of her inexperience with life and her ignorance of what was happening in Germany at the time. She held back the tears, but managed to talk about her two children with Felix. She was caught up with intense emotions as she related their deaths due to the bombing of the home in which they sought refuge from the Nazi's. Finally, she couldn't hold back her tears and broke down sobbing. I got her a glass of brandy and we decided the session was done.

Each session was an emotional ordeal for Sofia. They were an emotional roller coaster for her, but they were extremely revealing for me. I was amazed at the depth of her life and found that the book that I was going to write about it was slowly formulating in my mind. I almost forgot that Mary Long had hired me to write a book about her life. I sometimes felt that Sofia was actually writing her own biography. It was a strange sensation as we exchanged information so freely with each other. I was feeling very close to her and I started to feel that she shared the same feelings. We dined each evening, either at her home or at one of the local establishments. I learned about her past and began to put all the pieces of her life into a picture of her, as I saw her after only a brief introduction.

I was excited about writing the biography. I wanted to unveil the strong, shy woman behind the beautiful facade. I didn't realize how fond I was becoming of her, at least until that night that I was to leave to return to New York. My research was complete. She had prior commitments in Pittsburgh. We both knew that the sessions would have to end. We promised to keep in touch and to be in communication about the book. I knew that I was feeling something that I had never felt before. When I said "Good-bye" to her, I corrected myself and said that we shouldn't be saying "Good-bye" but rather "I'll be seeing you."

She agreed. Our eyes met and then our lips. We had our first and only physical contact during those meetings, but I knew it wouldn't be the last.

I arranged for the drive back to New York, saddened by the meeting's end. The next day, I felt an overwhelming need to talk to Sofia. It may have been that we developed a habit over the last two weeks. Whatever it was, I decided to call her. She was surprised and seemed excited to hear from me. We talked on the phone for over an hour. I was in New York and she was in Pittsburgh. She told me that she would love to have me visit her in Pittsburgh, as soon as I could come. I told her the same about the possibility of her visiting me in New York. Both of us decided that our schedules wouldn't permit either and decided upon a phone call each day until we could arrange another meeting.

As it turned out, Sofia and I exchanged telephone conversations for the next month. I looked forward to talking to her each day. She expressed the same thoughts. I knew that Sofia and I had developed a very close relationship in a short time, but I wasn't sure exactly what that relationship was. Sofia agreed and said that she felt comfortable with just noting that we were, "friends." She elaborated by saying that she never had a friendship, like this one, in her entire life. I agreed.

After that month of not seeing Sofia, we arranged to meet again. I flew to Pittsburgh and met Sofia at her Pittsburgh home. I arranged to stay at a Hotel in downtown Pittsburgh, but Sofia insisted that I should stay with her in her home. It didn't take much to persuade me. I accepted the invitation. Sofia and I spent a quiet evening at her home then, on the top of the hill, overlooking the City of Pittsburgh, known as "Mount Washington."

She prepared dinner and we talked until the early hours of the morning. From her home, we could see the beautiful skyline of Pittsburgh and the Three Rivers below. It was an enchanting sight – making me wonder why I had never realized the beauty of this city. Perhaps, it was because when I had traveled there last, I had not met Sofia Blackburn.

Sofia and I danced in the moonlight on the balcony, overlooking the city that she had come to know as home. A bright moon shed its light down into the large sliding glass door and a cool breeze whipped up from the river below. Afterward, we slept in each other's arms. At that moment, when I looked at Sofia lying quietly beside me, I knew that my life had changed.

I knew that 'Sofia Blackburn' was now the most important person in my life. I truly felt that I had waited my entire life for that night.

The next morning, I found my way from her bedroom down to the kitchen. I rummaged around, finding some coffee, juice, and toast, returning to the bedroom with them on a breakfast tray. I kissed Sofia softly on the cheek, wakening her. The tray surprised her. We sat in bed and enjoyed the small breakfast. I felt the overwhelming need to feed her. Therefore, I broke off a piece of toast and put it to her lips. She looked at me intently and only spoke one word.

"More?"

"Yes, darling, more and more," I said putting another piece in her mouth.

We enjoyed a remarkable breakfast. When we finished I told her, "I love you." She looked into my eyes.

"I love you too, Jeffrey, with all my heart," she whispered.

I knew she meant it. Then, as if it was an emergency, I spoke to her about the future. She put a finger on my lips, reminding me that we had agreed to talk about only the present, not the past, or the future. Now, she wanted to "enjoy the present."

"Sofia, I need you. Will you marry me?" I asked her.

"Jeffrey, I love you and I want to marry you, but I can't, not now."

Her eyes misted. "I have something to do before I can think of marriage, something very important."

"What could be more important that loving me the way that I love you?" I asked.

"I know it will sound silly, maybe even crazy, but I have been inspired by my reunion with my quilt. I feel compelled to complete a mission that I had promised my Oma when I had been just a little girl. I promised her that I would do something wonderful for people when I grew up, and that I would use her magical quilt to accomplish it."

"Sofia, you could still marry me and accomplish your childhood promise at the same time, couldn't you?"

"No. I can't. I'll not. I'll do nothing else – not until I have established the centers."

"What centers?"

"It is my dream to establish children's centers around the world. The centers will help all children, regardless of their financial status, their race, or their gender. I want to make a difference in the lives of children, Jeffrey. No, I HAVE to make a difference," she said with tears forming. "I am German."

"What does "being German" have to do with anything?"

"The reunion with my quilt did something to me, Jeffrey. I'll never be able to explain it, but when it had come back into my life, I knew that it was for a reason. I had a feeling that I could never explain to anyone; I can't even explain it to myself. Call it what you will – but, for the lack of a better word, maybe an 'awakening'. You see, the quilt isn't just a blanket – not to me. To me, it represents everything good about being German. To me, it is the embodiment of my grandmother. She was everything good. She taught me to love Germany and embrace its wonderful cultures and spirit.

However, all of that changed when the Soldiers had come to power, destroying my life. I abandoned Germany, vowing never to give her my allegiance again. I realize now that was wrong. My heritage as a German, as my family had taught me, is what has made me who I am. I must reclaim my pride. Now, I am in a unique position to use my wealth to do something good for the world, as I had promised my Oma when she had entrusted me with her quilt. I have a mission and a vision. The quilt is part of it. It is a part of me – just as my legs and arms are. I know what I have to do. I must establish these centers. I'll call them "World Organization of Quilts" or "W.O.O.Q" for short. I can't think of anything else – not right now. As much as I love you, Jeffrey, our time will have to wait." She had an unusual tone in her voice, one that forced me to relinquish any attempts to dissuade her.

"How can I help you with this plan of yours, Sofia?" I asked.

"You mean it, Jeffrey?" she asked.

"Darling, the sooner we get this plan of yours into motion, the sooner we will be together. Yes, I mean it."

"From that moment on, both of us focused on Sofia's dream. When she had accomplished it, I asked her again to marry me," he says with a look at the wedding band on his finger. Lucky for me, she said "Yes." I hope that my trip down memory lane was as helpful to you as it has been for me," he smiles.

"Thank you for sharing your personal thoughts, Jeffrey."

"I hope I haven't embarrassed you by talking so intimately about my relationship with your new grandmother. I guess I was carried away a wee bit. I am sorry. I never tire of talking about Sofia. I don't know what I'll do without her," he says softly, kissing Sofia on the cheek.

Janene watched as Jeffrey said good-bye to Sofia and left the room. She notices that Sofia still shows no response, continuing to lie in the bed with machines keeping her alive.

"Now, I know why Sofia hadn't shared that part of her story," Janene thinks as she taps on the keys again, sensing urgency. She pictures Sofia at their meeting and tries to capture in words Sofia's enthusiasm for starting the centers. The vision included Sofia grasping the pink square in the middle of the quilt. She recalled asking Sofia about that square and her reply and decided to type into her story:

"The pink square is the only one of its kind on the quilt. It was Oma's favorite. She told me it was cut from the hem of her first dress made by her mother, Julia Krause," Sofia had told her, moving her fingers away to show it to her.

"It is my favorite, too. The dress, just a little shorter than when my great grandmother Julia had made it, because of the squares being cut from it, was handed down to my mother and then to me. My daughter, Ana, wore it. It was in the old trunk in our house in Berlin. I left it there when I had run away. This pink square is the only thing left of that memory, a relic of lost times, and a place that will never be the same again."

"I can see why you are so attached to your quilt, Sofia."

"Yes. It worries me when I think about what will happen to the quilt after I die. It would be such a shame to bury it with me," Sofia said looking into Janene's eyes. "I'm saddened to think that its legacy, what it means to be a German as seen through my grandmother's eyes, would also be buried."

"That should never happen, Sofia," Janene blurted. She turned her eyes away from Sofia when she realized what she had said, hoping that Sofia wouldn't think that she was being too presumptuous. She wished that she could offer to take care of the quilt for her when she had passed, but lacked the courage to ask her.

"Jeffrey has promised to keep my centers operational. The story of the quilt is part of the program at each center. I hope that its story will inspire others to continue helping needy children. I truly believe that our children are our greatest resource."

"I agree. I would like to help you with your centers if you would allow me."

"All in good time, Janene, everything happens for a reason and in its own good time."

Janene had wanted to pursue the conversation about the quilt's future but she decided that it wasn't the time. Now, as she sits beside Sofia on her deathbed, she wishes that she had.

*

An Hour Later

Jeffrey caught Janene off guard when he tiptoed into Sofia's hospital room. Her mind was still on her writing when she blurted, "You know I have been thinking about something, Jeffrey. I want to put an excerpt in my story that is in Sofia's own words. Do you have any objections to my including the Prologue that she had written for her book, ONCE UPON A TIME?"

"No, of course not . . ."

"Thanks."

"How is your work coming?"

"Good."

"I talked to Bill. He is worried about you. He said you haven't called him."

"I'm glad you reminded me. I'll do that now, before I forget."

"You know that you can come back to the house and stay there. It might be more comfortable for you."

"No. I'm fine."

"I'll stay with Sofia. I would like a few minutes alone with her anyway."

"Okay. I'll just go to the lounge and get something to eat."

Janene gathered up her computer, briefcase, and purse and walked across the hall to the visitors lounge. She caught a quick look at Sofia and Jeffrey before setting up the computer to begin the next section of her project. She opens up her copy of the book, which Sofia had autographed before giving it to her at the meeting.

*

"12 December 1982 . . . Prologue . . . Once Upon A Time . . . Sofia Blackburn-Anderson," Janene reads. "I think these are probably the most revealing words that Sophie Simon has ever written," she thinks as she types them into her story:

"I sat at the keyboard with a dull look on my face. I had just finished my first full-length novel. The process had left me physically and mentally exhausted, but totally renewed. I had never set out to be a writer. The words just seemed to pour out, each becoming a piece in the giant puzzle of words, sentences, paragraphs and chapters which had created my imaginary characters, placing them in real time, allowing them to react to the real life circumstances of the times in which they had lived. Most of life is behind rather than in front of me. Perhaps, that fact gives me permission to proclaim a small amount of wisdom.

For a long time, I had secretly wished that I could have been born at a different time, wanting to select the circumstances of my birth, perhaps make a difference in how I would claim my heritage. However, at this point in my life, I am content that I have lived in my moment, realizing that time has little to do with it. It doesn't really matter when one lives, just that one does, and that one lives life to its fullest. It is the "how we live our

318

life" that matters, not only to the others in our lives, but also more importantly to ourselves.

For most of my adult life, I had believed the experiences of my childhood had been trivial, lacking substance and meaning. I was wrong. They have provided me with the inspiration that I have needed to overcome life's difficulties and rejoice in all of its gifts. After all, one needs courage to travel along this path called LIFE. My courage had materialized only after years of searching to find myself. In the process, I realized that the only way to find you is to look to others, emulating those who had stood out among the crowds with words and actions that demonstrated their strong characters.

Incorporating the stories of those whom I had admired as well as those who I had not into my writing has played an important part in the creative process for me. I began to write as therapy to cope with the unfolding events of the times in which I had lived. Like most things, it has evolved over the years. Now, Writing is a passionate release of creative energy, finally finding its voice. Through trial and error, I discovered what fuels my quest for immortality. It is the gift of creativity, providing me with an opportunity to continue my passion, an experience unlike any other in my life, with the exception, perhaps, of giving birth.

I like to think of the creative process as compared to childbirth. The labor is always long and difficult, but the delivery is purely cathartic. For it is through the weaving of words and sentences that a tapestry of life's experiences unfolds, becoming one's record of thoughts and ideas. I believe that reading is one of the most intimate of all human experiences, a pathway to the mind, whose destination is the soul or that special place, whatever you may wish to call it, that defines our humanity. I am proud to say, "I am an Artist – an Author" and I am privileged to travel to that special place where only I can go but I'll share with you, if only you allow me."

*

Sofia had written three more books in addition to her Autobiography, none was a book for children. All three had made the Best Sellers Lists," Janene notes, adding her thoughts into the draft of her own story. "Oma's greatest gift as a writer was her ability to touch her readers, especially the granddaughter that she had never known," she thinks closing the computer and walking back to Sofia's room, suddenly determined to make her life meaningful, if only to herself.

I'll not write the final chapter of my book until I find my mother and my sister.

*

"You're back, Janene," Jeffrey says as she walks back into Sofia's room. "Thank you for giving me some time with Sofia."

"Thank you, Jeffrey, for sharing her."

"I have been giving a great deal of thought to the doctor's suggestion, Janene. Sofia had expressed in her "Living Will" her wish that her life not be extended by any extraneous means."

"I understand, Jeffrey. You have to make a decision and it is a very difficult one, I am sure. I can be finished here anytime. I'll continue writing until you are ready. I wanted to write the chapter about Felix."

"Sofia would appreciate that."

Jeffrey kisses Sofia's cheek and slips out of the room.

Janene sets up her things and writes the final chapters, based on the last parts of Sofia's story as she had told it to her at their meeting. Although the meeting had only been a few weeks earlier, she thought it seemed like years ago. She looks at Sofia, sleeping so peacefully, the quilt covering her, the tubes keeping her alive. She remembers the look on her face as she had related the story of her first husband, Felix Fuerst, after she had found out the truth about him.

"Before I begin Janene, I must tell you that this part of my story wasn't revealed to me until many years after I had come to the United States," Sofia had said. Now, that Janene recalls the painful look on her face when she had shared the story, she thinks that Sofia looks very peaceful now, not showing any signs of a lifetime of tragedy. She starts to type, hoping that she will capture the essence of that part of Sofia's life in her writing.

*

6 June 1944, France

The long days and nights of traveling through Europe had taken their toll. It had been one stop after another, hiding in abandoned farmhouses and barns. She wondered if she would ever be able to get away and she worried about her parents and uncle but most of all she worried about Felix. She loved him despite her suspicions and fears. She was tired, hungry, confused, frightened, and feeling terribly guilty about her decision to leave and the ramifications of it, especially for her children. She had yanked them out of their beds in the middle of the night; hurriedly taken them away from the only home they had ever known, stolen them from the father whom they loved. They had no idea what was happening. They were too young to understand the war in Europe, why their father had not come away with them, or even why they were running away with their mother.

She wondered if she even knew why she had run away in the first place. As they lay sleeping, close to her in the latest farmhouse, she worried about their future. Enemies of the Nazi's had been hiding them. Every time she looked into their little, innocent faces, her heart ached recognizing the terrible ordeal that she had imposed on them. Max was quieter and timid. Ana wasn't sleeping, and she cried more than she had before leaving Berlin. Now that they were in France, her helpers finally shared her uncle's plan with her: getting to the coast and boarding a ship for America. As they traveled around the countryside, she began to think that they were just going in circles, moving from one destination after another under fabricated identities. She kept thinking that maybe she would wake up from the nightmare.

Several days earlier, they had heard gunfire and explosions in the distance. She was terrified for her children, trying to hide it from them in an effort to keep them calm. Now, as she sat quietly watching her children sleep, she began to wonder if she had done the right thing by leaving her husband. She wondered if their house in Berlin was still standing and what he was thinking about her leaving with their children.

She had taken nothing with her and still felt the loss of leaving her quilt behind. She missed its comfort and warmth. She thought of what she had left in Berlin, wishing that she could feel her quilt one more time. "I certainly could use a little magic now," she sighed. She compared the quilt to herself as a German. She knew that her life and that of her children would never be the same. She realized that the quilt was a symbol of her heritage. She had left it behind in Berlin. It was gone, never to be again – just as her life as a German was gone. She realized that the quilt wasn't just a legacy from her grandmother, but one that represented her heritage as a German. *That is all gone*. She reaches for her children, pulls them close, and feels a longing from a deep sense of regret that she will never pass on that legacy to her children.

She hears another explosion and hugs the children closer to her. They sob and stare at her, their faces asking explanations. As she lay on top of them, she hears another blast followed by the sound of breaking glass, shattering and falling over them. Frantically, she tries to pick the pieces off her children. Another blast brings the ceiling crashing down on top of them—everything went black.

*

Several hours later

The German and Allied Troops storm the countryside while French Freedom Fighters hide in the woods and watch as the shells hit the old farmhouse at the end of the meadow. They know that there were refugees hiding in the farmhouse and that they fear for their safety with each explosion. They wait until they think it is safe before they make their way across the meadow, hiding themselves behind the trees bordering the farm. Three of them move from the obscurity of the trees toward the farmhouse. They huddle close to the ground until they come near the house, crouching below the front window. Pieces of broken panes litter the ground as they inch their way to the door, kicking it open, expecting the unexpected. Three bodies are lying on the floor under a large beam. Two of the soldiers, drop their rifles and lift the beam while the third pulls the bodies out from under it. They feel for pulses in the throats of the victims.

"The two children are still breathing. The woman is dead," the young soldier says. He picks up the little girl and moves with her to the door. "Carry the little boy," he says to one of his comrades. Neither of the children moves. The third man checks the woman again. He shakes his head from side to side. "She's gone. We will just have to leave her for now. We should get the children back to camp quickly. They look like they both have head injuries," he says as he reaches into the woman's dress pocket searching for papers. "Her name is Madame Adeline Debauch and these are her children, Michel and Jacqueline," he says returning the papers to her pocket. "We should tell them in camp that her body is out here when we get back."

The group leaves the farmhouse and runs, ducking and dodging the continued shelling, carrying the children. When they get to the woods, they follow a path to their camp where they deliver the children to the arms of others. They tell the medic their names and the fact that their mother is dead in the farmhouse. After a quick examination, the medic advises getting them to another camp where they can get the proper medical help. They move north, cautious of the continuing sound of gunfire in the west. They see a steady stream of fighter planes flying toward the German lines. The planes wear the insignia of the United States of America. "Looks like the Yanks are here," one says.

"Yeah, the invasion is at Normandy, just like we had suspected," says the other.

*

A Few Hours Later

Thousands of troops invade Europe in one of the largest invasions in history. After a fierce battle on the beach at Normandy, a group of American soldiers found their way inland. When they saw the farmhouse, they approached cautiously, following military training. They survey inside the badly damaged house, moving toward a blanket covering a body on the floor.

One of the soldiers checks the woman while the others inspect the rest of the house. At first, the soldier thinks that the woman is dead. However, he notices that her body feels warm and places his fingers close to her nose, checking for a breath. Feeling for a pulse, he announces, "She is alive, but just barely." Another soldier radios their location, telling reconnaissance that they needed a medic for a civilian. They wait for the arrival of the additional patrol before carrying the woman out of the farmhouse, placing her into a medical vehicle.

"Hey, these papers in her pocket say that she has two little kids. Any sign of them?" he asks the medic checking her pockets.

"She was the only one in there . . . Guess they are gone, or dead, or something," one of the other soldiers says.

"Let's get her out of here before any Germans show up."

*

Several Days Later

Madame Adeline Debauch lay unconscious with head injuries, bruises, and abrasions in an American medical field camp. When she awakes, she is confused, disoriented, and unable to offer any resistance. Nor, does she ask about her children because she actually believed that the children were still with her. She subsequently boards a large ocean liner with hundreds of other European refugees. The vessel's destination is the United States of America and it is the final destination for Sofia on her flight out of Berlin.

*

A Refugee Center in the French Countryside

A little boy named Michel Debauch opens his eyes, startled that he does not see anything familiar. Opening his eyes further, he sees his little sister lying on a cot across from him. He gets up, feeling dizzy and nauseated.

"Jacqueline," he says shaking her arm, speaking in French. "Wake up, Jacqueline."

His little sister doesn't respond and he becomes concerned.

"Ana, wake up!" he says remembering his German.

"Your sister is all right, Michel," says a voice talking back to him in French. "She is just sleeping," says the woman wearing the nurse's cap.

"Where is my mother?" he asks in German.

"Don't worry about your mother right now. You have had a bad bump on your head; you should get back in bed," the woman tells him speaking in German. She leads him back to the mattress.

Glad to be back in bed but still worried about Ana, he tries to remember what has happened. "Where is Mutter?" he asks but his eyes close soon after his head finds the pillow.

He and Ana spend another week in the hospital and are then moved down the coast to Spain where they are become passengers on a refugee ship. They are designated 'French Orphans', joining hundreds of other children, all victims of the war. An American Relief Organization finds them a home in the United States; a family in Pittsburgh, Pennsylvania adopts them.

The family, Marcus and Harriet Stern, change their names yet another time. They become 'Michael and Jacqueline Stern', the children of a couple of German ancestry who had lost all of their family in the German Concentration Camps. Their lives as the children of Officer Felix Fuerst and his wife, Sofia, have ended. A new life in a new country awaits them across an ocean from the continent on which they had been born.

They are just two more of the newest immigrants to the United States of America, beginning their young lives ANEW.

*

June 1945 Berlin

He hid in the bombed out shambles of a German prison yard in Berlin, able to escape sure death by a firing squad simply because someone had opened the door to his cell. Captain Felix Fuerst wasn't surprised when they had arrested him. Rather, he was surprised that it had taken them that long to discover his acts of treason. When he had helped Adam to smuggle Sofia and the children out of Berlin, he thought they would surely suspect him. If they had discovered his betrayals, it would mean his certain demise and that of his wife and children. Not to save himself, but to save them, he had schemed to send them away.

"Sweet innocent Sofia, my God, what she must have gone through, thinking that I had never loved her and that I had only married her for the arrangement that her father had made, or worse, that I had wanted to impregnate one of their whores to satisfy their insane plan to create a pure race. She must have been terrified. I could think of no other way to get her to leave. Without the help from Gerhard and Adam, she never would have agreed to it," Felix thought as he recalled the sequence of events.

"Damn them! Damn them all," he cursed. He didn't think that anyone had heard, nor did he care but he felt very guilty as he trotted along the bombed out streets and buildings in the prison compound. *I am still alive. God only know what has happened to them.* The events replayed in his mind like a bad movie. "There should have been another way," he considered. "If they had stayed, they might be dead now or worse, knowing what they are capable of doing. Would they have used them to get a confession from me?"

The thought made him shiver. He feels moisture dripping into his eye and swipes the blood from his forehead with his hand. The cut above his right eye opened wider and blood oozed further. As he wiped the blood from his hand onto his pant leg, he thought that it was a miracle that he was still alive. He ducked into a doorway of a long dark hallway, remembering how, just hours ago, he had been sitting in his cell awaiting their next move. He had figured that they wouldn't send him to the firing squad before they had made sure that they had gotten every thread of information from him.

He had been dazed from the beatings and groggy when he had awakened, not sure of what was real. He noticed that the cell door was unlocked and slightly ajar. He pushed on the door and it opened. He looked for the guard, but none was there. He hobbled out, trying to be as quiet as possible, despite his excruciating pain. He knew that he only had one chance to avoid certain death. He was sure that this was the one. He dragged his body down to the main corridor, remembering when they had brought him back to his cell from their last torture session through the same hallway. At the end of the corridor, he crawled up a flight of steps, his legs weak from the beatings. He could see daylight beaming from an opened door and he checked over his shoulders before proceeding cautiously. He was looking for soldiers, but didn't see any men in uniforms. The lack of them puzzled him. He reasoned that maybe the government had fallen, but thought that maybe it was only his wishing. He was still wearing part of his former uniform and he realized the danger he would be in if THE THIRD REICH had fallen. He also realized that if it had fallen, members of THE THIRD REICH would want him dead so that he wouldn't reveal their secrets to the world.

He edged himself out of the door; blinded by the bright light, throwing his body down behind the opened door as he sought protection. After a few moments, his eyes adjusted to the daylight and began to focus. He was within eyesight of the courtyard. People were running in all directions creating a scene of chaos. The effects of repeated blows to his head made his head throb. He grabbed hold of a man running past him, almost losing his grip as the man tried to run away.

"What happened?" he asked him.

"He's dead. The Fuhrer is dead," the man shouted glancing at his tattered uniform before running away.

"I must get rid of this uniform," he thought as he made his way through the courtyard, ducking into doorways, and hiding as he went. In the far corner of the courtyard, he saw the gallows. Several persons hung from nooses, they were dressed in civilian clothes. One corpse, lying beneath the gallows, wore a soldier's uniform. There were three more soldiers lying face down on the ground. The ground under their heads was bloody.

He had an idea.

He tore off what was left of his shirt and pants as he climbed the steps leading to the galley where the victims hung. He tore the pants and shirt off a dead man. *They hung Officer Felix Fuerst for treason – that is what they will think.* He dropped his clothes down in front of the corpse and began dressing it with his uniform. The body was still warm, making it easier for him to slip the pants up over the limp legs. Fearing that someone might have seen him, he grabbed the dead man's clothes, bundled them in his hands and ran down the steps dressed only in his underwear, deciding to dress in them in a more secure place. He dressed under the steps of the galley.

"*The man must have been a little taller,*" he decides as he surveys the pants hanging over his bare ankles and dragging on the ground. *"I need to find some shoes,"* he thought, remembering how they had taken them. He started back out into the courtyard, barefoot. There appeared to be mass confusion with people running in all directions. His actions seemed to have gone unnoticed – *or maybe no one cares.*

He found his way out of the opened prison gates, thinking only of how to discard anything that would connect him to THE THIRD REICH. He remembered the military-issued underwear that he was still wearing as he darted into the doorway of a bombed out building. He removed them and dressed again. Weak and out of breath, he fell to the ground.

*

When he awakened, his eyes focused on the pile of underclothing lying in the dirt beside him. He used his fingers to dig up the ground and bury them. After eliminating every trace of a connection, he looked to his bare feet. He stumbled through the streets looking for some bodies and some shoes. He spied a dead man and he tried to remove his boots but they wouldn't come off his feet. He wiggled a shoe, back and forth several times, before he was able to dislodge it. The shoe didn't fit his foot but he was satisfied that it was too big rather than too small. He removed the other one and put it on. He checked himself one more time for clues to his past. He didn't want to broadcast his former affiliations to anyone, including himself. All that he could think of was escaping Berlin. He didn't know where he would go, or what would become of him, but he knew that he needed to disappear.

His thoughts go to Sofia, the children . . . and Frederick. The last word about Sofia had come from Adam. He had tried to follow their progress for several days after she had left, but couldn't run the risk. He suspected that they were investigating him. It was far too dangerous to have any contact with Adam. At their last meeting, Adam told him that Sofia and the children were still hiding in France, awaiting opportunities to escape to America. He also told him that a German patrol had killed Gerhard and Alexandra before they could get near Switzerland. He prayed that Sofia and the children wouldn't suffer the same fate and that help from the French Underground and Adam's close proximity would make the difference.

He and Adam had kept in touch after Adam had decided to leave Berlin when Frieda had died. Felix knew that Adam had lost his feelings for Germany. He knew that his unhappiness with the regime had led him to a membership in one of the many underground organizations in Europe. *"Why didn't I see it? I sent them into the biggest invasion in European history. If only there had been another way,"* he confessed as tears rolled down his cheeks.

Hearing the sound of gunfire in the distance, his thoughts return to the present. He had to enact a plan if he was to stay alive. All he saw around him was misery and devastation: fires burning and people wandering the streets, dazed and confused. Some were looking for loved ones, others not looking for anything at all, the horror of war indelibly marked on their faces. Lines of refugees formed a continuous ribbon of the war's depravity, walking behind one another like sheep, following, but having no destination. He thought that he might be safe if he joined the sheep and fell in behind the last group.

*

As he walked, he tried to formulate a plan that would help him to survive. He knew that he couldn't afford to be an ex-Soldier. "No one could have that title now – not if they want to live. The world will never forget what they did," he thought.

The long line was now behind him. He didn't want to think any more about yesterday or tomorrow. He could only think about today. Today, he was hurt. He was tired. He was hungry. He was thirsty . . . but he was *FREE*.

Where do I go?

What should I do?

"I have no family, no country, I have nothing left," he mumbled under his breath.

When he looked at the line of refugees in front of him, and the even longer line behind him, he knew that he wasn't alone. He decided that the first thing he would do would be to find Frederick, his illegitimate son. He hoped he was still there in the little town outside of Berlin where he had left him. He had fathered him with a German whore according to the grand plan.

"I'll find them – all of them . . . Sofia, Max, Ana, and Frederick . . . if it is the last thing that I do."

*

Janene closes her computer and gathers up her things. "I love you Oma," she whispers as she kisses her grandmother for the first and last time.

"I know exactly how Felix had felt when he had begun his search for his family," she thinks as she walks out of Sofia's hospital room.

"I'll find my mother and my sister if it is the last thing that I do."

* * * * *

CHAPTER 16
THE TAI FAMILY

The doctors turn off the machines that are keeping Sophie Simon alive on September 28, 2008. She takes her last breath as her family watches at her bedside. Jeffrey executes her final wishes to have her remains buried in the cemetery at the top of 'German Hill', a cemetery where many of the German members of the community of Pittsburgh bury their dead. News media flood the area, but respect Jeffrey's request for privacy. Her family gathers around the casket, covered in an arrangement of mums, poised over the hole in the ground. As they lower the coffin into the ground, a soft breeze blows a misty rain and, while the bright sun of a new day shines, a rainbow appears on the horizon.

*

The Next Day

Jeffrey calls the family together to read Sofia's Last Will and Testament in the library of the mansion. He decides that Sofia would have been pleased to have the remaining members of her "shattered family" together in one room. As he looks around at their faces, he knows that she is there with them *in spirit*.

"Everything is in complete order," he begins, "Except for the one final matter which Sofia had worried about most," he says with a very serious face and looking down at a highly varnished wooden box sitting on the desk in front of him.

"The content of this box is the most "precious" item in Sofia's estate; at least, it was to her. Before the reunion with all of you, she had worried about what would happen to it when she had passed. She agonized over what to do with every one of her valued possessions but this old quilt was the hardest one for her.

She didn't want to offend any of you by bequeathing it to just one of you so she deliberated the possibility of dividing the quilt into sections, but once her loved ones grew in numbers, she couldn't bear the thought of the quilt in so many pieces. She said that it would be like shattering her life again. Her next thought was to will it to one of her grandchildren, however, she couldn't decide which of her grandsons would appreciate inheriting a tattered, old blanket," he says as he looks at the smiling faces of Michael's and Jacqueline's children."

"I can't tell you how relieved she was and her great joy when Randy's daughter had found her. Once she had met Janene, her decision was easy. She told me that she knew her quilt would be safe but, more than that, she believed its magic would empower Janene on her search for her mother and her twin sister. She said and I quote: "I'll only rest in peace when Randy's daughters are together again." She prayed that she would live to see that day. I believe she is present with us in this room and she will continue to be instrumental in our lives," he smiles as he looks around the room.

"After I had found her in this very library, collapsed, and with the phone in her hand, I pieced together what had happened. The investigator had called her and told her he had found Janene's family in Vietnam. She must have taken notes from the conversation. From those notes, she must have written a short story about what he had told her," he says reaching for the file. "These are her notes and the story she had written, her last one. She must have decided to call you, Janene, to tell you more about your family. The phone was still in her hand. I would like to read this, her final writing to all of you."

*

"Mai-Linh Tai wants to look, but look away at the same time. Her goal: find her sister and her babies, the only three people left in her world. The twenty-year old Vietnamese woman is numb as she walks through what once was the peaceful village she had called home. Bodies lay on the ground, their blackened and broken faces staring back. They had been yesterday's survivors searching for loved ones after that attack, the second in as many days, had almost destroyed their village. As she looks beyond the path, she thinks that the Viet Cong may have finished the job today. The dirt path, now an obstacle course, led to the bombed mission, the sole place of refuge.

The smell of charred flesh choked her. She placed her hand over her mouth, swallowed hard and fought back tears. The shrill cry of her baby niece, Binh-Ly, almost hidden under her mother's still, bloody body startled her. "No. No. It can't be," she thought, reaching her hand to her mouth as she turned over the body of her younger sister 'Nhu-Suong' and releasing Binh. She picked up the baby, gave her a quick cuddle, trying to calm her and then touched Nhu's neck, thankful to find a pulse. Nhu never responded to her daughter's cries or to the sound of the shelling, lighting up the sky above them again.

Baby Binh cried louder. Frantic, thinking that she should seek cover, her eyes moved across the area in front of the mission, searching for An-Ly, Binh's twin sister. The ground shook and the loud noise hurt her ears, she pressed Binh down against her, wrapped her arm over her head, and ran towards the doorway of the main entrance to the mission.

Binh stopped crying.

Perhaps her infant mind recognized the futility.

Mai had stopped her crying years before, finding prayer the only option. As she lay huddled inside the doorway of the building where she, her sister, and her babies had gone after the demolition of their home near a rice paddy just south of town, her thoughts returned to An-Ly, regretting she had no time to look for her, and hoping that Nhu had left her safe inside the compound. She considered going back to search, but decided against it when another blast rattled the building. She curled her body tighter around Binh and asked God to protect her, keeping her from the same fate as her mother.

The day the twins had been born flashed in her mind. She remembered the happiness, mixed with anxiety. The normality of the great celebrations that had occurred upon the births of children in their village no longer existed. There was no rejoicing for new life, the celebration of their births, all tainted by the loss of so many of the villagers, all casualties of the continuing civil war between North and South Vietnam. Counting the twins, the Tai family now consisted of four. "If Nhu dies, it will only be three," Mai thought.

She remembered the day that Nhu and the American GI who had fathered her daughters had selected names, not knowing if the child would be a boy or a girl, never suspecting twins.   They had chosen the names of 'Binh-Ly' and An-Ly', both Vietnamese words for the English word 'Peace.' They believed that, if 'Peace' would come to Vietnam, there would be a chance for them to become a family. The American, who had pledged his love, couldn't keep his promise to return and take them to America. The war had taken his dream away and Nhu believed he would be waiting in heaven for her. As the attack continued, Mai thought that the possibility of peace seemed unlikely. Resigned and expecting her own demise, she vowed that she would do everything possible to insure that their daughters would live.

*

An hour later, the shelling had stopped. The quiet had an eerie ring. As she huddled in the doorway clenching Binh, she reasoned that the only thing worse than living through the shelling was what came after the smoke had cleared. The survivors faced the tasks of helping the injured and burying the dead. She left the shelter, Binh on her hip, and hurried to where she had left Nhu's body. A nun from the mission crossed her path and made the 'Sign of the Cross.' Mai's scream interrupted the nun's prayer.

"Alive! She is alive.

Nhu is alive!" she shouted hugging Binh closer.

"Nhu . . . Nhu . . . ," she whispers kneeling down, watching the blood ooze from a deep gash on her head. She reached to stop the bleeding with one hand while still balancing Binh with the other, but it did little good. Binh cries when she sees her mother, reaching out her little arms for her. Nhu-Suong opens her eyes, focuses on Binh's face for only a moment, moves her lips, and closes her eyes again.

*

Several days later, the two sisters leave the makeshift mission, replacing the one that once was. With one arm, Mai carries An-Ly, found safe and unharmed inside the compound. Her other braces Nhu, balancing Binh on her hip. With mixed feelings, they walk away from the only place that had offered them refuge. Nhu had not recovered from her injuries but the badly damaged, under-staffed mission could no longer offer them shelter. They had nowhere to go.

Soon after she had learned of their father's death, Nhu had decided to relinquish the babies for adoption. It had not been an easy decision. She had agonized over it, but finally had concluded that she had no other choice. With little hope of her own future and the realization that the twins' futures depended upon her, desperation forced her decision. Hoping to provide each one of them with the best possible chance of a new home, preferably in America as their father had wanted, she decided to separate them. Her plan was to take An-Ly to the American Army base, just outside Saigon. She had heard that there was a better chance of adoption for the children of the American GI's if the American soldiers found the orphans. She knew that Binh wasn't as strong as An-Ly, and she worried that she wouldn't survive the ordeal. Her plan was to take her directly to one of orphanages in Saigon and give her to the nuns.

When Mai and Nhu left the mission, they had no idea what the future would hold, or even if they had one. One thing they did know for sure, the babies' lives depended upon them. Their decision to join the group of refugees filing past the mission was a spontaneous one. Their destination was Saigon: the same as the Viet Cong.

*

Several Weeks Later

"They would never be accepted – no matter who wins the war," Nhu decided clutching Binh closer as she walked up the wooden ramp to the entrance of the orphanage. "Now that Randy is gone, there is no other choice to make." After spending weeks in Saigon, trying desperately to survive, she could think of only one thing: "Get my children out of South Vietnam before it is too late." Her country in shambles, her family destroyed, and her American soldier dead, she knew her mixed-race daughters would have a difficult life – if they survived at all. She finalized her plan. Binh would be the first to leave her loving arms. She wrapped her in a blanket and walked to the orphanage run by the nuns.

An hour later, she arrives at the orphanage. "Take her . . . She belongs in America," she said in a low voice and in response to the nun behind the desk. At first, she thought the good sister was going to turn her away but the nun surprised her by asking the baby's name and the names of her parents. After jotting the information down and reaching out for the baby, she gathered Binh into her arms and hurried off with her toward a doorway at the end of a long hallway.

Nhu's face relaxed. She felt relieved by the anticipation of food and shelter for Binh, but she couldn't bear to hear the echo of her screams, or to see the look of terror on her face when she had handed her over to an unknown fate. The sound of the door closing pierced her heart. She turned and ran away choking back the tears."

Jeffrey sighs and takes a deep breath. "Janene, the investigator has everything for you. Your round trip tickets to Ho Chi Minh City are in this envelope," he says handing it to her. Janene's hands shake and tears run down her face. As her biological family huddles around her and hugs her for a long time, her heart aches to go back to South Vietnam.

*

333

Two days later, Janene sits on the jetliner, holding the wooden box containing Sofia's quilt, now her own. Her destination is the home of her birth, Saigon, presently known as 'Ho Chi Minh City.' The trip will reunite her with her Vietnamese family. She hugs the box, hoping that her decision to have the quilt divided into two sections will prove to be a good one. She wants to share the quilt with her sister because she knows that was what Sofia would have wanted. She has come to believe in the quilt's magical powers as much as Sofia had. She had her own special reasons for how she feels about the quilt. *Whether I find her dead or alive, my sister will have one-half of our Oma's most prized possession.* A tailor, a friend of Sofia's in Pittsburgh, had divided the quilt so that the seam went right down the middle of the cluster of pink squares that Sofia had loved to touch. The quilt's design was symmetrical and it made Janene's decision to divide it into two identical quilts a very easy one.

While she looks out of the airplane window into the billowy clouds, her dream of the Vietnamese woman flashes in her mind, stirring her imagination again. She sees the woman riding the clouds holding her hand and the hand of her sister, an exact duplicate of her. Her mind floods with the many stories she will include in her book now that she has found her family. She closes her eyes, content that she is now riding the cloud with the woman in her dreams.

*

Janene has a strange feeling when her feet touch the ground in the airport. The anticipation of seeing her family for the first time had been gnawing at her since the moment she had found out about their existence. The bottoms of her feet tingle as the mere act of walking dispels the feeling of pins and needles and the warm tarmac sends sensations up her legs. She clutches the oak box closer to her as she walks down the steps of the plane, her mind reeling with Sofia's stories.

She thinks about her beginnings in Vietnam, picturing her mother giving her over to Corporal Robinson. Sofia's last story about her Vietnamese mother and aunt echoes in her mind. A sharp pain stings her chest when she remembers the meeting with Sofia. Although she had not had much of a chance to get to know her, Sofia had left a lasting impression on her, making her feel as if there had never been a time in her life when Sofia had not been a part of it.

She remembers that it had been Sofia's wish to reunite her shattered family and she recalls her promise again to "search the ends of the earth" for the mother of the granddaughters that Sofia had never known she had. Sofia's 'Last Will and Testament' had touched Janene in a way she had never felt before and her final wish of willing the quilt to her had surprised her. She decided that she would never bury the quilt and further she would make sure that her own children and grandchildren would hear Sofia's stories and have her memory in their hearts as well.

The sight of two women standing beside the gate interrupts her thoughts. The older woman looks like she belongs in Vietnam and, for Janene, looking at the younger woman is like looking into a mirror. The smiles on their faces tell her immediately what her tingling feet have already announced. *I have come HOME.*

Tamika Lyn Johnson and Janene Ann McDeenon stand silently, staring at each other as if each had seen a ghost. Janene moves toward Tamika and the two women embrace each other, holding each other for a long time. Their Aunt Mai-Linh stands motionless except for her quiet sobs and the tears rolling down her cheeks. In one motion, the twins put their arms around her and hold on tight.

*

Later, when the group arrives at Mai-Linh's home, Tamika explains to Janene that she had arrived the day before and had met with Mai-Linh. Sofia's investigator had found her in Chicago where she had grown up after an American GI had adopted her. She further explained that he had known about her from his experience of witnessing her abandonment while serving guard duty at a post outside of Saigon in 1972.

"My adoptive father, Dwayne Johnson, had told me that he had been touched by the actions of a Vietnamese woman abandoning her child to another soldier. He said he couldn't get the incident out of his mind, deciding that an African-American family should raise her. He moved to adopt the little girl himself and took the necessary steps," Tamika shared. "I have never known any parents but Dwayne and Yolanda Johnson."

Janene's mouth drops. "I can't believe it! That's the same story our Oma had told me," she blurts. "Oma said that I am 'An-Ly Tai'."

"Oh, no, you are not. I am. You are 'Binh-Ly Tai'."

Both of them look to Mai-Linh for an explanation.

With the help of an interpreter, Mai has tears in her eyes as she explains that Nhu-Suong had died in Saigon because of the severe injuries she had sustained and the lack of medical treatment. "When we had left our home after it had been destroyed, we were desperate. Nhu and I had discussed what we should do with her babies," Mai said her voice choking and trying to hold back the tears.

"Nhu was heartbroken after she had learned of Randy's death. She loved him and knew that he had loved her and wanted them to have a life together as a family in America. Under different circumstances and times, the village would have rejoiced with a great celebration of their love, but the war had taken all of that away. There was little about which to celebrate. She and Randy had to be content with the hope that peace would allow them a life together in the near future. They feared for the kind of life that the twins would have in Vietnam because the Vietnamese had treated the American war babies as outcasts. They couldn't see any future for their daughters in South Vietnam except one of more heartache. They looked forward to Randy taking them all to America as he had promised.

After she had learned of Randy's death, Nhu was devastated. She wanted to take An-Ly to the army base to give her to the soldiers and take Binh-Ly directly to the orphanage, because Binh wasn't as strong as An. She had believed that if she had separated them, making sure they were in the hands of the Americans, the babies would have a better chance of survival. An-Ly was stronger than Binh and she wanted to relinquish her to the nuns. When Nhu had returned after giving Binh away, she collapsed and died. "The next day, I took An-ly to the army base and I gave her to the soldier standing guard," she said with tears in her eyes.

"After Nhu had died, the twins were my only remaining relatives. I have never gotten over giving them away. When the war had ended, I went to the orphanage to see if I could find any information about Binh. I didn't know what had happened to An-Ly after I had given her to the soldier. Nhu had wanted an American family to adopt her. I prayed that would happen. At first, the nun wouldn't give any information but I didn't give up. I went back several times requesting records. I met 'Sister Mary Agnes'.

Sister told me that the nuns had decided to move An-Ly from the orphanage near the army base to the one here in Saigon when it had been shelled by the Viet Cong. Binh was already here because Nhu had brought her before she had died. Shortly after An-Ly had arrived at the orphanage, a request from an American GI came in to adopt her. Sister said that the soldier who wanted to adopt her had been very persistent. He wanted to adopt only one particular child, the little bi-racial girl whom the soldier from the army post had brought to the mission.

Because she thought that Binh-Ly would die unless she had medical treatment immediately, the nun decided to switch the girls, arranging for him to adopt Binh-Ly instead of An-Ly. She went on to explain that she had thought that she had made the right decision, because, not long afterward, another American soldier put in a request for adoption of the little girl whom he had brought to the orphanage, saying that he knew of a couple in America who desperately wanted her."

Mai reaches into her pocket and hands a yellowed sheet of paper to the interpreter. "Sister Mary Agnes had written the names of the couples who had adopted the twins on this paper. I have saved it all these years, praying that I would live long enough to see Nhu's daughters again. Today, my prayers have been answered." Mai sits very still looking into the twins' eyes and listening as the interpreter reads what the nun had written on the paper.

An-Ly Tai, twin daughter of Randolph Robert Blackburn III and Nhu-Suong Tai; Adopted by Dwayne and Yolanda Johnson, Chicago, Illinois, U.S.A.

Binh-Ly Tai, twin daughter of Randolph Robert Blackburn III and Nhu-Suong Tai; Adopted by William and Madeline McDeenon, Atlanta, Georgia, U.S.A.

*

After a brief visit and a long good-bye with their one remaining Vietnamese relative, the twins promise Mai that they will keep in touch with her and they board a plane together to fly back to Pittsburgh. The plan is for Tamika to meet Oma's family. In addition, they would both meet with Sofia's investigator to inquire about any new information about the Blackburn family. As they sit together on the plane, awaiting take off, they join hands. "I guess we really didn't get to play any of those 'twin tricks', did we, Tamika?" Janene grins.

"Now that we're together again, we better get our stories straight so that we can play some of those tricks," Tamika says with a smile and a raised eyebrow.

"No tricks for me, Tamika. I've had enough of them to last me a lifetime," Janene says. "My two adoptive brothers, Brian and Kevin, are identical twins. Funny, I had always wondered what it would be like for me to have a twin sister."

" . . . Me, too, Janene . . . Maybe we had remembered some things from Vietnam after all."

"You know, as much as I had longed for the opportunity to come back to Vietnam, I don't feel as if I belong here," Janene says looking into her sister's eyes, but feeling as if she is searching her soul.

"I agree, Janene. Although the United States isn't the country of my birth, it's where I belong."

"I think our parents would be pleased," Janene says gripping Tamika's hand tighter. "I can't wait to share everything I know about them with you."

"We have a lot of catching up to do, Sis," Tamika shares.

"We certainly do need to catch up and I have the perfect way to start," Janene smiles reaching for the carry-on-bag on the seat beside her. She opens the bag and takes out the quilt, now divided into two. "I didn't want to run the risk of putting these in the luggage compartment, Tamika. Our Oma's quilt is now my most precious possession and I hope that it will become yours as well," she says as she places one- half of Sofia's quilt on Tamika's lap and the other half on her own. "I promised myself that, when I had found you, I would share the quilt with you and all of the stories that our German grandmother had shared with me."

Tamika's eyes get big and the dimple in her cheek dances as she smiles, lifts the quilt, and rubs it against her cheek.

"I had the quilt separated into two equal parts because Sofia had believed so strongly that she would find you with its help and I knew that when I did, I would share it with you. It had worked out that the separation had divided the quilt into two perfect and equal parts – just as if our Great-Great-Grandmother Frieda had had a premonition that a set of twins who would be its heirs," Janene says as she points to the design of the quilt. "If it had not been for this quilt, the W.O.O.Q Center here in Vietnam would never exist. Without the center, I would never have found you. Now, I believe in its magic and I promised myself that, whether I would find you dead or alive, half of this quilt belongs to you."

"It's beautiful, Binh-Ly."

"I want to share Sofia's story with you and my own as well. I am very anxious to hear yours. Oma's story is long, but it is one that I think you will want to remember."

"Thank you; I want to share my story with you too," says Tamika reaching for Janene's hand. "I have always known that there was someone missing in my life," she says as she squeezes her sister's hand.

"I agree An-Ly."

"I guess sharing stories is in our genes . . . I know that Oma's story is safe with us," Janene says squeezing Tamika's hand tighter. As they share that special smile, the one reserved only for your twin sister, the Blackburn Twins say in unison, "You can rest in peace now, Oma Sofia."

*THE END

*It isn't really 'THE END' for Janene and Tamika –
They are just beginning ANEW.

ABOUT THE AUTHOR

Maura Patricia English
1950
Pittsburgh, Pennsylvania

Born 'MAURA PATRICIA ENGLISH' in 1947 in Pittsburgh, Pennsylvania, the author attended parochial school, graduating from St. Paul Cathedral High School in 1965. From 1965 to 1966, she worked as a secretary while attending classes in Painting and Drawing during the evenings at Carnegie Mellon University. In 1966, she enrolled as an Art Major, with a minor in Education at Edinboro State Teachers College of PA, now known as 'Edinboro University of PA'. She graduated with a B.S. Degree in 1970 in Art Education. She accepted her first teaching contract with the Pittsburgh Public Schools in September of 1970. She earned Masters Equivalency from Penn State Extension and the University of Pittsburgh, as well as her Pennsylvania Permanent Teaching Certificate.

In 1974, she married her husband, 'Robert J. Gallagher', a PA State Police Officer, affectionately known by most as 'Gallagher'. In 1978, she retired from teaching to become a 'Stay-at-home Mom' to their two daughters, 'Kelly Ann' and 'Patricia Jeanne'. In 1985, after working in the Wilkinsburg District and the Woodland Hills Districts as a 'Substitute', she accepted another contract with the Pittsburgh Schools as 'Replacement Teacher' for the Brookline Elementary Teachers Center. She taught Art in twenty-nine of the district's elementary schools, replacing teachers in order for them to attend retraining and development at the Teachers Center. In 1991, anticipating the close of the center due to funding, she accepted a classroom position where she remained until early 2001 when she was diagnosed with Fibromyalgia and Chronic Fatigue Syndrome, forcing her into an early Disability Retirement.

In 2007, she began writing in an attempt to overcome the devastating effects of her illness, in particular the one known as 'Fibro-fog'. "It was as if someone had taken a giant eraser and had wiped out parts of my memory," she commented. After years of looking to doctors for answers, she turned to herself, refusing to spend the rest of her life in a fog. She sat down at the keyboard and began to type the only thing that came to mind: "ASDFJKL; asdfjkl; . . . All good men should come to the aid of their country." Over four years later that simple exercise from Typing I class in 1964 had evolved into a manuscript she titled THE QUILT.

After entering it in a contest at Amazon (ABNA) and having it place in the Quarterfinals in 2010, she moved to self-publish it with Createspace.com. As she had prepared the manuscript for publication, she wanted to document what she had written about the quilt since she had never made one, nor had she known much about the history of quilt making. After searching on the internet for quilt dealers, she was surprised to find the exact quilt she had written about four years earlier. She called the dealer and asked about the quilt. He told her that he had no idea where it had come from or who the original owner might have been. However, he dated the quilt to the Victorian Time, the same time she had written that her character, 'Frieda Schmidt', had made hers. Further, based on its pattern, he called it AROUND THE WORLD. Since Frieda Schmidt's quilt had literally been around the world, beginning in Germany, traveling to the United States, then to South Vietnam, and back to the United States, she thought that it was certainly a fitting name. She bought that quilt. It is now one of her most cherished possessions, a relic of that time in her life when she had found that ". . . special place, the one where only I can go, but I want to share with others."

After becoming the new owner of the quilt about which she had written, she moved to share her work through self-publication. She learned everything she could about the self-publishing process and, in March of 2011, using a pen name, 'CLU GALLAGHER', a combination of a nickname for her first screen name, 'R.E.CLUSE', and her married name of GALLAGHER, she published her first manuscript, THE QUILT, changing the title to SHATTERED SEEDS: 'SOFIA'S STORY'. She not only wrote the novel, but she edited it, designed the cover, formatted it for publication, set it as Paper and EBook, and tried to market it.

In 2012 and to her great dismay, an association with another author who had begun a new type of publishing company and who had promised to market the book for her resulted in disappointment when he had failed to deliver his promises and never paid her any royalties. Not wanting to have her work associated with him and his publishing company, she retired the novel and moved to publish it again in several Special Editions, which resulted in another fiasco after she had her copyright violated when she had shared her files electronically. During this time, she moved to self-publish her second manuscript, another story about an immigrant to the United

States. Soon, she realized that several of her original writings all shared the common element in that they were stories about immigrants to America. In early 2013, she decided to create a series of her novels, all mainstream accessible fictions set in history and all stories about immigrants. She titled the new collection, THE SCATTERED SEEDS SERIES and moved to republish all of her work as volumes in the collection.

The first volume of this new collection is ANEW, a newly structured and edited version of her original manuscript THE QUILT and her first novel, SHATTERED SEEDS: SOFIA'S STORY, which she had self-published in 2011. She has issued several editions of the novel, striving to perfect it, continuing to get pleasure as a reader, hoping that the experience will be the same for others. The current is the Third Edition published on 4 August 2013.

The second volume in the series is **DARBY'S ROAD**, based upon her second manuscript, A MATTER OF DECEPTION, which she had self-published as THE ROAD TO RIGHTEOUSNESS in early 2012 but decided to rewrite with a new structure, edit, and new title. Presently at the proofing stage, she anticipates publishing it in August or September of 2013. She is currently working on the third volume in THE SCATTERED SEEDS SERIES. She hopes to publish the novel in late 2013. Based upon her original manuscript written in 2008 and titled FORGOTTEN, she has titled this novel, A MEMORY FOR MIRRY.

It has been a long process as a self-published author for Maura (CLU) as she has worked to establish her goal of sharing her work with others. She considers writing a *passion*, rather than a profession; she has developed a mission statement to guide her:

> "Reading is a pathway to the mind . . . The destination is the soul, or that 'special place', whatever you may call it, that we all share as humans. I take on the task of providing the written word with a great sense of responsibility, not only to those who have elected to allow my words to enter their most precious of all places, their intellects, but to myself."

In order that she may concentrate on that passion, devoting all of her creative energies to writing, Maura (CLU) is seeking representation for her work.

COMING SOON

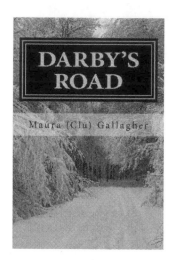

The Scattered Seeds Series, Vol. II

For more information, visit:

http://www.clugallagher.com/

Made in the USA
Middletown, DE
09 November 2017